Lady Gregory

Sir William Gregory, K.C.M.G.,

Formerly Member of Parliament and Sometime Governor of Ceylon

Lady Gregory

Sir William Gregory, K.C.M.G.,
Formerly Member of Parliament and Sometime Governor of Ceylon

ISBN/EAN: 9783337017286

Printed in Europe, USA, Canada, Australia, Japan

Cover: Foto ©Raphael Reischuk / pixelio.de

More available books at **www.hansebooks.com**

SIR WILLIAM GREGORY, K.C.M.G.,

FORMERLY MEMBER OF PARLIAMENT AND

SOMETIME GOVERNOR OF CEYLON.

AN AUTOBIOGRAPHY.

EDITED BY LADY GREGORY.

WITH PORTRAIT.

SECOND EDITION.

LONDON:

JOHN MURRAY, ALBEMARLE STREET.

1894.

LONDON :

PRINTED BY WILLIAM CLOWES AND SONS, LIMITED,

STAMFORD STREET AND CHARING CROSS.

PREFACE.

THE following memoirs were written during the last few years of my husband's life, from 1884 to 1891. They were at first intended only for me and our boy, but he afterwards showed them in part to one or two old and dear friends. He never spoke of their publication, and probably would not have thought them worth bringing before the outer world. I think differently, and my hope in publishing them is that his name, which was known, and kindly known, in many countries beside his own, may be kept alive a little longer, and that for his sake a friendly hand may sometimes in the future be held out to his boy.

I have, of course, left out a good deal of what he had written. Some detailed accounts of visits to Tunis and Egypt, when those countries were less in the beaten track than now, are no longer of general interest. In this age of hurry, when there are too many Parliamentary speeches to be read from day to day, it would have been useless to print those of half a century ago. And though he had written nothing that could be called unkind or ill-natured, yet I have left out many passages that seemed too personal, or that might have vexed the living or slighted the memory of the dead. This has been a difficulty, for every passage so struck out lessened the interest of the whole, but I have tried honestly to carry out a good intention, and may say—

> " What's done ye partly may compute,
> Ye know not what's resisted."

AUGUSTA GREGORY.

CONTENTS.

PART I.

CHAPTER VIII.

CHAPTER IX.

CHAPTER X.

CHAPTER XI.

CHAPTER XII.

CHAPTER XIII.

PART II.—CEYLON.

AUTOBIOGRAPHY OF

THE RIGHT HONOURABLE

SIR WILLIAM GREGORY,

K.C.M.G., F.R.S.

----◦----

CHAPTER I.

I FORGET the name of the writer who said that the auto-biography of every man, if honestly given, would be worth having. I therefore endeavour to give an account of my life for the benefit of my son. Some portions of it may be an encouragement, and some a warning to him. But before I turn to myself, I may as well tell the very little that I know about my family. It is a subject in which I never took the smallest interest, and therefore my knowledge is very circumscribed. We are directly descended from the Gregory family, of Styvechale Hall, near Coventry, who acquired their property in the reign of Stephen, in 1162, and in whom there is the dormant peerage of Marmion. All the title-deeds from that time, and various charters and documents, are preserved, showing that the property, not a large one, has remained without any break in the hands of members of the Gregory family till this date. The pedigree from 1162 to 1580 was completed by Glover, and is continued in the College of

Arms until now.   I was informed by my grandfather that his ancestor, a younger son of this Warwickshire family, came over with Cromwell, and settled in Ireland ; and this is confirmed by Burke in his " Landed Gentry."   The names of the owners of Styvechale Hall at that period show how strongly they had adopted the Puritan doctrines and politics.   " Love is God Gregory" died in 1654, and was succeeded by his son, also named " Love is God;" and it is from one of them that the Cromwellian sprang.

I distinctly remember having had in my hands—and I believe it is still in my possession—a letter from Colonel Gregory, the grandfather of the present owner of Styve- chale Hall, to my grandfather in which he remonstrates with him for having substituted a griffin's head as crest instead of the boar's head, and begs of him to return to the boar's head, to which he had a right, and to abjure the griffin's head, to which he had no right; mentioning, as if it were an undoubted fact, that the Irish Gregorys of Coole were the undoubted descendants of his family.   I also recollect the consultation between my grandfather and father as to the change of crest on the family carriages, livery, and plate, and that they both came to the conclusion—which was quickened by the entrance of my grandmother, Lady Anne, who said she would not listen to such nonsense—that it was as well to leave the crests as they were ; and so they have continued till this day.

My great-grandfather was the son of Henry Gregory, who lived in Galway.   He seems to have been a man of considerable vigour of character, for he ran away from home, made his way to India, got into the employment of the East India Company, and therein made a very large fortune.   In those days the pagoda tree had not shed all its golden fruit, and my relative was undoubtedly not behind his neighbours in gathering it. He married in India—whom I do not know; but I strongly suspect the lady had a good deal of native blood in her veins. This surmise is grounded on the personal characteristics of several of his descendants. He had three sons in India, Robert, Richard, and William; and when he left India finally, he placed the management of such funds as he had not remitted home in the hands of his eldest son Robert, who would naturally have been his heir, had matters run smoothly. But they did not. This Robert Gregory, junior, was passionately addicted to cock-fighting, which, in those days, was as irresistibly seductive as horse-racing is now. Some say that it is a better mode of gambling, barring the cruelty, because the cock has not got a jockey on his back to play tricks with him. But the cock, like the horse, has got a trainer who can manipulate his food, and if he has not got a jockey, he has a fighter who can disable him by a very easy and effective squeezing. All these modes of manipulating a cock-fight are well known in India; and Mr. Robert Gregory, junior, had lost, before his father's departure, very large sums, which were paid for him.

On leaving India, Robert Gregory, senior, informed his son that if he ever heard of his being again engaged in cock-fighting, he would disinherit him. And he was as good as his word, for, going down the Strand some time after his return, he saw a picture by Zoffany of the great cock-match between the Nabob of Oudh and Colonel Mordaunt. Mr. Gregory knew most of the portraits in this picture, and among them he recognized that of his son, holding under his arm a white cock, and in a very prominent position. He went into the shop, examined the key to the picture, and found that his surmise was correct. He made further inquiries in India, and ascertained that not only was he present at the fight, but that he was a partner of Colonel Mordaunt's. He immediately changed his will, and bequeathed his Irish landed property to his son Richard ; thence it came to my grandfather William, to my father, and myself ; and the print of the cock-fight hangs over the fireplace in the breakfast-room of Coole as a warning against gambling. It was not hung up there, unfortunately, during the early period of my life. I have never heard what became of this relative, except that he died on the 6th of December, in the year 1814, at Calcutta, in the East India Company's service, having never returned to England. But it is clear that he must have led a respectable life on his pay, and whatever he was left by his father ; for, a few years since, a speculative attorney offered to reveal, upon certain terms, the existence of a sum of money which had devolved to the heirs of this Robert Gregory. The terms were accepted, and it was found that a sum of £5000 had been gradually accumulating since his death, and this was eventually divided between the attorney and some members of the Gregory family.

My great-grandfather, on his return from India, did not sink down into the curry, mulligatawny, and indolence of many other returned so-called Indian "nabobs." He was a strenuous politician, a Liberal, the intimate personal friend and supporter of Lord Rockingham, Charles Fox, and Mr. Burke. He was returned member for Rochester in 1774, at the head of the poll, against Admiral Sir Thomas Pye and George Finch Hatton, Esquire, of Eastwell, and on the dissolution of Parliament in 1780, he again stood for the borough, and had made himself so popular there, that he was elected on one occasion while he was eating a mutton chop at the hotel. He was also an active and influential member of the East India

Company's board, and was chairman for many years at
a time when that position was one of the most powerful
and influential in the kingdom. He resigned in the year
1783, on the ground that the work was too heavy for his
health. His expenditure in politics was very great. He
had purchased an estate in Essex, another in Cheshire,
a house in Berners Street, London, then a fashionable
quarter, and a property in Ireland of over £7000 a year.
Before his death he had sold the Essex and Cheshire
estates, but he reserved that of Galway. From the accounts
I have heard of him, he was a most kind and polished
old gentleman, living in very great state, and considering,
as old Indians used to do, that a huge retinue of servants
was necessary for existence. I have heard my grandmother O'Hara speak of the procession of carriages in
which he and his suite travelled from London to Coole ;
but what particularly struck her were the numbers of
servants who came to the door, and waited at dinner in
black silk stockings, black breeches, and gold garters.
He was particularly courteous to young ladies, who had
good reason to remember their visits to Coole with
pleasure, as it was his habit to take them at their
departure to a drawer, in which were precious stones,
and let them fish out one of them without looking, taking
the chance of what it might turn out to be. One fortunate
maiden was mentioned to me—though I have forgotten
the name—who had the luck to pick up a very valuable ruby. He died at the age of eighty-three, September 1, 1810, with all his faculties unimpaired, and
his hair scarcely tinged with grey. There is an excellent
portrait of him by Dance, and a bust by Nollekens,
at Coole. The bust was done when he was eighty-three
years of age. His last letter to my grandfather, dated
August 13, just a fortnight before his death, contains the

following passage, which does credit to his sagacity and prescience :—

"In my opinion the whole of the European army in India should be under his Majesty's orders. The native troops to be commanded by officers bred in his Majesty's service, when they understood the language, and to be in the King's service also. This I suggested many years ago ; the patronage was the matter against it ; no Director will even hear of it with patience."

His two sons, Richard, my great-uncle, who succeeded, and my grandfather William, were both educated at Harrow, and went subsequently to Trinity College, Cambridge. Richard went into the Guards, and was, by all the accounts which I have heard, one of the most popular young officers of his regiment. Suddenly a blight, as it were, fell upon him. He was accused of having shirked active service on the plea of ill health, and of having thereby shown the white feather. The charge was entirely disproved—whether judicially or not, I am unable to say —but he left the army in disgust, a totally changed man. He gave up general society altogether, only seeing a few select friends. His marriage also affected his course of life. The young lady was at a school when he met her ; he contrived to take her away, and she lived with him in man's clothes in the present steward's house at Coole till his father died. When the fear of offending him was removed, he immediately married the lady, who thenceforth dropped the name by which she was known of "Jack the Sailor." I remember seeing her when a boy, and being greatly struck by her profusion of black, well-oiled curls. When we first came to Coole we used to hear from all quarters stories of her generosity and kindness to the poor. These good qualities, however, and her blameless life after marriage could not make amends in the eyes of my grandmother Lady Anne for her early indiscretion.

She refused to acknowledge her, and thenceforth to the day of his death there was a total separation between the two brothers, although at one time they were the most attached friends. The bitter feeling on the part of my uncle extended to the rest of the family, and it was not till I had won honours at Harrow that he saw any of us, and then only myself.

When I gained the annual prize for Latin Lyrics in 1835, I felt it my duty, as a matter of course without in the least thinking that anything would come of it, to apprise my uncle as the head of the family. I received by return of post a cheque for £25 in a letter of congratulation, beginning " Sir," and ending "your obedient, humble servant." When passing through London shortly after, I asked permission to call, but my letter was not noticed, and on knocking at the door of his house in Berners Street, was informed that I could not be received.

Next year I won at Harrow the Peel Medal, the Latin Hexameters, and the Scholarship, all of which I took care to announce to my uncle, and for each, except the last, I duly received a letter with " Sir " and " your obedient, humble servant," and with the cheque for £25. The last brought a letter with " Dear Sir " and the usual cheque, and in it also was expressed a wish to see me. I saw him several times, and he seemed at last, shortly before his death, to be gradually warming into a strong feeling of attachment. I really believe these cheques of £25 during my schoolboy life utterly demoralized my previous steadiness and decorum. He had at a comparatively early period of his life been afflicted with a most severe paralytic stroke, which ruined his previous good looks and twisted his head on one side. This affliction and his marriage, and the family separation in consequence of it, drove him, who had been the gayest of the gay

and the pleasantest of the pleasant, into complete
misanthropy. He lived a good deal at Rome and at
Florence, where he imbibed a taste for *vertu*, the results
of which are the very fine collection of books and the
marbles and bronzes at Coole. Shortly before his death,
and about a year or two after his first wife's death, he
married his wife's maid Christian ; but she, too, died
before him.

His death took place in 1839, and I attended his
funeral at Kensal Green, where he lies by the side of his
two wives. I remember being highly interested on that
occasion by the narrative of Carlo Lerandrei, the Italian
courier, of his successful efforts to keep out of the house a
certain young lady, a public singer, who charmed my poor
infirm uncle with her strains, and who was bent on marrying him. As he was by no means averse, great were the
difficulties which Carlo had to encounter, and the battle
went sore against him. But my uncle fell down and broke
his arm, and the courier won the victory, and kept the
hall door closed—as he said, on the chain—against the
invading fair one. Carlo professed to have so acted from
his regard for the family, being unwilling that they should
come into the property improperly charged with a heavy
jointure, which, by the way, as the lady is alive, would be
still paid out of the estate (October, 1883), forty-four years
after the settlement, if, indeed, the estate had not long
since been swamped by such a heavy additional burden.

We all accepted Carlo's exertions with much gratitude,
being perfectly aware, nevertheless, as the housekeeper,
who had a tiff with him, duly enlightened us, that he was
in much terror lest the new Mrs. Gregory should turn him
and all the existing *régime* out-of-doors, and render the
large legacy he was looking forward to very insecure.

All the books, bronzes, marbles, a sapphire ring set in

diamonds, and a most valuable emerald brooch, the only
survivors of his father's drawer full of gems, were left as
heirlooms by my uncle. A very valuable bequest was
made to Harrow School, of books and of a scholarship of
£50 a year for four years—the richest scholarship at
Harrow—in remembrance of my successes, as he himself
told me ; while he left to me his plate. This plate had
belonged to his father, and was very fine, as some of the
candlesticks which my mother bought from me testify ;
but in those days I was not impressed with the value of
early hallmarks, and the whole was forthwith sold to
Storr and Mortimer for a low price per ounce. To this
day I remember the tankards and salvers and dishes, and
bewail my errors.

The Coole estate and two small outlying properties,
Clooniffe in the barony of Moycullen, and Kiltiernan in
the barony of Dunkellin, which had previously been left
to my grandfather by his father, were now united. My
grandfather William only survived his brother a few
months. He died in Dublin, April 13, 1840.

My grandfather, though not at all a brilliant man, possessed many high qualities—excellent judgment, sound
sense, attention to business, great clearness and accuracy
in his transaction of it. He had a frank, open manner,
and was straightforward, true, and just in all his dealings.
Few people have been more popular in Ireland during so
long a period of great power, and though he was a Tory
of the Tories, he was not disliked by those who differed
with him in politics. My grandfather was originally a
man of Liberal opinions ; but his connections, and the
influential persons by whom he was surrounded, made him
adopt the extreme Tory opinions of that day, though I
never recollect hearing a violent expression from his lips
as regards Catholics. It is not, however, wonderful that

O'Connell was bent on removing all opponents of his views from Dublin Castle, and in several of his letters he lays the strongest stress on clearing out Gregory, though he subsequently acknowledges that " Gregory was turned out, though, to do him justice, he had some Irish feelings."

He had not thrown away his time at Harrow and Cambridge, for he was a very fair scholar, and used to show me, with well-justified pride, his early Latin verses, which were by no means amiss. In 1781 he was admitted to the Temple, and was High Sheriff of the county of Galway in 1799, following Giles Eyre of Eyrecourt Castle.

He married Miss Anne Trench, afterwards Lady Anne, daughter of Lord Clancarty, and had three children, Robert, Anne, and William.

In the year 1813 my grandfather was promoted to the position of Under Secretary for Ireland, and he held it for eighteen years, and in 1814 a pension of £500 a year was conferred on him and Lady Anne conjointly. The situation which he held was called " Under Secretary to the Lord Lieutenant in the Civil Department." There was at that time a military secretary, and both offices remained separate till 1819, when they were united in Mr. Gregory. He was also ranger of the Phœnix Park.

During the long period that he held his office, he secured the entire confidence of the successive Chief Secretaries and Lord Lieutenants, and with some of them established very deep and lasting friendship, especially Sir Robert Peel, Lord Whitworth, the Duke of Richmond, Lord Talbot, and Mr. Goulburn. His great knowledge of the country and of Irish business gave him an amount of power which, looking at the present position of the office of Under Secretary, it is hard to understand. But it was said, and with truth, that Gregory was the real Governor of Ireland, except, of course, where measures that had to pass through Parliament were concerned. I have an immense amount of his correspondence, private and official, also, which is curious, the amounts of the secret service money which went through his hands. On running my eye hastily over the figures, I was surprised to find the name of an editor, a great patriot and supporter of O'Connell, who seems to have secured a regular yearly stipend for some value received. In fact, while blustering in his columns for Repeal of the Union, he was furnishing the Castle with the fullest information of the intention of the leaders of that movement.

My grandfather had two residences, one in the Phœnix Park, and the other in the Castle. It was at the former that I was born on the 13th of July, 1817, and almost all the recollections of my childhood are connected with it.* It was a house devoted to hospitality. I can perfectly remember seeing there at dinner old Lord Norbury, the

---

* "On the morning of the 31st of January, 1891, Sir William and I walked away from 'Grillion's,' where we had been breakfasting, and where he had had Mr. Gladstone for his next neighbour. He told me that Mr. Gladstone had asked him, in the course of conversation, whether he remembered Lord Melbourne. 'Yes,' he replied. 'When I was a very little boy, my grandfather, who was then Under Secretary for Ireland, took me to the Chief Secretary's room, and formally introduced me to Lord Melbourne.' 'Did he swear at you?' asked Mr. Gladstone. 'I do not remember that he did,' rejoined Sir William ; 'but, for that matter, every one swore in those days. After I had been with him some time, however, he said, "Now, my boy, is there anything here you would like?" "Yes," I answered, pointing to a very large stick of sealing-wax. "That's right," said Lord Melbourne, pressing on me a bundle of pens, "begin life early. All these things belong to the public, and your business must always be to get out of the public as much as you can."' No one was less ready to put in practice this highly immoral doctrine, which, in his usual spirit of banter, he was ready to preach."—*From Sir M. E. Grant Duff.*

hanging judge, and Mr. Saurin, Attorney-General, and Chief Justices Bushe and Doherty, and old Sneyd, the wine merchant, always affectionate, but trebly so after a good pull at his own claret ; and there was no stint of the pull at the Under Secretary's Lodge. It used to go by the name of the Trench Hotel, a very excellent title, considering how many members of that branch of the family were ever quartering themselves upon it.

In 1827 it was intimated to him that his successor would be appointed, and he resigned his office with the offer of a baronetcy, which, after consultation with my father, he declined. The following correspondence passed between them :—

"Dublin, April 17, 1827.

"My dear Robert,

"I have resigned my office. Nothing could have been more kind than the Lord Lieutenant's (Lord Anglesey) expressions of regret at the decision I had made. I spoke to him of you, and he gave me every assurance that he would fulfil my wishes if he remained Lord Lieutenant ; if not, that he would mention to his successor what were his intentions. He said it was his wish to recommend me to be created a baronet and a Privy Councillor. I answered that, with respect to the first, I had declined it many years since ; that it was a matter more for your consideration than mine, and that I would write to you on the subject. Therefore, weigh the matter seriously before you decide, and I will act accordingly. I am to remain in office till my successor is appointed, which probably will be some time," etc., etc.

"W. Gregory."

My father answered this letter—

"I am fully aware that Lord Wellesley some years ago proposed to have you created a baronet, which you declined. If you have no further wish upon the subject now than at that period, and would now accept it merely on my account, I beg to assure you that I feel perfectly indifferent upon the subject, and entreat that you will act entirely upon your own opinion, as you have uniformly judged so well for the interest of those belonging to you."

The baronetcy was, therefore, refused ; but the distinction of Privy Councillor was accepted.   My grandfather, after all, retained his place till 1831, when he was
succeeded by Sir William Gossett.

My father was a light, spare man, passionately fond
of hunting, and the fastest runner of his day at Oxford.
His mother, Lady Anne, was devoted to him, but infinitely
more devoted to me, so that we were always welcome.
I doubt, however, if my mother was equally so.   She was
a very beautiful woman, and so thoroughly eclipsed my
aunt Anne, though she too was comely, that to neither
mother nor daughter was the rival attraction agreeable.
She was also, in those days of Protestant ascendency
and ultra-Toryism, of very liberal tendencies, being a
strong advocate of Catholic Emancipation.   She was,
moreover, constantly visited by persons whose political
opinions caused them to be held in execration by the
female inmates of the Lodge and their Trench relations.
My poor grandfather, though a stout Protestant and a
stout Tory, had no such aversions.   In early life he had
been a Whig, but was occasionally lashed into strong
language, particularly after dinner, by his womankind.   I
remember him so well at the mysteries of his toilette.
His shaving operations were to me a subject of great
awe, and I vividly recall the old grey dressing-gown in
which they were conducted.   Sir Philip Crampton, the
pleasantest *raconteur* and *brodeur*, used to tell a story
of the extraordinary appearance which Mr. Gregory
presented in the park one morning in this dressing-gown.
A duel had been arranged between Sir Valentine Blake
and Robert Burke of St. Clerens, two Galway men, and
the spot selected was close to my grandfather's gate.   He
was engaged at his important shaving operation, when he
heard first one, and then, after an interval, a second double

shot, which he knew to be from pistols. He did not hesitate a moment, but ran downstairs, bare-legged as he was. An orderly's horse was at the door; he sprang on it, and galloped to his gatehouse. As he neared the gate, he heard close at hand a third double shot, and just outside he saw a gathering of spectators round the seconds, who were discussing the subject of making a fourth shot effective. Just as he got to the ring, a huge fellow rode in and shouted out—

"Gentlemen, this is all child's play. Let's finish the business properly. Let each second advance his man two paces, and I'll engage they won't miss."

"Who are you, sir?" cried my grandfather, dashing his horse forward. "Who are you, sir, to give such bloody counsel?"

"Who am I, indeed!" said the other man, looking at the strange figure in a grey dressing-gown and bare legs. "I'll have you to know, sir, I'm Mr. Hickman, the Clerk of the Peace for the county of Clare!"

"Then, Mr. Hickman," said my grandfather, very quietly, "I arrest you and the principals and seconds of this duel in the king's name, and I'll have you all taken up before twelve o'clock."

After which, he rode home in his bare legs, chatting very pleasantly to Sir Philip, who had been on the ground acting professionally as surgeon for the belligerents.

Those who have read Sir J. Barrington's memoirs and Charles Lever's novels get a correct idea of the wild and reckless ferocity, mixed up with a kind of Irish drollery, during the days of duelling at the beginning of the century. Lord Clanricarde had a fund of stories of this character, which he told admirably, from the thorough sense of enjoyment which they seemed to give him. One day at Portumna he pointed out to me a field on the other side of the Shannon, about half a mile from the bridge which connects Galway with Tipperary. We had been talking of William Macdonough, the well-known steeple-chase rider, who was a kind of squireen and lived in the neighbourhood. He had recently shot himself through the head in a pistol gallery in Leicester Square, where Dunkellin and I went an hour afterwards to practise, and there he was lying stark and stiff behind a screen.

"I remember," said Lord Clanricarde, "seeing the poor fellow fight his well-known duel in that field. He had had a difference with some Tipperary gentleman, and it was decided that the duel should take place with pistols on the Tipperary side of the river. The decision as to the side of the river where the affair should come off was a matter of life and death, for the Tipperary man well knew that if he was victorious on the Galway side, he would be torn to pieces by the Galway mob, while the Galway man knew that if he killed his antagonist on the Tipperary side, his chance of escape from the men of Tipperary would be small indeed. On the morning of the duel there were at least two thousand persons present, all Tipperary men, as the Galway peasants did not dare to cross the bridge."

Lord Clanricarde went over from Portumna, and Macdonough rode his horse to the scene of action, and gave it to a man to hold close at hand. A regular lane was made, lined by spectators on each side. When the signal was given, both fired, and Macdonough not only shot his antagonist dead, but also one of the peasantry who, in his eagerness to see the sport, had pushed forward and received the ball in his head. Macdonough got to his horse and made for the bridge of Portumna. After taking one or two fences gallantly on the way, he found his retreat cut off, and the Tipperary men in occupation of the bridge. Without a moment's hesitation, he put his horse at the Shannon, amid the execrations of his baffled pursuers, and he reached the other bank in safety.

There is an excellent story, given by Lever, of a young subaltern having marched into a country town on the evening of the races, and when the ordinary dinner was going on at the hotel. He sat down, alone and weary, to his boiled chicken and cauliflower in a private room just over the public one. Suddenly a terrible row took place, which was shortly followed by the bang of a pistol, and then of another, while the cauliflower-dish sprang from the table, knocked to pieces by a bullet.

The waiter rushed in immediately, crying—

"Don't be alarmed, captain. Councillor Burke has received Mr. Keogh's shot, and has, in the handsomest manner, fired in the air."

This was a story of Lord Clanricarde's, appropriated by Lever, who left out the last words of the waiter, "But, by dad, he has destroyed the cauliflower!" The story is true, and Loughrea was the scene of action.

The first year (1841) that I came to live at Coole, I rode one day into Galway. When I got to Merlin Park, I asked a countryman the name of the place, and found him, as one always finds Irish peasants, most agreeable and communicative.

"I suppose you know all about that field?" he said, pointing to one opposite the wall of Merlin Park.

"No," said I; "I am quite a stranger."

"Well, sir," he said, "that's the place where the gentlemen of Galway used to fight their duels. Many's the duel I saw there when I was young, for I live quite convenient."

"Did you ever see a real good duel?" I asked.

"To be sure I did; and lots of them. But the best

I ever saw was between Councillor Browne and Dr. Bodkin" (I have forgotten the real names). "It was a beautiful morning, with a fine, bright sun. Young Lynch, the attorney's son, of Oranmore, was Councillor Browne's second, and won the toss. So he put the councillor with his back to the sun, and the doctor's second never saw what was going to happen till it was too late. The poor doctor came up, winking and blinking, and at the very first offer the councillor shot him dead. It was a grand shot, your honour. The doctor sprang up three feet in the air, and fell on his face and never spoke another word. Faith! young Lynch was a grand second that day!"

While on the subject of duels, I may mention that my grandfather told me a story of his introduction into Irish habits and customs, which was certainly not agreeable. He had just come over to Ireland, after leaving Cambridge, and went to his first ball in Dublin at the Rotundo. At the opening dance a man stood before him rather impolitely, but he attached no consequence at the moment to this action. Shortly after the dance was over, another man came up to him and said—

"Young gentleman, I knew your father and liked him, and am quite ready to do you a service. My name is Harrison."

My grandfather, always courteous, professed to be much obliged, but said he did not require any service at present.

"I suppose, sir," answered Mr. Harrison, "you have settled who your seconds are to be."

"Seconds! Why should I want seconds?" exclaimed my grandfather.

"Did you not see, sir, that that fellow, a notorious

C

dueller, insulted you on purpose ; and that to-morrow he will boast all over Dublin that he had done so, and that you took no notice ? You must let me at once put the matter in hand for you."

"Very well," said my grandfather, " I suppose it must be so."

"There is no supposition in the matter," said Mr. Harrison, and went his way.

After some time he returned and apologized for the delay, saying that the offender's manner had been impertinent, and so he had made the affair his own, and meant to deal with it himself. He did so effectually, by shooting him through the body, in the Phœnix Park, at six o'clock the next morning. Then my grandfather learned who his friend was, a mighty man of valour in the rolls of the duellists of that day, well known as " Featherspring Harrison," from the good use he made of that adjunct to correct shooting.

Another worthy was " Hero Keogh," another " Fighting FitzGerald ; " but the most formidable and deadly of this pestilent tribe of assassins was a fellow who went by the soubriquet of " Nickety Oily," as his sole occupation was the cleaning, oiling, and clicking of his pistols. I forget his real name.

But to return to the park. I was, at that early period of my life, subjected to the most thorough spoiling by my two very dear grandmothers, the remembrance of each of whom is most sweet even to this day. Both were to me everything that was kind and gentle, both most anxious that I should do precisely what I liked best, and nothing else, which meant entire idleness. But my mother's nature, with all her intense love for me, which she proved by the devotion of her life, was very different.

She did her best to counteract the spoiling process. She insisted on my being taught modern languages, in spite of many sneers of those who, during the war, had not seen their advantages ; and by the time I was twelve years old I was able to speak both French and Italian with the greatest fluency. I had a French governess, "Old Brownie"—in reality, Madame Le Brun, the daughter of a refugee, who taught my mother and her sisters French—and a very good instructress she was. She also instilled into my mind a love of gambling, by teaching me how to play cards for comfit stakes, and her lessons bore fruit in after days.

At that early period of my life most of my time was passed at the Secretary's Lodge, varied by a visit to my grandmother O'Hara at 15, Mountjoy Square. How I did enjoy those visits ! Both my grandmothers had been handsome women, but I think my grandmother O'Hara's was the gentlest, softest face I have ever seen, and yet in early life she had been a woman of rather domineering temper. Then there were my five handsome uncles, with whom I was a special favourite, and who amused themselves by noticing me.

Among the particular friends of my childhood days, no one stands out so strongly as W. Wilkie, the gardener at the Lodge, afterwards W. Wilkie, Esq., the under-ranger of the park, but to me always known as "Daddy Wilkie." He was a tall, gaunt Scotchman, with cavernous eyes and a strong Doric accent. He had a considerable amount of education and taught me many things. He was a thoroughly good, conscientious man, loving his garden and all that was in it, and perhaps loving me even better than his garden. As a proof of this assertion, I may mention that there were certain splendid peaches in the greenhouses which he fondly hoped would gain the prize at the Dublin Flower Show. In an unfortunate moment I got into the peach-house. So ripe and ruddy were the cheeks of the fruit, that I began to kiss them, and then to bite them, until at last nothing but their pale backs remained. Daddy Wilkie shortly after arrived, and, after seeing what had happened, merely remarked, but with tears in his eyes, "Oh, you cruel boy!" I have never forgotten the look and the words. I suffered far more from them than I should have done by ten floggings.

CHAPTER II.

I MUST now mention how I came across one of the greatest men of the present century, whose influence I really think brought me to a love of classic literature, and thereby tinged my whole after-life.

I well remember the occasion of my first meeting Lord Wellesley, although I was a very small boy at the time. It was in the summer of 1824, and I was busily engaged in landing a large roach which I had hooked in the pond of the Lord Lieutenant's Lodge in the Phœnix Park. When the conflict between myself and the fish was over, I became aware of the presence of a slight, short, elderly gentleman, who seemed to take the deepest interest in my doings. He asked me various questions about the fishing, and so completely fascinated me by his pleasant manner, that I told him there were several particular spots in the pond where one was sure to catch roach and perhaps, if it rained, a tench, and that if he would come out fishing with me, I would show him these spots on the condition that he was not to tell any one about them. He asked my name and promised me very faithfully he would not reveal my secrets. I was perfectly unaware of the greatness of the personage whom I was addressing, but I distinctly remember the impression he made on me, and that I would have gladly lent him my rod and line and have brought him to all the best places, so bright and sunny was his

manner, and his interest in the mysteries of roach fishing
apparently so deep. In the evening he informed my
mother of our meeting, and I then became aware that my
acquaintance was the Lord Lieutenant himself; and very
awestricken was I in consequence.

A few days afterwards I was summoned to the Viceregal Lodge, where I went with fear and trembling. The
great man was in his study, and in a few minutes my alarm
departed. He spoke about fishing, and said he was afraid
he could not come to catch roach with me, but that he had
got a book for me which some day or another I was sure
to read with pleasure. He then presented me with a
remarkably fine edition of Walton's "Compleat Angler,"
bound in Russia leather, with the inscription written on
the flyleaf—

> "1824
> To the Compleat Angler
> From his obedient Scholar
> Wellesley."

I remember accepting it with great pleasure and with
the remark, which caused him much amusement, that "I
was afraid it had cost him too much."

After that first visit, he was good enough constantly to
send for me, and he insisted on my beginning my classical
studies immediately. I had to decline my nouns and
conjugate my verbs for him, and it was my greatest treat
to be put through my facings by him. I always felt,
although such a very little fellow, that I must do whatever
he told me, and that I could do it. It seemed impossible
that he should impose anything unreasonable.

Amongst the presents he gave me from that time up
to 1827, when I was ten years old, were Ovid (Elzevir,
3 vols., duod.), Livy (3 vols., Elzevir, duod.), and Homer,
"Iliad" and "Odyssey" (duod.), which I still retain. When

I went to a private school shortly afterwards, I found that the grounding I had received in Latin gave me no small standing among my fellows.

After this there was a gap of many years ; but having been successful in gaining the annual Latin prizes for composition at Harrow, I ventured to send a copy of my composition to Lord Wellesley, recalling to his memory the little fisherman of the Phœnix Park. I received the following reply, far too complimentary, I am well aware, as regards the merits of the composition, but showing the warmth and affection of his character :—

> "Hurlingham House, near Fulham, Middlesex,
> "November 18, 1835.

' MY DEAR FISHERMAN,—

"For you must allow me to address you by that name, which revives the memory of past good and pleasant times, and recalls to my recollection the early lessons which I gave you, and which I flatter myself have contributed to encourage you in that career of honour where you now begin to shine with so much splendour. Be assured that I take the warmest interest in your success, and that I have read with sincere pleasure the compositions which you have been so kind as to send to me.

"They have all great merit. The two in prose are exceedingly excellent, not merely in the language, but in the sentiment, which affords abundant proof of a pure heart and sound mind, well grounded in every principle of virtue and religion. Your exhortation to your companions in study is truly admirable and indeed eloquent. The model you have recommended to their emulation is, I sincerely believe, the most perfect of these days, and if I were to select a character which, above all others, I should wish my own son to imitate, I should name the very person whom you have selected for your imitation. You have described him most justly and accurately, and with a full knowledge of him (which my political life has given to me) I confirm your judgment and deliberately advise you to follow his example. Your comparison of Cicero and Augustus is conducted with great knowledge of the subject, and with very great judgment and ability. Augustus was Father of the City of Rome, which he had greatly embellished ; Cicero, of the Roman People, whom he had saved more than once. Augustus, indeed, was not Father of Rome in the sense that Nicolas is of Warsaw ; but while he adorned the exterior of the city, he destroyed its liberties, or rather confirmed their destruction, for liberty had perished before Rome fell into his hands.

"In the dedication to Oliver Cromwell of a famous pamphlet called 'Killing no Murder,' you will find a good burlesque of the phrase 'Father of your Country': 'Your Highness may be truly called the Father of your Country, for while _you_ live we can call nothing _ours_, and it is from your death that we hope for the possession of our inheritances.'

"Perhaps Augustus had some claim on this ground. Nicolas has certainly no other claim to the title of Father of Poland. Your verses are very good, and the whole poem displays great poetical talent and skill; but before you write for the University prize at Oxford, I wish you to study the majestic harmony of Virgil more closely, and to discard all imitation of any other Latin poet. I am far from discarding all other Latin poets absolutely—many are entitled to high admiration—but Virgil is the best model for imitation in hexameter verse. Your lines on the ruins of Babylon are the best in your poem.

"In your prose you seem to keep 'a reverent eye' on Cicero; he is an excellent model, but still he is _Vitiis imitabile_. You should read the 'Dialogus de causis corruptæ Eloquentiæ' ascribed to Tacitus; it is very different from his quaint though forcible style, and truly beautiful. Whenever I have the pleasure of seeing you, I shall offer many other remarks which I trust may assist you in your progress towards that eminence which I have no doubt you will attain. I cannot more forcibly conclude than in your own words—

"'Parentibus ac patriæ mercedem reddes! Tene hunc cursum laudis; . . . firma eam stirpem virtutis, ex qua lætissimi gloriæ fructus gignentur. . . .—Ita Deus Optimus, Maximus, velit, ita faxit.'*

"Believe me always, with true regard,

"Yours sincerely,

"WELLESLEY.

"Pray write to me and give my best regards to your father and mother and to your excellent grandfather. I hope you are a complete Grecian. Study every word of Homer, Demosthenes, Plato and Thucydides, and the Greek tragick writers. I observe you quote Æschylus. Is he not sometimes rather extravagant?—W."

I may here mention that Sir Robert Peel was the person to whom Lord Wellesley refers as having been held

* From Gregory's "Concio apud Scholæ Harroviensis Gubernatores," in 1835.

up by me, in a Latin address read before the governors of
the school, as a bright example to be followed.

Encouraged by the kindness with which I was received,
I continued the correspondence for about three years. It
was unfortunately burned in the Pantechnicon.

I well remember replying to the last observation in his
letter, "I observe you quote Æschylus. Is he not sometimes rather extravagant?" and making the best battle I
could for him, whom I still consider the greatest of the
Greek tragedians. He combated this opinion, maintaining with much force and eloquence the superiority of
Sophocles. There was a remarkably fine passage in one
of these letters, in which he compared the writings of the
true tragedians with the sculptures of Greece. Æschylus
represented early art before the time of Pericles, with
undoubted lines of great beauty, but on the whole
uncouth. Sophocles represented the work of Phidias,
with not less strength than Æschylus, but with far more
beauty, sense of proportion, and self-restraint; and he
added that the plays of Euripides might be compared
with the works of the sculptors of the period of Alexander.
It is natural enough that the occasional turgid uncouth-
ness of Æschylus should be regarded with almost aversion
by Lord Wellesley, whose elegance—if I may use such
a proscribed word—in dress, manner, conversation, and
composition, was pre-eminent. No advice could be more
excellent for a young man, who, he saw clearly, was
rather disposed to admire what he considered to be
extravagant; and in almost every letter at that period,
I was urged to keep my eyes steadily on Virgil and on
Sophocles. It is a great loss to me, the destruction of
these letters. They were full of criticisms of a fine and
keen scholar, and of illustrations from modern writers;
and in many he referred to incidents in his own career.

I regret that the correspondence ceased during the time I was at Oxford, and entirely through my own fault; but when, shortly after leaving Oxford, I was returned for the city of Dublin, I thought an account of the severe contest which I fought with Lord Morpeth for the Irish capital would please Lord Wellesley, and I sent him a newspaper giving an account of our proceedings at the hustings. I received the following acknowledgment :—

"Kingston House, Knightsbridge, January 28, 1842.
"MY DEAR GREGORY,—

"For, although you might well be excused if you had forgotten me, I cannot expel from my heart my strong feeling of attachment to you, nor my ardent hopes formed in your most promising childhood, and now so gloriously fulfilled by the first dawn of your public life. Very soon after my last letter to you, I was seized with an illness which threatened the worst consequences, but which under Providence has led to an improvement of my constitution ; and now, in mind at least, I think I am as well as I have ever been, and I am assured that I may hope for the best as the weather improves. I was greatly obliged to you and to your amiable mother for calling on me, but at that time I was quite unable to see you.

"I have observed your progress with the greatest interest, and with the most heartfelt delight. Your rising sun gives more than a promise of a most bright and salutary day. I perceive by the initials on the cover that the report of your speech at the nomination comes from yourself. I am most grateful for this act of affection. Nothing can be more judicious (or, indeed, every way admirable) than your speech, which appears to have wounded very sharply and deeply. 'Perge modo.' I think your appearance a great blessing to our cause, to which I am most firmly attached. There is no other hope for this noble Empire, and I now rely most firmly and confidently on this hope. Sir Robert Peel and I are well acquainted, and my brother Arthur and I are now indissolubly united. All virtue and religion are with us. If I can be of any service to you, either here or in Ireland, you may command me. God prosper you! My kindest regards to your amiable mother. :

"Believe me always your much attached and faithful friend,

"WELLESLEY.

"Let me know your address. I have no objection to the publication of my strongest wishes for your success.—W."

On returning to London after the election, I had one interview, and one only, with Lord Wellesley. He invited me to luncheon, and after its announcement the servant closed the door. We remained talking for some time, until at length Lord Wellesley rose and led the way, and I ran forward to open the door for him. Lady Wellesley was also present, but did not accompany us. As I was leaving, she met me outside the door and said in a whisper, pressing my hand—

"I came to thank you so much for opening the door, as Lord Wellesley has not done such a thing for himself for very many years."

Afterwards we had a long conversation, which I shall not easily forget. He chiefly dwelt on the subject of Mr. Pitt, for whom he professed the most unbounded admiration. He mentioned that on one occasion when he was transacting business with Mr. Pitt, the subject turned on epidemics, and Mr. Pitt rose up and declaimed with all his majesty the lines at the opening of the "Iliad" on the plague among the Greeks. And Lord Wellesley followed his example. He, too, stood up and declaimed those magnificent lines with a majesty and strength which quite enthralled me. He then repeated the lament of Helen over the body of Hector, and the famous passage in the "Antigone" of Sophocles, where Antigone confronts Kreon and proclaims her intention to bury Polynices. I never saw Lord Wellesley again, but he was good enough to send me a copy of his classical compositions, containing a Latin Poem addressed to me on the occasion of my election, and an English translation of it. I received one more letter from him, dated the 1st of May, 1842 :—

"MY DEAR GREGORY,—

"For I cannot write 'Dear Sir,' and I do not wish to be answered 'Dear Lord.' Find some words that will express affection, friendship, and cordial regard. Alas! I have been very ill. I kept my bed almost the whole of last week, and I was in bed when you were so good as to call. Yet Chambers, my excellent medical attendant, says that my complaint is of no dangerous importance; but my *eighty-two* complaints make a whole of some weight. I am certainly getting better, and I ardently hope to be able to receive you and your dear mother (for whom I have and ever shall retain the warmest admiration and affection) and other dear friends, the comfort of life, without which, what is it? In the mean while, pray see Alfred Montgomery, who well merits your friendship. Pray present my best respects and regards to Lord Francis Egerton. I cannot give you a more just notion of my estimation of him than by assuring you that I never received more pleasure in my life than when you informed me that he had admitted you to the high advantage of his intimacy and friendship. Cultivate him, follow his example; in that soil good plants thrive (but I do not admire his law of marriage ! ! !).

"I hope to be able in a few days to have the high honour of seeing him. I was very well acquainted with his father and mother, and greatly respected them both.

"I wrote this immediately on receiving your note, with some difficulty; but I would not permit you to suffer another disappointment. Pray present my best wishes to your dear mother.

" Ever yours affectionately and truly,
" WELLESLEY."

On the 11th the following very sad note, written in his usual bold handwriting, was received by my mother :—

" Kingston House, May 11, 1842.

"My dear Mrs. Gregory,

"Be assured that I always feel the same love and affection for you and the dear Fisherman, but, alas! the hour of final separation approaches. I feel that I am dying; the hand of death is upon me, although my medical attendants say that I shall recover. I own I think otherwise. But the issues of life and death are in the hands of God, and whatever way His Almighty Will disposes, I submit. If I should recover, I hope to see you here, and to show you the most beautiful spot in the world, from which I send an humble tribute.

" Ever most affectionately,
" Your devoted
" WELLESLEY."

On the 26th of September, 1842, the great Marquis "qui super Garamantas et Indos protulit imperium" ceased to live.

I was about ten years old in the spring of 1827, when I was first sent to school to Mr. Ward's, at Iver, Buckinghamshire. He had been chaplain on board Lord Gambier's ship, and was on the whole not a bad schoolmaster, though very far from a good scholar. I had no particular love for him or for his family during the four years I was with him ; rather did I dislike them. He had one or two good ushers, and I got on pretty well, though not nearly as well as I ought to have done, had the tuition been better. Some of my holidays were passed at Styvechale Hall, and some at Ingestre, at Lord Talbot's, who was my grandfather's very dear friend. To run to and fro by the Holyhead mail to Dublin was too serious a matter in those days, and so most of my short vacations were spent in England. There were two festivities annually at the school, which gave me extreme pleasure. The one was on the 5th of November, when a boy was selected to have his face blackened and painted, and to play the part of Guy Fawkes. He was carried in this guise on a chair into the presence of the Miss Wards and other Iver ladies, and had his mouth and nose tickled with a straw till he laughed and thus disclosed who he was, which was, however, perfectly well known before. We then had a glass of wine and a bonfire, and greatly enjoyed our innocent dissipation. The second festivity was a whole holiday during the early summer, which was spent with a picnic at Blackwood, a place some miles from Iver. It well deserved its name. It was a very large wood of dark pine trees, with a large pond and small lake in the centre, and there we picnicked and caught butterflies and hunted out caterpillars—for entomology was the fashion of the school—and returned in the evening, tired and as happy as little kings. The remembrances of Blackwood have always lingered so freshly in my memory that a few years ago I made a pilgrimage to it, expecting to see a very uninteresting place; but it was not so. There was the old Chequers publichouse at the entrance of the wood, and the old oak paling covered with lichen, and the old pine trees and the high ferns and crisp carpet of pine spikes, and even the lake looked a very respectable and picturesque bit of water. I was rejoiced after nearly half a century to see the old spot again, and to find, what is, alas! so rare, that I had not lost as regards it the illusions of my boyhood.

In 1831 Mr. Ward drove me over in a postchaise to Harrow, where I was placed in the house of Dr. Longley,* afterwards Archbishop of Canterbury. I was put into what is called "the shell," a kind of limbo between the fourth and fifth forms, between the fagged and faggers. It was divided into the lower and upper shell, and it was in the former that I made my *début*. The upper shell, immediately above me, was composed of extremely big and extremely ignorant boys, whereas ours were small boys, but some very clever and well educated. Among these was Wilson, son of Professor Wilson, the eminent Sanskrit scholar; Tom Kent, stepson of the Bishop of London (Blomfield); Benjamin Brodie, afterwards Regius Professor of Chemistry at Oxford; Hugh Pearson, afterwards Canon of Windsor, the dear friend of Dean Stanley; and Edward Bouverie, now Right Honourable, the only one of these living at the time I write. Taking these boys as a lot, there was, undoubtedly, a very high aggregate of ability, rarely to be seen in the division of one remove. After this observation it must seem conceited for me to

---

* The late Lord Clonbrock told me that Dr. Longley said William Gregory was the cleverest boy he ever had under him.—A. G.

mention that I almost immediately rose to the top lot of
my remove. At the half-yearly examination it was always
Kent, Pearson, Gregory, or Pearson, Gregory, or Gregory,
Pearson, and so on. My two dear and special friends were
Pearson and Brodie, very different boys ; the one the most
gentle and refined of human beings ; the other vigorous,
hard-headed, sarcastic, and already a Radical in politics,
but a young fellow of strong feelings, inflexible honesty,
and a deep love of poetry. His father, Sir Benjamin
Brodie, often invited me to his house, and impressed me
more than any man I ever met, except Lord Wellesley,
with the idea of concentrated power. I was fortunate
enough to have for my tutor that fine scholar, Benjamin
Kennedy, afterwards Head Master of Shrewsbury School,
and now Regius Professor of Greek at Cambridge and
Canon of Ely. He was one of those men who, if he saw
in a pupil an appreciation of his beloved Greek writers,
could never do enough for him. He thought he perceived
this in me, and he showed me his own trophies at Cambridge, his admirable poems both in Greek and Latin. He
declaimed his favourite passages for my benefit. Nothing
is so contagious as enthusiasm. Fired by his energy, and
having my studies rendered easy by his constant readiness
to explain and illustrate every passage that barred my
way, I soon began to love my classics with all my heart.*

* These lines were written by Dr. Kennedy in 1880, in return for
a pot of honey of Hymettus we had brought him from Greece.—A. G.

EQUITI INLUSTRI
GULIELMO GREGORY
GRATIAS AGIT
MELLITUS ELIENSIS.

I.   Σύ μοι φίλως ἔδωκας Ἀττικὸν μέλι ·
      Δέχου τόδ' Ἀττικίζον ἐξ ἐμῶν μέλος.

Sweet Attic honey by your gift I gain :
Accept from me this Atticising strain.

There were at that time very few prizes at Harrow compared with the number and variety of them at present. There were three annually for poetry, Latin Hexameters, Latin Lyrics, and Greek Iambics, and one for Latin prose, a gold medal given by Sir Robert Peel, a distinction greatly prized; but the blue ribbon of Harrow was the scholarship, of which some years there were two, and some years only one.

Shortly after getting into the fifth form in the year 1833, Dr. Kennedy recommended me to try for the Latin Lyrics. He said—

"Of course you won't get them, as you have all the sixth form against you; but you may as well try. It will be good practice for you to have to do your very best."

I took his advice, wrote a very moderate set of Alcaics, and sent them in. The subject was "The River Ganges." About a month after, I met one of the monitors in the street, who said—

"Dr. Longley wants to see you. I rather think you have got the Lyrics."

II. Γρηγορίου πέμψαντος ἰοστεφάνων ἀπ' Ἀθηνῶν
Φημὶ τεῶν ἀνθῶν ἄνθος, Ὕμηττε, λαβεῖν.
Τοῖσι γὰρ ἐξ Ἀσίας ὅδε Γρηγορίοισιν [1] ὅμοιος
Ὡς γλυκὺ γευσαμένοις Ἀττικόν, οἶδε, μέλι,
Οἶδε μαθών, φιλέων δ' ἄρ' ἐμοὶ φιλέοντι παλαιῆς
Μνῆμα διδασκαλίης τοῦτ' ἀπέδωκε γάνος.

From violet-crowned Athens Gregory sends
Thy bee-wrought bloom, Hymettus, to his friends.
Like Asia's Gregories,[1] he, with learning graced,
Knows well how sweet is Attic honey's taste,
And my old service of tutorial aid
With that sweet bloom his heart has well repaid.

K.

---

[1] Gregorios dico, saeculo p. C. n. quarto nobiles, alterum Nazianzi, alterum Nyssae episcopum: quorum Athenis doctrinae studuisse illum scimus, hunc credimus, qui frater esset Basilii Magni, et ipse rhetoricae peritus.

It was true enough. Although the verses were nothing to boast of, those of the other candidates were less so. To this day I cannot forget the delight of my dear tutor Dr. Kennedy.

"Come along ; come along and see Mrs. Kennedy !"

Mrs. Kennedy was a pretty and a very winning woman, and apparently very much gratified also. He walked up and down the room with the tears in his eyes, repeating aloud for the benefit of his wife, who did not understand a word, the passages he most approved of in my prize poem.*

Dr. Kennedy's enthusiasm and my own delight, and the welcome present of £25 from my uncle, already mentioned, converted me from being an idle boy into a genuine hard-working student. The following year I again got the Latin Lyrics, and ran second for the Greek Iambics. The subject of the Lyrics was "The Temple of Jerusalem," and having just found a copy of them among my grandfather's papers, I honestly think they were a very creditable composition. But, unfortunately for me, without in the least intending to take any advantage over my competitors, I showed my verses to my tutor, Dr. Kennedy, the day before I sent them in. There were no alterations made by him—I believe he suggested the

---

* From that day till now, I have never been unfaithful to the classic muse. By land and by sea, at Newmarket and at Ceylon, under the palms in the oases of the great desert, and under stephanotis bowers in Cuba, I have never neglected my classics. Hardly a day, or rather a night, has passed that I have not read some portion of Greek or Latin literature. Unfortunately, my memory is defective as regards retention. I can get up for the moment any amount of matter, but after a time only a hazy remembrance remains.

About the year I mention I got a prize for repeating the whole of the "Bacchæ" of Euripides excepting the choruses, and a thousand lines of Claudian, at a stretch. Five years afterwards I could not have repeated fifty lines of one or the other.

omission of some stanzas. There was no secret about the matter, but it seems that some one made a representation to Dr. Longley on the subject. On his informing me that I had won the prize, he asked me if it was true that my tutor had seen and corrected the Lyrics before they were sent in. I said it was quite true he had seen, but untrue that he had corrected them, beyond inducing me to strike out some portions. Dr. Longley, with very great grief, then told me it would be impossible to give me the prize, and that it must go to Pearson, who was second. It was a terrible blow to me, and for the time had a very bad effect. I gave up my books and reading and got into every kind of scrape, until it ended by my being turned to the bottom of my remove, one of the heaviest punishments that could be inflicted, in consequence of a series of consecutive offences, the culminating one having been absence for a whole day. I was, however, only fishing. At that time fishing and shooting were my constant occupations, and there was not a field within miles of Harrow in which I had not poached by day, or a pond I had not dragged at night, with a celebrated loose character, Billy Warner by name. I really cared very little what I did or what became of me, so bitter and so enduring was the disappointment. I think I should have gone quite to the bad had I been under any master except Dr. Longley. I loved him so very dearly, that when I found him distant in his manner and yet at times looking upon me so kindly and so sadly, and when I could bring myself to think dispassionately upon his decision and recognize its justice, the better principle prevailed. I mended my ways, took to my books again, and next year (1835) got the Latin Hexameters, the Peel Medal, and the scholarship, and wound up my career by being head of the school for a considerable time.

It was when I was turned down that I became intimate with Anthony Trollope, who sat next to me. He was a big boy, older than the rest of the form, and without exception the most slovenly and dirty boy I ever met. He was not only slovenly in person and in dress, but his work was equally dirty. His exercises were a mass of blots and smudges. These peculiarities created a great prejudice against him, and the poor fellow was generally avoided. It is pitiable to read in his autobiography, just published, how bitter were his feelings at that time, and how he longed for the friendship and companionship of his comrades, but in vain. There was a story afloat, whether true or false I know not, that his father had been outlawed, and every boy believed it was the duty of a loyal subject of the crown to shoot or otherwise destroy "old Trollope" if possible. Fortunately, he never appeared among us. I had plenty of opportunities of judging of Anthony, and I am bound to say, though my heart smites me sorely for my unkindness, that I did not dislike him. I avoided him, for he was rude and uncouth, but I thought him an honest, brave fellow. He was no sneak. His faults were external; all the rest of him was right enough. But the faults were of that character for which schoolboys would never make allowances, and so poor Trollope was tabooed, and had not, so far as I am aware, a single friend. He might have been a thoroughly bad young fellow, and yet have had plenty of associates. He gave no sign of promise whatsoever, was always in the lowest part of the form, and was regarded by masters and by boys as an incorrigible dunce.

At the end of the summer half, for so it was called, of 1835, I raced away from Harrow, as was our custom, in one of Newman's postchaises, and was first past the Marble Arch at Hyde Park for the last time; thanks, I presume, to the heavy tip my uncle's successive presents of £25 enabled me to make the post boy. How we escaped breaking our necks and killing Newman's horses in these annual races from Harrow to London is to me a wonder.

I had been head of the school for a year, and had gained every prize which was to be obtained, except one—Greek Iambics—and for that I ran second. It was strange I did not get it, for I was a far better Greek than Latin scholar, and I had over and over again beaten my competitor in other examinations.

Harrow was a fine, manly place. It was a little world in itself, and boys were the arbiters of their own happiness or unhappiness in it. A bold, bright boy was sure to be a favourite, and even a studious, retiring boy was never unkindly treated ; but woe betided the sneak and the snob. On the whole, there was but little bullying, and the fagging was a salutary discipline for young gentlemen who had been made much of at home. They were brought to a level with their fellows, and it did them no harm to lay their master's tablecloth, make his tea and toast, and run messages. All the old rough work of brushing boots had been done away with. I do not think that even the coats were touched by fags. The only hardship was cricket fagging, when the small boys had to run after the cricket balls of their masters, whether they liked the game of cricket or not. I hear that this duty has been considerably modified since my time. I wish I could give the school a better character than I am forced to do as regards its teaching. It used to be most defective. The masters, with the exception of Dr. Kennedy, were bad. The system was bad. I came there, as I said before, with a considerable knowledge of French and Italian ; I left it having in a great

measure forgotten both. I came thoroughly grounded
in arithmetic from Mr. Ward's; I left it without the
power of doing a rule of three sum. Of Euclid and
algebra I was entirely ignorant. There was, it is true, a
French and mathematical master, the same man perform-
ing the double function. But good-natured, laughing
M. Marillier was a perfect Gallio as regards tuition. He
"cared for none of these things." He was quite willing
to help a boy who desired his help, but the nonfulfilment
of the task brought no evil consequences, and so no one
learned anything from him. My French was good
enough for a limping conversation, and with that he was
satisfied; but French literature, and the grammatical
rendering of the French language were unknown to me.
In one word, our whole course of studies was thoroughly
bad. I learned, it is true, a good deal of Latin and Greek;
but, except when with Dr. Kennedy, it was in a dry,
formal manner. A knowledge of Dawes's canons, and
Parson's, and Elmsby's rules and emendations was held
to be far more important than a genuine appreciation of
classic literature. I look over my commonplace books,
containing the notes of the masters on the various authors
we were studying, and nothing can be more dry, unattractive, and useless. We were condemned to learn by
heart the Eton grammar, written in crabbed Latin, which
we only half understood, and cordially detested. Our
time, both in and out of school, was wasted in writing
silly Latin verses. There was hardly any attempt to
make a boy think. A Latin essay or theme was written
once a week; but far more attention was paid to the
grammatical accuracy than to the thoughtfulness of the
production. History was little more to us than a collection
of dry facts and dates; it was anything but philosophy
teaching by example. We knew when Pericles lived and

died, when Brasidas and Callicratidas fell, when Epami-
nondas gained for his State the Hegemony of Greece,
but we heard little of the social life, the political neces-
sities, the religious influences, the artistic developments of
the different states ; in short, all that renders a knowledge
of early Greece and Rome invaluable. The husks of
history were thrown to us to digest as best we might, and
we were punished if we did not digest them. It was not
likely it could have been otherwise, considering that our
textbook was the " History of Greece," of the " Library of
Useful Knowledge," in one thin volume. Nor were we
more judiciously dealt with in regard to modern history.
We derived our notions of it from Hack's " Revolutions in
Europe," and those who have had to get up a portion of
it will not readily forget how intolerably dry and distasteful it is. We had no lectures or comments on English
history and literature—no essays on such subjects were
thought of.   We were not asked to think in our own
language, or to write it with vigour and correctness ; and
so much was this the case, that, when I went up to Oxford,
the very first thing my tutor—the present Dean Liddell
of Christ Church—enjoined upon me, was to read Dryden's
Prose Works, and to write English composition twice a
week, for he said, " Except in the case of the Rugby boys,
slovenliness of style and incorrectness in writing English
were the characteristics of public schoolboys." It is hard
to speak thus of one's Alma Mater, but it is strictly the
truth. The only thing to be said is that, besides the advantages of boyish public life, Harrow was just as good as
other schools at that time, always excepting Rugby, where
Dr. Arnold had revolutionized the whole discipline and
teaching system, and whence has proceeded that remarkable and salutary change apparent in all our scholastic
institutions, though not yet carried as far as it should be.

Before going up to reside at Oxford, I went for four months to the Rev. Nutcombe Oxenham, a fine scholar and charming gentleman, who had the parish of Modbury, in Devonshire, near Ivy Bridge. I read as honestly as he could wish, and improved my scholarship considerably by his tuition. There was very little to interest one at Modbury except the church, in which were buried many members of the Champernowne family at a most remote period. I went in after years to see their old family residence from Torquay. It is a long, straggling edifice, the hall being of the time of King John, and the rest of the building of various periods up to the time of Richard the Third. The owners have there dwelt in peace and quiet, none making them afraid, the eldest son being squire and the younger parson from remote ages. I carry away no other reminiscences of Modbury than of this old family, of very hard reading, and great kindness.

CHAPTER III.

IN the winter of the year 1836, I passed some time at
Garbally. At that time it was owned by Lord Clancarty,
the grandfather of the present lord,* who had been our
representative at the Hague and Brussels for many years,
and at the Congress of Vienna. He was a charming old
gentleman, extremely plain, most hospitable and genial;
and Lady Clancarty was one of the most high-bred women
I ever met. Garbally was at that time stiff, and the
general atmosphere was of the greatest propriety, from
which one person alone seemed anxious to break loose,
Lady Emily Trench, afterwards Cozzeres. She was a
peculiarly ill-favoured maiden, with the sweetest voice,
the kindest manner, and a very apparent desire for a little
dissipation. (When at Brussels she and some foreign
inamorato meditated flight, but her parents got an inkling
of what was going to take place, and she was stopped.
Her disposition was very docile, and she turned back
readily enough with her travelling kit, which consisted of
a pair of cuffs and a toothbrush.)

One day she informed me that an invitation had come
from a certain Mrs. Handcock of Carantrila to her, requesting her to make one of a party; and I also, as being a
possible future Galway squire, was asked to accompany
her. How we obtained permission is still a mystery.
I believe it was understood that we were to dine at

* Written in 1884.

Carantrila, and after the ball that followed were to go on
to the Palace of Tuam, a dwelling of the very odour of
sanctity and of frizzled eggs. We made our journey in
one of the state yellow Garbally carriages, and on arriving
at Carantrila (which is about six or seven miles from
Tuam) late in the evening, we found that not a soul of the
large party had been out that day, or, indeed, for several
days. The ladies were mostly dancing in a large new
ballroom erected for the occasion, and the gentlemen
were, many of them, more drunk than sober. The party
consisted of Lord Clanricarde and a favourite satellite
of his, Tom Nolan, better known as Tom the Devil; Sir
John and Lady Burke, then very handsome, and their
son Thomas, a young soldier in the Royals, looking like
a youthful Apollo with his beautiful complexion and wavy
golden hair; Mr. and Mrs. Persse, she my future mother-
in-law, a very pretty woman not long married, dressed
in white of an evening with pearl decorations; Mr. and
Mrs. L——, of County Clare, she clever and piquante; a
Miss R——, now Mrs. C—— in Galway, who was then lovely
with dark hair and eyes, and a rich complexion like a plum.
It was only the other day that I destroyed, among other
love tokens, a mitten she gave me, and which at the time
I greatly prized. There was Granby Calcraft, the brother
of Lady Burke, a London dandy and swell out at elbows;
and one or two more of no great note. But I must not
forget the daughters of our host and hostess. The girls
were just rising into womanhood, and nothing could have
been more captivating, such charming manners, sweet,
pretty, innocent ways, and a determination to make the
house pleasant.

On our arrival we proceeded to dance, and kept up
our afternoon ball with great spirit till nine o'clock, when
dinner was served, to which we sat down, about twenty-

eight to thirty in number. Lord Clanricarde took the
head of the table and did the honours. At about
eleven we adjourned to the drawing-room and danced
and flirted till one o'clock, when supper was announced.
After a decent interval the ladies retired to bed, and the
fun became fast and furious, and the drinking steady,
Lord Clanricarde, Sir John Burke, Tom Burke, Mr. Persse,
and myself being the only shirkers. It was my first
acquaintance with Lord Clanricarde, and he left an impression on me which I never forgot by the manner in which
he preserved his self-respect even in the midst of this
riotous license. Although full of the wildest fun, he
never allowed the slightest liberty to be taken with him,
or rather, never put himself in the position of having
familiarities reciprocated. It was about three o'clock in the
morning; A. Z——, of C——, had just drank off a tumbler
of almost raw whisky which I had given him, I believe
intentionally, and had dropped from his chair like a felled
ox; Tom Nolan had placed his chair on the table, and
was singing some rollicking song, when the door was
suddenly thrown open, and Mrs. Z——, in her night-dress,
with her hair down her shoulders, and in naked feet, stood
in the doorway and surveyed the scene. A deep silence
ensued. Suddenly she perceived her prostrate husband,
and rushed to his assistance as he lay upon the floor.

" Get away ! " was all he could mutter.

" You wretches, you are murdering him ! " shrieked
Mrs. Z——. " I arraign you as murderers. I arraign you,
Lord Clanricarde, as chief murderer."

" Easy, easy, ma'am," said his lordship ; " we will soon
bring A—— up to his bed all right enough. A drop of
whisky don't kill a man in this country."

So he took him by the head, and I took him by the
heels, and some other sober guest lent a hand, and, preceded

by Mrs. Z——, we slowly and solemnly bore him upstairs, and laid him on the matrimonial bed.

The next day when I awoke and looked at my watch, I found it was half-past twelve o'clock, so I dressed in all haste and came downstairs rather ashamed of myself. On reaching the drawing-room, all was dark. I made my way then to the dining-room; all was dark there also. At last I heard a sound from the kitchen regions, and saw a glimmering light, which proceeded from a candle carried by a very feeble old woman, apparently for no purpose. I asked for news about breakfast, and she said—

"The divil a mouthful you'll get before three o'clock, so you had much better go to bed again."

I took her advice, and, as she escorted me through the dining-room, I gazed with admiration at the long files of claret bottles, the contents of which had been consumed at dinner and at supper.

At three o'clock I came down, and by degrees the party dropped in to breakfast.

Such was the mode of proceeding during the next two days. The only person who went out of doors during that time was young Tom Burke, the most abstemious man of the whole party, who started forth with unshaken nerves, and supplied the table with snipe. Such was our life during those three glorious days, and as we drove to the respectable Palace of Tuam, Emily Trench and I bound ourselves by dreadful oaths to profound silence, and the archbishop and my great-aunt Trench to the end of their lives believed that the party at Carantrila was not only merry but wise.

I have gone at some length into this visit, as hardly any scene narrated by Sir Joseph Barrington could be more amusing. It was the dying-out flicker of old Irish revelry, as told by him.

In the spring of 1837 I went up to Christ Church,

Oxford, having some months previously matriculated to the satisfaction of the dreaded Dr. Gaisford, known as the "Learned Blacksmith," from his swarthy face and uncouth manner. At the time of my matriculation, I remarked, among the other students undergoing the ordeal, one in particular, who struck me much. He seemed very old, very ugly, very unclean, and very uncouth, and I wondered what could have brought such a creature to such a smart college as Christ Church. Shortly after my coming up there were three exhibitions or scholarships for Christ Church men alone. They were pleasant things to get, as they about paid for the food of the holder of them. I went in, thought I had done a most successful examination, as many subjects were given with which I was thoroughly conversant, and when the result was announced it was Linwood first, Gregory second. My antiquated and dirty companion at matriculation was the victor, and by all accounts an easy winner. It was hardly a crumb of comfort to have got the second. A rumour pervaded the college that he wrote off sixty or eighty of the most unimpeachable Greek iambics, whereas I felt rather elated at having produced about twenty during the same period of two hours, all of which were not unimpeachable.

The same year I contested the Craven Scholarship, open to all the University, and there I found my old antagonist. I had still great hopes that I should be able to turn the tables on him, but alas! it was again Linwood first, Gregory second. I had only the barren honour of being the second best scholar of my year. It was truly unfortunate my coming into contact with this remarkably learned man, a kind of modern Porson in Greek, the author of the profound "Lexicon Æschylaus," and the subsequent master of Birmingham school; for not only had I to submit to the bitterness of defeat, but I became dishcartened and gradually estranged from the steady reading set of men, with whom I had allied myself at the beginning of my Oxford career. Still, however, I continued to read on, though in rather a desultory manner, and the result was that, on going in for the Craven Scholarship the following year, I again ran second, this time to Mr. Marshall, a fellow-pupil of my tutor Henry Liddell, now Dr. Liddell, Dean of Christ Church, whom he had assured me I was sure to beat. He was, however, in thorough good training, and I was not ; and such has been the case in many a race.

A circumstance occurred about this time which exercised a most fatal influence over my whole future life. I went, for the Easter vacation in 1837, to pay a visit to some old Harrow friends at Cambridge, and in their society I met several undergraduates who were bitten with the love of racing. They brought me over to Newmarket, showed me all the favourite horses for the great events, introduced me to one or two jockeys, minor stars, of course, and sent me back to Christ Church full of racing information. From that out I deserted my old studious friends, and thought of nothing but Epsom and Newmarket. Still I read on for my degree by fits and by starts. I had two of the best coaches in Oxford, Osborne Gordon for classical scholarship, and Elder for logic and philosophy, and I kept myself pretty fairly up to their requirements. Gordon was famous for a Greek epigram which he wrote during a splendid examination for an Ireland scholarship, which he won. The subject was "the two children sculptured by Chantrey on a monument in Lichfield Cathedral." They are represented as sleeping in each other's arms. As well as I recollect the words were—

"'A Μοῖρ' ἁ κρυερὰ τὼ καλὼ παῖδ' 'Αφροδίτας
"Ηρπασε—τῶν καλῶν τὶς κόρος ἐστ' 'Αϊδι;

'Ἀλλὰ σύ γ' Ἀγγελία, τὸν ἀμδέα μῦθον ἔχουσα
Βάσκ' ἴθι παγκοίταν εἰς Ἄϊδαο δόμον·
Λέξον δ', 'Ω δαῖμον, τὰν καλὰν ὤλεσας ἄγραν,
'Οὐ γὰρ τὰς ψυχὰς οὔδε τὰ σώματ' ἔχεις·
'Αι μέν γὰρ ψυχαὶ μετέβησαν ἐς οὐρανὺν εὔρυν,
Σώματα δ' ἐν γαίᾳ νήγρετον ὕπνον ἔχει."

I believe I am quoting correctly, though it is forty-six years since I committed these lines to memory. I mention them because, some thirty years after Osborne Gordon and I parted, we met in the British Museum, and looked hard at one another. He said—

"I wonder if you remember who I am?"

"I wonder," I replied, "if you remember a certain Greek epigram." And I quoted the first of the lines above.

I need hardly say how immensely gratified he was. He had then subsided into a country parson, but was well known as a man of great ability, and was, moreover, to the best of my belief, connected with the *Times*.

In 1838 I went abroad for the long vacation to Germany, to read with Mr. Massey, fellow of Wadham, and subsequently head of Durham College. Mr. Edmund Oldfield, afterwards of the British Museum, and the life and soul of the Arundel Society from its birth to the present time, was my companion. Mr. Massey was a most admirable scholar and a capital companion. We first established ourselves at the Gasthof of the Goldenen Krone, at the little town of Nassau, about two miles and a half from Ems, and there we took long walks, read very hard, and flirted with and learned German from our host's nieces in the evening. At last, however, the temptation of the gambling tables at Ems proved a greater attraction than the German lessons and the Mädchens, and I hired a pony from a miller and used to ride over of an evening in order to enjoy a mild roulette or "trente et quarante." My tutor

made no objection so long as I returned with a good
number of silver pieces, but when luck turned, and I began
to fancy myself in love with a young lady from Hamburg,
and my work became neglected, he thought it high time
to decamp, and we proceeded to finish our vacation at
Rudesheim.   Nothing could have been more delightful
than the time we spent there, and the glorious long walks
we took in the Niederwald and on the other side of the
Rhine.   We had one famous episode, the glory of which
is still green in my memory.

One night, as I and Mr. Oldfield were returning home
rather late, we were assailed with abusive epithets from
four young fellows who had just emerged from a Gasthof,
full of wine and insolence.   The epithets we bore, but
when they proceeded to emphasize them by throwing
gravel at us, the British lion was aroused, and we resolved
to try the hazard of battle ; and so, having agreed to stand
back to back, I hit one of our assailants with closed fist
full in the face with all my strength.   Well was it that
I had devoted some of my spare time in learning the art
of self-defence, and in being knocked about by Mr. Sambo
Sutton, the black prize-fighter, at Oxford.   We had a
desperate encounter which lasted twenty minutes.   Our
adversaries rushed in, boxing our ears with open hands,
while we struck their faces at each approach with the closed
fist.   Fortunately, we repelled these rushes, and thus won
the battle.   Had we been thrown we should have had a
sore bad time.   At length they retreated, leaving a coat
behind.   We erected this into a trophy in the most classical
manner, and had we been possessed of a trumpet, would
have sounded a triumphant fanfare.   The next day we
presented a sad appearance, our ears being swollen to the
most enormous size ; and we were oppressed by the dread
of the appearance of a policeman to haul us off to a court

of justice on a charge of assault and battery. No such misfortune happened, but on the third day our little maid informed me that a baker from Assmanshauser requested to see us, and announced that he had been desperately beaten by us. We went down in much alarm, and found the young baker with a lip split open and closed with plaster, and with two terrible black eyes into the bargain. But instead of meeting us with threats, he came forward and shook hands, and said he came over to make friends, as the fight was fair and free. We celebrated the reconciliation with copious Rudesheim, and discovered that one object he had was to be shown the English mode of fisticuff, as he often got into quarrels and would soon settle them if he could only serve his antagonists as he had been served. We gave him a lesson, but found it hard to convince him that I had not a stone in my hand on the night of the fray. We parted capital friends, and so ended the " Battle of Rudesheim."

Next year was the time for my degree, and I had every reason to expect getting my first class, the great object of our Oxford ambition—the credentials, in fact, for the start of an ambitious young man in life. I had left Christ Church and had gone to New Inn Hall, not in the least from any disapprobation of my conduct, but because I had out-stayed the usual number of terms. Unfortunately, at New Inn Hall no discipline was observed. I lived in the town and could do just as I liked. The consequence was that I went to the Newmarket spring meetings, and afterwards signalized myself by riding from Oxford to Epsom and back on relays of hacks, cantering all the way. There I saw Bloomsbury win the Derby during a snowstorm, and there I won £300 on him, which confirmed my fatal love of racing. On sitting down to my work, I underwent a close examination from my coach, Mr. Elder. He pronounced me to be perfectly safe as regards classics, but that I had a long leeway to make up both in divinity and logic, two subjects of no mean importance. I had, in fact, totally neglected them. I had no long time for preparation, and I worked literally night and day, until I felt almost dazed and stupid.

The day, or rather the night but one before the examination arrived, and I was taken violently ill by a rush of blood to the head. The doctor was sent for at once, as I was perfectly prostrate. I was ordered to leave Oxford at once, and not to open a book of study for six months. At the end of the six months I tried to begin work again, but it was useless and hopeless. I left Oxford in broken spirits, and did not go in even for a common degree. I had not the heart to do so, after feeling confident that I should be on the first class list. Such was the first result of my visit to Newmarket.

The winter that followed this unfortunate fiasco I spent at Rome with my father and mother. Our journey through Italy was very imposing—two carriages, two maids, two manservants, and a courier, "*cosi viaggino i ricchi,*" as Byron says. We took apartments at Cerny's Piazza d'Espagna, and practised on a liberal scale the virtue of hospitality. Whether it was the badness of the dinners or of the atmosphere, I cannot say ; but shortly after the Christmas religious festivities, I was taken ill with gastric fever, and for two or three weeks lay between life and death. At last, however, a good constitution and the skill of Dr. Gloque prevailed, and I gradually recovered. At certain times one almost feels it a comfort to have been ill, so rapturous is the return to health again. How well I remember being taken out day after day just to sit on a cushion propped up upon

the steps of St. John de Lateran in the warm early spring.
I was too weak to speak, but not to look at and drink
in the soft outline of the Alban Hills, and the solemn
beauty which gives to "the mother of dead nations" that
indescribable fascination which ever holds captive those
who have once come under its influence. All the while
strength seemed to be pouring in, and I gradually was
strong enough to mount a horse and take a gallop with
the hounds on the Campagna. That same night the
enemy returned, and attacked my heart. I had previously been suffering tortures during my long illness,
but there was temporary relief. This time the agony
was dreadful ; it seemed as if my chest was bursting open
and I prayed for death, so intolerable was the pain. Dr.
Gloque said it was impossible I could hold out much
longer, and he proposed that which was contrary to all
accepted practice, to bleed me, as the only chance left.
He did so, and the effect was something quite extraordinary. As the blood flowed out, so flowed out the
pain, and the next day I was well again. Dr. Gloque
recommended me to be most careful in avoiding sudden
chills for some years, as there was every probability of
gastric fever returning, and he was right in his warning.
Two years afterwards I was again attacked in Paris, and
all the painful symptoms had recommenced. I was
attended by Dr. MacLaughlin, a physician of much
eminence at the time. I told him what had occurred
at Rome, and begged of him to bleed me, which he
positively refused to do. At last, on giving him a written
paper taking all the responsibility on myself, he agreed
to be present while the bleeding was performed, though
not to do it himself. Again the same salutary effect
was produced. In one day the swelling of the joints
had subsided ; in three days I was able to walk about

my room, and at the end of the week I was about
as usual.

On the present occasion I did not recover strength
so soon ; but I felt myself obliged to return to England
well or ill, much to the consternation of my parents, as
I had backed Coronation, the favourite for the Derby,
to win a large sum of money, and it was necessary to
make financial arrangements in case he was beaten. I
therefore started off, though scarcely able to crawl, to
meet the French steamer at Civita Vecchia. Owing to
some delay on the road, I arrived at the port just in
time to see the smoke of the vessel making its way to
France, and so I had to spend a week at the little inn
of the place. To this day I recall with gratitude the
kindness of the people belonging to it ; but the one who
specially devoted herself to me was the daughter of the
host, Steffa by name. I was young, feeble, rather nice
looking, and she pitied me with the whole strength of
her warm, impulsive, Italian nature. She was a pretty,
gentle girl, about seventeen or eighteen, and every day
she took me out to a place overlooking the sea, and there,
in a sunny spot among lentils and broom, we watched
the classic antics of the goats and talked for hours.
Steamboats and railways, which were just beginning to
be generally constructed, were a great topic. They were
evidently, in her mind, under the patronage of the devil,
the "nemico di Dio," and she strongly urged me not to
place myself voluntarily under his influence.

"Why not go to England in a *carrozza*, or by the
diligence, of course ? "

"But still I should have to cross the sea, as England
is an island."

"Why not go there in a *barca* with a sail, and so
avoid all bad influences ? "

But the main subject of conversation was religion. She could not understand why I was a heretic, as I professed to believe in the Holy Virgin, St. Joseph, and every other saint she mentioned, besides my namesake Pope Gregory, to whom she was convinced I was related. At last she discovered to her satisfaction that I had only two sacraments and she had seven. This was a sad blow, and we talked it over very gravely one afternoon amid many tears on her part.

The next day, wishing to comfort her, I said, " Steffa, I have been thinking during the night over these sacraments, and I am quite ready to accept the seven."

" Do you really say so ? " she cried, seizing me in her arms. "Why, then you can stay here and marry me, for you will be as good a Catholic as I am, and you will soon be well," and so on.

I could not exactly explain my connection with Coronation which compelled me to return to England. I could only say that I had a father and mother who had great objections to seven sacraments, and that I was sure I never could overcome them. So it was agreed that unless I wrote within a moderate space of time that there were no obstacles—she should be quite free to marry whom she pleased ; for she was an only child, and her father wished much to have some one to keep the inn, which would have to become very large when the devil should bring the railway from Rome ; not that I need trouble myself about its management ; she would do that, and I could sit upstairs and write letters.

At length the Messageries boat arrived. It was on some particular saint's day, and Steffa presented herself to me in full dress, with a white veil floating from her head to the ground. As I had accepted the seven sacraments, she insisted on my giving her my arm and

attending Mass with her. We made a fine show going
down the street, and, to my great shame and confusion
of face, who should I see watching us with much amusement but two young Englishmen with whom I made
subsequent acquaintance, Captain Fitzhardinge Berkeley
and Major Everett, well known afterwards at the viceregal court of Lord Morpeth. They had landed during
the stay of the vessel, and were seeing the sights of the
place. This confusion of face was still more increased
at my departure by the farewell of Steffa, by whom I
was bewailed and kissed in a frantic manner before all
beholders. The child of Nature utterly ignored even the
presence of my stolid English servant.

On our arrival at Marseilles, Captain Berkeley and
myself voted diligence travelling to be low and a bore
and slow, so we hired a phaeton and posted to Paris. It
cost us each about three times as much as would have
done our places in the *coupé*, and we arrived nine hours
after the diligence. The same evening we went to dine at
the Trois Frères Provençaux, and had rather an amusing
adventure. We had nearly finished our dinner when two
tall over-dressed men came swaggering in. Shortly afterwards one of them got up and crossed the room to us.

"I see," said he, "you are two English gentlemen.
I dare say you can decide a bet between my friend
and myself as to whether Macleod has been hung
or not."

Macleod had been made prisoner by the Americans
as having taken a chief part in the burning of the *Caroline*,
a piratical steamer in Niagara river, when moored on the
American side and flying the American flag. We replied
we were all abroad as regarded recent news, having only
just come from Italy.

"Now," said I to Captain Berkeley, "are you up to

a little amusement? I have not been on the turf for a short time without having picked up some knowledge of rogues and swindlers. These fellows are both one and the other. They are sure to ask us to sup or dine, then to introduce play, and to cheat us if they can. We know no one in Paris, we are here only for three days; why not enjoy ourselves at their expense?"

"By all means," said Captain Berkeley, only too happy for the adventure.

Presently the same man came back and said that, as we had mentioned our being perfect strangers, perhaps he and his friend might be of some service in showing us the lions of Paris, about which we professed entire ignorance. He introduced himself as Mr. Reynolds and his friend as Captain Elliott. I remembered all I had heard about the pair. Elliott had been concerned in a recent duel, in which he had shot a man under circumstances which smacked of murder after a row in a most disreputable night-house, the Piccadilly Saloon, now extinct. The other, Reynolds, was a cheat and gambler, who lived by fleecing young men who were fools enough to play with him.

We adjourned by invitation to the Hôtel Mirabeau, where the party had a very handsome suite of rooms, and where we were presented to Madame Reynolds, a remarkably good-looking woman. Her real name was Emma Kaye, and her relations with Mr. Reynolds were but of a temporary nature, in which she served as a decoy duck. We went first to a *café chantant*, and then returned to the hotel, where we had a game of what they called "jeu Napoleon," but which was neither more nor less than Blind Hookey. While we were so engaged, a gentlemanly man came in who was introduced to us as Mr. Baring. He, too, was a well-known character, and went by the name

of "Bruiser Baring" from his proficiency with his fists. In
the course of the evening some bets were made on our
ages, the loser to give a sumptuous dinner next day at
the Trois Frères.

"This is the opening of the campaign," said I to
Berkeley, as we walked home. "They mean to give us
a most beguiling dinner, to make us drink too much, and
then to pluck us." And I adjured him by all his gods
to keep the muzzle on.

Next day we did have a gorgeous dinner indeed, and
Emma Kaye, as Mrs. Reynolds, put forth all her seduc-
tions to induce us to exceed, and to my horror I saw
Berkeley, not only making free with what was before him,
but suggesting that the most rare and expensive wines
should be called for.

"I saw," said he afterwards, in reply to my scolding
for his imprudence, "that you were taking sufficient care
for two of us, and so I determined to work them." And
work them no doubt he did, to a considerable tune.

After dinner we adjourned to their rooms, and cards
were proposed. After playing a short time for small sums,
Mr. Bruiser Baring proposed so to arrange the game that
any player might have power to raise the stakes to a
considerable amount. Captain Berkeley demurred, and
Baring replied in a very insolent manner, upon which
Captain Berkeley remarked in the coolest way—

"I'll see you all d——d first. I am not going to be
'rooked' by any of you."

A fierce uproar ensued. Bruiser Baring declared he
would instantly inflict chastisement upon my friend unless
he apologized; but Captain Berkeley very calmly, in spite
of the Chateau d'Yquem and the Lafitte of '30 which he
had been imbibing copiously, replied—

"If you raise your hand I will break every window

in the room, and you will have the police on you, which
you will hardly like."

Mr. Reynolds, who had preserved his head in order to
manipulate the cards and do the cheating, now interfered
and tried to make up the misunderstanding ; but Baring and
Elliott, who had both taken too much, and were determined
on a quarrel, insisted on blood and a meeting next day.
This was accepted, and we departed highly delighted with
our evening's entertainment.

On the morrow we were waited on by Mr. Elliott,
demanding a most ample apology. This I refused
peremptorily, so a meeting was arranged for that evening
in the Bois de Boulogne.

" Pistols," said Mr. Elliott.

" Pistols, of course ! " said I.

But the last card was still to be played. As I was
bowing him out—

" There is one matter of importance," I remarked with
much emphasis ; " you know nothing of us, we are strangers
to you and may be adventurers quite unfit for you to meet.
We, on the other hand, do not know you. I must therefore request of you to go with us to the British Embassy
where, of course, we shall all be known, and can be formally
presented to each other."

Mr. Elliott looked extremely dumfoundered, merely
said, " Oh, of course ! though we are satisfied about you,"
and departed.

In about half an hour in came Mr. Reynolds, who said,
" I am thoroughly disgusted with this wretched business
caused by Baring's bad temper. He is very sorry for what
occurred since I spoke to him, and begs of you to think no
more about it."

The reconciliation was sealed by an engagement for us
all to go to Chantilly races the next day ; but we had had

enough of disreputable society, and departed to London by the train.

In about a month after I met Monsieur and Madame Reynolds walking in Hyde Park.

"Tiens," said madame ; "voilà Monsieur Gregory."

"Oui, madame, c'est bien moi et j'ai l'honneur de vous saluer ! " was my reply, and our last expression of recognition.

The whole gang were subsequently arrested and imprisoned in Belgium for some gambling and gross cheating transaction.

One must be very young to enjoy such adventures.

Meanwhile the Derby was approaching and Coronation becoming daily a greater favourite. I still continued to back him, even till he was saddled, so that when the time came for the race my losses would have been very heavy had he been beaten. However, he won in a canter, and my gains were over £5000, a large sum at that time, before the heavy betting began.

In the year 1877 I dined with the Prince at Marlborough House, and there met the late Lord Clanwilliam. He told me that he perfectly recollected, in the year 1841, just after Coronation's Derby, standing by a very young man in the corner of the Jockey Club stand, who was making up his book ; and that the young man, after the close of his calculations, said, in a soliloquy to himself—

"Well, I am sure I don't know how I shall spend all this money ! "

And the young man was myself.

My father and mother were returning at this time from Italy, and were dining one day at the *table d'hôte* at Frankfort. The conversation turned on the Derby, which had just been run, and one of the convives remarked that he

heard that one of the heaviest winners was a young Irishman, who had hardly left Oxford, of the name of Gregory.
This was pleasant news wherewith to greet anxious parents,
and fully explained my strange departure in such feeble
health from Rome.

CHAPTER IV.

In the spring of 1842 we were paying a visit to Gar-bally, when the news arrived of the death of Mr. West, the member for Dublin city, and there seemed to be some difficulty in getting a suitable candidate. The late Lord Clancarty suggested that on every ground I should stand ; that my family was well known in Dublin, where my grandfather, the late Right Honourable W. Gregory, had been very popular and much respected. He was, more-over, the great personal friend of Sir Robert Peel, the Prime Minister ; and Sir Robert himself had been very complimentary to me when he attended Harrow speech day, on the occasion of my having won his gold medal for Latin prose. Accordingly negotiations were entered into with the political wire-pullers in Dublin, of whom Remmy Sheehan, the editor of the *Evening Mail*, assumed the chief importance. He was a funny looking little man, like a peg-top, full of self-conceit and pomposity, but of con-siderable ability and vigour. He had known my grand-father, who, I believe, had done him some good turn, and I am bound to say that throughout the election he behaved towards me loyally, considerately, and like a true friend. Lord de Grey was then Lord Lieutenant, Lord Eliot Chief Secretary, and by them my candidature was accepted. The Dublin people welcomed me very heartily, and an agreement was come to that I was to pay £4000 down, that the balance was to be made up somehow, and that I was to have nothing to do with bribery. The election ultimately cost about £9000; where the balance came from I know not, but among the vouchers in possession of my committee was one which was afterwards placed in my hands: "For 1500 freemen, gratification, at £3 per head, £4500."

The next thing was the issuing of an address, which at that time was an absolutely impossible feat for me, for I knew as little as I cared about politics. That difficulty was surmounted by the Right Honourable Fred Shaw, the Recorder and member for the College, who composed for me a grandiloquent proclamation, pledging me to a strong Protestant programme. Then came the canvassing, which I got through pretty well, thanks to the self-confidence acquired at Harrow and Oxford. I am bound, however, to confess that the speeches made by me to various bodies during this canvass were not of that degree of excellence which gave any hope of the uprising of a rival to Grattan and Plunkett. They were, however, noisy, and did well enough to get up the steam, as it was called, among the Protestant voters; and they gave me confidence in the sound of my own voice, and taught me to think on my legs.

Among the extreme partisans distinguished by the virulence of their language and uncompromising hostility to Roman Catholics as well as to their religion were a Protestant clergyman, the Rev. Tresham Gregg, and Professor Butt, of Trinity College. They were both admirable mob speakers, and they "got the steam up" with a vengeance. Tresham Gregg was a mighty man of valour among the Protestant operatives. He was a fluent, vigorous orator, with a voice of Stentor, and a remarkably fine presence. He was supposed, perhaps unjustly, not to be quite trustworthy in money matters, and some difficulty arose because my committee refused to entrust to him the handling of "gratifications" for the freemen. He sulked, in consequence, for some days, and refused to "get up the steam;" but the committee made it all right subsequently by a direct largesse, as I was informed at the time. I doubt if he was sincere, but, at all events, he was consistent, and that is more than I can say for Butt, who was at that time the extreme of the extremes in all religious and financial questions, the very type of ultra-domineering, narrow-minded, Protestant ascendency. These two men did me much harm at the time by hinting at my half-heartedness, and by urging me "to come out" against the Catholics at the various meetings during my canvass. I resisted them as far as I could, but I certainly entered Parliament burdened with admissions which, had I known better, I never should have made, and which were a millstone round my neck. I was so highly amused at the time with the account of one of these meetings at Fishamble-street Theatre, where I addressed a large gathering of freemen, that I preserved it, and insert it here :—

"THE TORY CANDIDATE—EXTRAORDINARY SCENE.

"The following report appears in the *Freeman's Journal* of this morning :—

"'The ruined theatre in Fishamble Street—which, for the last two months, has been devoted exclusively to the domestic purposes of mice, rats, and other vermin—was last night devoted to a more ignoble use, and was desecrated in being made the scene of the insane caperings and tumblings of the "Protestant" operatives of the city, who hired the mouldering edifice for a spree, and had "a regular night of it." The house was crowded, not to the ceiling, for there is none, but to the rafters, and the audience, the most plebeian we have ever found ourself amongst, fooled themselves to the top of their bent, fulminating anathemas against O'Connell, committing the Pope and Popery to the regions of Orcus, and shouting, screaming, yelling, and hallooing till they grew black in the face (blacker, we should say, than they were on entering), in approval of the lofty tumblings of the various gentlemen who kindly consented to exhibit for their gratification. In the orchestra a band of music was located, which ever and anon struck forth some party air, such as "Croppies lie Down," "Derry Down," "Boyne Water," "First of July," "Protestant Boys," etc., etc., which were performed amidst the most vociferous exclamations of wild delight, unmerciful thumpings of the mouldering timbers of the edifice, and ubiquitous wavings of orange and blue handkerchiefs, filthily dirty. The meeting was called for seven o'clock, but a great deal of delay took place, and the "operatives" would probably have grown highly incensed at the want of punctuality in taking the chair, were it not that various devices were had recourse to by accommodating persons in various quarters of the house to beguile the wearisomeness of delay. One gentleman especially, who was located in the dress circles, and who consulted for the freedom and coolness of his person, by omitting to wear a shirt, was particularly successful in banishing *ennui* by his Tory skilful performance of various Orange songs, which he gave with great gusto, the company joining in full chorus.

"'At half-past eight o'clock, on the motion of the never-to-be-half-enough-honoured T. D. Gregg, the chair was taken by Mr. William Paisly, amid a hurricane of yells, indicative of applause.

"'The chairman advanced to the foot-lights, bearing in his arms a huge bust made of plaster of Paris, which he fondled to his breast, evidently being at the time under feelings of the deepest mental emotion. Presently he took out an enormous pocket-handkerchief, orange and blue, with which, having affectionately kissed the nose and upper features of the clay figure, he rubbed his own face with infinite zeal and violence, amid thunders of applause.

"'This affecting ceremony evidently excited deep emotion in the performer, nor did the witnessing of it produce a less powerful effect upon the audience, for the tear of sympathy rose unbidden to the eye of hundreds. The chairman then assumed the presidency, and, having done so, he gave the meeting to understand that he was the owner of the bust which they all admired so highly, and the possession of which he looked upon as the source of the deepest gratification that the human heart could experience. That bust was the bust of the Right Honourable William Gregory, grandfather to the gentleman who would be member for Dublin, and he would put it under the table if they liked (shouts of "No, no!").

"'Chairman: "Shall I put it on the table?"

"'A thousand voices: "Yes, do."

"'Chairman: "Very well, let it stay there; I'll now be quiet." (Great applause, in the midst of which one gentleman having been detected in the act of transferring another gentleman's handkerchief from the owner's pocket to his own, was, after a long scuffle, given into the custody of the police).

"'Order having been at length restored, a Mr. Marlow came forward to propose the first resolution, which was to the effect that the association pledged themselves to support Mr. Gregory at the ensuing election. The speaker made an interminable speech, in the course of which he took a very extended view of society, and spoke with great aptness on things in general. He spoke of what he termed the "greeviances" of Ireland in particular, and said that the master grievance of all was Hutton's Bread Bill. (This intelligence had evidently all the charms of novelty, for the audience clapped their hands in approval, until blisters of enormous size must have been raised upon their palms).

"'The name did not transpire of the gentleman who seconded this resolution, but for the benefit of posterity be it recorded that he was a tall athletic gentleman of unique appearance, who read his speech out of his hat—

> "And still he spoke, and still the wonder grew,
>   How one small hat could compass all he knew."

"'The speech was to us unintelligible.

"'Mr. Gregory then came forward, and the operatives, as soon as they caught a glimpse of his shadow, made heaven re-echo with their vociferations. The trumpeters blew "See the Conquering Hero comes" until they were black in the face, and the drummers whacked the implements of their vocation till they were sore again, to the same tune. Gregory then proceeded to address the meeting, and many and wonderful were the things he said. He would support the present Government, because he considered it a conscientious one, and one that would not bow the knee to an insolent and disappointed faction (shouts). He did not like the manner in which the grant was made to Maynooth, and would try, with other members, to bring the question to a solution (screams). He hated the system of national education (yells); and he would endeavour to abolish it (indescribable noises). He called upon the freemen to support him (shouts of "So we will," from a dozen ragged men in the gallery); and he trusted they would not be prevented from doing so by the present corporation. The man who called himself the Liberator of Ireland (grunts), thought that he was the only man in the world who was entitled to use an Irish word, but this was a mistake. He (Mr. Gregory) was a Connaught man (immense cheering), and he would say *nabocklish* *

---

* Humbug.

to whatever would fall from the lips of O'Connell. They should not mind O'Connell at all, but they should come and give their votes to him, and thus make him one of the units which made up the glorious Protestant majority in the House of Commons. The Protestant party had a majority of eighty in the House ; but that, after all, was but a small majority, and might soon be reduced to nothing if they were not energetic to the last. But triumph was sure (shouting, bawling, screaming, yelling, and squeaking). Win they must. *Faugh a ballagh !* That meant "clear the way "—clear the way to a great moral victory (shouts of " More power to your elbow "—the right elbow, it is to be presumed). Would they desert their post (vociferations of " No, no; we'd be blowed first ; " and cries of " No surrender ! ")? If Dublin was lost, it would be the greatest blow ever inflicted on the Protestant party. But they should all vote for him, for his political and religious principles were the same as those held by his forefathers. Mr. Gregory resumed his seat, amid a volley of indescribable noises, wavings of pocket-handkerchiefs, and various other demonstrations of applause.

" 'The Rev. T. D. Gregg then bounced upon his legs ; but the scene which followed baffles all description, and, for this very potent reason, we will not attempt to pourtray it. As for his speech, it was the funniest thing ever listened to, but it is out of the question to think of reporting it, for if we attempted we should fall asunder from force of laughter. The audience were in ecstacies.

" ' Several distinguished tumblers followed, and threw such summersaults as astounded and delighted every spectator. It was altogether a glorious night. Heavens ! when shall we look upon its like again ?

" ' The fun was over at eleven o'clock.' "

In the meanwhile my opponents were not inactive. They had selected a most formidable adversary, Lord Morpeth, recently Chief Secretary for Ireland. No one was more generally respected, indeed, beloved. His most bitter political enemies had not a word to say against him personally. He was at this time travelling in America, having lost his seat for the West Riding of Yorkshire, and his farewell speech was so beautiful and touching, that every one, friend and foe alike, felt that the absence of such a man from the House of Commons was a national loss. The seat for Dublin was one of no small importance. The Whigs felt that to win it from the Tories would be indeed a triumph, and they were sanguine of success, having such a candidate. But they had to deal with the Macedonian phalanx of fifteen hundred freemen voting solid at £3 a head.

At last came the nomination day. The Court House was packed with the partisans of the two candidates. The Honourable Mr. Caulfield proposed Lord Morpeth, and Mr. O'Connell, Lord Mayor of Dublin, seconded him. In the course of his speech, which was severe but not abusive in his reference to me, Mr. O'Connell accused me of having listened to and encouraged the cries of "To hell with the Pope," which, he said, resounded through the streets after the meeting at Fishamble-street Theatre, to which I have just referred. He spoke of Lord Morpeth with the highest though not exaggerated praise, as a politician and as a nobleman of the most illustrious birth, the lineal descendant of the famous belted Will Howard, and he contrasted this mature statesman with the boy who had the presumption to enter the lists with him, and to seek the representation of such a constituency as Dublin.

My proposer and seconder were Sir John Kingston James and George Ogle Moore, both of them highly esteemed leaders of the Conservative party. When my turn came to speak, I really made a first rate speech; part of it I had carefully conned over, part was quite unprepared; but I had most valuable hints given to me as to the points which O'Connell would most likely raise, by my staunch friend Tom Sheehan, brother of Remmy, and London correspondent of the *Evening Mail*. These hints served me greatly, and I was able to give back pretty nearly as much as I received. To the eulogium on Lord Morpeth and his lineage from Belted Bill, I

F

retorted that this compliment came strange from one who had not long since denounced " the scoundrel aristocracy of England," and as regards the charge that I had identified myself with the cries of " To hell with the Pope," I denied it with strong expressions of no simulated indignation. "It has been," I said, " gravely asserted that my voice had lately mingled in a cry of ' To hell with the Pope and Popery.' I cannot bring myself to think that a man occupying the high position of Lord Mayor of Dublin, could have ever uttered these words, knowing them to be false. I know well that he did not ; but I tell him that he has been grossly and wilfully misinformed. Were these the last words I ever were to utter, I should declare as solemnly as I do now, that never did my voice mingle in such a cry, that I never heard such an expression, and that, were I present and were such words made use of before me, I should manifest nothing but the most unqualified disgust. I have passed too many happy and peaceful days in the Eternal City, I have too much respect for any prince or ruler, I have too much reverence for the grey hairs of an aged and venerable man, how wide soever we may be sundered by differences of religion, ever to participate in such a cry. But, as I said before, this is no apology to soften the rancour of political animosity, but as a mark of respect to many Roman Catholic friends, excellent and upright men, who may derive their notion of my words from a profligate partial press, I owe this explanation. God forbid that my voice ever should be raised in louder accents than those of expostulation ! God forbid that my hand ever should be extended, except to meet theirs in the grasp of friendship. I owe this explanation, not to Roman Catholics alone, but I owe it to those Protestants whose character I esteem, whose opinion I respect."

I am afraid there were some good grounds for O'Connell's statement that the offensive words were shouted, though my conscience was clear enough. I was much rebuked for the violence of my disclaimer, and the Rev. Tresham Gregg, in a speech next day to the Protestant freemen, when alluding to these allegations said, " No, my friends, we must not cry ' To hell with the Pope ; ' we must cry ' To heaven with the Pope ; ' but all I can say is, if ever he goes to that place, there will be but a Flemish account of his Popish principles."

It will give some idea of the religious rancour which prevailed in those days among the lower classes of Protestants, that one of the first petitions I was requested to present was a supplication to the House of Commons to pass a measure to prevent the Roman Catholics from using bells at their chapels, which, as being summonses to idol worship, greatly distressed the ears of the petitioners. Another was to refuse all further measures of relief to " millions of factious idolaters." I need hardly say that, with the concurrence of Sir Robert Peel, I refused to present such documents, which did not increase my popularity with the lowest class of Dublin voters.

I remember as a child, the horror and dread which O'Connell's very name inspired in my young mind was so great, that it became a superstitious terror, a kind of Mumbo Jumbo, and the fear of him absolutely affected my spirits. They were, however, restored to their natural buoyancy, when one day our man-servant, who had been in the Lancers, asked me why I was so downcast.

" Because," said I, " I hear O'Connell is going to have emancipation and to kill us all."

" Don't be afraid, Master William," said Sergeant Lawson, " if O'Connell tries on that game, my regiment will run him through with their lances."

Mr. O'Connell was so pleased with my indignant protest, and with the plucky way in which I stood up against
him, that at the conclusion of the nomination, he leant
over and said to me—

"May I shake you by the hand, young man? Your
speech has gratified me so much, that if you will only
whisper the little word 'repeal'—only *whisper* it, mind
you—I will be the first to-morrow at the polling booth to
vote for you."

From that day forth O'Connell was always most genial
and warm in his manner to me. Shortly after the election
was over, we crossed the channel in the same packet.
O'Connell was in the cabin when I came in, and I hesitated
about going to him from bashfulness rather than from
any other reason. But he at once called out—

"Come here, young man! You are not ashamed to
come and sit by old Dan, are you?"

Colonel Connolly, a most ultra-Tory politician, was
also in the cabin, and O'Connell, seeing him glaring at
me, said—

"Don't mind him; you're just in the proper place,
where you ought always to be—by my side." And we
talked away merrily and gravely for fully an hour.

Forty-seven years have since passed away, but the
impression is as vivid as ever of the charm of that hour.
Full of humour and pathos was his conversation. He spoke
much of the political condition of Ireland, and how hopeless it was to obtain anything, in consequence of the
inveterate prejudices of Englishmen against Irishmen and
Roman Catholics. He said—

"I have heard a good account of your family as landlords, and they say your tenants are attached to you and
you to them?"

"How could I not be attached to them?" I exclaimed.

" I think them the most lovable and loving people in the world."

" Well," said he, " has it not often happened to you to see on a Sunday morning this lovable and loving people kneeling outside a miserable chapel, while the rain poured on them, there being no room within, and they themselves being too poor to make it a commonly decent house of God ? "

" I have seen such sights," I replied.

" And when you have gone to your own parish church on a Sunday, have you found it crowded with worshippers, and the rain coming through the roof, and no means of making it decent?   And do you think a population treated with such unfairness in a matter that goes home to their hearts is loved by those who rule it, and can be loving to them?   Surely you will not fail me in my endeavours to redeem this great iniquity ? "

I could not help being deeply impressed by his eager, earnest expostulations on that and other subjects ; and, till 1869, when religious equality was obtained, at the bottom of my heart there was always a recognition of Jeremy Taylor's famous saying, that " a prosperous iniquity was the most unprofitable condition in the world." After this he used constantly to beckon to me to come across the House of Commons and sit next him for a chat ; and he always, in his droll way, when I got up to depart in deference to the scandalized looks of my Tory friends, found some pretext to detain me.   One evening he said—

" If you could only see yourself in a glass, my dear boy, how much better you look than over the way, you would never go back to those fellows."

He constantly and urgently pressed me to pass some time with him at Darrynane, but I said it could not be,

that I would give anything to accept his invitation, but
that I could not wilfully throw away my seat and cause
bitter disappointment to the many friends who had worked
hard for me. "When you have turned me out of Dublin,"
I remarked laughing, "then I shall be free to pay you a
visit."

"And if I do," he rejoined, "it will be the best day's
work that ever was done for you."

I recall a conversation one night with him in the
House of Commons. He had been descanting on the
insult and injustice of the State Church, on the mode
in which Irish education was regarded, and other similar
topics.

"But surely," said I, "Mr. O'Connell, a reform in these
abuses is possible without the extreme resort to the
repeal of the Union, to which the North is opposed, as
well as all the upper classes, landed and mercantile ? "

"We can never get perfect equality without it," he
replied. "The English elector regards 'them Hirish,' as
he calls them, like pigs, and he thinks any concession
to them, no matter how harmless and how just, is something taken away from his own superiority over us."

"But," I insisted, "let us suppose that it were feasible
to wipe these injustices and grievances off the slate, would
it then be impossible for you to forego demands which
will never be agreed to by such a large and influential
portion of your countrymen ? "

He laughed and said, "I am too old and too busy to
indulge in such dreams ; but let me recommend you to
read an account of what happened at Mallow in 1835,
when Lord Normanby paid that town a visit."

I have found, and copy, an account of Lord Normanby's
visit in the book called "Ireland and its Rulers," and I
believe it to be correct :—

"In 1832 the Repealers of Mallow ejected Mr. Jephson from Parliament, and in 1835, when Lord Normanby passed through the town, they thus addressed him : 'We stand before you in numbers amounting to over a hundred thousand, and the greater part of us avow ourselves as having belonged to that political party in the country who advocate the repeal of the Legislative Union between Great Britain and Ireland, in the eager pursuit of which we dismissed or aided to dismiss from the representation of this great country and borough in Parliament, individuals who on other public questions were entitled to confidence and respect. From the expectation which we entertain that the principles indicated by your Excellency's Government will be carried into effect, namely of having the inhabitants of this country to rank in the eye of the law on terms of perfect equality with the British people, we tender your Excellency our solemn adjuration of the question of the repeal of the Legislative Union and of every other question calculated to produce an alienation of feeling between the inhabitants of Great Britain and those of Ireland.' "

I had no opportunity of again referring to this episode in Irish agitation. Our conversations were generally short and merry enough, interspersed with extremely droll allusions by him to the things said and the men who were saying them.

One evening he remarked a peculiarly listless and lifeless English member, whose appearance amused him, and he said—

" He seems to have no more life in him than the dead man in Tralee."

He then told me the story, the details of which I had only indistinctly preserved, but which is so well recorded in the " Correspondence," that I feel sure Mr. Fitzpatrick will forgive me for borrowing it :—

"One of O'Connell's earliest displays of forensic acuteness took place at Tralee. The question in dispute touched the validity of a will which had been made almost *in articulo mortis*. The instrument seemed drawn up in due form ; the witnesses gave ample confirmation that it had been legally executed. One of them was an old servant. O'Connell cross-examined him, and allowed him to speak on in the hope that he might say too much. The witness had already sworn that he had seen the deceased sign the will. ' Yes,' he went on, ' I saw him sign it, and surely there was life in him at the time.' The expression, frequently repeated, led O'Connell to suspect that it had a peculiar meaning. Fixing his eye on the old man, he said, ' You have taken a solemn oath before God and man to speak the truth and the whole truth ; the eye of God is on you, and the eyes of your neighbours are fixed on you too. Answer me, by virtue of that sacred and solemn oath which has passed your lips, Was the testator alive when he signed that will?' The witness quivered, his face grew ashy pale, as he repeated, ' There was life in him.' The question was reiterated, and at last O'Connell half compelled, half cajoled him to admit that, after life was extinct, a pen had been put into the testator's hand, that one of the party guided it to sign his name, while, as a salve for the conscience of all concerned, a living fly was put into the dead man's mouth to qualify the witnesses to bear testimony that ' there was life in him' when he signed the will. This fact preserved a large property in a respectable and worthy family ; and an incident in Miss Edgeworth's ' Patronage' was suggested by this occurrence."

O'Connell always exercised a strong fascination over me. His humour and his passion carried me away. I always felt that he had led his countrymen out of the house of bondage and made them free men ; and if his language was at times violent, abusive, and odious, God knows he was only giving back what he got. As to his being the "Big Beggarman," as he was called, never was there a man more indifferent to money. He had great expenses. He had given up his lucrative position at the bar to carry out his political career ; and he accepted, and was justified in accepting, a national tribute from a grateful country. I had always a soft spot in my heart for "old Dan," and when he died I mourned him, however glad I may have been at the dispersal of the contemptible satellites who surrounded him. In July, 1887, I wrote to the Right Honourable G. Shaw-Lefevre, who had recently published his book on Peel and O'Connell, the following letter. It gives more fully my relations with O'Connell and the opinions I held of him.

"MY DEAR LEFEVRE,

"I told you when we last met that I intended to bring 'O'Connell and Peel' with me to Ireland, where I could read it carefully and quietly. I took it up with rather adverse prepossessions, as I differ from your views as regards Gladstone's Home Rule schemes. But I am bound to say that I go with you almost entirely in the opinions you express as to the treatment which Ireland experienced throughout the whole career of O'Connell, and specially as to the manner in which he was regarded and dealt with. I am glad that a person in your position has had the courage to treat his career with justice.

"When I came into Parliament in 1842 I was young in years, and still more young in political knowledge. In fact, I knew but little, and took my opinions from the men by whom I was surrounded. They were the representatives of the narrowest views, the most staunch opponents of all change, the most violent advocates of Protestant ascendency. I looked on O'Connell as a kind of wild beast, or something worse, as influenced in his career by the most sordid views, and as a would-be rebel, but refraining through cowardice from trying to carry out his aims by action. When I stood for Dublin, I had only been a short time in Ireland. It is true I was born there, and had passed my early days at the Castle and in the Phœnix Park, where I had known nothing but denunciation of Liberal policy, distrust of Roman Catholics, and where as a child I was brought down on the occasion of dinner-parties to stand on a chair and drink the Glorious Memory. I then went to Harrow, Oxford, and abroad, and it was not till 1841 that my father succeeded to his Irish estates, occupied by Catholic tenants exclusively, and with Catholic gentry around us. The only antidote to the impressions I then imbibed came from my mother, who was an ardent supporter of Catholic claims ; but she too was pervaded by a dislike of O'Connell.

"The constituency which I contested, that of Dublin, was one of the most extreme in Ireland. . . . I was urged to get what they called 'the steam' up by making violent speeches against the Roman Catholics. All my feelings revolted against such a course, and I was considered by no means up to the mark ; but no other candidate could be got, and I was returned." (Here follows the account already given of friendly relation with O'Connell.) "I believe, in spite of all personal ill-treatment and injustice to which he was subjected in England, that there was not a more loyal man in Ireland. He hated revolutionists. Had he been treated with common justice, and had not English narrow-minded prejudice prevented the reform of gross abuses, we should have heard very little of Repeal from him. A

national feeling had not possession of the country. The Catholic
hierarchy had no sympathy with Repeal, always excepting Dr.
MacHale, though the younger clergy had. It was the marvellous
power of O'Connell over his countrymen which caused the feeling
of sentiment at that time, and even more so during the temporary
Young Ireland movement. After that, it completely died out, and
was the subject of joke. I do not believe when I stood for Galway,
in 1857, that I should have had twenty-five additional votes by a
profession of Repeal, and yet a considerable number of votes in the
towns were perfectly independent. Much has been said of O'Connell's
virulence, bad language, and exaggeration. All that I admit readily
enough ; but first of all, he was an Irishman appealing to the *per-
fervidum ingenium* of his countrymen, who saw and see nothing
amiss in violent and abusive words, and who are generally (certainly,
if excited) incapable of a strict adherence to facts. And secondly,
there never was a man so grossly abused. Coward, rogue, beggarman, liar, were the ordinary expressions applied to him. Those who
recognized his great position and his great qualities did not dare to
do justice to them.

"In England he was a kind of social and political leper, and no
wonder the *sæva indignatio* broke forth. I don't excuse him, but
I should like to know how many of us, if similarly treated, would turn
our cheeks to the smiter.

"I do not think that O'Connell was ever a hearty redresser of the
tenants' wrongs. He did not feel their abject position. He spoke
out loudly when widespread destitution prevailed, but he never
brought his powerful intellect to bear in formulating measures for
the improvement of the condition of the Irish occupiers. His own
property was a model of everything that ought not to be. In fact,
Irishmen in those days lived in the happy-go-lucky state ; not a word
was said or thought of a landlord who evicted non-paying tenants.
It was the eviction of solvent men which caused outrages. American
sympathizers and American newspapers had not come over to stir up
the peasants by a recital of their wrongs, and I am certain that the
Devon Commission exercised the English conscience far more than
the Irish, even the Irish liberal one. The clearing of estates left
behind it in every case where it was resorted to a burning sense of
wrong; and yet, bad and ruthless as it was, the country was improved
where it was resorted to, and the peasantry who are left are in a
far better position than they were. On some estates the landlords
allowed unlimited subdivision and never ejected while rent was paid.
Such is the case with the property of Lord Dillon, who in former
days was blessed and prayed for as the most indulgent landlord by

his four thousand cabin holders, but who now is cursed for asking rent from such a nest of paupers. However, the short and the long of the chief source of Ireland's troubles was this, that the wretched position of the tenantry was never till within the last twenty years a prominent plank of the Irish platform ; and that, had measures of improvement been insisted on when O'Connell was in the zenith of his power, a different system would have gradually sprung up, especially if the privilege of selling the good-will had been everywhere confirmed with a limitation as to the raising of the rent, though, indeed, I hardly believe it would have been possible, without a convulsion, to have passed such a measure through the House of Lords. I am quite sure, moreover, that O'Connell would not have liked it." *

To conclude, however, the tale of the election. I took the lead the first day, and kept it till the close of the poll,

---

* " I stood last January by the marble slab in the Church of Santa Agata at Rome, which contains the heart of O'Connell ; and I recalled the notable description of him in ' Ireland and its Rulers.' ' Those who have seen and heard him in committee fighting against the Coercion Bill can never forget that huge, massive figure, staggering with emotion—the face darkened with all the feelings of scorn and rancour, while he vengefully prophesied a future Irish rebellion, and with gloomy smiles exulted in the troubles of England. Coarse, stern, and real, he was a powerful representative of the people in whose name he spoke ; the man was far grander and more impressive than his matter. How much more would such a man have done for the popular cause than a legion of Henry Warburtons and Joe Humes ! Mechanical utterers of first principles, dogged calculators, who fancy themselves public representatives because they prove popular wrongs statistically, and tell the national agonies in £ s. d.' And then he came before me as he used to stir the blood within me while sitting by him on the front bench of the floor of the House of Commons, when he told me of Darrynane and of the great cliffs on which the Atlantic thundered, and of the great sea in all its moods, and of the music of his beagles, and his home happiness ; and I wondered that the image of such a man could ever have grown faint in the hearts of his countrymen, and that his name should have ceased to be a household word, as it has done ; and I thought, after all, it was well that he should long since have been at peace, and that his relic should be consigned to that quiet church.

'. . . ubi sæva indignatio
Lacerare cor ulterius nequit.' "

W. H. G., in *Nineteenth Century*, April, 1889.

when the numbers declared were — Gregory, 3825 ; Morpeth, 3435. Majority for Gregory, 390. It was a well-fought, well-conducted, good-humoured election, though there were a few rows and some window-breaking. Only two Roman Catholics voted for me, one of them being a solicitor, Mr. Keogh. It was said at the time that he was recognized dressed as a shabby artisan, and busily engaged in breaking his own windows. He undoubtedly considered that he had a strong claim on the Government by reason of his martyrdom, and pressed it incessantly. Whenever a clerkship of the Crown fell due, it became my duty to accompany " Mr. Conservative Keogh," as he was called, to the Castle, to enumerate his sufferings, and to impress on the Government the strong effect which would be produced on the Catholic mind of Ireland by his appointment. At length we were successful ; the county of Kilkenny was entrusted to his jurisdiction, and I was then relieved, to my great comfort, of Mr. Conservative Keogh, who positively besieged me, and once was nearly shot by me at a shooting party at Coole, when he lay in wait behind a thick brake of blackthorn. On receiving his appointment, his native land knew him no more, as, owing to his pecuniary difficulties, he retired to France, and only appeared at the Assizes, when his person was safe from his creditors.

Another of my supporters requested me to procure him a Government situation, on the ground of having voted for me under thirteen different names.

CHAPTER V

THE great success of beating so prominent and popular a statesman as Lord Morpeth, backed up by Mr. O'Connell, and the very good speech I made at the hustings, caused me to be something of a hero when I took my seat in Parliament. I was loudly cheered on entering the House, and was presented to the Speaker by Sir Robert Peel, who greeted me with much warmth, and to the members of the Cabinet, among whom no one was more glad to see me than old Mr. Goulburn, the Chancellor of the Exchequer, who had known me as a little fellow in the Phœnix Park when he was Chief Secretary there. I used to play with his two boys—Edward, now Colonel Goulburn, late of the Guards, and Frederick, afterwards Sir Frederick, and Chairman of the Customs, who died a few years ago. He was in those days remarked for his beautiful brown curly hair. One day when we were having an amiable scuffle at play, the whole of the beautiful brown hair came off into my hand, and nothing remained of that handsome head but a gleaming white skull. I was so horrified that I sprang out of the ground-floor window, wig in hand, and ran across the park to my mother, at the Under Secretary's Lodge, as fast as my feet would carry me, crying out to her, "Oh, see! I have pulled off the top of Freddy's head, and what shall I ever do!" In the meanwhile, poor Mrs. Goulburn was consternated, as she thought I had carried off Freddy's wig as a kind of scalp or war token, and she had no other. I was at once forgiven, but I could not bear to go back to my playmates; and on the present occasion, when I called to renew acquaintance, Mrs. Goulburn said, laughing, "Come as often as you like to see us, and you need not be afraid, as Freddy has got his own hair now."

Among the great ladies who took me up, and were particularly civil, were Lady Ashburton, the predecessor of the present Dowager Louisa, and the great friend of Carlyle and Charles Buller, the rising light of Whiggery, and the real author of Lord Durham's famous Report in 1839, on Canada. She was very clever, very impertinent, and her drums at Bath House were most exclusive; but she was to the last particularly kind to me, and I was always invited. Then there were Lady Londonderry, equally exclusive, the mother of the living Dowager Duchess of Marlborough; and Lady Jersey, also exclusive to the last degree. Her house was always open to me; I dined there constantly, meeting the most eminent men and women of the day; and at Middleton, their country place for several years, I met with the warmest reception. To give some idea of her exclusiveness, I asked her one day if she knew Baron Lionel Rothschild, the head of the firm in England. "I know him by name," she answered; "but as of course I could not receive him, I have not allowed him to be presented to me."

The old Lord Jersey of that day was the very type of an English Grand Seigneur. Tall, slight, singularly handsome, nothing could be more captivating than his address, and he was quite as good and kind as he looked. He was often president of the Rooms at Newmarket, where the racing *élite* used to dine. It is, or was, the custom of the president to drink immediately after dinner the health of the youngest member, and Lord Jersey

used always, during the time I was the junior, to address
me, as soon as the cloth was removed, with "Mr. Pope, we
drink your health, Mr. Pope." I was so named after Pope
Gregory, and the name still sticks to me among my old
Newmarket friends. There were never parents more
sorely afflicted than Lord and Lady Jersey. I used
always in my mind to compare her with Niobe, for her
pride was equal, and her family misfortunes still greater.
They were the handsomest family I ever saw. The eldest
daughter, Sarah, married Prince Nicolas Esterhazy, and
received the cold shoulder from the aristocrats of Vienna
because her mother was a granddaughter and heiress of
Child the banker. This beautiful Princess Esterhazy was
the first that her mother had to mourn, for she died
young in 1853. Then died young Lady Clementina, in
1858. She was one of the most charming girls I ever
met, lovely and lovable. Her life was a very sad one.
Gentle, affectionate, and fond of quiet, she was dragged
through an incessant turmoil of London dissipation by
her imperious mother, till her health broke down, and she
passed away without any particular disorder. Her mother
had set her heart on her marrying some great magnate, at
one time the Duke of Cambridge, at another the Duke
d'Ossuna. Never was a girl less of a flirt, and yet Lady
Jersey guarded her with every possible restriction.
Knowing her intimately well, I sent her some book she
wished to have, together with a note. I received the
answer, a civil one, from Lady Jersey, thanking me, but
informing me that she never allowed her daughter to
receive any letters except from her near relations. The
third daughter, Lady Adela, also very pretty, ran away
with a Captain Ibbetson, a man without fortune, and of
no position. She, too, died young, in 1860, having only
obtained a formal forgiveness. Then, for the sons, there

was Jack, the second son, a fine young man, an admirable rider, and very pleasant, who also died early, wasting away. The same decline carried off Fred Villiers, a singularly handsome, high-bred looking man, who married Lady Elizabeth de Ginkle, the sister and heiress of Lord Athlone; and Frank, the youngest, died also young, an exile at Bilbao. He was one of the best-looking men of his day. He had seen much of the world, and was, when he pleased, remarkably agreeable. He had been aide-de-camp to Sir Colin Campbell, in Ceylon, and he never tired of his vivid descriptions of that glorious island. It was he who inspired me with the strong, permanent desire to go there as Governor—the great ambition and object of my life. He was member for Rochester, and had ability to be anything, though he never spoke in Parliament. He was the favourite of father and mother. Last of all I come to the first-born, who was no favourite at home, Lord Villiers, "Old Willows," as we all called him. He had not the beauty of his race, nor its arrogance and pride, and he was looked on in consequence with compassion as a poor creature; but he was one of the very salt of the earth, honourable, high-minded, gentle, the best of husbands, the best of fathers, and the best of friends. He also died young, just a month or two after succeeding to the title. Old Lady Jersey died in 1867, having outlived all her family except Frederick. I mention them particularly, as I lived greatly among them for some years, till Lady Jersey chose to quarrel with me, through no fault of mine, in consequence of my having, on the recommendation of her own sons, Fred and Frank, been brought to fight a duel in Osterley Park, which was her property, with Captain Vaughan, of which more at the proper time.

From the day I entered Parliament till his death I was

treated almost as one of the family by Sir Robert Peel.
" My good fellow," said he one day (he always called me
" my good fellow "), " come in and out of my house
whenever you like ; Lady Peel will always have a seat at
lunch for you. If you hear I am by myself, tap at the
library door, and if I am not busy we can have a talk."
I often availed myself of this permission, and he used to
speak to me in the most unguarded manner of his policy
and intentions. I am bound also to say that he often
wound up by a story of rather a free description, which
he told extremely well, and with fits of laughter. It was
a curious feature in the character of that statesman that,
though cold and haughty to his superiors in rank and
equals in position, he was the most open and gayest of
men to his young official friends. George Smythe, afterwards Lord Strangford, when Under Secretary for Foreign
Affairs, has told me repeatedly that he has been astonished
at the unreserved manner in which he discussed the various
questions of the day with him when he called in the
morning for instructions, as well as with his perfect good
humour and merriment ; and Lord Normanton, then Lord
Somerton, who was also rather a favourite, lately remarked
to me the same characteristics of Sir Robert.

As a proof of his great good nature to me, I may
mention that when Lord Ashley (afterwards Lord Shaftesbury) made one of his magnificent speeches in committee
on the Factory Bill, in 1844, to limit the period of labour
of young persons to ten hours daily, the House was in the
greatest excitement. Sir Robert Peel, backed up by
Cobden and Bright and the political economists, opposed
the bill, and it was confidently predicted that if English
children were not to be allowed to work till they dropped,
our manufacturing supremacy would be endangered. Lord
Ashley stood forth the helper of the helpless, and fought

the battle of humanity. His grand presence, his fine voice, which rang through the House, his deep sincerity, and the noble words of his peroration, caused a sensation such as I have seldom seen equalled. The young members deserted their leader and went with him. The division appeared to be a close one, but when the tellers advanced to the table, and the Clerk handed the numbers to Lord Ashley, we who were supporting him knew he had won ; and so he had, by a majority of nine against the Government. The House broke out into cheer after cheer, and I, oblivious of all Parliamentary decorum, jumped up and unthinkingly waved my hat over Sir Robert's head, who was sitting just below me. He turned to me when the turmoil had subsided, and said, laughing, "My good fellow, I shall give you a scolding if you wave your hat over my head whenever you beat me ; and the Speaker will give you a scolding if you wave it at all." This was a lesson, but it was administered in a pleasant way.

In those days—I speak of the time of the Ministry of Sir Robert Peel—there were four great salons to which it was a distinction to be invited. Lady Ashburton's, chiefly political; Lady Londonderry's, where the heavy aristocracy, great titles, and men of many acres resorted; Lady Jersey's, also political, but of the strictest Tory type, with an admixture of the *haute diplomatie*, chiefly Russian, Austrian, and Prussian, as the French was too *bourgeoise;* and Chesterfield House, the most restricted and the paradise of the expiring dandies who were in their zenith about twenty years previously. It is difficult to explain the qualifications which were regarded as the "Open, Sesame !" in this case. High birth, good looks, quickness of repartee, a stable of race-horses, a notorious *liaison* with some *demirep habituée*, all these advantages might obtain admission which would have been scornfully

refused to the lofty and ponderous magnates of Holder-
nesse House (Lady Londonderry's).   I used to be invited
there occasionally, and was always very glad to go, as the
society was sure to be light and merry, though extremely
ignorant and unprofitable.   I am ashamed to say that I
lived much in that class of company, having all the time
the most supreme contempt for it.   I find the following
passage in a kind of spasmodic diary which I then kept,
and which I much regret I did not carry on :—

" *Wednesday, July* 8, 1846.—Elected member of the new club,
the Coventry ; something pre-eminently *muscadin.*   The *Cercle des
Prétentieux*, and I may add of many of them *précieux ridicules*, a
kind of expiring effort to lift old tottering, decrepit dandyism to a
pedestal.   It is worth belonging to, besides the incomparable *cuisine*,
if only to watch the last death-struggle of these priests of that foolish
false god, before which simple and honest Englishmen so long submitted to bow down.   There have been dynasties of rank and ancient
lineage, dynasties of wit, and dynasties of wealth ; but of all dynasties
that ever strutted its little day, the most contemptible was that dynasty
of exclusivism—an idol ideal with face of brass, but with feet of mire
and clay.   One can understand the insolence and vulgarity of wealth
reigning supreme, one can rejoice in the domination of intellect giving
law to society, but that imbecile, ignorant, useless dandyism, without
the prestige of rank, the splendour and material enjoyments of wealth,
the fascination of genius, or the high desert of a great deed, should
have been tolerated so long as a domineering power, proves that in
the wisest of nations, as well as in the wisest of human beings, there
may be intervals of infatuation.   So far as either regard or respect for
such men goes, I would as soon be elected a member of some Chartist
lodge, among men rude indeed and prejudiced, but earnest, fresh,
and true."

The most fashionable club before the establishment of
the Coventry was Crockford's, and I was elected to it
immediately after being returned for Parliament.   It was
admirably kept.   Francatelli, the cook, was unequalled :
there was a first-rate supper, gratis, with the best champagne
for those who hungered and thirsted after midnight ; and
in a little room off the supper-room was the gambling

table, at which too many an ardent admirer of hazard had lost all his fortune. We who played all knew one another very well, and whatever may have been our run of luck, we had no fear of foul play, either with the dice or with our fellow-players. Of course heavy sums were lost and had to be obtained forthwith. There was a well-known Jew of the time always ready to advance a loan, but somehow he had never quite the amount required, so he compelled the unfortunate borrower to take as part payment "a musical mouse," which squeaked and ran about on wheels, telling him that such a person, naming some tradesman, would buy it from him. And so he did, at half the price at which it was valued by the Jew. This "musical mouse" was always brought to Crockford's and made to run squeaking over the hazard table. The question used to be asked, "Who has the mouse this evening?" I was wont to try my luck very often, and began to feel the love of play coming strongly over me; but one night, fortunately, Sir Sandford Graham and I accepted the wise and kind suggestion of Lord Newport (now Lord Bradford), who recommended us to let him tie us up—that is, he gave each of us a sovereign and we were bound to give him each in return £500, to be applied to charity, if we ever lost more than £5 on any one night at the club, and we were on honour to inform against ourselves. Owing to this salutary precaution and the determined steps taken by Sir James Graham, when Home Secretary, to suppress gambling, I was not a sufferer by my connection with this famous club.

At the time of which I write, the state of London as regards gambling was scandalous. There were copper hells, silver hells, gold hells, where pence, shillings, and pounds were played, scattered over the town, but especially in the region of St. James. They were nominally

illegal, but were carried on with perfect impunity, ruining
servants, tradesmen, and gentlemen alike. Sir James
Graham set to work with no half-measures ; the police
were ordered to break into every hell and bring the
keepers and the gamblers also before the magistrates, by
whom they were severely punished. But that was not
all. In spite of the remonstrances of that class who,
while honestly disapproving of evil things, cannot bring
themselves to attempt their removal, in spite of prophecies
that the youth of England would betake themselves to
private play if they had not the vent of public play,
Sir James Graham sent word to Page, the manager of
the club who had succeeded "Old Crocky," that the
police had orders to enter it with as little ceremony, and
to arrest its inmates, as if it were a coffee hell frequented
by costermongers. The consequence was that in a month
or two it was closed. No private play resulted from this
closing, and I and other members, not having the
temptation before us, never troubled our heads about
hazard playing again.

In 1872 I cited to the Legislative Council in Ceylon
this action of Sir James Graham as my justification for
a very large reduction of arrack taverns in that colony.

I have often wished I had the same power here that
I had in Ceylon, and Gort, with a population of fifteen
hundred, would not be cursed with twenty-eight public-
houses.

The political men of the day who were most civil to
me were members of Sir Robert Peel's Government,
Sidney Herbert, Lord Dalhousie, and Lord Lincoln,
afterwards Duke of Newcastle. Mr. Gladstone I scarcely
knew. I had little notion in those days that the quiet,
reserved Lord Dalhousie was about to be the mighty
pro-consul, the overthrower of ancient dynasties in India,

and one of the most ambitious Governor-Generals that ever swayed the destinies of Hindustan. I met him in Cairo in 1856, utterly broken down by overwork, and coming home to die. Among the very handsome, the most refinedly handsome men of that time was Sidney Herbert. No one told an improper story, and he certainly told many, especially when in company with his friend, Henry Corry (Lord Rowton's father), with more grace and bashfulness. He was a special favourite of Sir Robert Peel, who commended me to him.

[Since the publication of the first edition of this book, various discrepancies have been pointed out to me in the story connecting Sidney Herbert with the disclosure of the secret of the repeal of the Corn Laws. I have, therefore, thought it best to withdraw it altogether.—A. G.]

Of all the young lieutenants of Sir Robert Peel, the one I knew best and liked the most was Lord Lincoln, afterwards Duke of Newcastle. He was very pleasant, very resolute, and not the least conceited, and thoroughly liberal in his opinions. I have several letters of his, one written on the death of my father in 1847, which is quite affectionate in its tone. I knew Lady Lincoln, from whom he was divorced on account of Lord Orford, and I was astonished to meet a woman of her rank and position at rather a free and easy kind of house, the Riario Sforzas, Neapolitans, where we used to go to dance the polka of an afternoon, during the time it was the rage. She was very pretty, and evidently not only up to but in quest of an adventure. One of her first lovers, possibly the first, was young D——, a Lifeguardsman, and remarkably handsome, who became quite infatuated about her, and left for her sake another lady of high rank to whom he had previously been devoted. He and I had been very good friends, and I liked him extremely, but we had a

misunderstanding, for which I dare say we were both
very sorry, and we became mere nodding acquaintances.
Towards the end of the season of 184–, he came up to
me laughing, and said, " I can't bear to keep up this
ridiculous tiff, let us just be as we were. I am off to the
Isle of Lewis or of Skye to-morrow, and if you have
nothing better to do let us dine together." I was very
placable and much pleased to get rid of a silly quarrel
with a man for whom I had so much regard, and we
dined together. After dinner, during which he was in
low spirits, he said, " I want to ask you a great favour.
You have a house in London where you can keep things
safely. I go to-morrow to Scotland, and I have an odd
kind of feeling that I shall not come back. Will you
keep a parcel of letters for me, and burn the parcel unopened in case of my death ? I am afraid to leave them
in barracks, as we shall be shifting to Windsor, and things
get constantly broken open during these transits. You
will naturally ask why I do not burn them. It is the
wish of the writer that I should preserve them, and I
cannot disobey." A very short time afterwards I heard
he was ill, and in a few days his death was announced to
the unfeigned sorrow of all who knew him.

    Among the other men of note with whom I was on
intimate terms, during my first Parliament, were George
Smythe, member for Canterbury (afterwards Lord Strangford), Lord George Bentinck, and Mr. Disraeli. George
Smythe had recently come up from Cambridge with an
enormous reputation, not derived from anything he had
done in the way of academic honours, but from a general
belief that he was the coming young man in politics. He
was quite the first speaker at the Cambridge Union,
though he never spoke without great preparation, and,
indeed, elaboration. He was the most brilliant talker I

ever heard, eloquent, imaginative, and paradoxical, and, in consequence, although his appearance was unattractive, small, and dingy, he exercised a fascination over women which was quite remarkable. It was a bad day for every one of those who listened to the voice of the charmer, for he was as remorseless as he was capricious, and rolled in the mud and destroyed the reputation of the woman whom he had been adoring the day before. He commenced his career of Lothario by making love to Lady ——, a most charming old lady of a great French house, who was old enough to be his grandmother. For a time, never was there anything equal to his mad devotion, and, after completely turning her head, compromising her, and making her the talk of the whole town, he left her suddenly one day, and hardly recognized her afterwards. He was not a successful debater, though he made one or two fine prepared speeches. His maiden speech was, to the horror of his Cambridge friends, a decided failure ; he broke down, and could never bear the slightest allusion to it. But in 1843, on the Maynooth debate, he did better, and really made a fine speech, upon which he was congratulated, not very felicitously, by Sir Robert Peel, who said, " It was impossible for me to listen to his" (G. Smythe's) "speeches without great satisfaction at the bright views they indicate of great future eminence. I remember having foretold to the honourable gentleman— I know not if he recollects it—when, through the embarrassment of youth, others thought he had failed, I remember I tried to console him, and I told him my conviction was that he was destined for future eminence." George Smythe did not like it, and on my congratulating him upon having been so "buttered up" by Sir Robert Peel—"Yes," said he, "with his usual dose of rancid butter." Sir Robert made him Under Secretary for

Foreign Affairs, but he paid no attention to his work, and was thought very little of at the Foreign Office.

He died young, worn out by dissipation, brandy and water, and a delicate chest. He published one book, called "Historic Fancies," of which he gave me a copy, now in Coole Library. Some of the short poems in it are very remarkable, full of spirit and fiery declamation. The prose essays are also most graceful compositions. It gives one the highest opinion of his talent and refined taste. He also left after him an unfinished novel, called "Angela Pisani," subsequently edited by Lady Strangford, which is unequal, but contains passages of singular brilliancy. These are all the remains of a man who entered the world amid the acclaim of his contemporaries as a second Praed or Canning. He was selfish and heartless, but a most delightful, fascinating companion. It was during the early period of his Parliamentary career that the Young England party, so called, of which he was the leader, came into notoriety. It was chiefly composed of men of his own standing at Cambridge, and he, Lord John Manners, Baillie Cochrane (afterwards Lord Lamington), Beresford-Hope, Peter Borthwick, were the prominent members. It was a kind of High-Church-divine-right-of-kings-philanthropic band of brothers, in which the working classes were to be looked after and elevated on the principal of everything for the people, but nothing by the people. It had, undoubtedly, high and honest views, but it died of ridicule, chiefly brought on it by the memorable lines—

> "Let kingdoms fade, let art and commerce die,
> But give us still our old nobility."

Mr. Disraeli was also a good deal connected with this party, but he was far too intelligent to identify himself very much with their unpractical views, though they were constantly his guests, and George Smythe and Lord John

Manners were prominent characters in the novel, famous at the time, of " Coningsby ;" in fact, George Smythe was the hero Coningsby, and Lord John Manners figures as Lord Henry Sydney.

In those days I lived at No. 14, Park Street, Grosvenor Square, not far from his house at Grosvenor Gate, and we used constantly to walk home together from the House of Commons. Hardly a week passed in which I did not dine with him and Mrs. Disraeli. His dinners were small, not over good, but always gay and amusing ; not that he himself was at all brilliant in conversation ; on the contrary, he was generally silent, unless there was an opening for some epigrammatic or paradoxical or startling observation. Though bitterly sarcastic if it suited his purpose, he was very far from being cynical by nature. On the contrary, he was remarkably placable, and, though he had few strong dislikes, he had many strong friendships. He has been reproached with har- bouring unrelenting vindictiveness, and with no just reason, to Croker, and that in " Coningsby " he vented on him all the envy, hatred, and malice of a malignant nature. It is undoubtedly true that in " Coningsby " he employed all the vigour of his pen to crush the man whom he had reason, and good reason, to believe never missed an opportunity of vilifying and ridiculing him. It was war to the knife, and I am bound to say that, when " Coningsby " appeared, public opinion did not regret that one who had wielded his pen with such unscrupulous ferocity, and had caused so much misery by his unfeeling criticism, should have met with an antagonist well able to cope with him. Disraeli, too, looked on it as an act of policy to make himself formidable—

> " . . . Cet animal est dangereux
> Quand on l'attaque, il se defend."

I am aware that it has been generally thought that he
had a bitter hatred of Peel, on account of not having
been offered office by him, or of having been refused
office. I knew he did not like him, for he missed no
opportunity for a jibe and a sarcasm upon him. Disappointed at not receiving office at a time when a salary
would have been a godsend, almost a salvation, had,
doubtless, some influence; but his character was so
entirely the opposite to that of Sir Robert, as to be
certain to produce antagonistic feelings. Disraeli was
eminently Bohemian, imaginative, without a particle of
belief in anything, totally unprincipled—I do not use the
word in an offensive sense, but as being devoid of all
principles of policy. Such a man was the very antipodes
to the prudent, cautious, unimaginative, and somewhat
pompous Prime Minister, whose correctness was a reproach to Disraeli's Bohemianism. As for the belief
that the fierce and dreadful attacks which he made on
Sir Robert when he proposed the repeal of the Corn
Laws originated from resentment alone, I much doubt
the correctness of it. With that quickness which pre-
eminently characterized him, he saw an opening for distinction, and seized on it at once. There decorous and
ordinarily forcible speeches would have been ineffectual.
Something was required to meet the resentment of the
infuriated Conservatives. He felt he could say all they
felt but could not express. A leader was wanted, and
at once he sprang into the place, ready to pander to the
one passion which animated the bulk of the Conservative
party—desire for revenge. Lord George Bentinck had,
from the first, taken the lead in the secession, and was
looked up to as its mouthpiece; the organization and
marshalling of his forces he was well competent to
manage, but he felt himself quite unable to do the

speaking part, and he knew that Disraeli could do it well, so he forced him, as captain, into the front of the battle. It was in vain that the squires and aristocracy kicked at the supremacy of one whom they looked on as mountebank; in vain their gorges rose at being directed by a Jew. Lord George overruled all this squeamishness, and convinced them they had only the alternative of falling to pieces, and having to come back like froward schoolboys to Peel, or else of heartily adopting as their leader the man whom in their hearts they thoroughly despised. They resisted for two years, but had at length to yield.

Looking back on all that has since happened, how different would events have been, and how much the future of England would have been changed, had Sir Robert Peel recognized Dizzy's talent and given him office. Of course he would have stood firm to that office and his salary. The Conservative seceders, powerful in numbers, powerless in debate and experience, would have been as sheep without a shepherd, for Lord George Bentinck died early, and they would have accepted the leadership of Mr. Gladstone, as it was nothing but Mr. Disraeli's claim to lead the party prevented Mr. Gladstone from joining it in 1852. All his instincts were with it, he would have brought his friends with him and have established the great Tory party, in spite of all its recalcitrations, on grand principles of finance and of enlightened, well-considered progress. Democracy would have been retarded by half a century.

One remarkable and grand trait in the character of Disraeli was his noble demeanour to his wife. She was the widow of Mr. Wyndham Lewis, his former colleague for Shrewsbury. When he died, Mr. Disraeli was in a most embarrassed state, on the very brink of ruin. He was intimate with Lady Blessington and Count D'Orsay, and he consulted the latter as to the complete break-down of all his ambitious hopes, owing to his financial difficulties.

"Why don't you marry your colleague's widow? She is very rich," said Count D'Orsay.

It was a happy thought, and accepted with alacrity. He proposed at once, was accepted, and did marry the widow. She relieved him from his distress, set him on his legs, and verily she met with her reward. From the day of his marriage to the day of her death he treated her with the deepest, most trusting affection; indeed, with a chivalrous devotion. And yet she was a most repulsive woman: flat, angular, under-bred, with a harsh, grating voice; and though by no means a fool, yet constantly saying stupid things, most frequently about him, which tended to make him ridiculous; as, for instance, when the conversation turned on some man's fine complexion—"Ah," said she, "I wish you could only see Dizzy in his bath, then you would know what a white skin is." There was hardly any circumstance in their domestic life which she did not take a pleasure in narrat-ing in public, and marvellous were the stories daily afloat of her escapades, especially after her husband's great position had considerably turned her head. One night after dinner she said to her guests, three or four young men, myself among them, "Would you like to go and see the room where Dizzy was brought to bed of Con-ingsby?" We all expressed much interest in the revered spot, and were invited by her to go upstairs to the bed-room floor, and to enter a certain door. George Smythe took the lead in a regular scamper, amid roars of laughter, upstairs; he burst into the wrong room, which was quite dark. We heard a splash and a cry, and down came our leader wet through and dripping. He had fallen into Dizzy's bath. He presented himself in a drenched condition to Mrs. Disraeli, who asked him placidly if he had seen the room where Coningsby was born. "I know nothing of his place of birth," said Smythe, "but I know I have been in the room where he was recently baptized."

It was ludicrous the tokens of affection and apparently of admiration which he lavished on "Marianne," as we irreverently called her. One evening, on coming up from dinner, he knelt before her, and as they say in novels, devoured both her hands with kisses, saying at the same time, in the most lackadaisical manner, "Is there anything I can do for my dear little wife?" And yet this ungainly, repulsive-looking woman was deserving of his affection. She had saved him from perdition and set him on high among the people. All her wealth was valued by her only so far as it could assist his objects. She watched him like a faithful dog, understood his every fancy, habit, thought; in fact, lived in him and for him. I know few anecdotes of devotion finer than her conduct when one afternoon she had driven him to the House of Commons. He was speaking to her at parting, and somehow she got her finger inside the carriage door, which he shut forcibly. Though dreadfully crushed and in agony, she never even exclaimed or mentioned the matter till he returned home. He was going to make a great speech, and she thought if she uttered the least cry, or had even given him to know he had hurt her, his thoughts might be distracted. George Smythe allowed himself now and then, on the strength of their great intimacy, to make observations of wonder at the warmth of Dizzy's attention to "Marianne," more particularly on one occasion after she had told him, with a grim grin intended for a simper, that he always treated her more like a mistress than a wife. But he never again

ventured on the liberty. Disraeli looked at him straight
between the two eyes and said, "George, there is one
word in the English language of which you are ignorant."
" What is that ? " asked Smythe, somewhat taken aback by
his manner. " *Gratitude*, George," said Dizzy, in his deep,
solemn voice. George Smythe felt the rebuke deeply,
and accepted the lesson, but not the slightest coldness
ensued in consequence. Disraeli was never prone to take
offence, and was entirely devoid of touchiness. At the
end of 1856 or the beginning of 1857, when the question
of the Lorcha "Arrow" and the impending war with
China were the topics of the day, he was leading the
Opposition, and sent for a captain of the Royal Navy just
arrived from Hong Kong to give him information. He
received him in the dining-room, and the officer, when
going away, took a look round the room.

" Ah ! " said he, " I remember this room very well, and
those curtains. I dined here several times, many years
ago, with a rum old girl, a Mrs. Wyndham Lewis."

" Yes," said Dizzy, " the curtains certainly are old and
rather fusty, in fact, we must do up the whole room
when our ship comes in."

My connection by marriage, James Clay, the Radical
member for Hull, was the man for whom of all others
Dizzy had the greatest affection, and the regard was
mutual. Clay, who was singularly adroit, and who had
the ear of the House of Commons, used constantly to do
him good turns when the Tory Government were very
hard pushed by the attacks of the Liberals. Often he
got him out of a difficult position by building him a bridge
to pass over, and the movement was effected with such
judgment that no one supposed it was dictated by friendship. They had been companions in early life, and had
travelled in their yacht through the Mediterranean, among

the Ionian and Ægean Islands, and thence to Constantinople and Asia Minor.   Clay told me that it would not
have been possible to have found a more easy, agreeable,
unaffected companion when they were by themselves, but
that when they got into society his coxcombry was
intolerable.   At Corfu and Gibraltar he made himself so
hateful to the officers' mess, that, while they welcomed
Clay, they ceased to invite "that d——d bumptious Jew
boy," as they called him.   His appearance was certainly
against him ; long, hyacinthine curls, rings on his fingers,
gold chains, and velvet dresses of the most gorgeous
description.   His conversation, too, was of a most offensive
nature, calling in question every preconceived and revered
opinion, together with flights of sarcasm, against all
accepted maxims of the British Army.   What rendered
matters worse was his great knowledge and memory, which
enabled him to make short work of any bold soldier who
encountered him in argument.   When I knew him, he had
given up his absurdities of dress, but he still retained the
love-locks and curls, and the Charlie on his chin.   At the
time Lord Derby was forming his Ministry in 1852, Lady
Jocelyn, who was nominally favourable to him, as Lord
Jocelyn was supposed to be Conservative, but who was
in her heart a thorough opponent, being the daughter of
Lady Palmerston, came up at an evening party and, with
every appearance of deep interest, asked him—

"Well, Lord Derby, how are you going on ? "

He replied, " Will you promise not to tell if I let you
know an important matter in our favour ? "

"Oh, of course I will promise ! " said Lady Jocelyn.

"Well," said Lord Derby, " Mr. Disraeli has just
announced to me his readiness to allow himself to be
shaved and to have his hair cut, in order to smooth all
difficulties."

He had always a dislike and distrust of Lord Jocelyn, whom he looked on as a kind of emissary from Cambridge House (Lord Palmerston's), although professing to be one of his followers.

One evening, when Lord Jocelyn was speaking in a half-hearted manner, one of his friends sitting by his side said—

"You don't seem to be paying much attention to your noble friend?"

"No," replied Disraeli; "I have no particular pleasure in listening to a great Saracen's head creaking in the wind."

No description could have better hit off Lord Jocelyn, who was a big handsome man, with a large round face and a profusion of jet-black hair, and his manner of speaking was exactly "creaking in the wind." To me, long after our intimacy had ceased, in consequence of his attacks on Sir Robert Peel and my adherence to the Peelite party, he was always most friendly. One day in 1867 we met in St. James's Street, and he took my arm as far as the Carlton. He spoke with much kind feeling about old times, hoped that although I could not be his political supporter, I would always continue out of the House our pleasant relations of former days. I answered that I thought he must be aware I had not forgotten them, for though on many occasions I had made speeches adverse to his policy, I had carefully avoided ever saying one word which could be personally disagreeable to him. He said, "My dear Gregory, I should be blind if I had not noticed your invariable courtesy to me, and I have been anxious to get the opportunity which has to-day occurred, of renewing our old friendship; and now let me ask you to do me a great favour. If during my term of office I can serve you or yours in any way, of course

I don't mean politically, give me the pleasure of allowing me to do so." Some months afterwards there was a vacancy amongst the trustees of the National Gallery, and I said to Colonel Taylor, the whip of the Tory party, that I wished he would mention to Mr. Disraeli my desire to be named to the vacancy. Taylor said he would do so, but he feared Mr. Disraeli could not comply with my wish, as he already had conveyed to him the desire of several of his supporters, peers and M.P.'s, for the honourable appointment. For all that, the next day came a note offering it to me in the handsomest terms. This was pure disinterested friendship, as he knew well enough he would not gain any support from me by the compliment, nor would it in any degree mitigate my political opposition. On a later occasion, when I was trustee, in the year 1867, Mr. Robinson, of the Kensington Museum, reported that he had been shown at Madrid the celebrated Colonna Raffael, which had always been kept in the bedroom of the King of Naples and been carried by him to Gaeta. Don Bermudez de Castro, Duke di Ripalda, the Spanish Minister at Naples, and a great friend of the king, had been presented with the picture by his royal friend, and his brother mentioned that it might possibly be for sale. Sir William Boxall, the Director of the National Gallery, went to Madrid, saw the picture, which was then in fine order, indeed, quite intact, and was anxious to obtain it. I went to see Mr. Disraeli (in May, 1868), who was then in office, and told him all about the picture. He listened, and said, "Get the picture." I remarked that I was certain' it would cost £20,000 at least. "Get the picture," was all he replied. On my saying that I could not manage the negotiation, he agreed to confide it to Baron Rothschild, who commissioned Mr. Bauer, his agent at Madrid, to buy

it. In the meanwhile, the knowledge that the picture was
in the market, and that England was disposed to obtain
it, got wind, and the French began to nibble at it. The
Duke di Ripalda (Bermudez de Castro) was a great friend
of the Empress Eugénie, who was always ready to serve a
friend. Forty thousand pounds were asked for it, and the
French press was subsidized right and left to declare that
the honour of France was involved in the purchase, and
that it was cheap at the money. It was sent to Paris to
M. Reizet, the Director of the Louvre, and I here trans-
cribe an account of what followed and which I wrote at
the time, May, 1870, from Paris :—

"The Colonna Raffael was a few months ago one of the most
perfect and important pictures of that master. In an evil moment
it has been submitted to the cleaner, and a piteous spectacle it now
is in the eyes of gods and men. It is said that on the old frame
being removed, and the iron band which kept it together being
unscrewed, it fell to the ground in three pieces. I believe there is
no doubt as to the truth of the story, which is confirmed by the
extraordinary winking appearance of the eye of one of the female
saints, through which, unfortunately, one of the cracks runs, and
which, therefore, had to be repaired by a modern hand. I cannot
say that I feel any great rapture about this picture. Very grand it
is, no doubt, in its whole arrangement, but the infants Jesus and St.
John are uninteresting, and the figures of St. Paul and St. Peter,
usually so majestic, are squat and dwarfy. At present it looks as if
it had undergone the fate of St. Bartholomew and been thoroughly
flayed, so that I hardly think even the great name of Raffael or its
former reputation will induce a bold purchaser, public or private, to
give the sum demanded for it, nothing less than £40,000. Over it
should be engraved the well-known epitaph, ' I was well ; I would be
better. Here I am.'"

And now to return to and conclude with Mr. Disraeli.
I have already shown good reason for a strong personal
regard towards him, and this regard would naturally lead
me, if I could, to express respect for him as a statesman.
Truth prevents me from doing so. I willingly admit that

he was one of the most remarkable public men that England has ever known. He has been called a man of genius. If the definition of genius be true that "Genius will do as it must, talent will do as it can," he was not a man of genius, for I do not believe that he ever acted from impulse or from the prompting of deep-seated opinions, in spite of his assertion that "Man is never so manly as when he feels deeply, acts boldly, and expresses himself with frankness." He had no deep-seated opinions ; every subject was regarded by him as having reference solely to the Parliamentary triumph of his party, and consequently the advancement of his own power. He was ready to be free-trader or protectionist, liberal or illiberal, on questions of land, religion, and the franchise, just as it suited the exigencies of the moment. That he was really a most advanced Liberal in heart upon all questions of trade and religion I have not a doubt, but I doubt if he at all trusted the people, though I have heard him a hundred times in private proclaim his preference for the working-man over the sleek, narrow-minded, dissenting rulers of the boroughs. His mind was essentially a mocking one, and before those who knew him well he made very little secret of the tendency to dissemble.

In the year 1868, one day, in the lobby of the House of Commons, Colonel Taylor, the whip of the Tory party, told him that many of his friends were dissatisfied at the distant manner in which he treated them. Mr. Disraeli asked who the malcontents were.

"Here is one of them," said Taylor, pointing to Admiral ——, M.P.

"Pray introduce me at once," said Mr. Disraeli.

Accordingly he was introduced, and quite fascinated the old sailor, who, on shaking hands, said—

"Mr. Disraeli, I am extremely glad to make your

acquaintance. I am not a novel reader, but my daughters
are ; they have read all your novels and constantly express a high opinion of them."

" This is indeed fame ! " replied Mr. Disraeli, in a
solemn tone, but with an indescribable look at Colonel
Taylor.

At a somewhat later period, when in the fulness of
his greatness, he sat next at dinner to Mrs. Stonor,
daughter of the great Sir Robert Peel. He immediately
began expatiating in a very fulsome manner on the
career of her father. She was one of the family who
had never forgiven the attacks, and she answered very
curtly that she presumed he had a different opinion of
her father's merits at the time he so bitterly assailed him.

" Oh, Mrs. Stonor," said Disraeli, " you should not
be angry with me about that. Have you not remarked
that little dogs always take delight in barking and snarl-
ing at great dogs ? I was a very small dog, and followed
the example of other small dogs by attacking the great
dog of the day, although at the time I had the greatest
admiration for him."

It was, however, the clergy of the Established Church
on whom he chiefly lavished his blandishments. There
never was a minister who to the close of his life retained
ecclesiastical confidence to the same degree. It is perfectly
true that in his early writings, such as " Coningsby," he
had vented sarcasm upon sarcasm upon the Established
Church. " We cannot conceal from ourselves," says
Coningsby, " that after nearly two centuries of Parliamentary Government and Parliamentary Church, the first
has made Government detested, the second religion disbelieved." " The only consequences of the present union
of Church and State are that on the side of the State there
is a perpetual interference in ecclesiastical government,

and on the side of the Church a sedulous avoidance of all those principles on which alone Church government can be established." "There is no society, however great its resources, that could long resist the united influences of chief magistrate, virtual representation, and Church establishment." The novel of "Coningsby," in which is to be found the exposition of his political creed, teems with denunciation of a Church establishment. It was written in 1844, when he was still a political adventurer, and had not foreseen the political uses to which the clergy could be put ; but he had come to great power in 1861, and looked to the clergy in three-fourths of the parishes of England as potent allies. Accordingly, at Aylesbury, in 1861, he addressed the following language as his manifesto to the Church of England :—"How can it be denied that in this country the union of Church and State is menaced and attacked? It is attacked in the most exalted place in the realm, in Parliament ; it is menaced in an assembly in which the power of the Church would be irresistible if Churchmen would combine together. How many bills were introduced in the last session of Parliament, all under different forms, having one sole end in view, to undermine the Church and the most precious privileges of Churchmen. Our mode of distributing charities is called in question ; our cemeteries threatened with invasion ; our *adversaries* aim at changing our marriage law, at facilitating our public worship as they pretend, and in despoiling of its national character the sound constitution of our Church. As to Church rates, my opinion is well known. I believe their abolition would be a terrible blow struck at the *alliance between Church and State*, and that under no possible or imaginable circumstances should such a concession be made." A more mischievous appeal to sacerdotal pride and to religious

domination cannot be conceived. It is resistance to the
reform of our charitable bequests in which every species
of abuse and fraud was rampant ; it is resistance to allow
a Nonconformist to lay his heretical carcase in the church-
yard of his fathers ; and as to Church rates, they have
passed away, and their abolition, like the reform of the
other abuses which he maintains, have immensely
strengthened and not weakened the Established Church.
On February 22, 1861, writing to Lord Malmesbury, he
says, " The fact is, in internal politics there is only one
question now—the maintenance of the Church. There can
be no refraining or false liberalism on the subject." It
was just about this time that I asked him why he never
went to Ireland. "I have no taste to go to a country,"
he said, "where people are always quarrelling about a
thing they call Religion," jerking out the last word with
a tone of supreme contempt. Later on, when walking
from the House of Lords with Lord Orford, after a
division on some question connected with religion, he
turned to him and said, "It is strange that you and I
should be walking out here together after an attempt to
prop up an exploded theology." Throughout all his conversation there ran a constant vein of scorn for any fixed
principle, and his actions were in harmony with his words.
In spite, however, of all hollowness and flattery, yet to his
praise be it said he never faltered in his allegiance to his
own race, and invariably supported the emancipation of
the Jews when the Tories to a man were rabidly opposed
to it.

There is no more flagrant instance of unscrupulousness
in the annals of the public men of this century than his
conduct in 1867 in respect to the Reform Bill. He and
his party had, with the aid of the so-called "Cave of
Adullam," combated the Reform Bill of Lord Russell the

previous year. The "Cave" had on the motion of Lord Dunkellin proposed the moderate restriction of a £6 rating instead of a rental franchise, and the whole Tory party, led on by Mr. Disraeli, supported and carried the motion by a majority of nine. The Liberal Government resigned, and Lord Derby and the Tories came in. After a series of childish and disreputable manœuvres, Mr. Disraeli came down and proposed Household Suffrage, with the view, as Lord Derby with his usual levity called it, of "dishing the Whigs." There was never a more profligate act, or one which more lowered the character of the great and respectable county party. Many of the most prominent members of it, Lord Salisbury, Lord Carnarvon, and General Peel at once seceded.

That I am not unjust will be manifest to any one who tries to labour through Mr. Disraeli's speeches. Not one of them indicates a policy or a conviction. They were admirably adapted to the exigency of the moment, but are now heavy, uninteresting reading, barring the occasional brilliant jibes or turn of phrase which now and then lighten their dulness. Most pathetic was his answer when he was reproached for having done nothing during the Tory Ministry of 1858. "What could we do," said he, "crushed by an overwhelming majority? but let us get your majority for a time, and see if we will not do great things." The Tory Government came into office in 1874; it was a powerful majority; I fully expected great measures to follow, and yet what great or good measure was effected by it either in England or in Ireland? And as for the colonies, his expressions were always those of contempt and a contented impression that we should sooner or later be rid of them. It is true that his party was leavened by stupidity, inefficiency, inexperience, and prejudice; but his overwhelming personal influence could easily have swept aside every obstacle, had he ever conceived any important measure and been resolved on carrying it. He might have effected immense reforms in dealing with land, which the squires would have accepted from him, but his Government did nothing except carry a law to permit arrangements between landlord and tenant, if both were consenting. No doubt towards the close of his life his great object was Imperialism, the extension of England's power, and her taking a more decided line in Continental politics. As such he obtained for himself a great reputation throughout Europe, and unquestionably dissipated for the time the growing belief of the decadence of England. That he was a man of immense talent not even his greatest enemy can deny; but even I, his personal friend, must confess that from his entrance into public life until his last hour he lived and died a charlatan.

CHAPTER VI.

LORD GEORGE BENTINCK was of a very different nature. Proud, overbearing, persevering, brave as a lion morally as he was physically, once he took up a subject he never let it drop to turn his thoughts to something else. He thoroughly worked it out. His amazing and undaunted energy made him almost invariably successful. His motto eminently should have been " *Nil actum reputans dum quid superesset agendum.*" He was the first man who ever put a racehorse into a van, and when the blacklegs at Doncaster thought his famous horse Elis was safe on the Hampshire Downs, and were betting against him as if he were dead, he was trotting in his van into the town of Doncaster, to win the St. Leger in a canter two days afterwards. It was his vigour which inspired the Government to sanction the passing of an Act of Parliament to stay all vexatious proceedings in the case of the celebrated Qui Tam action, which was the endeavour by a set of low attorneys to levy enormous penalties in pursuance of an obsolete Act of 9th Anne for sums won by betting. His intelligence and perseverance worked out the discovery of the infamous fraud by which Running Rein, a four-year-old of falsified pedigree, was enabled to compete with three-year-old colts in 1844 and to win the Derby. But for him it would have succeeded, and enormous sums been won by a gang of blacklegs. He thoroughly reformed the turf regulations,

in spite of the obstruction of Newmarket fogeyism, and
he succeeded in sternly enforcing at other race-courses
the enactments he first set on foot at Goodwood for
expelling from the precincts of the grand stands the
welshers, levanters, touts, and ruffians who had previously
infested them. The same determination he soon manifested
when he took to politics. He was not a well-educated
man, and scarcely ever read a book, though he had been
private secretary for three years to his uncle Mr. Canning.
In writing to Mr. Croker in October, 1847, he speaks thus
modestly of himself—

"Virtually an uneducated man, never intended or attracted by taste
for political life, in the House of Commons only by a pure accident,
indeed, by an inevitable and undesired change, I am well aware of
my own incapacity to fill the station I have been thrust into. My
sole ambition was to rally the broken and dispirited forces of a
betrayed and insulted party, and to avenge the country gentlemen
and landed aristocracy of England upon the minister who, presuming
on their weakness, falsely flattered himself that they could be trampled
on with impunity."

Over and over again he spoke to me in that strain. For
eighteen years he had slept soundly upon the back benches
every night when not at a race, and when the House of
Commons was sitting, for he rarely went into society.
He dined at White's regularly, and then drove down to
the House. He always voted steadily with Sir Robert
Peel, but when it became bruited abroad, in the autumn
of 1845, that Sir Robert was disposed to repeal the Corn
Laws, his indignation knew no bounds. He considered
that the Prime Minister had led his party into power on
the faith of Protection, that every member of the great
Tory majority had pledged himself to it, and that to
violate such a pledge was fraught with dishonour.

In writing to me, in November, 1845, from Welbeck, on
the subject of some experiments made for storing potatoes,
he says, " When the pits were opened they were whitened

sepulchres, and stank as the present ministers will stink in the nostrils of every honest man, if they try to carry out the intentions attributed to them." When the announcement appeared in the *Times* that the Cabinet had resolved on Free Trade, he placed himself at once at the head of the large portion of the Tory party who were resolved to resist the change. Racing, so recently the darling object of his life, his sole thought, became at once a secondary consideration. To resist the Government and to punish them was henceforth his fixed idea. Never did man work as he then worked. As he said to me, " I am profoundly ignorant of political economy, and have to learn the rudiments of it to understand and meet the arguments of the Free Traders ; I am unable as a speaker to put two words together ; and, worse than all, the long confirmed habit I have of sleeping after dinner causes me the greatest misery while endeavouring to break it off." But he gallantly persevered. It is quite true that he never really understood Adam Smith, and that he clung desperately to every exploded economic fallacy, and never became a fluent speaker, but he was able to express himself, and knew thoroughly what he was about, and he never faltered or despaired. With signal perspicacity he selected Mr. Disraeli, as I said before, as his lieutenant, and then forced him on the party as their leader. He was totally devoid of personal ambition.

It was early in 1846 that Lord George Bentinck took the field, and before the end of the session, to quote Mr. Disraeli's words, he

" had rallied a great party which seemed hopelessly routed, he had established a parliamentary discipline in their ranks which old political connections led by experienced statesmen have seldom surpassed ; he had proved himself a master in detail, and in argument of all the great questions arising out of the reconstruction of our commercial system."

He continued to act as leader of his party till the end of
1847, when he resigned. The cause of this formal resignation was his having spoken and voted for Lord J. Russell's
bill for the admission of Jews to Parliament. He had
done so on two former occasions, but on this one he
received a letter from Major Beresford, one of the Conservative whips, to the effect that a considerable portion
of his party was dissatisfied with him. Although Major
Beresford tried to reduce the offence by saying he was
only stating his private opinion, Lord George's proud
spirit would not brook such an intimation, and he at once
resigned. I believe he was glad of the opportunity of
doing so, though evidently deeply wounded by the want
of confidence expressed. Whatever may have been his
heresies on currency and banking, on all religious matters
his early connection with Mr. Canning had freed his mind
from bigotry, and he was ready and anxious to concede
to the Catholic and to the Jew alike the fullest equality.
"As for the Jews," he says, in one of his letters to Mr.
Croker, "I don't care two straws about them, and heartily
wish they were all back in the Holy Land;" but he
protests against leading a party based on such miserable
sectarian principles with all the scorn of his generous,
fiery spirit. He writes, December 19, 1847, to Mr.
Croker—

"The great Protectionist party having degenerated into a No-Popery,
No-Jew party, I am still more unfit than I was in 1846 to lead it. A
party that can muster a hundred and forty on a Jew Bill, and cannot
muster much above half those numbers on any question essentially
connected with the great interests of the Empire, can only be led by
their antipathies, their hatreds, and their prejudices, and I am the
unfittest man in the world to lead them. I think it very unfortunate
that things have been brought to that pass, that I see no chance of the
party being kept from melting away except by the choice of a new
leader, and he a No-Popery man. I wrote this to Stanley long ago. I
have resigned with a good grace and in a tone of good feeling, and I

hope that the result will be that the party will henceforth act with more concord and zeal, and may thus on the only subjects which concern the Empire be led by their prejudices to muster more strongly than they could be by argument or reason so long as they were led by a man who endeavoured to lead them by their understandings, but knew not how to sympathize in or to pander to their religious prejudices."

On the resignation of Lord George Bentinck, Lord Granby was selected to lead the Protectionist party, but refused this very questionable position ; and a triumvirate consisting of Mr. Disraeli, Lord Granby, and Mr. Herries were appointed as "joint leaders in the House of Commons ;" " an evident failure," wrote Lord Malmesbury at the time, "the latter two being in the way of the first." Lord Malmesbury had throughout recognized the sagacity of Lord George Bentinck in placing Mr. Disraeli in the front, for shortly after Lord George's death he writes : " No one but Disraeli can fill his place. Although of perfectly different natures, they pulled together without any difficulty. It will leave Disraeli without a rival, and enable him to show the great genius he undoubtedly possesses without any comparisons."

I have recently heard persons declaiming on the extraordinary astuteness of Disraeli in putting forward Lord George Bentinck as a leader, knowing that he could not possibly hold the post for long, but just long enough to enable him to assume the direction of and gain the adhesion of the party. But those who make such an assertion little know Lord George's clearness of vision, and that he was the very last man to be an instrument in the hands of any one. They are entirely ignorant, moreover, of what was then Disraeli's position ; that he was spoken of contemptuously as a somewhat ridiculous though very clever adventurer. It is true that his great speeches against Peel opened men's eyes to his ability, but it required all Lord George Bentinck's strength of will, tenacity of purpose, and high rank to force him into the prominence which culminated into leadership. Over and over again did Lord George, before we were estranged, speak with almost fury of the resistance of the squires to the prominence of the " d——d Jew," as they chose to call the man whose memory they now adore with primroses in their button-hole. To use what would have been Lord George's racing language, " It was he who gave Dizzy the mount, it was Dizzy's riding that won the race."

It was the custom of the Whigs and Peelites to sneer at Lord George as an ignorant intruder in the political area, and to proclaim that Newmarket alone was his proper sphere. I entirely disagree with that view. I regard him as a man of remarkable ability, unflinching perseverance, of high moral as well as physical courage, and believe that had he devoted himself in early life to politics, he would have taken a prominent, perhaps the most prominent, position in the history of the day. It is true that he was unyielding and tenacious of his own opinion, but that fault would have been modified by the exigencies of office. He never would have been, like his friend Disraeli, a man of expedients, but would have formed a decided policy, would have fashioned measures of great importance in his mind, would have worked the details to as near perfection as intelligence and industry could bring them, and would have influenced his party in support of them by the contagion of his own enthusiasm. Witness his famous measure, at the time of the Irish famine, for the prompt and profitable employment of the people of Ireland, by lending a sum of sixteen millions to railway companies who were prepared to come forward with half that amount and to open up the whole of Ireland. This proposal was ridiculed and rejected by the Whig

Government which succeeded Sir Robert Peel; but it was a grand scheme, every detail worked out, every difficulty met. It would have been the greatest blessing to the country, and it would have provided a vast amount of profitable relief to the suffering poor. It is calculated that employment to 110,000 able-bodied men would have at once been given, whereas under the Labour Rate Act 500,000 persons were employed idling, and doing in many cases absolute mischief at a cost of £700,000 monthly. I do not recollect one work of utility completed under the Labour Rate Act, but I know too well, and every Irishman who takes a part in country business knows that it has left an insatiable desire for public works, because they bring with them reckless expenditure, jobbing, and fraud. This labour, moreover, would have been honest and reproductive, and unaccompanied by the demoralization which the ineffectual system of relief adopted sowed in the country, and which has become as it were ingrained in it. And now, after an expiration of thirty-seven years, the Government is engaged in partially carrying out the views of Lord George Bentinck which were sneered down in the House of Commons on February 4, 1847, and with what loss to Ireland!

My friendship with Lord George Bentinck began at a very early period of my life, when I had just left Oxford. He was extremely civil to me and often invited me to see his horses. The following letter, written just after my hustings speech, shows the very friendly relations which existed between us :—

"Welbeck, January 29, 1842.

"The news of your majority on the first day's poll gave every Conservative here, and especially me, the greatest pleasure. I sincerely congratulate you upon it, but still more do I congratulate you upon the distinguished fight you made upon the hustings against the great O'Connell at the nomination, and even the Whigs have acknowledged their admiration of your speech. I need not say that I anticipate no reverse upon the poll. I doubt not that you will maintain and improve the strong lead you have taken, but should it be otherwise still I could not but congratulate you upon the triumph of talents evinced in your first day's battle upon the hustings. Verily if Auckland " (the first favourite for the Derby) "has done as much with the old ones in private as the 'tipsy boy' from the Curragh has done with the great agitator in publick (*sic*), there is no fear but that he will win the Derby in a canter. With sincerest wishes for your continued success,

" Believe me always very truly yours,

"G. BENTINCK."

The reference to the " tipsy boy from the Curragh " was to one of the amenities employed towards me by the *Freeman's Journal* during the time of the election. Though at that time I had never been at the Curragh, truth compels me to admit that Remmy Sheehan, the editor of the *Dublin Evening Mail*, had recently given a dinner-party to myself and my chief supporters. We were all in high spirits, and the wine was excellent and our host somewhat overpressing, so much so that when Lord Jocelyn and myself adjourned to a ball at Lord Eliot's it was manifest, though only slightly manifest, that we had been dining out. I need hardly say the *Freeman* made a mountain out of this mole-hill.

I had constant letters from Lord George, on all manner of subjects, till the break up of Sir R. Peel's Government, when a coolness arose between us in consequence of his employing the epithets of " janissaries " and " renegades " to the Peelite Free-traders, and this lasted till within a few days of his death, which occurred shortly after the Doncaster Meeting of 1848. One day at Doncaster, when the races were over, there were several men, whom he knew well, standing together, and he said, " Will you come to the paddocks and see the mares and foals ? " and, turning

to me, he added, "And I hope *you* will come too." He
laid so much stress on the word "you" that I very
cordially accepted the invitation. After the inspection
of the young stock was over, he turned to me and said,
"We have plenty of time before dinner—suppose you and
I take a walk. It is long since we have had one." There
was not a word about our former coolness during the walk,
but he seemed to do his best to efface all memory of it.
In fact, he was for the time quite gentle and unlike himself
and the proud obdurate race to which he belonged. He
spoke a great deal about himself—how unfit he was to lead
a party, how much he regretted his deficient education, and
the absolute torture it was to him to give up his habit
of sleeping after dinner. I asked him if he did not at
times regret having sold his famous stud and his great
horse Surplice. He said at times he longed for the
pleasant windy mornings on Newmarket Heath or Stock-
bridge Downs, seeing his young horses gallop and trying
them, but, he said, "I have given up every thought of
racing. I know nothing of it. I have put my hand to the
plough and cannot turn back." When we parted it was
quite clear that we were to be for the future on the
old footing. This walk and kind conversation were a
great satisfaction to me when a few days afterwards I
heard that he was picked up stone dead in a field near
Welbeck.

If ever a man killed himself by sheer hard labour and
privation, that man was Lord George Bentinck. Mr.
Disraeli mentions that for some time before his death
he worked for eighteen hours a day, and he has told me
repeatedly that he was in a state of inanition, because if
he tasted food till his day's work was over, he would
become liable to the drowsiness which only starvation
overcame. He died, it is supposed, of spasm in the heart,

produced by over anxiety and toil, for he was perfectly
sound in every respect, and one of the finest and handsomest men I ever beheld. I mourned his death at the
time deeply and unreservedly. I felt that a great Englishman had departed; but subsequent reflection brought me
to the conclusion that his death was, so far as his reputation was concerned, not disadvantageous either to himself
or his country. In two years he had risen from the ranks
and become one of the most prominent men in England.
Had his early life been more disciplined, had he been
subjected to the chastening influence of office, and to the
responsibility of administration, he would have been more
pliant, more ready to look around him, more disposed to
listen to argument and to objection. This was not his
way—a strong difference from his views was tantamount
to a moral offence. It would have been impossible for
the Tory party ever to shake themselves clear of the
economic fallacies which he laid down as the basis of
faith with an Athanasian dogmatism. The slightest back-
sliding from what he considered the immutable principles
of right and wrong would have brought down even on his
best friends his unsparing denunciation. Friendship or
party consideration were no shield against his wrath when
the fire burned hot within him. His anger was too often
unreasonable, as when he fell foul of Lord Derby, during
a political dinner at the Carlton, in consequence of Lord
Derby expressing an opinion that it was unwise to persist
in denunciations of the followers of Sir Robert Peel who
might, perhaps, if gently handled, be induced to rejoin the
Tory party; and again, when he assailed Lord Lyndhurst
for having jobbed his patronage, an accusation which was
proved to be altogether unfounded. These outbreaks were
the result of the want of discipline to which I have alluded,
and would undoubtedly have been attended with much

unhappiness to himself and with the disruption of his party, which the ability of Disraeli with difficulty kept together. I cannot, therefore, regret his untimely death, though I am by no means prepared to say that I should have regretted the disruption of the Tory party. In that case we might have formed a powerful, moderate, and enlightened Government, with Mr. Gladstone as its leader. A careful and progressive policy, with his great financial skill, would have secured the confidence of the country, and democracy, though irresistible, would have been retarded for a quarter of a century, instead of being fostered and egged on.

With the exception of my five and a half years' government of Ceylon, these first five years in Parliament were the happiest period of my life. I was young, strong in health, well off through the generosity of my father, who never denied me anything. I was popular, and welcome to the best houses in London. I should qualify this by writing the best Conservative houses in London, for party spirit ran high, and there was but little love lost between Whigs and Tories. I always have regretted that I never had a chance of penetrating the charmed and charming circle of literary society, which was even then expiring, but there were still Rogers, Lockhart, Luttrell, Macaulay, Hayward, Sidney Smith, and others. My acquaintance with Sidney Smith was rather amusing. Shortly after my election I was asked to dine with Lord and Lady Clanricarde, at 2, Carlton-house Terrace. I arrived, as I considered myself bound to do, at the very minute indicated. On being shown into the drawing-room I found there was one guest before me, a fat elderly parson, whom I supposed to be the domestic chaplain, and with whom, to set him at his ease, I entered at once into conversation with the most condescending affability. To

my amazement my advances were met with something
that was very like chaff, and in a few minutes I found
myself an object of the broadest banter by the old fat
parson. My dignity was a little rubbed, but he was so
extremely droll that we were shortly in fits of laughter
and excellent friends. So I relaxed my self-importance
and said to him, "Let us make an arrangement. I am
sure I shall know no one of the great people who will
be here, and I dare say you will be in the same predica-
ment, so let us sit together, and we shall get on famously."
"That will just suit me," said he, and at that moment
in sailed Lady Clanricarde and introduced me to the
wittiest and best known man in England, the Canon of
St. Paul's. I almost sunk into my evening boots, but, as
we were going out to dinner, he said to Lady Clanricarde,
" I have made an engagement with my young friend here
to sit next to him. Pray put us next each other." This
she did, and, after a little temporary abasement, I passed
a most pleasant evening. I do not think I met him
again. I knew Thackeray at the time, and until his
death, extremely well. We made acquaintance at the
house of Thoby Prinsep, M.P. and East India Director,
where we both worshipped at the shrine of the most
beautiful woman I have ever seen, the present Lady
Somers, then Virginia Pattle, sister to Mrs. Prinsep.
There were many other worshippers. George Smythe,
Lord Lansdowne, Alfred Montgomery, and Watts the
painter. When Lord Somers came, in 1850, and carried
off this lovely and most lovable girl, we were all very
sad. I saw her first at a Highland ball, in Hanover-
square Rooms, in 1844. She and her sister, Mrs. Dal-
rymple, also very beautiful at that time, were sitting
together covered with folds of white gauze. Every one
was looking at them with the greatest admiration, but

no one knew who and whence they were. Going out into
the passage, I met Lord Altamont, the present Lord
Sligo, and I said to him, "Come in here without losing
a moment, there are two angels who have just floated
into the ballroom through an open window, and if you
don't make haste they may fly out of it." "Why," said
he, "these are the Pattle girls, daughters of old Blazer
Pattle—I knew them well at Calcutta. Come and be
introduced!" I came, was introduced, and was "burnt
up at once into kabobs," as the Persians say. To this
hour she retains some of her wonderful beauty, and in
goodness of heart she remains, and ever will remain,
unchanged.

It was not, however, merely in London or in Parliament that I took my pleasure. I regret to say that very
soon Newmarket and the great race meetings began to
exercise a far stronger attraction than politics or society,
and undoubtedly there was in those early times a fascination about Newmarket which was irresistible. The style
of racing was totally different from the present. There
was plenty of betting, no doubt, but the betting was on
the weight for age races, and on matches. Handicaps
of any importance were comparatively rare. The Derby
was the one great object then; there were but few two-
year-old races to throw a light on it, and in the spring
meetings there were every day weight for age races for
three-year-old colts, many of these being of the deepest
interest as regards the great event. There was not the
system then of gigantic training stables; many owners of
racehorses had their private stables, and in most cases
the trainers had only two or three employers. John Day
and John Scott, the great representatives of the Northern
and Southern stables, were the exceptions, both of them
training large studs. Nothing was more delightful than

to get up early in the morning, mount one's hack, and
watch all the champions for the great events taking their
gallops, and listen to the comments of the *cognoscenti*.
Never were eggs and bacon more punished than after our
return from the Heath.   In the daytime we were all on
horseback—there were only about half a dozen races in
the year witnessed from a stand.   A pleasant dinner, full
of fun, at the Rooms, matching horses after dinner, and a
rubber of moderate whist ended a healthy day.   Besides
the old-established meetings there was one set on foot
by old Lord Verulam, father of the present lord, at
Gorhambury, which was very pleasant.   I used to be a
guest at the house, where there was invariably a large
party of smart, good-looking women, and of fast young
men of opulence.   We kept late hours, had excellent fare.
The race-course, if not very good, was very pretty, and
we always looked forward to the meeting.   In the evening
all sorts of amusements prevailed, and I shall never, while
I live, forget the performances of Paul Methuen, the present
lord, and what came of them.   He was reputed to be one
of the strongest men in the army, and his strength must
have been prodigious, as he actually lifted from the ground
by the waistband of his trousers the present Sir Watkin
Wynn, then weighing certainly over fourteen stone, and
held him out with one hand.   Unfortunately the material
of the trousers was not equal to the strain.   They gave
way—and I leave to the imagination the sight that met
the eye of all the ladies assembled in the great hall, and
of the maids above in the gallery.   There was a dead
silence for a moment, then every one broke out into a
roar ; the ladies ran into the drawing-room and hid their
faces in the cushions, and the gentlemen laughed till
they cried.

Although young and inexperienced I held my own

very fairly at these meetings, but I did not bet heavily except on the Derby, when one had plenty of time to look about and get advice. The year after my success on Coronation I had a reverse on Attila, not so much from what I lost on the horse himself as by reason of some heavy defalcations. But in the following year, 1843, my good fortune was again in the ascendant. One morning, early in the session, Mr. Bowes, M.P. for Durham, a great friend of mine, called on me and asked me, in strict confidence, to back his horse Cotherstone for the coming Derby, and he advised me to follow suit. Cotherstone was an outsider in Scott's stable, little thought of, and at forty to one in the betting. Mr. Bowes gave me plenty of time to do the commission, which I returned to him as £22,000 to £1000. The horse came to Newmarket in April, won the two great races there, the Riddlesworth and Two Thousand Guineas stake, for which I backed him heavily. He then went to Epsom and won the Derby in a canter, and I had the gratification of handing to Mr. Bowes £22,000 on the Monday following, and of lodging £5000 to my own credit at my bankers. Two years afterwards, on the Sunday fortnight before the Derby, I made a very remarkable bet. A large party was dining at Greenwich, of whom Jack Mytton, the son of the celebrated Squire of Halston, was one. He was offering to bet extravagant odds against outsiders for the Derby, and I proposed to take £1000 to £5, ten times against each of two horses, one an outsider in Scott's stable, and the other, called "Merry Monarch," trained by Forth, of whom I had received a good account from a trustworthy source. He won the Derby, and Mytton would have had to pay me £10,000, but I hedged off £6000 with him before the race, when he was warned the horse was dangerous. As it was his dinner cost him £4000.

CHAPTER VII

I MUST now mention some of my doings in Parliament.
I have a few notes still remaining written at the time. It
is most unfortunate that I did not pursue the practice
of keeping a record of the sayings and doings of the men
of mark with whom I came in contact, and of my own
honest, unbiased view of the questions of the day. As
I became better educated in politics I found that the
intimations—I will not call them pledges—which I gave
to my most intolerant constituents were serious impedi-
ments in my way. At the time when I canvassed the
constituency I was entirely, owing to my political ignorance
in the hands of others, of men who had fought to the bitter
end against Catholic Emancipation, and I was recommended
by them to denounce the Maynooth Grant and the system
of National Education and to take the high Protestant
line. My early associations had been entirely free from
religious bigotry ; there was no animosity towards Roman
Catholics and their religion among the young men with
whom I lived at Oxford. My mother and the O'Haras
were decidedly Liberal in politics, and all of them enthusiastic advocates of Catholic Emancipation. My father,
though nominally a Tory, was totally free from the Trench
traditions and perfectly liberal in his religious opinions.
If he was not so in general politics it was because he was
timid and had not given much heed to them, rather than
from any force of conviction.

When I went over to England as a member of Parliament I found English Conservative opinion to be very different from Irish. The former was desirous of raising up the Irish Catholics to an equality with the Protestants and to do away with all disabilities and inequalities ; the latter was desirous of keeping down the Roman Catholics and retaining every anomaly, every insulting distinction, and of preserving their own social superiority. " Always make a nigger feel he's a nigger, or else he'll grow saucy," says Sam Slick, and such was exactly the feeling of the great majority of middle-class Protestants, and of a considerable number of the higher class. I was seriously requested to bring before Parliament the conduct of the Catholics in having and using chapel bells, and I remember Lord W—— wanting me to join him in throwing overboard the Dublin packet two tin cases belonging to some fellow-travelling Roman Catholic prelate. I asked him why we should do such a thing, and his answer was, " Because he is a Catholic priest, and of course a scoundrel." I find in the diary to which I have alluded various entries at this time, expressive of the intense disgust which I felt at this intolerance and of the irksomeness of my own position. I copy one made at an early period :—

"Occupied all day about the Maynooth Grant, which comes on to-night. Read all the former debates on the subject—weary work enough. Hope we shall be spared having our opposition disgraced by the abominable fanaticism of Messrs. Plumtre and Co. Tresham Gregg and the operatives of Dublin are sufficiently bitter pills without having 'the Man of Sin,' 'Antichrist,' 'Priests of Baal,' and 'the Scarlet Lady of Babylon,' crammed down our throats."

During the first session of 1842 I only made a few remarks in reply to some observations by Mr. Shiel, who commented on my having attended a meeting of the Protestant Operative Association at which the Rev. Tresham Gregg presided, and having there declared

myself against Maynooth and National Education ; Lord
Jocelyn, who was on the Lord Lieutenant's staff, was also
hauled over the coals for having accompanied me, and
aided me in my canvass.   Lord Eliot, then Chief Secretary,
threw me over by regretting my language on the subject
of education.   I said I was in favour of religious education,
and that I would do all in my power to obtain a system
founded on religious principles.

A few days afterwards Sir Robert Peel called me into
his room and said, " My good fellow, the days of extreme
religious opinions are over.   I was sorry to hear you
identify yourself at all with the intolerant section of your
countrymen."   I told him the whole truth, and with much
bitterness of heart.   " Well," said he, " if you have unfortunately given any pledges you must stick to them or resign
your seat.   At all events, take every opportunity of dis-
sociating yourself from those ultra men, who if they
had their way would create a fresh rebellion in Ireland."

As regards the views I held on National Education
I might now boast that my object has been attained, as the
National Education system is virtually denominational,
and the higher education is becoming more so.   I have
always held the opinion I expressed in 1842, for I
am certain that the ties of religion are the only influences
which can beneficially affect the unruly wills and lawless-
ness of the Irish lower classes.

I felt the most unbounded admiration for the courage,
as well as political foresight, with which George Smythe,
a young man like myself, treated Irish questions, social
and religious, although he represented the extreme Tory
and, indeed, retrograde element of a cathedral city (Canterbury).   I chafed at the pledges or, as I called them in the
preceding page, " intimations " which I had given to my
Dublin constituents, and felt resolved to break my bonds

at the next election, and to tell the voters that, while loyally supporting the Government of Sir Robert Peel, I should speak my mind and act freely on all questions. I took no other part in the House of Commons during 1842.

In the following year I was equally silent, except that I made two short speeches on "fishing piers" and "polling places," but even then I had come to the conclusion that food taxes were doomed, and, much to the indignation of my Tory friends, I paired in favour of Mr. Hutt's motion for the free importation of Australian corn, and was thereby the first seceder from the Protectionist phalanx. In 1844 I made a good, though somewhat laboured speech on the Dublin State Trials, and the general condition of Ireland. Mr. Macaulay told the oft-told and too true tale of English misrule, I contended that it was useless to go back, but it was our duty to go forward, and I was applauded when I described Macaulay's historical allusions as "Hatchments over the memory of departed grievances, with the word '*Resurgam*' ostentatiously inscribed in the most conspicuous characters." In the course of this speech I used these words, which are not inapplicable to the present state of things in Ireland:—"In England you may extend the elective franchise in the counties if you will, property there will have its legitimate influence. In Ireland, however, the case is different. The more extensive the augmentation of the constituencies there, the greater power you lodge, not in the friends of Ireland, but in the hands of those who are the determined enemies of British connection and of the establishment of tranquillity in the country." I also spoke indignantly of the ill-treatment of the poorer Irish tenants, who were encouraged to multiply during the time of the forty-shilling franchise, "but who, because they could no longer minister to the political ambition of their master or the extortions of the middleman, were driven out roofless and homeless on the wide world, to swell the lists of those to whom any change must be a godsend."

In April, 1845, Sir Robert Peel brought in his bill to increase the Maynooth Grant. I made a moderate speech on the introduction of the bill, not opposing it, as many did, on the ground of its encouraging religious error, but because the priests brought up at Maynooth had proved themselves to be so essentially turbulent and disloyal. On the 14th of April I again spoke against this grant, and made a very bad, ill-argued speech. I so acted partly because I had most unfortunately compromised myself at the election that I would oppose the Maynooth Grant, and, *à fortiori*, I was bound to oppose an increase to it, but also because I had been constantly assailed by the Dublin Tory press on account of my Laodicean luke-warmness. What were my real opinions at that time I expressed in my diary, which, for many reasons, I never intended that other eyes than my own should see. On the 3rd of April I write—

"All last night at the House of Commons. Peel introduced his measure for the increase of the grant to Maynooth College. I never saw a man look more downhearted than he did during the time of private business, when petitions against his bill poured in from every village and hamlet, city and county, throughout the land. There might be seen, with the same pile of earnest and sorrowful protests, Sir Robert Inglis and Tom Duncombe, Church and Chartism, the Anti-Corn League and Young England, Cobden and John Manners, Plumptre, the man of devotion, and Disraeli, the man of sneers. All, all are present, laden with the orthodox terrors of the whole of England and Scotland and half Ireland, lest the Roman Catholic priesthood of the last-named wretched country should be elevated one half-inch in the scale of humanity, lest the students of Maynooth College should, through the liberality of Parliament, be enabled to sleep two instead of three in a bed.

"And oh! what a miserable falling off was there in our Premier's attitude and demeanour. Where was that jaunty air, that ponderous jest, that emphatic thump on the red box, when, with coat thrown back in days of yore, he turned to drink in the enthusiastic cheers of his working majority of ninety? All this had passed away. Like a man accused of some great crime he took his stand, and pleaded his cause slowly, painfully, despondingly. No turning round now behind the Treasury Bench, not a cheer from thence."

It was in this year, on June 6th, that her Majesty gave her celebrated Bal Poudré, to which I had the honour of receiving an invitation. The costume was limited to the period between 1730 and 1750. My dress cost between £70 and £80, so I may as well describe it. High red-heeled shoes with diamond buckles ; white silk stockings with gold clock ; cherry-coloured velvet breeches ; a deep waistcoat with flaps of white satin, embroidered with arabesques ; a turquoise-coloured velvet coat with gold buttons, from whence emerged a sword ; and on my head a small three-cornered hat trimmed with ostrich feathers. The costume of the time required a small bob-wig with a couple of side curls. Most of the guests cut off their hair and invested in a horsehair wig. I allowed mine to grow, and had it well curled and pomatumed and powdered just before starting. The dances of the evening were minuets, Sir Roger de Coverley, and country dances. After her Majesty had danced her minuet the other minuet parties came forward and danced before her. I never saw so striking a sight as this ball. Besides our own national attire, civil and military, we had Hungarians, Venetians, Russians—in short, the inhabitants of all Europe in the dress of the period ; and the ladies looked superb in powder, rouge, and patches, especially ladies in the autumn of life, who, for that night at all events, completely cut down the younger and more blooming *débutantes.* I always wonder that ladies just in the descent of the hill of life have not made the introduction of rouge

and powder a *sine quâ non* of the highest fashionable evening attire. They have everything on their side, experience,
a common bond of union, and desperation to enforce their
decree.   Could they but succeed their attractions would
be extended and paramount for at least another five years.
Surely such an object is worth a struggle.

At about half-past two in the morning I felt a very
unpleasant laxity in the state of my curls, and found
that the heat of the atmosphere and my dancing exertions were gradually relaxing them into straightness, and
so I took my departure.   It was a lovely warm morning
and the streets quite deserted.   I walked up to St.
James's Street on my way home, and found Crockford's
Club still open.   On going upstairs, the supper-room
was full of men from the ball, and not one in ordinary
attire.   It was an exact representation of Hogarth's
" Rake's Progress."   The Rakes of 1845 were not drunk
to be sure, but there they were as in 1780, with their
legs up and their swords thrown on the table or the
ground, their bob-wig either on the back of their heads or
altogether off.   It was one of the most curious sights I
ever saw.   I only wish I had had the power of Hogarth
to record it.   I am not aware that any drawings were
made of the costumes, but well do I remember the extraordinary beauty of Lady Waterford, Lady Canning, and
Lady Douro (now Duchess of Wellington), and how
fascinating and picturesque Lady Villiers looked as a
French marquise.   I can still see Lord Cardigan striding
proudly through the rooms in the uniform of the 11th
Dragoons at Culloden.   How strange my friend Robert
Curzon looked in a quaint Venetian dress, how high bred
Lord Wilton and Lord Alford, and how odd the guards-
men, in their long white infantry gaiters and old-fashioned
high-peaked caps !

In 1846 came the great conversion. The Conservatives deserted Protection in platoons, that is, almost all
the leaders, except Lord Derby, Lord George Bentinck,
Mr. Henley, Mr. Herries, and Mr. Disraeli, though the
last-named, at that time, had not emerged from the rank-
and-file. Sir Robert Peel, on the meeting of Parliament,
brought forward his motion for Free Trade. I took an
early opportunity of supporting Sir Robert to the best of
my power. Early in February I made a speech on the
abolition of import duties on corn, which was long, extremely dull, and received with attention, and nothing
more.

My speech was better thought of by Sir Robert Peel
than I thought of it myself, for, two days after it, I
received a note from him, requesting me to call on him.
On my doing so, he asked me if I thought my seat was
safe, and, on my expressing my belief that it was so, he
went on to say that the Irish Lordship of the Treasury
was vacant, and that he wished me to take it ; and not
only that, but, in consequence of the Chief Secretary for
Ireland, Lord Lincoln, having resigned his seat in Parliament, it was his intention to place the conduct of the
Irish business in the House of Commons in my hands.

I need hardly say that I was completely taken aback
by such an offer ; but I was more alarmed than pleased.
I remarked to Sir Robert Peel that it was impossible for
me to make head against O'Connell and Shiel, I had not
the political knowledge or power of speaking to do so.
"You will do well enough," he answered, "after one or
two encounters ; and, moreover, Sir James Graham has
promised always to come to your assistance if you are
hard pressed." Most unfortunately for me, my father and
mother were passing through London at the time, and I
asked permission to consult them. Peel concluded the

interview, during which he appeared to be in high spirits, by saying, " Of course your father and mother will be very glad that their son should get such an opening ; but remember, my good fellow, that henceforth the days of Newmarket are over. You will have to give up racing. And now let me say one word. You are a young politician, and, as you would say at Newmarket, a good start is everything. It will be hereafter a matter of pride to you to be associated with measures of a wide and generous character which may entirely change the aspect of Ireland to England. Do not think the opposition of last year to the increase of the Maynooth Grant indisposes me in the least to go much further, and to endeavour to place the Roman Catholic clergy in a position of comfort. There are other measures, too, indispensably necessary to your country, in which I hope you will take a part."

I went home and found my father so averse to my accepting the proffered office that I at once declined it. My mother was unable to make up her mind. On the one side was the brilliant position ; on the other was the speech I made advocating protection at the hustings and the imputations that would be poured out on my head by the rabid Dublin press. My father was exceedingly sensitive ; he could not bear that it should be said I had spoken and voted in order to obtain office. He had not the least objection to the line I had taken, and he considered that my refusal of office would justify the course I adopted. To this day I bitterly regret that I refused Sir Robert's offer. It would have put me fairly in the political groove, and would have enrolled me in the corps of those famous young men whom Sir Robert had selected, and had shown his eminent sagacity in so doing —Mr. Gladstone, Lord Dalhousie, Lord Elgin, Lord Canning, Mr. Cardwell, Lord Lincoln, Sidney Herbert. It

K

might have been that, absorbed in politics, I should have weaned myself from racing, which was every day encircling me more tightly in its noxious coil. I feel also that, up to the day of his death, Sir Robert Peel was not the same to me. He was as kind as ever, but he did not show the interest he always took in my doings. He no doubt thought he had done his duty by his old friend, my grandfather, in giving me a great chance, but as wilful men must have their way he could do no more. As it turned out, however, had I accepted office, my tenure would have been but a short one. Within four months of the circumstance I have narrated, Sir Robert Peel's ministry was overthrown by a combination of the Whigs, Radicals, and Protectionists, on the second reading of the Protection of Life and Property Bill, Ireland. I find in my journal the following entry :—

June 27, 1846.—"More than a year's blank in my journal, and what strange events have happened in the meanwhile. The sacrilegious hand that touched the altar and remained unscathed has assailed the wheatsheaf and been withered up. A protection House of Commons has, by a majority of seventy-three, defeated the minister who perished in his endeavour to protect life and property in Ireland. To think of the farce of Lord George Bentinck and Bankes and Major Beresford grounding their opposition to the bill on the plea that they could not confide powers, beyond the constitution, to a minister in whom they had no trust ! Yet if ever there was a minister scrupulously and morbidly sensitive as to the slightest encroachment on the constitution it is Peel. It is his great fault of want of nerve and daring that made George Smythe, at Manchester, exclaim, ' Oh, for one hour of George Canning ! ' "

Well might I write this, recalling, as no doubt I did, the action of Sir Robert Peel on the Coercion Bill of the Whig Government in March, 1833. Had he then chosen to indulge in a party triumph, he might have rallied round him all the Conservatives, all the Irishmen, and the discontented Radicals. But the safety of life and property

in Ireland were his first considerations, and he saved the
Government he might have undoubtedly overthrown.
Three days later I find the following passage :—

"Attended the last speech and dying words of our departed
Premier. ' *Requiescat in pace.*' He seemed happy enough, and sang
his death dirge with the complacency of undoubted euthanasia.   He
had indeed much to show, and did show, for his five years' government.   Chartism extinct, manufacturing prosperity restored, decrease
of crime, alleviation of distress, monetary system placed on a secure
foundation—all but poor Ireland flourishing and happy ; and abroad,
Afghanistan reconquered and the captives restored, China humbled
and her ports opened to English commerce, Scinde annexed to
British India, the victories of Ferozeshah and Sobraon in the
Punjaub, two difficult questions settled without hostility in America—
the North-east boundary and the Oregon—the matter, as Mr. Pack-
enham states, arranged according to our own proposals, without the
addition or diminution of a single word ; the most pacific relations
with other European nations, and the ' *entente cordiale* ' with France
almost tightened into a Saddlers Wells' stage embrace ; Ireland and
New Zealand, the latter thanks to the tutelage of Lord Stanley, being
the only dark spots on the political horizon."

Dean Stanley, in a letter of the same date, writes under
quite the same impression as myself—

" Peel's speech is to me the most affecting public event I ever
remember ; no return of Cicero from exile, no triumphal procession
up to the temple of Capitoline Jove, no Appius Claudius in the Roman
Senate, no Chatham dying in the House of Lords, could have been a
truly grander sight than that great minister retiring from office, giving
to the whole world free trade with one hand and universal peace with
the other, and casting under foot the miserable factions which had
dethroned him.'

There is, however, another passage in my journal,
written on the day which intervened between the vote in
the House of Commons and the resignation of Sir Robert
Peel, which throws a light on the generous nature of Peel's
character, so little understood, owing to his reserved disposition, for with him the right hand knew not what the
left hand did.

Sunday, June 28.—"Read the account of poor Haydon's suicide. What a miserable gang of tradesmen we are! We give testimonials amounting to thousands of pounds to a successful and bloated speculator, and the first ladies in the land jostle for the arm of Hudson, the haberdasher of York, a vulgar brute; but he who adorns his country by the creation of his genius is left to die by his own hand, crushed to the earth by shame and penury. Poor Haydon! and poor Chatterton! How many other poor ones are ye whose intellects should have borne you up and yet who have been entombed beneath the avalanche of want and woe which has overwhelmed you in this wealthy country? What dreadful disappointments must have prompted a devoted husband and a loving father to this fearful deed. He was found with his head against his unfinished picture, his feet touching the portrait of his wife, a most shocking sight. He appears to have committed suicide literally from the shame of being dishonoured by not meeting his liabilities. He had written to all the great men he had known for a temporary assistance. He received one answer, from Sir Robert Peel, enclosing a cheque for £50. The rest forsook him. The poor man writes in his journals with profound gratitude, 'And yet they say this man has no heart!' Cold and uninteresting as is Peel outwardly, I believe his acts of unknown munificence and kindness to be unequalled, and, strange to say, in the conversations I have had with him, I never met a more unreserved man. In this instance, the appeal to him alone met with an instant reply and unhesitating aid. From the midst of circumstances and controversies, under a pressure of unexampled burdens, in the hour of peril and in the day of defeat, Sir Robert Peel found time for an act of charity, and if this should be among the last acts of his official life, it will be more to his comfort in his chamber that he cheered the last moments of a dying artist with the means of leaving a little legacy to his desolate family, than if he had carried all his measures over the heads of an exasperated House, and crushed his combined foes, with the swoop of a conqueror, into a helpless humiliated mass."

During the rest of the Parliament I was in nominal opposition to the new Government of Lord John Russell, but hardly so in reality, and the Peelite party gave it a general support. The result of this uncertain position was that I devoted myself to racing more than ever, and was far too slack in my Parliamentary attendance. For all that I think I made considerable way in the opinion of the House in the following session. On the 2nd of

February, 1847, I made a good speech, on which I received many compliments, notably from Sir Robert Peel, on the Labouring Poor, Ireland, Bill. I warmly defended Lord George Bentinck's scheme for giving employment by lending money for the institution of railways, which was so much sneered at, and I commented strongly on the doctrinarian policy of leaving the people in such an unprecedented calamity to be fed by private enterprise— considering that throughout a large proportion of Ireland there was no one of capital and experience in the least degree equal to such an undertaking. Three days previously, I said, there was not a ton of Indian meal to be purchased in Galway, though there were a thousand tons in the stores of the Government at that place. Sir Robert Peel said most solemnly and emphatically to me, "You were quite right. The feeding of the people was the first duty of the Government, and they could by Government agency alone be fed in many parts of Ireland."

Shortly afterwards I spoke in support of Lord Lincoln's motion for an address to her Majesty, praying that she would take into consideration the means by which colonization may be made subsidiary to other measures for the improvement of the social condition of Ireland, and by which, consistently with full regard for the interests of the colonies themselves, the comfort and prosperity of those that emigrate may be effectually promoted, and Lord Lincoln seemed pleased with my backing, for after this date we became very intimate. I spoke also in March on Poor Relief, Ireland, in answer to Powlett Scropes's ruinous proposal to organize a general and continual system of outdoor relief for the able-bodied, and I introduced and carried two important clauses into the new Poor Law Bill. These clauses have been explained and commented on by Mr. Oliver Burke, in the *Dublin University Magazine* of August, 1876, and I borrow an extract written by him :—

"The dreadful potato disease of 1846 engaged much of Mr. Gregory's attention. Ireland, at that period, was chiefly peopled by a peasantry in the wretched condition of squatters, whose miserable holdings were quite inadequate to afford more than a precarious support to their occupiers. Comforts were out of the question, because a worse than French *morcellement* had split up farms into mere squatter holdings. The low standard of life thus caused amongst the agricultural classes, and the facility of obtaining that low standard so long as the potatoes lasted, had encouraged the pernicious subdivision of the land and stimulated such an increase of population as has never elsewhere been witnessed in a country with a moist climate, and where the population is utterly dependent, from the absence of manufactures, on the produce of the soil. Here, then, were two difficulties for the statesman, the one how to manage matters so that none but the destitute should receive relief, and the other how to provide an outlet for the redundant population.

"Mr. Gregory was amongst those who devoted their thoughts to these twofold difficulties. As to the latter, he proposed to the House that any tenant rated at a net value not exceeding £5 should be assisted to emigrate by the Guardians of the Union, the landlord to forego any claim for rent and to provide such fair and reasonable sum as might be necessary for the emigration of such occupier, the guardians being empowered to pay for the emigration of his family any sum not exceeding half what the landlord should give, the same to be levied off the rates.

"This clause was agreed to without opposition. Of the humanity which dictated it there can be no second opinion ; it was surely humane to try and provide an outlet for the famishing people. At home there was want, at home there was a vast population depending for food upon a soil which seemed to be excepted from the primeval blessing that ' the earth should bring forth herbs and fruits according to its kind.' Fever was at home, and, worse than all, despair as to the future. But a few days' sail away, across the Atlantic, there lay a land with millions of unoccupied acres, teeming with natural riches. Why not open a career in that New World for those who were willing to go there, and thereby diminish the pressure on the resources at home? Surely such an effort would be humane, and that effort was made by Mr. Gregory. But there remained that other difficulty of which we have spoken, namely, the absorption by undeserving persons of a large portion of the public funds. How was this evil to be met? If it were not arrested, and that, too, speedily, the tax for the relief of the poor, already a frightful burden on the land, would become intolerable. The poor rate was already so heavy that in many cases it exceeded the amount of the yearly rent of the land. Something must be done, or else the dream of Pharaoh would again be realized, and the seven lean kine would devour the seven fat kine, if indeed there would be then remaining any fat kine to be devoured ! Something must therefore be done, but what? Mr. Gregory proposed that a test be applied to insure that no undeserving person should get relief, and his test was that the possessor of more than a quarter of an acre of land should not be entitled to assistance. This suggestion became law, and has since been known as the ' Gregory Clause.'

"That this clause has been perverted to do evil no one can deny, and those who only look to one side of the question have often blamed its author for some of the evils that were inflicted by its provisions ; but such men might fairly be asked, was not some test then necessary? and if so, what other effectual test could have been proposed ? Was not the country in truth demoralized ? and if the ' quarter acre clause ' was made to operate oppressively, on whom should censure fall ? On him who proposed and on them who supported it, or on the peasants, who, without requiring it, became recipients of the public charity, and on those locally influential persons who were aware of their deceit, and either supported or did not oppose it.

"It is very easy to prophesy after the event, but on the night when the ' Gregory Clause ' passed the Committee of the House of Commons, there were present in the House 125 members, many of them Irish members, and of these 125 only 9 voted against the measure. Mr. Morgan John O'Connell spoke strongly in its favour. The evil results we have alluded to were not then foreseen, certainly they were not believed in by Mr. Gregory, whose advocacy of the emigration clause is the best proof of his good motives to those who do not know the humanity and the kindness which, then and always, have marked his dealings with the tenants on his own estates."

I may mention that in the minority of nine there were only two Irish members, while there voted in favour of the clause, G. C. O'Brien, M. J. O'Connell, O'Conor Don, Archibald C. Lawless, Layard, Monaghan, Sir W. Somerville, Sir Thos. Wyse, all staunch Liberals. There is no doubt but that the immediate effect of the clause was severe. Old Archbishop MacHale never forgave me on account of it. But it pulled up suddenly the country from falling into the open pit of pauperism on the verge of which it stood. Though I got an evil reputation in consequence, those who really understood the condition of the country have always regarded this clause as its salvation.

In the month of August this year Parliament was dissolved, and I again stood for Dublin. I have no doubt that my hold on the constituency was not so strong as it was in 1842. My vote in favour of free importation of corn had alienated some, chiefly of the higher classes, and it was pretty well known that I was determined for the future to depart altogether from the bigoted clique which exercised considerable influence over the lower class of Protestant voters. On both these points my friend and colleague, Mr. Grogan (now Sir Edward), entertained views differing from me. Still he was on this occasion, as on every other, honest, straightforward, and friendly. In spite, however, of the differences alluded to, my election was considered perfectly safe, and so it was but for one fatal obstacle. In writing of my former election I referred to the widespread bribery of the Protestant freemen, which up to that time had been recognized as a necessary incident in every Dublin election. We determined to take this favourable opportunity of abolishing it for ever. There was no candidate in the field, there was every appearance of a walk over, and so instead of minding my business I went off to Goodwood races. On my return I found that a local, noisy, and rather disreputable fellow, John Reynolds by name, a great spouter at Repeal meetings, but never recognized by O'Connell as a friend or ally, had come forward and offered himself to the electors. All my friends laughed at his pretensions, and said he would never go to the poll, but he did go. Had the electoral law continued unchanged since 1842 I have no doubt I should have won the battle easily enough,

but the number of polling days were reduced from five
to one, and the polling booths were largely increased.
The consequence was a general scene of confusion, no
proper accounts were kept of the polling, my agent lost
his head and got drunk ; one hundred and fifty freemen
offered at the last to vote if paid their day's wages, but
were told to go to ——, and the poll closed.

E. Grogan	...	...	...	...	3353
Reynolds	...	...	...	...	3220
Gregory	...	...	...	...	3125
Majority of Reynolds over Gregory				...	95

When Parliament met in 1848 there was a petition
tried against the return of John Reynolds. It cost me
much money and lasted a long time. The main point
turned on the invalidity of many of Reynolds's votes in
consequence of non-payment of taxes. To this principle
Mr. Bright, a member of the committee, was opposed,
and his strong will much influenced his colleagues in
requiring such an amount of proof and so many witnesses
that the contention was felt to be hopeless, and after
reducing the votes at great expense by a considerable
amount the petition was abandoned, and John Reynolds
declared duly elected. Curiously enough the same John
Reynolds, who had a small property in Galway, was
one of my most staunch supporters at the election of 1859,
and made some useful and "agitating" speeches in my
behalf.

The day after I was beaten in Dublin I betook myself
to Galway, and issued an address to the county, where the
election had not yet begun. I was well enough received,
but the electoral list was in such a state that there were
not more than five or six hundred voters on it, and no one
knew anything about them. Captain Burke, my future
colleague and afterwards Sir Thomas Burke, and Mr.

St. George were elected. Mr. St. George was detested
by the popular party, but he had got his own voters and
the voters of the barony of Ballinahinch in a stable, about
a hundred and twenty in number, and as there was no
use in courting a second defeat, I resigned after being
nominated, and after making a very telling speech at the
court-house. After this I had nothing more to do with
Parliamentary life for ten years, except that once when
I was abroad, I was put up for the borough of Dungarvon,
without my knowledge or wish, and was well beaten by
Mr. Maguire. A petition was instituted against Maguire's
return, but altogether failed. He was, however, a very
good, placable, and clever fellow, and we became excellent
friends when I was subsequently returned to Parliament
in 1857.

CHAPTER VIII

I MUST now leave my political career and refer to the events of 1847 as they affected my private life. In that year, in April, my father died. He was one of the victims of duty during that terrible time when fever followed famine. Among the other landowners of my country that perished from their intercourse with the sick, were Lord Dunsandle and Thomas Martin owner of the great Ballinahinch estate. From the moment that my father saw the extent and nature of the catastrophe, he and the priest of Kinvara, Father Ford, whose name should be recorded, worked together incessantly to meet the emergency. At last my father was stricken down, and Father Ford shortly after was added to the roll of victims. I was in London in April and knew nothing of my father's illness till I received my mother's letter with the ominous words, "Make haste or you may be too late." I was too late. In those days there was no telegraph, nor was there a railway to the west of Ireland. I had to post in a hired carriage all the way from Dublin, and when I reached my gatehouse I saw, by the faces of those who were there, that I need ask no questions. I was one day too late. There never was hope from the first day of the seizure. I was quite overwhelmed, for I loved my father very dearly and respected his honest, honourable qualities. His great fault was too much kindness to me. Had he

been a sterner parent I should probably now be narrating
past events of far more credit to me than I am bound to
do while professing to write the truth and nothing but the
truth. I found that he had left a considerable amount of
debt, which, together with my own liabilities, I should probably have soon reduced to small dimensions had I devoted
myself to my country duties, but I was one of those who
made haste to grow rich, and I preferred the prospect
of wiping off all liabilities by some stroke of good fortune
on the turf to steady economy and supervision. Moreover,
though at that time our rent roll had been a well paid one
of £7800 a year, still the poor rates and other charges
swallowed up everything. The rates on the division of
Kinvara were eighteen shillings in the pound, and that
a fictitious pound, for it was never paid. I did, however,
all I could to alleviate the dreadful distress and sickness
in our neighbourhood. I well remember poor wretches
being housed up against my demesne wall in wigwams
of fir branches. There was no place to which they could
be removed. The workhouse infirmary and sheds were
crowded. Fortunately these patients did better in the
pure open air than those who were packed together within
four walls. There was nothing that I ever saw so horrible
as the appearance of those who were suffering from
starvation. The skin seemed drawn tight like a drum
to the face, which became covered with small light-
coloured hairs like a gooseberry. This, and their hollow
voices, I can never forget, and yet they behaved with
the greatest propriety. I believe a few sheep were stolen,
but in my neighbourhood at least there was a total absence
of crime. There seemed to be a general race to get out
of the country at all hazards ; farms were abandoned, even
where no rent was asked, fences were broken down, houses
unroofed ; in short, if an army of Huns and Vandals had

swept over the country they would hardly have created greater terror, desolation, and despair, and yet within two years all this gloom had passed away and Ireland seemed brighter, richer, and more hopeful than before. But the disastrous perversity of the Government in throwing the feeding of a starving population on private enterprise to be exercised for the first time to any such extent, has never been forgotten or forgiven by those who remained at home, and of those that went in those days the *Times* wrote: "The Irish are pouring out of Ireland *with a vengeance*."

It was about that time that I contracted two friendships, that of Lord Dunkellin and of Mr. Edmund O'Flaherty, of Knockbane, near Galway. If I were asked who was the most generous and honourable friend, the wittiest and brightest comrade, the easiest and most sweet-tempered companion I ever had, I should without hesitating name Lord Dunkellin. From the time when I first met him, as an Eton boy at Roxborough, I conceived the greatest affection for him, which endured without check or shadow till the hour of his death, in 1867. I have letters from him for a long period, during the Crimean War, during the period of the Indian Mutiny, when he was aide-de-camp to his uncle Lord Canning, during the Persian War, when he contracted the seeds of the disease of which he died at last, and during the years in which we sat together in Parliament, the latter portion of which, from 1865 to 1867, he was my colleague for the county of Galway, having, on the retirement of my former colleague Sir Thomas Burke, exchanged the town of Galway, which he had previously represented, for the county. At the time of his death he had secured a considerable Parliamentary reputation. Although he joined the so-called " Cave of Adullam," and, by his successful motion in favour of a rating as against a rental franchise, overthrew the Government of which he had been previously the supporter, he was still a staunch Liberal, and volunteered to propose a vote of confidence in the Government, but the offer was rejected. His early death, when just arrived at the fulness of his powers, was a catastrophe from which our county has never recovered, as his sound judgment and good sense would have been exerted against the fatal contest of 1872, which utterly annihilated the political power of the landed gentry of Galway, and sowed the seeds of bitterness between them and the priesthood, which has grown a hateful crop.

Edmund O'Flaherty made my acquaintance in 1847, when, after losing Dublin, I endeavoured to obtain a seat for Galway county. He took up my cause with great warmth, and though he had little influence, still his cleverness and quickness and inexhaustible resource would have been of great use had there been any contest. I had a high opinion of his dexterity and ability, and introduced him to the Duke of Newcastle, who was anxious to secure for the Peelite party the alliance of the Irish members. This was the more easy as the Peelites had to a man opposed the Ecclesiastical Titles Bill, to which William Keogh, a very dear friend of Edmund O'Flaherty, headed the resistance. The duke invited O'Flaherty to dine with him, was immensely taken with him, constantly communicated with him, employed him as an emissary, and gave him a Commissionership of Income Tax in Ireland, with a promise of something better. He was one of the pleasantest men I ever met, full of fun and spirits and singularly soft-hearted and kind. His hospitality was unbounded, and when I remarked on his large expenditure, which my intimacy with him permitted me to do, he always said that he was engaged with the Birmingham

Attwoods in iron speculations, which brought him in at times good sums of money, and that, *en attendant*, he had no scruple in running into debt. He was certainly the most avowedly unscrupulous man I ever met, but he was so open and candid about his laxity that I always treated it as a joke. Not so, however, my mother and Lord Dunkellin. Neither of them could bear him, and both warned me over and over again that I should have reason to regret the intimacy. To all this I turned a deaf ear. I know that he had a sincere affection for me, and to this day I fully believe he would have suffered much rather than have done me any injury. My affairs, too, were in a most embroiled state, and he constantly advised me with great ability upon them, and rendered himself a kind of William of Deloraine "good at need" by obtaining loans for me in all directions. This ultimately continued for several years, till one morning, in the early summer of 1854, I met Keogh coming down the steps of the Reform Club. He was evidently much discomposed, and said, "Can you tell me about Edmund O'Flaherty?" "What about him?" said I. "Don't you know that he has gone either abroad or to America, and that warrants are said to be out against him for extensive forgeries?" was Keogh's reply. I felt utterly overwhelmed, for I was sure at once that the accusation was true. It was but too true. He had forged the names of Lord Bolingbroke, Lord Dunkellin, Bernal Osborne, Mr. Godley, and my own upon bills, besides those of other persons I have forgotten. An action was tried against me in Dublin on two of these bills. It lasted two days, and the jury almost immediately gave a verdict in my favour. The plaintiff sought to prove two things—that I was so involved in money matters with O'Flaherty that he was, as it were, empowered to sign my name, and, secondly, that both I and my witnesses might be mistaken as to my handwriting, and that the signatures were really mine. A very curious test was employed, which, had I made the slightest error in dealing with it, might have lost me the case, but which gained me the suit at once by the correctness of my answer. Half a dozen closed envelopes were placed in the hands of my witnesses, a small piece of the corner of each of them was cut out, and in this open space there appeared my signature, but to what document it was affixed it was unknown. Some of my witnesses were very doubtful as to the signatures, and refused to swear whether they were mine or not. Some they thought were decidedly not mine. When my cross-examination came on these envelopes were, towards the close of it, produced. I was asked the question about the signatures, and I declared, looking at them one after another, that they were all mine. " Do you swear that ? " said FitzGibbon, the counsel. " I do swear it," said I. " Give me back the envelopes," he replied in a sullen way. " No, my lord, I claim to have these envelopes opened on the spot and handed to the jury," cried I to the judge, looking up steadily at the jury, and from whom I never took my eyes. The document in each envelope was a letter of mine to O'Flaherty of which only the signature appeared. I saw in one second that my cause was won.

Among the many forgeries was one on Bernal Osborne. O'Flaherty was dining one night in company with a naval officer, who expatiated on the readiness with which a Jew at Plymouth, named Marcus, lent money to officers, and he mentioned that Marcus had done business with some admiral's official, who was supposed to have given him a favourable contract in consequence. O'Flaherty said, " I am going shortly to Plymouth, and, as I am doing up my house in Dublin, I should like to borrow a small sum, even at usurious interest, in a remote place, for I don't wish to apply to my bankers, and it would be all over the town if I, a Commissioner of Income Tax, went to the house of a London or Dublin lender." The officer offered him a letter of introduction, in which he described him as a man of position, Income Tax Commissioner, etc., etc. A few days afterwards O'Flaherty presented himself to Mr. Marcus with his introduction. He said he called on him desiring to speak confidentially to him. The fact was that Mr. Bernal Osborne, the Secretary to the Admiralty, had been spoken to by the heads of the Government on account of his want of hospitality, and that he was obliged to set up an establishment and give dinners ; but he had, owing to the bad times, drawn but little rent from Ireland, and he wished to borrow £1500 for six months. The Jew hesitated. "Who told him about me?" said he. "Why, Captain So-and-So," naming the captain who had given him the letter, and adding that the letter was given in order to carry out the transaction from Mr. Osborne. Still hesitation on the part of Marcus. Then O'Flaherty played his trump card. "By the way, Mr. Osborne mentioned that I might say to you that certain contracts would be shortly advertised." "Have you got the bills?" said Marcus. Two bills for £1500 were produced, signed by Bernal Osborne. "I must have a second name on them," said Marcus. "No," said O'Flaherty, "Mr. Osborne will never allow it. He demands positive secrecy." "My God!" cried Marcus, "what can I do! My father-in-law won't give the money without two names. Why won't you put your name, Mr. O'Flaherty, on the bills, to serve your friend?" "I have never put my name to a bill in my life," said O'Flaherty, very solemnly ; "but I am afraid I shall have to do so shortly for £300, as I want to fit up my reception-rooms, and render them suitable to my position. I must then get the money for Mr. Osborne elsewhere; and as for that navy contract, remember I made no allusion to it. I treat you, Mr. Marcus, as a man of honour." "Stop, stop, Mr. O'Flaherty," cried the Jew, in an agony. "Why won't you serve your friend by giving him your name? You know he is quite safe, and, though my father-in-law cashes the bills, I promise you no one will ever hear a word about them, and let me lend you the £300 you want." O'Flaherty consented with reluctance, signed the bills, and returned to London, with about £1700 in his pocket, just one week before his final disappearance. Marcus told the whole story to several persons as I have narrated it; among others, to William Keogh, who was my informant, and who repeated it often in my company.*

I was greatly grieved at this lamentable conclusion of O'Flaherty's career. The accompanying letter from John Robert Godley will show that I was not the only person who had formed a strong regard for Edmund O'Flaherty :—

"June 23, 1854.

"MY DEAR GREGORY,

"I am deeply shocked by the contents of your letter. Though I was quite aware of poor O'Flaherty's obvious faults, yet his

---

* "Of this O'Flaherty, the late Sir J. Pope Hennessy used to tell a very characteristic story. He paid a visit to Dublin, and was invited to dinner at the Mansion House by the Lord Mayor. The poor dignitary was, of course, on his knees before the great London financier and politican, as O'Flaherty was then supposed to be, and spread before him one of those gorgeous and appalling feasts for which civic entertainments are noted. There were four soups and half a dozen kinds of fish, and *entrées* by the score. O'Flaherty passed dish after dish, until the hapless Lord Mayor at last asked the great man what would tempt an appetite at once so lordly and so fastidious. 'I would like a mutton chop,' quoth O'Flaherty. It was, as Talleyrand said of Lord Castlereagh, when he appeared without any decorations in the midst of the dazzling splendours of the Congress of Vienna, *bien distingué.*"

This ancedote is given by Mr. T. P. O'Connor.—A. G.

good nature and simplicity had quite won upon me, and I really felt a strong sympathy for him. Of all the extravagant men I knew there were few whom I should less easily have suspected of a dishonourable action, in the ordinary sense of the word, but I suppose he became desperate from want. I would not judge him too harshly. His character was utterly weak, and I am sure there was more weakness than wickedness at the bottom of his crime. I pity you, my dear Gregory, more than I can tell you. I used to think your attachment to him undue and exaggerated, yet I can imagine him being very lovable, in his way, before he became spoiled. Anyhow, you must indeed be wretched now ; it is hard enough to lose a dear friend, but to have him turn out unworthy is a blow for which there is no consolation to be offered."

I always remember that he never did me any injury intentionally, but would have gladly spent money, time, and trouble to do me a kindness. He did not foresee that his forgeries on me might have been ruinous. He was so versatile, so self-reliant, that he always looked to some lucky chance or speculation or marriage to put him on his legs again. He went to America, and there assumed the name of Captain Stewart. He began by writing for one of the papers, made some money, and then took a theatre, the Winter Garden, if I recollect aright. He was at first very successful, and he rapidly rose to be one of the most popular men in New York, famous for his hospitality and little pleasant supper-parties. It was well known there was something against him, but it was supposed that he had left England being unable to pay his debts ; moreover, at New York, a high standard of morality is not a requisite. Over and over again I have been surprised at hearing from Englishmen of great position, on their return from America, how they had been entertained by the pleasantest and wittiest of Irishmen, Captain Stewart. When I went there, in 1859, Mr. Brewster, afterwards Chancellor, warned me on no account to allow old feelings of friendship to prevail and to renew my former acquaintance ; that my character would be seriously compromised were I to do so. I did meet him once in the streets. We looked hard at each other and passed on. I have heard that he spent the large income he was making, and had fallen into poverty. In spite of all his errors I have always kept a soft corner in my heart for him. He died, 1887, in great poverty.

There was ten years' interregnum in my political life, six of which I would fain have blotted out. These six years were a time of struggle and humiliation, during which I abandoned society and public life for the turf only, during which I became deeply involved, chiefly through liabilities for friends, and during which I was forced to sell two-thirds of my ancestral estate. But at last, by a strong effort, I turned over a new leaf, and, though a poor man, became a free man, and once more in my right mind.

*   *   *   *   *   *

The flight of O'Flaherty and the revelation of his doings came upon me like a shock, and I felt that there was only one course left to me, instantly to abandon the turf altogether, to face all my liabilities, to sell sufficient land to pay off all charges on the estate, and to make the best terms I could with usurious creditors, to whom I was largely indebted, partly on account of myself, but chiefly on account of friends who had taken their departure to other lands and left me to bear the brunt. I was guided in every step by Mr. Brewster, afterwards Lord Chancellor, and by that advice I placed my affairs in the hands of Mr. Bate, a Dublin solicitor, who proved himself to be an able counsellor and a true friend. Most fortunate for me and for my property was the large jointure of my mother and the arrears due on it, which protected the estate and secured the most valuable part of it to me, together with

the demesne of Coole.   Most fortunate was I in having
such a mother, whose whole life was one of devotion to me.
Under any circumstances it would have been necessary to
sell a large portion of the property to clear off the mort-
gages not of my creation ; but when the question arose
whether more should be sold, to pay off my mother's
arrears of jointure, there was considerable difference of
opinion.   The object in doing so was to obtain a fund to
settle my private debts.   Some of my friends urged us to
cling to the land, looking forward to a great rise in value
of it hereafter ; but my mother took a different view, and
insisted on selling the outlying portions of the estate up
to the full amount of the arrears due to her, in order to
relieve me, so far as it lay in her power, from the misery
and humiliation of debt, and every pound that came to
her was thus expended.   How wise was her resolution
present events testify.

I cannot recall during that period of six years a single
event worth dwelling upon, but as I had the misfortune
to fight a duel in 1851, and as the causes of this conflict
were but little understood, there being no society papers
in those days, I may as well explain to my son why I
was induced to commit an act so foolish, so wrong, and
so contrary to public opinion, even in those days.   In
1847 I bought, at Doncaster, a mare called Moss Rose,
with a colt foal at her foot, subsequently named Damask.
When he became two years old I tried him, found him so
slow that I did not think him worth training, but sold
him to my trainer Treen, who insisted on it that the
horse was not so bad as we thought.   The colt ran as a
two-year-old, and was beaten.   In the year 1850 he was
entered for the Ascot Stakes.   His weight was very light,
and his owner, my trainer, thought he had an excellent
chance, and asked me to borrow a horse to try him with.

I borrowed a horse called Wanota, from Lord Clifden, which was also in the same race, and the two were tried together, the result being that Damask won very easily and Lord Clifden and his friends, and I and my friends, backed him heavily for the race. Suspicious circumstances soon occurred ; the more the horse was backed the more ready were certain persons to bet against him, and, to use a turf phrase, Damask was laid against as if he were dead.

I traced the movement to a sporting blackleg baker named Glen, who lived in Regent Street, and also to the Hon. Captain G. Vaughan, a fellow-member of the Turf Club. I wrote to my trainer, who informed me the horse was well and sure to win, but the more he was backed the more shaky was he in the betting. On the Sunday before Ascot, having heard that Treen's horses had arrived there, I went down and saw him. He then confessed to me that, in the previous winter, being in great distress, he had sold the horse to Glen for £400, but that Glen had made him promise secrecy, as the fact of his having racehorses would interfere with his business. He said he had written to Glen about all the present business, imploring him to mention his intentions about the horse, and that Glen had promised to let him run, and had stated that he had backed him. On my return to London I went at once to Glen, who did not deny having promised the trainer that the horse should start, but said he had changed his mind and was determined to scratch him for the race on the morrow, and so he did, and thus Lord Clifden and his friends, and I and my friends were audaciously robbed by this ruffian and his associate the Hon. G. Vaughan. It was clear that Damask would have won the race, as Wanota, the horse with whom he had been tried, won it very easily. I need hardly say that my anger burned hot within me, and I

and my fellow-sufferers cut the acquaintance of Captain
Vaughan, though I inwardly determined to take an opportunity of paying him out for his iniquity. This opportunity
did not present itself till next year. On the Saturday
after the Derby, at the Turf Club, in the afternoon, a rubber
of whist was proposed, and I sat down to the table.
Although Captain Vaughan saw that I was one of the
party he came up and joined it, as I thought, in a defiant
manner. Some discussion took place about some im-
material point, hot words passed, and I struck him across
the face with my glove, saying at the same time, most
unfortunately, " I have waited long for this, but I have
got you at last!" Of course there only remained one
thing to be done, and I placed myself in the hands of Lord
Bolingbroke; while Captain Vaughan deputed Captain
Campbell, of the 32nd Regiment, to act for him. Usually,
under such circumstances, the affair would have come off
the following day. Providentially it did not, for pistol-
shooting had long been a favourite amusement of mine,
and I was a perfect master of that weapon. I had fully
determined, whatever might be the consequences on my
future life, not to spare my antagonist. The affair could
not come off on Sunday, and Monday and Tuesday following were the settling days for the Derby at Tattersall's.
I had won ten thousand and fifteen pounds for myself and
some large sums for friends, and it was considered that
I was bound not to risk my life until after my account was
settled. The meeting was therefore fixed for the following
Wednesday. In the meanwhile, Lord Bolingbroke, finding
that the matter was a very serious one, took fright at the
consequences, and I was placed in an awkward situation
to find another second of good position resolutely determined to see the affair out to the bitter end. In this
emergency my old friend, the present Sir Robert Peel,

called on me and said, " I hear Bolingbroke has refused
to act ; here I am, quite prepared to take his place
and to see you through it." I need hardly say I was
deeply grateful, more especially as, when I told him that
his office was a dangerous one, he replied, "Never mind,
you may rest confident that I shall not leave you in the
lurch." I again told him that I had provoked this duel
with the full intention of not sparing life, and he again
assured me of his determination to see me through it.
Of course we met often during the intervening days, and
more than once he spoke of the dangerous position in
which we both stood, more especially owing to my observation that I had long waited for the opportunity. "Of
course," he said, " if we escape hanging, we shall have to
live abroad for the rest of our lives," and he discussed our
future residence.   He then discussed the cause of conflict,
and, while adroitly admitting that I had been grossly
offended, he asked me if I thought it was an offence
deserving of death, as he did not.   By Tuesday morning
I was in a far more placable state of mind, and when, the
same afternoon, he told me he had seen Captain Campbell,
who had described the state of Captain Vaughan's family
as perfectly heartbroken, I relented completely, and gave
him my promise that, though I would make no apology
for the blow, yet that I would not fire at my antagonist,
but that, if he missed me the first shot and asked for a
second, then I should undoubtedly do the best I could
to put him *hors de combat* for ever.

The place of rendezvous was Osterley Park, a place of
Lady Jersey's.   It was a lovely spring morning, by no
means one for leaving the world, especially with £10,000
in one's pocket.   We were placed at twelve paces and
ordered to fire at the word of command.   My opponent's
bullet sung close to my ear ; I raised my pistol, took

deliberate aim, by way of giving him a comfortable moment, and then fired in the air. They said they did not require a second shot, and so we went home on our way rejoicing. When I look back, and think of the frightful consequences which Sir Robert Peel by his tact avoided, I cannot but feel that I owe to him as deep a debt of gratitude as one man can owe another. He offered his services as second with the full determination of saving me, his old Harrow friend, from committing a deed which would have been the ruin of my life. The following year, when I lost heavily on the Derby, he came to me and said, " I know you have lost heavily, I can't lend you the money, for I have not got it, but I can lend you my name, and you can borrow what you want." I gladly accepted the offer, and did what is rare on such occasions, and what I wish others had done by me, repaid the money borrowed when it became due. A few days after the duel I called on Lady Villiers (the present Lady Jersey), and she told me, with much amusement, that her children, who had been passing the day at Osterley, came home highly delighted at having seen from the terrace some gentlemen shooting at each other in the park. The result of this duel was that old Lady Jersey abjured my acquaintance, considering herself insulted by my going to be shot at on her land without asking her permission, though it was her own son, Fred Villiers, who suggested the place, and though her other son, my friend Lord Villiers, told her that I was not the intruder, but was taken there by the seconds without having had a word in the matter. We made it up at last, but our old friendship was never restored.

It seems strange that in after years I should have met Captain Vaughan on terms of good fellowship, if not of friendship. He sent me word that he bitterly regretted what he had done, that he well knew how ill he had behaved, and hoped I would shake hands with him. The burning of powder clears the air, and so it was in this case. After the pistols were fired I had not a particle of enmity left, though my opinion of the transaction remained the same.

I have often since thought how strange are our hallucinations. For a whole year my mind was bent on inflicting the retribution of death on this man for the affront and injury to which he had subjected me, and in one minute all feeling for vengeance disappeared, and in subsequent years we met pleasantly. I fear that in too many of us, in spite of culture, education, refinement, something of the tiger lingers in our blood. As regards my old trainer Treen, I was obliged to take my horses from him, in deference to public opinion, though he was perfectly guiltless of everything except having told a lie, and this he told to save his masters. It seems, as I before mentioned, that he remonstrated with Glen for betting against the horse, that he told him he would inform me that it was no longer his property, but that he had sold him to Glen. This scoundrel wrote back to say he had only laid a small sum, to drive the horse down in the betting, but that he was going to back him heavily, but only in case the secret was kept, otherwise he would at once withdraw him from the race. Poor Treen was as much bamboozled as the rest of us; and so ended this rascally affair.

Considerable time elapsed before all the preliminaries for the sale of a portion of my estate were completed, and in the interim, during the spring and autumn of 1853, I devoted myself with enthusiasm to the construction of a pinetum in the nut-wood of Coole. I ransacked the nursery grounds of Bristol, Liverpool, and Exeter, and planted all the specimens that were invented and got up by ingenious nurserymen for the benefit of Coniferomaniacs, as we were then called. Judging from the amount of the bills paid, and the little result which followed, the appellation in my case was not misapplied. Half the conifers, indeed more than half, which would flourish exceedingly on any soil but limestone, died forthwith with me, and only a few seemed really to enjoy life. Among those who have done pre-eminently well are the *Pinus insignis*, and the giants in the nut-wood were only planted in 1855. They are the finest I have ever seen of their age.

My pinetum being well launched, I (1855) determined to pay a winter's visit to Egypt, and, on my return to Coole, I occupied much of my time in preparing a full account of my journey, and of the various places I visited, which included every spot of interest from Cairo to the Second Cataract. This, together with a narrative of a tour in 1857 with Sir Sandford Graham through Tunis, I had printed, in 1859, in two volumes. There was so much in these volumes written carelessly and playfully that I determined on not publishing them, but kept them for private circulation only. They were all burnt in 1873, in the Pantechnicon, except two volumes I still possess and a few I had given to friends.

The rest of the year 1856 I devoted to completing my pinetum, and in preparing for the intending sale of my estate. In order to have the carriage of the sale, it was necessary to have a friendly creditor to place the property in the Landed Estates Court. This friendly creditor was my uncle, the Rev. William Gregory, who in every dealing which I ever had with him showed invariable kindness and consideration. On his recommendation, I appointed Mr. Henry Harrison Briscoe to be my agent. He was a man of high reputation, having been elected by the Poor Law Board to act as vice-guardian on several

occasions. I had previously been most unfortunate in my
agents, but with Mr. Briscoe my troubles came to an end ;
he had every quality for an agent, especially at a critical
period for his employer—uprightness, temper, and judgment. I fully believe that if he had been employed from
the first there would have been no necessity for the sale of
the estate, though, most fortunately, it was sold at good
prices, and the remainder cleared.

The sale was announced for the ——, and before
going into court I was warned by a very astute friend,
who had been through the same ordeal, that there was
great danger, in so large a sale, of many lots being knocked
down at an inadequate price, as well as of a combination
among buyers. He had got over this danger by means
of the assistance of friends who had bid for him. I
talked over the matter with Mr. ——, afterwards M.P.
for ——, a well-known railway and dock contractor
in those days, with whom I was on intimate terms.
He said, "Trust to me, I will send you over an Englishman, a very clever fellow, who dresses the capitalist, and
has all the manner of one. You must give him a list of
the lots of the estate, with the lowest prices at which you
consider it advisable to let them go, and he will bid up to
that price. It will be impossible for the judge to put up
the lots again for sale under a year, and in the meantime
you can dispose of them. Of course the judge will be
furious, and if he can lay hold of my friend he will make
him acquainted with the interior of an Irish jail ; but there
is not much likelihood of that, and he will willingly run the
risk for a ten-pound note, which you will hand him after
the sale. He will present himself at Kildare-street Club
the morning before the sale, and will present my card."
Sure enough the capitalist, calling himself Mr. Almond, of
Bolton, presented himself at the club in due time, and

looked all over a well-to-do Englishman—the very picture
of neatness; in short, rather Quakerly was his attire, and
his whole aspect denoted wealth.   The sale came on, and
Judge Hargreave presided.   The chief purchaser of the
Kinvara estate was a Mr. Comerford, who had been a
carpenter, and had made money ; but he bought, as the
tenants had reason to know, with borrowed capital.   It
was only the Kinvara lots which went badly ; the land was
stony and poor, and by no means in general favour.   Here
stepped in Mr. Almond, and was declared the purchaser
of the first lot which did not reach the price named.   The
judge asked for his name.   "Mr. Halmond, my lord, of
Bolton," was the answer.   "Halmond," said the judge,
"do you write it with an H ?"   "No, my lord, with a Hay.
Halmonds and raisins, my lord," replied Mr. Almond,
quite facetiously, and rubbing his hands.   Several lots
were knocked down to him, apparently by the encouragement of the judge, who urged him continually with, "Now,
one more bid, Mr. Almond."   "Well, one more, my lord,
but I am afraid I shall get very little return for my
money," and so the acute Englishman just gave a bid
sufficient to cover my margin, and was either beaten by
Comerford or declared the purchaser.   I could hardly
keep my countenance, so infinitely droll, and so perfect
was the manner of Mr. Almond.   When the sale was over,
I pressed a ten-pound note into his hand, and said I hoped
he would leave me his address.   He said, with a benevolent
smile, that for some time to come he was not likely to
have any fixed abode to which he would like to invite the
very civil Judge Hargreave, but that his services would be
always available if I wrote to Mr. ——, and so began and
ended my relations with Mr. Almond.   I need hardly add
that Judge Hargreave was furious ; but his wrath was
of no avail.   The sale on the whole was a fair one ; much

was disposed of at twenty-five years' purchase, and much of the poor land at eighteen. The average was about twenty years' purchase. Though I parted with it in regret, I cannot now but regard this transaction as my salvation.

I may here mention that the result of this sale had a very strong influence afterwards in my political career, and rendered me a very advanced politician on the tenants' side, on the landlord and tenant question. Shortly after my father's death I visited every holding on the estate, and was struck with the results of the unflagging industry of the tenants who occupied the light, stony land about Kinvara. They had by their labour, and with no allowance from the landlord, cleared large portions of their farms, and the great monuments, as they called them, of stones, attested their industry. From these clear patches they had excellent barley crops, and were in prosperity. My great-uncle and father were both just men, and allowed them to enjoy the fruits of their toil for many years without raising the rent. On the occasion of my visit, when I was about to drive away, I said to these tenants, who had assembled to greet me, that I was surprised to see so much good land, and that I thought it was capable of bearing a higher rent. Of course this called forth a general protestation, and very sad were their faces; but they soon cleared up when I said to them, "Were I to take one shilling out of your pockets on account of the additional value you have given to my property by your industry I should be a robber and ashamed to look you in the face. You can go on in good heart with your work, and be assured that while I own this property your rent shall never be raised on account of your improvements." Such were my intentions, and such was the confidence of those tenants that they never asked for a lease, or I should have gladly given it to them. When the sale came on I was so occupied with other matters that I quite forgot their danger. Indeed it never crossed my mind, for I had then heard of no particular instances of rapacity on the part of new purchasers ; but I very soon had a terrible account of my remissness in not securing these poor folk. Mr. Comerford, to whom I have referred, as soon as he was placed in possession of the lots he had purchased on which those tenants dwelt, lost no time in dealing with them in the most remorseless fashion. The rents were raised so as to pay £5 per cent. on the borrowed capital, and a large income besides for himself. They were almost invariably doubled, and in some cases £5 was charged where £2 had been the rate of the former rent. But he killed the goose for the golden egg, the town of Kinvara was all but ruined, and the best tenants ran away. I met one in Australia, at Ballarat, and he assured me he was well off when I was his landlord, but a pauper three years after, when he emigrated. Such were the proceedings of the man whom the excellent parish priest, Father Arthur, never called by any other name than Holofernes ; and it was such proceedings, which I found were too common elsewhere, which made me a tenant righter, and the advocate of measures which, in a different state of society, I should have opposed.

CHAPTER IX.

On the 3rd of March, 1857, occurred the event which laid the foundation of what I may justly call the second period of my life. Mr. Cobden's motion of censure on the Government in regard to its dealings with China, in the affair of the famous Lorcha "Arrow," was carried by a majority of fourteen. Lord Palmerston accepted the challenge by an immediate appeal to the country and a dissolution, and on the 31st of March the general election took place.

As soon as the news of the impending dissolution reached my county I received many communications inviting me to stand. I had serious misgivings. The expense might be great, and I could little afford it. The sitting members, Sir Thomas Burke and Captain Bellew, were both personal friends of mine. The former was the most popular man in the county, and I had not the power or the wish to enter into the lists against him. With regard to Captain Bellew it was different. A more honourable or more warm-hearted fellow did not exist, but he had made himself extremely unpopular among his friends and supporters by giving himself what they considered to be "airs;" while several of his votes in Parliament, especially one in connection with the extension of the income tax to Ireland, caused very general dissatisfaction, and brought on him a public denunciation by

John, Archbishop of Tuam, and his priests. I was specially urged to stand by J. Cowan and J. M. O'Hara, both men of considerable interest in the county. The former had been sub-sheriff to my father, for whom he entertained a genuine affection ; he was a man of remarkable astuteness, knowing every person of any influence in the county, and he offered to conduct the election gratuitously, and to bring my expenses within a very moderate limit. J. M. O'Hara was the acting sub-sheriff, and he, too, had a general knowledge of the county. They both assured me that my chances were excellent, and that, if I could only secure some of the largest interests, my return would be certain. The great voting interests were those of Lord Clanricarde, Lord Clancarty, Lord Clonbrock, and Lord Dunsandle. Lord Clonbrock at once promised me his support, and Lord Clancarty followed suit, as there was no Conservative in the field. Lord Clanricarde hesitated at first, but, on my declaration that, if elected, I should vote with Lord Palmerston, he also came over, and with him a very large number of the Liberal Catholic county gentlemen, who looked on "the marquis" as their leader. Lord Dunsandle, pressed by a strong letter from the Carlton Club, urging that I was a much more dangerous opponent to their party than Bellew was, opposed me. But Sir George Shee, who represented a powerful interest in the far off barony of Dunmore, where I was weak, was one of the most valued accessions to my side. It now seems strange, so vast is the revolution caused by the Land Bill and the ballot, so absolute the inability of a landlord to secure a single vote, to write of an election upon the results of which one could reckon with certainty, by simply counting up on the registration lists the names of the tenants of each landlord who had promised or refused their adhesion.

M

Lord Carlisle, whose support I had invoked, sent me the following very graceful letter, referring to my having defeated him in Dublin, fifteen years previously :—

"DEAR MR. GREGORY,

"I have written in your behalf to Sir Thomas Redington, Lord Campbell, Mr. Gough, Sir George Shee, and the Dean of Kilmacduagh, in spite of his orthodox precedence. You know I am bound to think highly of a candidate from whom I once sustained such a licking, for which believe me

"Your very grateful servant,

"CARLISLE."

At first everything seemed propitious ; the great proportion of the landlords had promised me their votes, the town voters, comparatively independent, were divided, and the priests seemed disposed to take no part in the struggle. Sir Thomas Redington, in view of standing, had visited Dr. Derry, the very able and influential Bishop of Clonfort, but had received a stern refusal of assistance from him, and a like answer from Dr. McHale, the great archbishop of the west. It seemed as if I were about to win in a canter. The tide, however, ebbed. Dr. Derry was induced to intercede with Dr. McHale for Captain Bellew, who was again taken into favour. His Grace issued a violent denunciation of "Quarter Acre Gregory," the cry was taken up by several, though by no means all, of his priesthood, and it was feared that, through their influence, many of the voters would, in the dioceses of Tuam and Clonfort, refuse to come to the poll. In the two other dioceses of Galway and Kilmacduagh, I had not only the landlords on my side, but the Bishop of Kilmacduagh, Dr. Fallon, was my most ardent adherent. He even wrote my letters for me when I was confined to my bed by a severe cold. Dr. McEvilly had just been appointed Bishop of Galway. He, too, was a staunch friend, and said to me, I well remember his expression, "If the consecration oil were not still moist upon me, you would see how I would exert myself for you." He did exert himself, nevertheless, and we had thus the spectacle of two dioceses arrayed on the side of Bellew, and two on my side, and, as for the mob, it was droll enough.* At Tuam, the hussars were charging with drawn sabres to enable my voters to come up, while in Gort and Galway popular feeling was as demonstrative on my side, but the preponderance being all one way, matters went off comparatively smoothly. Unfortunately, just as the election was coming on I was taken extremely unwell from a violent cough, but my lieutenants worked so admirably and energetically that everything went as well as if I had been commanding in person. In the western baronies, James Martin, of Ross, and George Burke, of Danesfield, took the lead in bringing up the voters. My dear old friend Tom Joyce took charge of the district about Craughwell, Andrew Comyn of that of Ballinasloe, while, at Eyrecourt, John Eyre worked the baronies of Longford and Leitrim with unflagging zeal and energy, and

---

* "I can write with some confidence on this subject (De-Protestantizing Ireland), as for fourteen years I represented the county of Galway, in which the mass of the voters were Roman Catholic, and naturally much swayed by their clergy. During the greater part of that time I was in constant, indeed I may say in confidential relation with the bishops and priests of the county. In this unrestrained intercourse I never perceived the slightest symptom of hatred of Protestants as such. I may, perhaps, here refer to a somewhat ludicrous incident which illustrates my contention. At a public meeting, in which I was canvassing before an election, some one in the crowd called out, 'But he's a Protestant!' Upon this the parish priest, who was by my side, exclaimed, 'Who dares make such an observation?' And, having discovered the offender, he sprung into the thick of the throng, and then and there, amid general acclamation, administered to him a sound castigation with a stick" (Letter to the *Times*, 1890).

brought carriages and cars full of voters to Loughrea, amid much noise, cheering, and enthusiasm. I was confined to my bed on the nomination day, and unable to appear at the court house of Galway, which was a great drawback, but the tumult and disturbance which raged in it would have rendered my eloquence of very little avail. The polling days were fixed for the Thursday before Easter and the Saturday following, April 10th and 12th, Good Friday being blank, but on the Thursday evening the reports from the different polling stations showed such an immense majority in my favour that Bellew, who was in Galway, came to my uncle, William O'Hara, and said, " I see I am beaten, and there is no use in prolonging the contest. I do not wish to put Mr. Gregory to another penny's expense, and will not poll a man on Saturday, so give orders at once to your agents to stop all further proceedings." He issued the following dignified and kindly notice :—

"Gentlemen,

" Finding, from the result of Thursday's polling, that I have not received the amount of support which I had been led to believe would be given to me, I have determined no longer to prolong a contest which cannot terminate in my favour, and which could now be only productive of inconvenience to many of the electors. Although an unforeseen combination of circumstances and interests has been the cause of my defeat, yet I feel convinced that, upon cooler reflection, this county will acknowledge the error of dismissing from its representation one whose study it has been faithfully to represent the opinions on which he was elected. I have now only to return my warmest thanks to those kind friends who have supported me ; and to those who have opposed me the regret consequent upon their opposition is, I assure them, mingled with none but kindly feelings.

"T. A. Bellew."

This action of Bellew's was entirely in harmony with his honourable and warm-hearted character. We had

always been warm friends, and the election did not cool
our friendship in the slightest degree. My poor pockets
were then light enough, but, thanks to the admirable
management of J. Cowan, these two severe contests only
cost about £750 for the first, and £650 for the second,
and, what is still more strange, I had not one subsequent
application or claim for unsettled demands. Well, the
election was over, and I was proclaimed duly the knight
of the shire for the county of Galway.

On proceeding to London and taking my seat I was
received with cheers by the old friends who had still
retained their places in the House of Commons since I
was their comrade in 1847; but the changes during those
ten years were very great. I felt strange among the new
faces. It seemed to me, from the minute on which I
entered afresh the House of Commons and shook the
Speaker's hand, that my former life had been shifted as a
scene from the stage, and that I had become a totally
different man in character, and objects, and thought. I
had cared very little for politics during the time I sat
for Dublin; I believed Sir Robert Peel could not do
wrong, and that was enough for me. I had seen enough
of the old Tories to be utterly estranged from them, and
a process contrary to the usual one in the case of public
men, who enter life ardent and advanced Liberals and
end their days in quiet Conservatism, was going on in my
mind. I began by being Conservative, and every day
became more and more Liberal. I have already mentioned the causes which made me such an advanced
politician on the tenants' side. It was clearly conviction,
and not the mere desire of popularity, as to be a prominent
tenants' advocate was by no means the way to hold one's
own in a constituency controlled by landowners. As
regards religious matters, again, there were few took more

advanced views than myself. I was in favour of every
fair claim, alike of Catholics and Dissenters, being granted.
I had no objection to a State Church, both in England
and in Ireland, but I had the strongest objection to a
State Church of a minority. The time had not come for
the abolition of the Irish Church; there were discussions
on it, but they were academic and nothing more. In my
heart I was the strongest advocate of a total change in
our Irish ecclesiastical system ; the change I wished for
was not the subsequent levelling down measure, whereby
the religious endowments should be strictly applied to
religious purposes, and divided among the different
denominations. I held the claims of the Irish Roman
Catholic clergy to have confided to them the full education
of their flocks, in accordance with the wishes of these
flocks, to be well justified and sound. I believed then in
the arguments of the Roman Catholic prelates who said,
" Give us the education of our people, and when you have
done so, but not till then, hold us responsible for their
conduct." I thought of all religious teachings theirs was
best for the unruly wills and affections of Irish nature.
I thought Presbyterian teaching essentially suited to the
sturdy Scotch-descended population of the North, and I
thought the Church of Ireland, so-called, had, by reason
of its shortcomings in the face of overwhelming encouragement, the least claims to continued support. Had
the English Church been the same pampered, rickety
establishment, kept up for the benefit of a rich and
comparatively small minority, I should have joined the
Church Liberation Society, and been among the foremost
to demand its overthrow. But the Church of England is
the Church of the majority, it is the Church of the poor
essentially, far more than is any other denomination ; it
is not pampered, and it is not rickety, for it gives good

work for what it receives, and it is ever getting a stronger
hold on the confidence of the people. I therefore see no
reason for its overthrow. These were pretty much the
arguments I used with myself, and with the few friends to
whom I ventured to open my mind in those days. I was
reproached with being indifferent to religion, as I seemed
to draw no distinctions, and to treat all alike. To
dogmatic religion, I replied, I was comparatively indifferent, but to religion in general terms I considered
the State was bound in policy to afford every possible
encouragement and assistance. I never could look with
aversion or displeasure on a religion not my own. I
regarded it as having its particular merits, its special
adaptation to its followers, and, instead of searching to
explore its demerits, I was quite satisfied, seeing many
dwelling in it safely and content. I acknowledge myself
to be eminently latitudinarian. My theory has always
been that we cannot feed the human mind with moral
sentences and ethical admonitions, and that, as Robespierre
said, "If there were not a religion it would be necessary
to invent one," and undoubtedly no religion has been, or
could be invented so thoroughly adapted to the wants of
modern society as the Christian. It insists on order,
obedience to laws, humanity and beneficence, love of God
and love of our neighbour. All the Christian denominations profess the same, and all should, therefore, be
encouraged and maintained. I have ever looked on the
Roman Catholic Church as the great central fortress of
law and order, resisting wild theories and destructive
innovations, and I have regarded other religious minor
denominations as auxiliary forts, having the same common
object, the defence of society. I have entered on this
lengthened disquisition because it is the keynote of many
a speech of mine, and of my policy during the fourteen

years I was member for Galway county, and I maintained
the same policy, and with much success, in Ceylon, where
I had opportunities of putting it into execution. I have
not included the Eastern Church among the Western
denominations, which I should regard with equal favour,
because, though I may form a wrong estimate of it, I
believe it to be, except in the great towns, a religion of
mere forms and superstitious practices, without the active
and beneficent piety of the West. It is quite true that in
Ireland, of late years, the Roman Catholic prelates seem
to have abandoned the high standard of their Church, and
to have acquiesced in, if not encouraged, dishonest and
lawless combinations. But the authoritative voice of
Rome has condemned such practices, and it must be
remembered that it has been misgovernment which has
placed the Irish hierarchy in the position of being
swayed, and even commanded, by its flocks. My object
during the time I was in Parliament was to sweeten the
relations of the heads of the Catholic body in Ireland with
the Government of the day, and to render them as
independent as possible of extraneous influences.

During the session of 1857 I took no part in the
debates beyond moving and carrying a clause in the
Industrial School Bill, having for its object the prevention
of any tampering with the religion of a child by his being
sent to an industrial school, and not to any other. This
very fair clause was suggested to me by Dr. Derry, and
gave satisfaction to my Roman Catholic clerical supporters.

The extraordinary pleasure of my Egyptian expedition
of the past year had sown the seeds of that constant
longing for travel which I have never to this day succeeded in appeasing. My old friend Sir S. Graham
volunteered his company, and we agreed to proceed in

the autumn (1856) to Tunis, and make our way thence to
Tripoli. An account of this was written in the volumes
before mentioned.

The following letter which appeared in the *Times*,
September 7, 1881, gives a description of Kairwan, one
of the places visited on this journey :—

"SIR,

"I see by the letter of your correspondent from Tunis,
dated the 17th of August, that an attack on Kairwan, either by the
forces of the Bey of Tunis or by the French, is imminent. If the
forces of the Bey succeed in putting down the insurrectionary movement in that district not much difficulty will ensue. It will be merely the
case of Mahommedan encountering Mahommedan. But if the French
take the city it is impossible to foresee what will be the effect of the
violation of a spot which, after Mecca, is the most holy in the eyes of
every believer in the Prophet throughout Tunis, Algeria, Morocco,
and Tripoli. I have not a doubt that it will arouse a feeling of the
bitterest hatred which will last for years, and which nothing but
overwhelming force will suppress. I can speak with some authority
on this point, as I am one of the very few Christians who ever entered
its walls ; and I well remember the intense veneration with which it
was regarded by the Tunisians, and the respect which greeted myself
and my friend when it became known, as we proceeded on our journey,
that we had penetrated the sacred precincts and dwelt there securely,
enjoying much courtesy and honour.

"A few lines taken from my notes written at the time of my visit
may at this moment be of some interest to your readers. In the year
1858, in company with a friend, Sir Sandford Graham, now no more,
I thoroughly explored the Regency of Tunis. Our start from Tunis
was first to Zaghouan ; thence due west to Kef ; thence to the south to
Kissera, Sbaitla, with its temples and its tombs ; Feriana, Kafla the
treasury of Jugurtha ; to Tozer and Nettah, the furthest of the oases of
the Great Sahara ; then, striking due east across the salt lake, called
the Sea of Marks, the Lacus Tritonis of the ancients, to Cabes, on the
seashores of the Lesser Syrtis. We thence proceeded northwards by
the coast of Sfax, the scene of the late bombardment by the French,
where we were most courteously received, and thence, striking inland
after a stay at El Djem, famous for its magnificent amphitheatre, we
reached Kairwan.

"I should mention that previous to starting on this expedition we
had an interview with the Bey, who furnished us with letters and an

escort. Nothing could have been more kind than he was in granting us every facility to visit his country. When the question arose as to the possibility of our entering Kairwan, he made no difficulty about it, provided his lieutenant on the spot could guarantee our safety, but he remarked that he could not give us an order for admittance to any mosque, as it would cause excitement and expose us to much danger.

"I shall not readily forget the morning of the 20th of January, 1858, when we entered the famous city. The weather had previously been dreadful, and we were a draggled *cortége*, our horses covered with mud, and we ourselves not much more seemly; but the sun burst out as we approached the lofty white crenelated walls, which rose up from the wide plain surrounding it and gave it the brightest and gayest appearance, for there were no suburbs or a single house about it, and so every eye was fixed on the sacred city, and on it only, and its innumerable minarets and domes. The fear of marauding Arabs kept the citizens within the safeguard of the defences, which were strong enough and high enough to resist all attacks without heavy artillery. We had sent forward before dawn a spahi, to announce our coming to the Kehaya, or Governor, and when within sight of the town, we waited his return with no little anxiety, not feeling at all sure of the reception we were likely to obtain. We were not long kept in suspense. The spahi soon appeared, galloping back with joyful countenance, and he informed us that the head men of the city were prepared to give us a warm greeting, about a mile from the town, and to conduct us through it to the Bey's Palace, which was placed at our disposal. We found the city sheikhs at the places indicated, and, after a hearty reception, they marched before us into the town. One portion proceeded in front and cleared the street of every human being, while the other half remained behind and blocked it up, allowing no one to enter it till we had passed through. It recalled the procession of Lady Godiva along the streets of Coventry, in the days of Peeping Tom. At last we reached a large and excellent house intended for the use of the Bey when he visited Kairwan. Stables occupied the basement, and were of great extent, supported by a number of white and red marble and porphyry columns, evidently the spoils of some ancient structure. The house was in good taste; the flooring being chiefly composed of encaustic tiles, and the walls lined with the same material. In summer it would have been cool and comfortable, but at the time it was cold and damp, and, as there was no outlet for the fumes, it was impossible to bear the brazier in the room for more than a short period. The Kehaya, or Governor, called at once, accompanied by a *cortége* of grave and bearded elders. He was a singularly handsome man, magnificently dressed, very civil, and very ill-informed. He supplied us with the best of everything, and volunteered to show us the town next day, and on my asking if it would be possible to see the mosque of the famous saint Sidi Sabi, he did not seem put out by the enormity of the request, but promised we should see the interior of it, though he could not permit us to enter the sacred precincts. And he was as good as his word, for when he rode through the streets the next day, he conducted us to the gates of the mosque, which had previously been thrown open, and he bade us to look in with a reverential spirit. Nor was this all, for we were brought to visit the famous well, Baroota, which communicated with the still more sacred well, Zem-Zem, at Mecca, and is held equally sacred in consequence. It is curious that they have here precisely the same story with regard to their holy well that the Cairenes have with regard to theirs in the Mosque of Amr. In both cases it is stated that a pilgrim, having dropped his wooden drinking bowl into Zem-Zem, on returning to his native city found the identical bowl floating on the surface of his own fountain—a fact which, of course, proves the connection of the two sources. The elders professed much gratification on being informed that we had come from far to drink this celebrated water, and to do honour to their saint Sidi Sabi, about whom they were curious to hear if his name was known in England. Having read about him when at home, I was able to answer these questions very honestly in the affirmative, and so they handed us water from the well, and bade us quaff it into our bodies, and with it Islam into our souls. They also showed us a very seedy-looking old camel, who is perpetually engaged in drawing water for the faithful, and who is exhibited to them on state occasions in magnificent velvet housings. This animal they said was an object of great respect, and were rather amused when I observed that I thought he would prefer a little more food and a little less respect. Both on this and the following day we were conducted through the streets and round the walls, and were treated with respect, and even cordiality, being invited on more than one occasion to enter houses and have coffee. What struck me most was the neatness of the town, its excellent private houses, and the cleanliness of the streets, in spite of the heavy rain which had recently fallen. It was a remarkable contrast in these respects to the many other Moorish towns in which we had been sojourning. There was little sign of any business going on, it was sleepy enough to all intents, but its citizens seemed to attach importance to propriety and neatness. It seemed a kind of Mahommedan Bath, or rather Oxford, to which Tunis and Sfax would play the part of Wapping. I attribute this to the fact of numbers of highly religious Moors, who, finding themselves jostled elsewhere by Christians and Jews, determined to remove themselves from the contagion and retire here to live and die in the odour of sanctity. To dwell within its holy walls is the very next thing—indeed, an approximation—to being actually in heaven, so they informed me, and so also affirmed many Moors elsewhere, lamenting that their poverty or avocations prevented them from taking up their quarters in this abode of the blessed. We had large *levées* every evening of the chief persons, and much discourse on religious matters, which Mahommedans are always eager to discuss. They were also most desirous of understanding how a powerful country like England could remain powerful or have any taxes collected under a female sovereign. I endeavoured to ascertain if it were true that some of the old families who had taken refuge in Kairwan from Spain still preserved the keys of their houses in Grenada and Cordova; but though they said there were many families of the refugees from Spain, they were not aware of their having retained their keys. They told us that their present saint was a female, and that the last marabout, who had recently died, was a man of extraordinary sanctity, and a performer of the most wonderful miracles. Our landlord at Tunis, a Frenchman, told us that when accompanying the Bey as cook to Kairwan, he had the misfortune to lose his horse, and was in despair, as he could find no one to sell him another. In this emergency some one advised him to consult this famous marabout. He accordingly went to his abode, and as he was about to state his perplexities, before he had time to open his lips, the holy man said to him, ' Return to your tent, and you will there find what you require.' The saint then shut the door in his face, but on my host arriving at his tent he found there a man holding a horse, who handed him the bridle, and without a word departed. Among other information which we received from our visitors we heard that the women of Susa were famous for the beauty of their eyes, those of Tunis for their good taste and knowledge of the becoming in dress, while those of Kairwan bore away the palm for the symmetry of their legs. As in these matters we were profoundly in the dark, we had to take our informant's word for the accuracy of these characteristics. After three days' sojourn in Kairwan we went on our way rejoicing, having had a most cordial reception ; but throughout the whole of the Beylik we experienced hospitality and kindness, both from Moors and Arabs. The Tunisians have always had a better reputation than their Algerian neighbours, and the fanatical and ignorant inhabitants of Morocco.

" I have no doubt that much of the kind treatment we received was due to the strong feeling of reliance on England which was at that time entertained by the ruling classes in Tunis, and mainly inspired by the great ability and high character of our Consul, Sir Richard Wood. Some remarks which I wrote in my journal in 1858, after an interview with the Bey, are so applicable to the present state of affairs, that I ask leave to reproduce them precisely as they were written :—

" ' The allusions made by the Bey to his friendly disposition towards the English were not mere compliments. He is perfectly alive to the fact that France is only waiting for the propitious moment to extend her African frontier to the borders of Tripoli. There is one fixed idea innate and uppermost in the mind of every Frenchman, and that is, that it is a necessity for the glory and destiny of France that the Mediterranean should be a French lake. The possession of Tunis is essential for this project. Its fine secure bay, in a coast devoid of good harbours from Morocco to Alexandria, would be invaluable to their fleet. Its position would be a counterpoise to Malta ; its inexhaustibly fertile plains and excellent climate would attract population, and redeem the failure of Algerian colonization. Already, quietly and silently, every preparation is being made. Two military roads are in course of construction ; one from Bonar to the frontiers of Tunis, near Kef, the other to the south of Tebissa. When these are completed, it only remains to march one column to Kef, and thence to Tunis ; while the other, penetrating the southern part of the Regency, can traverse the country, and occupy without impediment the towns along the shore of the Mediterranean and Gulf of Tripoli. Whatever Tunisian forces there are would thus be taken in the rear. French officers in Algeria do not scruple to open their minds to you upon the subject. With perfect ingenuousness they show you the value of the conquest, both in a military and commercial point of view, and they tell you very frankly that Morocco, Algeria, Tripoli, and Egypt will be a fair set-off to our empire in India. The position of the Bey, however, as vassal of the Porte, created some difficulty in the way of the execution of these schemes of conquest, consequently the policy of France has been since the occupation of Algeria to inflame the minds of successive Beys with visions of independence. Every inducement is held out to their vanity, and to their fears to allure them to proclaim themselves sovereign princes. At one time they were told that were they not mere feudatories they would be admitted into the fraternity of the great European Powers. At another they are alarmed by rumours that the Sultan is about to assert a right of appointing, and of superseding his vassals, and of converting Tunis into a Pashalik, as Tripoli has been converted ; the

Government of which was at one time in much the same position as that of Tunis. Another plan is, by intrigues, to disorganize the country, and render the inhabitants ready for a change. The late Bey was unwary enough to be dazzled with this scheme of independence, and determined on paying Europe a visit, and obtaining from the Western Powers a recognition of that independence. Louis Philippe gave him every encouragement, but, fortunately for Tunis, there was one man who had the sagacity to penetrate these projects, and who had the firmness to prevent the foolish dupe from becoming the victim of his short-sighted vanity. Lord Palmerston was then Foreign Secretary. The Bey notified to him his intention of visiting Her Majesty as a foreign prince. Lord Palmerston replied that he could only come as a vassal of the Sultan, and be presented by the Turkish Ambassador. His Highness returned to Tunis in dudgeon, complaining of the treatment he had received from his English friends. But they were, if unpalatable friends, true, at all events ; for it was clear that Lord Palmerston meant to maintain the Sultan's territorial rights. Thus no excuse was sought to pick a quarrel with Tunis in the days of the late Bey, who at last thoroughly understood the wisdom of the course pursued by Lord Palmerston. On the accession of the present Bey the same artifices were employed, and it is said that he was disposed to lend too ready an ear to them, until, from the instruction of our Consul-General, Mr. Wood, he became thoroughly acquainted with their object.'

"I cannot but feel regret for the evil times which have fallen on the Tunisians, for personally I received much kindness in their country, and undoubtedly they have some claims on England's goodwill. The last Bey but one was the first Mahommedan prince who abolished the slave trade in his dominions. He did it at the risk of his life and throne, and through the instigations of Sir Thomas Reid, then our Consul. His people were most indignant, but a noble example was set, and travellers in Central Africa state that no heavier blow - was struck at the slave trade, and the horrible system of slave hunts in the interior, than by this good act of the Bey of Tunis. He asked for a slight recognition from this country, was refused, and on his death-bed expressed his regret that he should die without an honour from England. The late Bey, on the breaking out of the Crimean War, behaved admirably to the allies. With the greatest alacrity and good will, he fitted out and sent 10,000 men, well disciplined and appointed, to the seat of war. Services like these ought not to be forgotten at the present crisis.

"I remain, sir. yours, etc.,

"W. H. GREGORY."

I did not return to England till February, and the only speech which I made in the House of Commons of any length was in seconding Lord Harry Vane's motion for deferring all legislation for the transfer of India from the Company to the Crown, which was proposed by the Government. I am bound to say the speech was by no means good; it went against public opinion, and was badly received. Still there was something in it, though I am now quite satisfied I took a wrong and needlessly unpopular course. I thought it advisable there should be an intermediate Government between India and the Government of the day; that was the pivot-point on which my arguments turned. There were strong objections to the House of Commons ruling India. The East India Directors were uninfluenced by the politics of the hour, and while their position was maintained there was no fear of India becoming, like Ireland, a battle-field of party, and disturbed by popular cries echoed by ignorant men. No doubt all double governments are bad, like all dual ownerships of land, as we in Ireland know to our cost; but still the steady conservatism of the Directors had many advantages, and doubtless moderated great ambitions which the Board of Control could not have done alone. They were elected by middle-class voters, they were not appointed or removable by the Minister of the day, a Ministerial crisis in no way affected their course of action. The interference of Ministers in Indian appointments, and the danger of favouritism over-riding merit, could not be lost sight of. The telegraphic "Take care of Doub" in the Crimea gave warning of similar telegraphic messages to India. We had seen enough of favouritism in the generals sent out by the Horse Guards, where to the lame, gouty, paralyzed, and incompetent pets of the powers that be, were entrusted, as we had known to our cost, military operations of the greatest importance in India. The East India Company was not guilty of having involved us in the annexation of Oude, the Afghan War, and the unjust and violent attack on and conquest of the Emirs of Scinde, all of which were causes leading up to the Mutiny. They had steadily opposed all those schemes and acts of aggrandisement. The Indian Empire was founded by the middle class ; place it in the hands of a Minister and it will soon become an appanage of the Crown and aristocracy, and a dangerous instrument from the enormous patronage which it might be made to confer. Such were my views at the time, and there was certainly a certain amount of force in them ; but Lord Palmerston made short work of them, and the House of Commons and country were in no mood for delay. The terrible crisis we had passed through during the Indian Mutiny was attributed by the majority to the faulty system of dual government which had prevailed, and a clean sweep was demanded, of such a drastic nature that Sepoy mutineers should become impracticable. The transfer, however, was not effected by Lord Palmerston, but by Lord Derby, as, in February, 1858, Mr. Milner Gibson carried his amendment against the Conspiracy Bill of the Government by a majority of nineteen votes. I voted with the Government with all my heart. I thought their object a proper one, to enable them to prosecute the foreign assassins who resorted to our shores to mature their murderous designs or to escape the consequences of them. It simply purported to make conspiracy to murder a felony. But the country was in no mood for such a measure. The menaces of France had thoroughly aroused English pride, and though there was no doubt of the co-operation of well-known refugees with the recent attempt by Orsini, the Government failed to carry their bill. It was a proper bill. It would have gratified and strengthened Louis Napoleon, supposed to be our special friend, and it would have removed the accusation, too justly made against us by every foreign power, of being a refuge for the most atrocious criminals, if they could only claim the privilege of political action. Lord Palmerston undoubtedly failed in his conduct of the bill, and received a lesson he never forgot. And so India was transferred from John Company to the Empress-Queen, and very properly, in spite of my reasons to the contrary.

I had good fortune in the next session, 1859, in bringing in and carrying a bill in relation to the religion in which deserted children should be registered in Irish workhouses, and also providing for the outdoor maintenance of orphan and deserted children. Lord John Browne, the member for Mayo, cordially assisted me, and added his name to the bill. This bill was rendered necessary by the decision of the Poor Law Board that all children in workhouses, whose religion could not be ascertained, should be brought up as belonging to the Church of England, and much dissatisfaction was the result, as the probability was strongly in favour that these children were the offspring of Catholic parents, considering the numerical preponderance of the Catholics, and that habitually these poor waifs and strays came from the lowest classes of the community. Constant conflicts between the guardians of the Poor Law Board were the result, and religious zeal was stirred up whenever any of these children were introduced ; the Protestant guardians insisting on the decision of the Poor Law Board being maintained, the Catholic guardians sturdily resisting it on the ground of its manifest unfairness. My bill set this vexed question at rest, much to the relief of the Poor

Law Board, and was received with general satisfaction by the Roman Catholic clergy.

I took the important step in this session of moving for a Committee of Inquiry into the British Museum ; rather a venturesome step for a member of no standing and of small experience, but the necessity for inquiry was so manifest that the Government acceded to my motion. So far back as 1854, Dr. Grey, the keeper of the Zoological Department, reported that the zoological collection was almost inaccessible, and, if not transferred to dryer quarters, would before long be destroyed. In 1857 Mr. Panizzi, the principal librarian, had renewed the complaint, stating that no specimen could be examined without removing two or three others ; that a vast number of the most valuable objects were stowed away in the basement ; that the Trustees were, from insufficient accommodation, unable to exhibit their prints and drawings ; that the colonnade was defaced with a glass conservatory, crammed with the marbles of Halicarnassus, and that those from Carthage had been relegated to subterraneous regions of Nox and Erebus. I proposed various heads of inquiry, chiefly as to the question whether, in order to relieve this scandalous state of things, resort should be had to obtaining increased space in contiguity with the present site, or to the removal of the natural history collections elsewhere, and if so, where ; also as to whether duplicates of books in the Library might not be rendered available in loan to provincial libraries ; also whether it would be advisable to appoint more men of science on the Board of such a great scientific institution ; also as to the mode of transacting business by the Board, and as to the expediency of some kind of lecture or exposition being given by the officials, to illustrate the vast, and to the great majority of visitors, incomprehensible

treasures of the Museum. The statement was well received by the House, and with acclaim by the heads of
departments in the Museum, with the exception of Mr.
Panizzi, who could not bear any interference with this
great establishment over which he ruled with absolute
authority, and was highly exasperated at any changes
being proposed which did not directly emanate from him.

The following evening I had to move, formally, the
appointment of the Committee, at the end of other public
business, when, to my astonishment, Mr. Gladstone got
up and, without notice, opposed it, at 1.30 a.m. There
were only twenty-one members in the House, and out of
them he got but one supporter. We divided, nineteen
to two, and that was the commencement of a continued
antagonism between Mr. Gladstone and myself on all
subjects connected with the British Museum.

Parliament was dissolved, and so my Committee fell
through for that year.

At the earnest request of Captain Vivian, who had
taken office, I became his successor to a motion he intended to bring before the House to inquire into the
grievances of Mr. Ryland, the Clerk of the Council in
Canada. I was met by Mr. Chichester Fortescue, on the
part of the Government, and my motion was defeated, I
believe very properly, by a large majority. It had the
effect, however, of laying the foundation of much friendship with a charming family in Canada, that of Mr.
Ryland, from whom I received much kindness when I
visited the country.

CHAPTER X.

WHEN the session of 1859 was over I determined on paying a visit to Canada and the United States. I had often received letters from my uncle, Colonel O'Hara, who had settled at Toronto, which had greatly impressed me by their ability, and I had heard so much of the charm of his society and of his family that I had long looked forward to the trip. Two days before starting I met Geoffrey Browne, now Lord Oranmore, at Kildare-street Club, and, on my mentioning my plans, he proposed to join me. I agreed; he telegraphed to Liverpool and obtained the vacant berth in my cabin.

We sailed in the *Anglo-Saxon* on the 1st of September. We were to have started the day before, but the hurricane which raged caused a delay. It was terrific. Several ships had gone ashore in the Mersey, and the sight of these wrecks was not a pleasant one as we made our way by them. We got on board with great difficulty and danger, and after a few had reached the *Anglo-Saxon's* deck at the risk of their lives, the tender was obliged to sheer off till low water. For eight days this tremendous storm raged, and was the grandest and the most fearful sight I ever witnessed. At one moment we were perched on the summit of an enormous rolling wave, and then descended into an abyss, with a wall of green water rising right above us, but the ship went up bravely and easily.

For a day and a night we made but little way. It was almost impossible to remain on deck except on all fours, and, as the cabin was battened down, our time was not spent agreeably. But not a rope or bolt gave way, the engines did their work nobly, and the captain, a God-fearing, hard-headed Scotchman, never once, during those eight days of danger, took off his clothes, and inspired general confidence, even among the ladies, by his un-ceasing care and calmness. Once, however, he showed what he thought of our danger. At dinner one day, a young pert cockney said to him, in a chaffing manner, " I say, captain, if the rudder-chains gave way, what would you do? " I shall not readily forget the captain's solemn reply : " Young man, if you knew how near you are to meeting your Maker, you would not ask such questions."

One of our fellow-passengers was John Head, the son of the Governor of Canada, who was going out to join his father, Sir E. Head, and family. He was a most charming young fellow, full of originality, and evidently of a very high order of ability. His mind was directed to scientific studies, and he was to enter at Cambridge next term, where every one prognosticated for him a distinguished career. When we reached Quebec we received an invita-tion from his father to join him at Montreal, and to proceed thence to Trois Rivières, a town at the mouth of the St. Lawrence river, from which we were to make an excursion of four or five days into the wild country on the banks of that river. We joyfully accepted the invitation, and had a most amusing public dinner at Trois Rivières, where the jolly mayor gave the health of the jolly Commander-in-Chief, Sir Fenwick Williams, of Kars, who accompanied us from Montreal. He wound up with a musical outburst, accompanied with the beating of a big drum, with a " bomm, bomm, bomm, and a boom. boom.

boom—our artillery general's health, and boom, boom, boom." It was extremely comical, so much so that we all continued singing "boom, boom, boom," with the big drum beating time, and the mayor in the greatest fury in vain endeavouring to lay the spirit he had let loose.

Next day we started in boats of birch bark manned by half-breed Indians and employés of the Hudson's Bay Company. Nothing could be more delightful; the marvellous tints of Canadian autumn had coloured the woods in purple, orange, and crimson of every shade. The weather at first was perfect. When we came to rough water on the river we got out of our canoes and carried them till the water was smooth again. Then we entered a chain of lakes, and the scene was very pretty. We had five or six boats, all rowing in procession; each of the rowers was clad in a red flannel jacket, and at a signal the steersman of the foremost boat tossed up his paddle and gave the signal for one of the old-fashioned Canadian songs, this was taken up by the next boat, and so all along the line, and the lake was full of music. I remember the beginning of one song, the refrain of which was extremely pretty—

> " Le fils du roi il est méchant,
> Il a volé mon canard blanc."

Our first day's excursion was to the magnificent Falls of Shaweegan, the finest I had ever seen, not having yet visited Niagara. The great river comes tearing down a gorge, and, turning suddenly, meets a huge rock in midstream which bars its progress. It dashes itself high up in the air with a crash and turmoil heard far away. We bivouacked near it our first night.

Our party the first day consisted of Sir E. and Lady, Miss and John Head, Sir Fenwick Williams, and some friends from Trois Rivières, G. Browne and myself and Monsieur

Cartier, the Prime Minster of Canada, once a rebel, and I
believe out in the Papillon rebellion, but now as loyal a
subject as her Majesty ruled over, and a most delightful
companion, full of fun and with exuberant spirits. We halted
toward evening near Shaweegan, where there was a house
which the Governor and his party occupied, but we put up in
tents and slept most comfortably and soundly on spruce
branches, after a merry dinner. The evening wound up
with Canadian songs and dancing, and M. Cartier, in the
fulness of high spirits, seized a fiddle from one of the
voyageurs, jumped on an empty barrel and kept us in
continual laughter by his songs and drolleries. I have
known all our Prime Ministers since 1840, but I hardly
think any combination of circumstances would have made
any one of them give way to such friskiness, not even
Lord Derby, in spite of his love for a practical joke. The
next day the cares of office carried off Monsieur Cartier,
to our universal regret; but for two more days we had
delightful journeys through beautiful woodland scenery
and by magnificent waterfalls, passing occasionally the
house of a settler, which was indicated by the smoke
curling through the forest. It was on the second day that
we arrived at the fine Falls of Grande Mère, and there we
were forced by rain to remain two days. The weather
clearing up we went on to the Falls of Les Pelles, and
thence returned to our camp at Grande Mère. At dinner
there was a good deal of banter at the expense of John
Head for not bathing as the rest of us did, and Sir Edmund
said laughingly to his son, "If you do not get up and
bathe to-morrow, I shall send the boatmen into your tent
to pull you out of bed and duck you," and I added, having
just had a swim before dinner in the river, a strong warning
to all not to bathe from a very tempting spot, as the sand
was almost a quicksand, and that had I not been a good

swimmer, I should have run great risk. The following
morning, at about nine o'clock, Sir E. Head had gone out
fishing, the ladies had not yet appeared, the boatmen were
all sitting on the bank, and G. Browne and myself
finished or were going to finish our breakfast in the cottage
close to the falls, when a cry arose from the river, and
there was a running to and fro of the boatmen in great
agitation. Presently Captain Kettallich, the aide-de-camp,
ran up and said, "John Head is drowned." We ran down
immediately, a canoe was rapidly brought to the spot, and
the boatmen dived all around the place where John Head
had disappeared. He had run down from his tent, and,
although quite unable to swim, he had entered the water
at exactly the spot against which I had warned him and
others. His feet slipped from under him, owing to the
impalpable sand on which he tried to make a footing.
Three times he rose above the surface, three times he sank
in the full view of the boatmen on the bank, they merely
remarking what a capital diver he was. It was not till
he sank for the last time that the alarm was given, but
the body had been nearly twenty minutes under water ere
it was reached. He was close to the shore, not more than
three or four yards, and apparently on all-fours, but there
were sixteen feet of water where he lay, and a strong
under-current. We set to work to endeavour to revive
him, and in a short time Sir E. Head, who had been
bathing and fishing, came and took the direction with
perfect calmness and self-command. For three hours we
rocked the body to and fro, and sometimes inspired by
hope from air-bubbles which came from the lips, but at
last the hopelessness of our task became apparent. Sir
Edmund looked me in the face and said, "It is hopeless."
I could only bow. He turned to his poor wife and
daughter, held up his hands, and fell flat on his face,

perfectly senseless, as, in the words of Dante, "Caddi come corpo morto cade." One can readily imagine the misery which had succeeded all our joyousness. For two days we had to make our way down the river with the body of the poor boy wrapped up in a blanket. It was not till we reached Trois Rivières that we obtained a coffin. Sir Edmund was completely unnerved, and could do nothing, but Lady Head bore up wonderfully, and I was able to help them a good deal during that dreadful journey. When we parted she took my hand in both of hers and said, "May God thank you for your kindness to us. Come and see me when you can ; it will be a relief to me to see one whom I associate with the recollections of my dear child." And Sir Edmund seemed also to be much gratified when we expressed our intention to go down to Quebec to be present at the funeral. The cemetery at Quebec is a lovely spot overlooking the broad St. Lawrence. The people flocked in from all quarters to the funeral, and their conduct was admirable. There was no appearance of idle, vulgar curiosity, but they came as if their object were to fulfil a melancholy duty. The maple in its gorgeous beauty was waving over the grave, and solemn ancient pines added to the impressiveness of the scenery. I did not think the poor parents could have had the courage to face the ceremony, but they did.

JOHN HEAD,

AGED 19 YEARS AND 7 MONTHS.

Died September 25, 1859.

This was the inscription on the coffin. I could not help recalling the words of Tennyson, which seemed to come home to my heart as we looked from Spencer Wood and saw the ships with their white sails sweeping down the St. Lawrence to Quebec—

"The stately ships go down
    To the haven under the hill ;
    But O for the touch of a vanished hand,
    And the sound of a voice that is still ! "

From Ottawa I went to Pictou, to pay my friend Mr.
Ryland a visit, and thence to Toronto, to my uncle
Walter. I had heard that the establishment was extremely ree-raw, but, on the contrary, everything was
orderly, very good living, and the warmest welcome. I
was greatly taken with them all, but was only able to stay
with them a day or two, having to go on to Niagara to
meet Browne, who had preceded me. I need say nothing
of Niagara, except that it was perhaps the only sight
of my life which exceeded my previous expectations.
No picture can give an adequate idea of the wondrous
majestic calmness of that ceaseless fall, of its treacherous
slate-green water, and of the pools of foam below. From
Niagara I went to Chicago, and my letters are full of
admiration of this great and ever-rising city, and from
Chicago I traversed the State of Illinois to Quincy, a
place of evil fame for rowdyism. I attended a fair held
there, where there was a race between the ladies of Illinois
and of Missouri, which was extremely amusing. As the
Missouri lady won I fully expected there would be an
outburst among the Illinois citizens ; but everything was
orderly, though I heard in the hotel that a murder or two
was expected during the night, not premeditated, certainly,
but owing to difficulties arising among gentlemen from
transactions during the fair.

We left Quincy and the rival female jockeys without .
regret, and took steamer to Louisville. The steamer
was, as Mississippi steamers always are, of immense
proportions, with very comfortable cabins, excellent
living, and gorgeously fitted up. I had hitherto been

under the impression that the Mississippi was a slug-
gish stream, flowing through swamps and fever-haunted
morasses, but this higher part of it is extremely fine.
There are, for some miles ere reaching Alton, in Illinois,
high banks or bluffs, as they call them, which were
of remarkable beauty, and at that time, October 13,
decked in all the magnificence of the American autumn.
At Hannibal, quite a new place, and the point of departure for gold-diggers to the west, we took on board
a lot of adventurers just returning from the Rocky
Mountains to Pike's Peak. Such a set of ruffians in
appearance I never saw before; but they were extremely
well behaved, and, though in rags and unkempt, very
excellent, fine fellows. In the Western States at that
period, for this was thirty-nine years ago, the disregard
for human life was rather a striking feature. An Englishman on board told me he had been at Quincy only two
years, and that during this time eight men had been
pistolled or stabbed to death in quarrels, to say nothing
of wounds, and yet Quincy was but a small place. While
we were discussing this phase of society an American
gentleman, wishing to do the honours of the customs of
these regions, rushed up and urged me to go forward at
once, if I desired to see a difficulty. On proceeding to
the scene of action, I found the captain surrounded by a
crowd, and remonstrating with a most ill-favoured, ragged
young scapegrace, who was threatening to make some
other man "smell hell." I asked a bystander what was
going on, and he replied coolly, sending forth a squirt of
tobacco juice, "Wal, I guess that 'ere gentleman wants to
let blood from that other gentleman;" and so it was, the
youth had the sacrificial knife quite ready, and was only
calmed down by the assurance of the captain that he
would put a bullet through him if he heard any more

nonsense. The youth believed the assurance and slunk away, cursing with remarkably strange oaths. The wild adventurers from Pike's Peak and myself became fast friends during this voyage. By good luck the *Times*, of which I had several recent numbers, had been giving very interesting descriptions of gold-mining districts, and among them was one, if I recollect right, of Pike's Peak ; at all events they were highly pleased with the accounts, and requested me to read them aloud to them. This was the cause of our friendship, and most warm were the invitations to Pike's Peak. On my hinting at the in-security of life and property in those remote diggings, one of my friends replied, "I calculate, sir, your property is safer than on board this boat ; if a man steals we jest hang him up right off at once." And so they did, and the consequence was that in no part of the United States was there more honesty than among these wild desperadoes. I was highly amused at meeting my friends the day following our arrival at St. Louis ; they had discarded mocassins and leather leggings, and were arrayed in polished boots, sticking-plaster waistcoats, black coats, and chimney-pot hats, and seemed as conceited as butter-flies just escaped from the chrysalis state.

From St. Louis, but recently the last stage of civilization, just on the outposts of savagedom, but now a fine flourishing town in a flourishing and settled district, I proceeded to Louisville, in Kentucky, partly to see that State, and partly to see the Mammoth Caves, which, however, I was unable to reach. At Louisville I was standing, in the evening, under the lamplight of the door of the hotel, when a waggoner rushed from his car and horses and almost embraced me, crying out, "Oh, my dear master, don't you remember me ? " I had not forgotten him. He was a tenant's son, and had crossed the Atlantic to seek his fortune some years previously. He told me the waggon and horses were his own, and that he was running, though quite a young man, into much money. The next day he brought a concourse of former inhabitants of my property, and of the vicinity, and we had a long and pleasant chat on home matters, and on their own affairs and prospects in America, which were certainly very encouraging.

At Cincinnati, to which I next proceeded, I had more gaiety. The porter of my hotel discovered that he had married a daughter of one of my tenants, a certain Mrs. Regan, of Lissatunna, and invited me to visit his wife that evening. She had been housemaid at Coole, a very good-looking and remarkably clever girl. I found her in snug rooms, well furnished, and full of friends from Gort, and the region thereabout. Nothing could be pleasanter than the evening which, with the help of tea, and I am afraid not a little whisky punch, was prolonged to a late hour. The whole assembly accompanied me to the hotel, and at parting my hostess whispered something to her husband, who with a smile said to me, " I hope your honour won't be offended with the request, but my wife wishes your honour will, for the sake of old times, give her a kiss at parting." I willingly acceded, and gave the asked for accolade, and the party broke up with a cheer to celebrate it.

From Cincinnati I made my way to Cumberland, Virginia, to Washington, to Baltimore, and finally to New York.

I must mention Harper's Ferry. It is a small town at the junction of the Potomac and Shenandoah rivers, but of importance as being one of the armouries of the United States. Three days before my arrival it had acquired an immense notoriety, and, from the 17th of October to the

19th, the main topic of conversation, through the length and breadth of America, was "The Revolution of Harper's Ferry." On that day a band of desperate men, inflamed by religious fanaticism, and without a particle of sordid motive, seized, and held for a whole day, this armoury of the United States. This foray was contrived by Commander John Brown, a God-fearing man, deeply imbued with religious convictions, and perfectly convinced that he had received a Heaven-sent mission to act as a second Moses, and lead the slaves out of captivity. He seems to have inherited from remote ancestors a profound hatred of injustice, coupled with strong religious convictions. He was descended from John Brown, of Ashford, who was burned at the stake in his native village during the per- secution of Henry VIII., and his more immediate ancestor had left England to worship with freedom in America. His early career was that of a tanner in Ohio, whence he removed to Kansas, then the theatre almost of civil war between the advocates of slavery and the abolitionists. There he made himself known and feared by his bloody retaliation of the murders and spoliation of the slave- holding party, and thence he removed to the Alleghanies. All this long period of his life he had ever before him, as his paramount act of duty, the liberation of God's children, as he called the negroes, by some signal insurrection. Emerson, writing of him, says, " It was not a piece of spite and revenge, a plot of two years, or of twenty years, but the keeping of an oath made to heaven and earth forty-seven years before."

For some time he had lived in the hills near the town, had obtained arms, and had inspired with his enthusiasm other fanatics like himself. Their plans were well laid ; the arms, being seized, were to be handed over to the negroes, and emancipation proclaimed right and left. He

confidently reckoned on a fierce and unanimous rising of
the negroes, but, fortunately, he was disappointed, for a
scene of bloodshed, robbery, and violation would have
ensued which would have laid waste some of the fairest
provinces of the Union. Not a negro stirred. He said in
his letter, " The true object to be sought is first of all to
destroy the money value of slave property, and that can
only be done by rendering slave property insecure." The
attacking party got possession of the arms and the stores,
took the chief persons and the Government workmen
prisoners, and then entrenched themselves in one of the
public buildings, expecting vainly the rising of the black
population. When the troops and volunteers arrived the
following day they refused to surrender, and fought till
thirteen were killed, and the rest, except one, who contrived to escape, desperately wounded. During the fight
his son was shot dead. He laid down his rifle for a
minute, and arranged his limbs decently, then took it
up again, merely remarking, " This is the third I have
lost in the cause." John Brown was made prisoner, and
was being taken to Washington either by the train in
which we were travelling or by the preceding one. He
was supposed to be dying of his wounds. The Governor
of Virginia, Henry Wise, one of the most fierce fire-eaters
of the South, got in at Harper's Ferry with some other
officials, and invited us to his carriage. Of course the
conversation was on the subject of recent events. Some
one of the party applied to John Brown the opprobrious
name of "coward." " Sir," said Henry Wise, in a tone
the sternness of which I still remember, "you know not
him whom you are defaming. He is the bravest man I
ever saw." But he had fully made up his mind to hang
him, and did so very rightly. He was hanged at Charleston,
and his dying words were of remarkable power and

solemnity. He spoke to time and to eternity, and even at that moment, when the minds of his audience were furious against him, they listened to him with respect, almost with awe. These were his last words, noble and simple and fearless : " Now, if it is deemed necessary that I should forfeit my life for the furtherance of the ends of justice, and mingle my blood with the blood of my children, and with the blood of millions in this slave country whose rights are disregarded by wicked, cruel, and unjust enactments, I submit. So let it be done."

His memory has been venerated in the North as that of a martyr, and the " Marseillaise " of the Northern army, as they crushed and trampled on the Southern chivalry, was the refrain on the chant of his death—

> " John Brown's body lies mouldering in the grave,
> His soul is marching on."

Nothing could exceed the panic of the slave States caused by this attempt. They felt they were resting on explosives, and when men are terrified they are cruel. An English gentleman, Mr. Wynne, was in the train that arrived during the conflict ; the dead and dying were lying on the grass. One of the unfortunate wretches, dreadfully wounded and rolling in agony, called for water, and Mr. Wynne asked permission to give him a cupful. " If you do," said a volunteer, who was standing close by, " I'll jest shoot you as I shot him. I guess he shall die an uglier death than a dog or a horse." Had we not been delayed accidentally at Cincinnati we should have come into the fray, for the train by which we were to have travelled had its baggage-master shot dead, and the guard's hat was perforated ere they could retire out of bullet range. The guard was so infuriated by the majesty of his hat being outraged that he borrowed Mr. Wynne's

X.]   A SHOOTING EXPEDITION.   193

rifle, and, in the capacity of captain of militia, went "a shootin'," as he called it, that is, he joined the fight. The bullets of Mr. Wynne's rifle were conical, and one of them blew open a poor fellow's breast in such a style that the guard "traded" half a dozen bullets he had left at half a dollar a-piece, as he triumphantly informed his audience.

After a very short stay at Baltimore I went on to New York, and lodged at the Fifth Avenue Hotel, then vaunted throughout all Christendom for its magnificence. It put up a thousand beds, and fifteen hundred persons could, and did at times, sit down to dinner. This enormous block of building was constructed of polished white marble. The *cuisine* was excellent, and every possible convenience and amusement were to be found in it. Eleven shillings a day covered all expenses. It is now considered old-fashioned, and its day has gone by. I had excellent introductions in New York, and was inordinately feasted during the few days I stayed there; but I was bound to shoot with the young Mr. Rylands in the Illinois prairies, and started off, thinking nothing of the journey of fifteen hundred miles. I passed by beautiful Lake George and met my friends at Toronto, and, with them, started forth to the Illinois prairies. I forget the name of the station at which we were advised to stop. I remember that we arrived there at night, and, on asking at a small tavern, the only one in the hamlet, if we could have beds, we were told there were none vacant; however, they made up something for my friends the Rylands, and offered me the choice of the kitchen table or to share the room of the "School Marm" upstairs. I preferred the kitchen table.

Our shooting destination was about nine miles from the station. We hired a kind of butcher's cart, and were

O

told to drive straight to the "Lone Tree," and then to keep straight on, and retain the cart as long as we liked. We found the "Lone Tree" by the aid of a patent compass, and reached our destination, which was a log house in a grove of oaks. The master of the house had gone away, but the maid made us welcome, and stowed us away in her master's room and beds. When he returned he insisted on our staying where we were. We had capital butter and milk, fried pork for breakfast, and boiled beef and tea for dinner. No fermented liquor was allowed. The labouring men, about eight or ten, and ourselves all dined together. They were rough fellows enough, but most obliging. The weather was dreadful, and but for this we should have had the most marvellously fine shooting. Wild ducks of all kinds, and wild geese and prairie chickens were literally destroying acres of Indian corn which lay between two lakes. There was no need of a dog; we walked to and fro among the corn and put them up, or else shot them as rocketers flying over us. We brought back to Toronto a prodigious quantity and variety of game, which, being frozen, lasted our friends there during the whole winter till the following Easter. The owner came back the second day, a most excellent man, the very salt of the earth, I should say. He was from New England, very grave, very slow, very honest, and of strong religious views, and with a fine New England nasal twang; he was also well informed, and our evenings were pleasant enough in his society. It is usual on such occasions to pay for one's board, and on my proffering what would be the recognized amount for myself, two friends, and horse, he said in his slow, sententious way, "Not a cent from you, sir. I am amply paid by the company of a gentleman from the old country. I don't forget my father was a Yorkshireman.

If you wish to repay me, come again next year and stay a good long time with me." Such was the feeling everywhere.

The same reception awaited me in Baltimore. I had an old friend there, John Morris, a member of one of the principal families, and every house was open to me, every one anxious to make my stay pleasant. Well do I recall the merry suppers of roast oysters at the club, and the bright eyes of the pretty girls for which Baltimore is famous. It has given us a duchess (of Leeds) and a marchioness (Wellesley), and is about the most dangerous place a susceptible man can enter, for not only are the girls singularly beautiful, but they have the grace and sunniness of the South. Lucky is the man who departs heart whole! It is one of the most aristocratic towns in the Union, and the society is refined and polished; but, politically speaking, it was, thirty years ago, one of the most mob governed. The respectable portion of the community had retired in despair from political life, and violence and corruption carried the day. The judges, magistrates, ay, even the constables, were elected by universal suffrage; criminals virtually did as they pleased, under the ægis of rowdyism; and the decisions of the legal tribunals were notoriously influenced by bribery, or by a desire for popularity, as every four years the legal functionaries were re-elected. Human life was of as little value as that of a dog; no election took place (and they were constantly taking place) in which several persons were not shot, and a gang of rowdies called "plug-uglies" ruled the city. This association armed themselves with gimlets, or awls, which are fastened to the arm under the coat by an indiarubber band. They consequently fly up the sleeves when not held in the hand. These instruments they were in the habit of thrusting into the body of any

voter whom they considered to be opposed to them, and
the result was to deter every timid person from the ballot-
box. I find the following comments in a letter to my
mother from this place :—

"As for the ballot-box here it is a farce, every man's vote is
known, and corruption and intimidation are ten times worse than with
open voting. Matters are just as bad at New York, and in many of
the other large cities. The mob have got the upper hand, judges are
elected by them, many of them are notorious scamps, justice is a
mockery, all respectable men hold aloof from the jury box. It is now
occupied by professional jurymen, who attend for no other object
than bribes, and it was stated publicly to me before twenty persons
who all agreed that hardly a crime can be committed which may not
go unpunished if a proper distribution of money be made in the right
quarter. All this is the legitimate and immediate effect of universal
suffrage. I wish every member of our Parliament were forced to
travel through the United States, and to converse with men of all
classes in them, and, rely on it, he would modify many a democratic
opinion, and become apprehensive of extensive constitutional changes
at home. I have travelled a good deal in my life, and would rather
live under any of the despotic European Governments than here. As
for liberty, it is nonsense to use such a word. There is no such
tyranny as mob tyranny" (we have of late years seen its effect in
Ireland), " no such uncompromising and unrelenting master as the
party organization here. The greater proportion of the men of
refinement and sensitiveness in the Northern States have retired from
political life. The press is altogether different from ours. It is low,
abusive, vulgar, and declamatory, and not argumentative. No public
man is presumed to act on purely patriotic motives. We, at all
events, give both parties credit for occasional honesty. I have
touched on these topics briefly, perhaps crudely, but the *résumé*
is that I shall return to England with relief. But, having said this
much, I am bound to add that I have the strongest regard for
Americans, and always shall have. From them, high and low, I have
met with invariable civility ; as a general rule they are entirely free
from that inquisitive obtrusiveness of which they have been so
unjustly accused. Reserve and great self-possession is far more the
characteristic of every class. I have experienced a warmth of
hospitality and kindness from every one to whom I had introductions
which I never can forget, and, personally speaking, it is impossible
not to feel regard for such really fine fellows as these American
gentlemen. They are brave, off-hand, kind, cheerful, honourable

men, sensitive to a fault, but thoroughly sincere. My fault-finding is not with them, but with the tendency of the system under which they live, which lowers the tone of society, of education, and of ambition."*

I have inserted this long extract as my experience of America mainly influenced my course of conduct in regard to the Reform Bill, and, indeed, I may say, my future political career.

I betook myself at length to Washington, where I found everything in a perfect maelstrom of political excitement. There had been bitter bad blood before between the North and South; now the feeling on the part of the South had been roused to fury by the recent foray of John Brown on Harper's Ferry, and by the tone of the Republican section of the Northern press commenting on it. By Lord Lyons I was presented to President Buchanan—better known as "Old Buck"—and by General Breckenridge, the Vice-President, I had the honour of being made free of the floor of the Senate, and of taking a place and sitting, during the debate, among those distinguished politicians. I confess I was not struck with the debates, either in the Senate or in the House of Representatives. The fluency of the speakers was remarkable, but the object of every speaker seemed to be to play for the gallery, in other words, to speak for his constituents, and them only, and very long, washy orations they were. The city I thought detestable, and the Capitol equally so.

The night before I left Washington I was dining at the Southern mess, and a large party was invited of Southern friends. After dinner Mr. Mason, the Virginian Senator, said in very grave tones, "You are now going back to England, Mr. Gregory, and you will tell your friends that you are able to announce to them the

* To Mrs. Gregory, October 25, 1859.

disruption of this great Republic." "Indeed, Mr. Mason,"
I replied, "I shall do no such thing. I know well that
men, when excited, speak rashly and act rashly. But I
have great faith in American good sense and steadiness."
"Well, sir," said Mr. Mason, still more emphatically,
"what I say will turn out to be true." I then felt that
his language and demeanour were very serious, so I
turned to the company and said, "Now, gentlemen, may
I ask you, one after the other, if there were a document
lying at this moment in the Capitol embodying separation
from the North and the establishment of a Southern
Republic, would you sign it?" Each of them in turn,
except Mr. Hunter, said gravely, "I would!" Knowing
Mr. Hunter to be one of the most moderate, long-headed,
and universally respected of the Southern leaders, I turned
to him and remarked, "Mr. Hunter, you are silent."
"Yes, I am silent," he answered; "for though at present
I would not assume such a responsibility, yet, if a Republican President were elected, and if the document was
in the Capitol, I should claim my right as the senior Senator
of Virginia, to be the first man to put my name to it."

I returned to my hotel most amazed by the gravity
of this conversation, and that same night I wrote the
account of what had happened to Lord Palmerston.
When I met him in England he thanked me for my
letter, but he added laughingly, "You pay more heed to
American tall talk than I am disposed to do."

I find in a letter to my mother from New Orleans,
the following results of my journey from Richmond to
that place :—

"It was a long one of fourteen hundred miles, during which I
passed through North and South Carolina to Montgomery, in Alabama,
and thence I made my way three days and two nights down the
Alabama river to Mobile. I witnessed on the journey one of the

institutions of this free and enlightened country, namely, that of the tarring and feathering of an individual whose opinions were obnoxious to the majority of his fellow-citizens. At Columbia, the seat of government in South Carolina, a stonemason from Phila-delphia, on the strength of his earnings, indulged in too many cock-tails, and on the strength of them proclaimed his opinions to be in favour of the abolition of slavery. The chivalrous spirit of his fellow-tipplers would not stand any reflection on the 'peculiar institution,' and they haled him before the mayor. When sobriety returned he was ex-amined by that functionary, and he denied all remembrance of having said a word on the subject, but, being pressed if he was, in theory, favourable to emancipation he replied, ' Them's my sentiments, sartainly,' whereupon he was instantly handed over to the Vigilance Committee. They administered to him thirty-nine strokes of a cow-hide at the hands of a nigger, then stripped him naked and tarred and feathered him from head to foot. It was in this condition that I saw him. He had just arrived by the train in the hands of his executioners, and he was exhibited to me with that consideration which prompts them to exhibit to strangers every object calculated to excite their admiration or wonder. The man seemed in a dying state from ill-usage, and is probably dead, but they seemed hurt at my not enjoying the spectacle as much as the rest. I shall never forget the dreadful appearance of this wretched man. He seemed like a gigantic fowl covered with feathers and clotted tar—'put on pretty hot, too, I can tell yer,' said one of his guardians. He was crouched up in the corner of the van, and was poked up by a bystander's stick that I might fully enjoy the sight."

No wonder this dreadful scene aroused my strongest indignation, and I find the following in my next letter :—

" I am sorry not to be able to remain longer at New Orleans. My Christmas dinner I eat to-day with Dr. Mercer, a planter of great wealth, and a most agreeable, well-informed, polished old gentleman. The character of this town is quite French—in dress, appearance, everything. I have already made acquaintance with some of the Creole young ladies, families of pure blood, but of French and Spanish origin, and they are charming ; but it is a murderous, blood-stained city, not a night passes without assassinations. Every one goes armed to the teeth, and in the St. Charles Hotel, the best here, where I am putting up, eight men have met with violent deaths in the last four months. One man was shot down the night before I arrived. Still I like New Orleans and the people. The weather is warm and genial, and the citizens are like the weather."

At the Christmas dinner of Dr. Mercer, to which I
have referred, I was introduced to a most agreeable, handsome, black-whiskered, middle-aged man, the judge of
Baton Rouge, the capital of the State of Louisiana. Dr.
Mercer begged me to note him, and said he would tell
me an anecdote of him after he had gone. This judge
was a very pleasant *convive*, and as merry as a cricket,
and yet he had the recent blood of two men on his hands.
Only a short time previously he had considered it his
duty in court to speak in the strongest manner of the
dishonesty of an attorney practising before him. The
man was old, but had two grown-up sons who publicly
announced their intention of shooting down the judge
"at sight." This intention was notified in court to him,
and he was shown from the windows the two men waiting for him. The waggons, or, as we should call them,
buggies of suitors were drawn up at the door of the court.
Directly the judge appeared one of the brothers drew
out his five-shooter, and they fired at each other as they
dodged between the waggons. The judge brought his
man down stone dead with the last shot. Then the other
brother, who had kept aloof while the bullets were flying,
rushed in full confidence at the judge, knowing he had
discharged his last shot; but a provident friend stepped
in and handed him a shot-gun, with which he brought
the conflict to an end by killing his assailant. I hear
the acclamations of the citizens were tumultuous, remind-
ing one of Bon Gaultier's ballad, "The Alabama Judge"—

"They raised him with triumphant cheers : in him each loafer saw
  The bearing bold that could uphold the majesty of law.
  And raising him aloft they bore him homeward at his ease,
  That noble judge whose daring hand enforced his own decrees."

I heard of a narrow escape of a man I knew very
well, a certain Captain Campbell, of the 32nd, supposed

to be the best and craftiest billiard-player in England ;
in short, no one ever knew how good he was. Being of
a predatory nature, and a clever man withal, he won considerable sums at billiards and play, and especially in
the United States, through which he made a tour. He
came down to New Orleans, and was playing one night
in a huge, rickety, but very fashionable, gambling saloon,
at the favourite Southern game of monte. He had won
a very large sum, and had stowed away the notes, but
he had a considerable pile of gold and silver on the table.
He looked up and saw, from the glances of the ruffians
about him, that he had not the slightest chance of getting
home alive with his spoils. Like a man of decision he
made up his mind at once. He left his cash and his hat
on the table and asked his neighbour to look after them
while he, assigning some reason, went out for a minute.
He had hardly got to the bottom of the stairs when the
gamblers suspected the ruse and in a body made after
him, but they had to catch the fastest runner in England,
and he escaped with his life and his bank-notes to his
hotel. I asked him if the story was true. He said it
was, but that the best of it was omitted, namely, that
the gambling-room was upstairs, and supported by piles,
like many houses in New Orleans, resting on very insecure foundation. When the rush was made the stairs
and the saloon gave way, and the whole lot were pre-
cipitated to the bottom. There were a terrible amount
of contusions and broken limbs, and, he believed, some
deaths, which he regarded as a merciful dispensation of
a well-inclined Providence.

I left New Orleans with regret, though my heart was
always constant to Baltimore. It is amusing to read in
my home letters the dread I had of being forced to go
back from America by the Galway Line, and to encounter

bad fare, worse company, and still worse ships; but I
really think, had I started from the North, and not gone
home by one of these rickety vessels, I should have
incurred the lasting displeasure of Galway and of the
Rev. Peter Daly, so I determined to make my way by
Cuba, and found myself at Havannah early in the New
Year of 1860. The hotel to which I was commended
was one of the most abominable that can be well conceived—dirty and noisy and foul-smelling. I paid a visit
to our Consul, Mr. Crawfurd, and was lamenting my hard
fate when a gentleman came into the room whom I
thought I had seen before; and so I had, but not since
I had been at Harrow, where he was an upper boy when
I was a new-comer. He was introduced to me as Mr
Ryder; he was slave arbitrator, on a salary of £1500
a year, one of the Harrowby family, and brother-in-law
of Sir George Grey. In the kindest manner he insisted
on being my host; he said he had a nice house in the
Cerro, the most fashionable quarter, that his cook was
not bad, and that he had a particular tap of claret which
he could confidently recommend, and he carried me off
at once, bag and baggage, and fulfilled every inducement
he had held out. I liked a little of Havannah life. That
city was then in full swing of wealth and gaiety. My
great delight was to go to the Domenica, a famous
ice-shop, and see the Spanish beauties dashing in on
their *voläntes*, the postillions vying with each other in
sumptuousness of uniform. The *volänte* is a pretty
vehicle, like a gentleman's private cab, thrown back with
very long shafts, and drawn by two horses, one of them
in the shafts, the other running by the side. Nothing
could be more gorgeous than the harness and accoutre-
ments—silver everywhere, winding up with massive silver
stirrups. Generally there were three ladies in each,

one prominently forward in bodkin, but all dexterously managing their fans, and prepared to flirt like fury.

I had heard so much of the beauty of the interior of Cuba that I took a trip to Matanzas one Saturday to pass my Sunday there. The beauty of the place is quite remarkable, as is the fertility of the soil and the remarkable produce of sugar. I visited one sugar plantation which was worked by an American, and heard a great deal of the characteristics of the Chinese, who were employed in all work wherein accuracy and care are necessary. The owner praised them highly for intelligence and industry, but complained bitterly of their habit of forming secret associations. If any grave offence was committed on the estate, and any Chinaman was accused, each of his countrymen in turn came forward and confessed the act was done by him; if one was severely punished he hanged himself, and thereby the owner of the plantation incurred the loss of his advances and cost of importation. He gave many instances of their sturdy independence and maintenance of their rights. In their agreement their various duties were specified, and if a Chinaman was desired to do anything not within the four corners of the agreement he immediately pulled out his book and asked his master wherein the performance of that particular kind of work was specified. Still, on the whole, he regarded them as most valuable and intelligent servants, and easily led though impossible to drive. Matanzas is about thirty miles from Havannah, and as we approached it the stations were filled with *aldeanos*, peasant farmers, dressed in white, with white straw hats, the very pink of dandyism. Every stopping place resounded with the crowing of cocks, for every peasant had one either under his arm or tied to his leg. The next day there was to be a solemn and grand cock-fight at Matanzas, and all who could afford were to be in attendance. I received a formal invitation from the *alcalde* and *ayuntamento*, the mayor and corporation, to be present, and after Mass we all walked in great state, they in their robes, I in my Sunday best, to the cock-pit. It was a most extraordinary sight. The cocks were not armed with steel spurs, but fought with the weapons nature had given them, which made each battle rather long. The betting was very heavy in those fine large pieces, the *onzas*, representing nearly £4. During the fight the cries and shouting were loud: "Ten ounces to one on the Platero," the silver-coloured cock; "Five ounces to one on the Indian," the black cock, and so on— and the bets were all taken by motion of the fingers. When the fight was over there was a dead calm, and one heard the clink of the large pieces of gold as they passed from one to another. Some men had piles of them on the rails before them, heaped up one on the other like crumpets. The member of the corporation who sat by me, said, "I am not a better on cock-fights, though I delight in seeing them. Now let us have a small bet of a dollar on each fight. I will give you your choice when the cocks are produced." I accepted the offer and rose up the winner of one dollar, and highly elated at my judgment having been correct. The love of cock-fighting in many countries seems extraordinary to us of the present generation, but up to the end of last century it excited the greatest possible interest in England, and old pictures give the portraits of famous victorious cocks.

On my return to England, when stopping at St. Thomas, young Mr. Crawfurd, the son of our Consul, was on board, and he invited me to mount the hill and pay a visit to General Santa Anna, the old dictator of Mexico, a stout soldier in his day, with one leg, the other lost in the war.

He was in exile, but had a nice country place. All along his avenue were dog-boxes, but the inmates were cocks, not dogs, and they told us that any person who wished for a fight at any time had only to come up and name his stake. He was not kept a minute, for all other business was set aside for the battle. He offered to fight *a main* for our edification, but the steamer was puffing below, so we refused the offer, and reached Southampton, without any incident, just before the meeting of Parliament.

CHAPTER XI.

THE Committee on the British Museum was appointed in 1860, and the reference was to this effect :—

To inquire how far, and in what way it may be desirable to find increased space for the extension and arrangement of the various collections of the British Museum, and the best means of rendering them available for the promotion of science and art.

The Committee was a strong one, and I was appointed chairman. This arrangement imposed much labour on me, as I was but imperfectly acquainted with many of the questions which were to be considered, and had to learn them as the inquiry proceeded. I had also to settle with the witnesses the various topics on which they had to be examined. Among the witnesses were Professors Owen, Huxley, Bell, Sir Charles Eastlake, Sir Benjamin Brodie, Mr. Layard ; and the members of it were Sir P. Egerton Sir G. Grey, Mr. Gathorne Hardy (now Lord Cranbrook), Mr. Lowe, Mr. M. Milnes (Lord Houghton), Mr. Puller, Lord Stanley, Mr. Stirling, Mr. Walpole, Lord Elcho.

The main point of the inquiry was whether the natural history collections were to be removed elsewhere, or whether additional space was to be found on the ground contiguous to the present building. We commenced our sittings on the 3rd of June, and did not conclude our report till the 10th of August. The arguments in favour

of removal were—that visitors were bewildered by the vast
extent and variety of the collections ; that in no age or
country were such multifarious collections kept together ;
that if all the houses proposed to be taken for the increase
of the Museum were to be applied to its wants, present
and immediately prospective, the space thus acquired
would soon be filled up and fresh demands be made
involving immense expense ; that an extension of the
present site would involve far greater cost than a new
building elsewhere. On the other hand, a memorial of
114 of the most eminent men of science was presented in
1848, strongly opposing a separation of the collections,
among whom was Professor Owen, who was supposed to
have written the memorial with his own hand, but who
now was one of the prominent Separatists.   He grounded
his present advocacy of change on the necessity of having
a site of five acres if the new Natural History Museum
was to be of two stories, or of ten acres if of one, and he
actually advocated this preposterous proposal before the
Committee.

On the other hand, those whom I may call the
Unionists claimed for the present site the advantages
of its central position. They gave statistical proofs of the
far greater number of visitors resorting to the Natural
History Galleries than to the rest of the collections.
They liked the advantages of the connection with the
great library. They contended that though the cost of
the land at Kensington might be cheaper, yet that, considering the Museum must, under any circumstances, be
enlarged, this enlargement would suffice for the antiquities
as also for the natural history ; that a natural history
library would have to be purchased and kept up ; that the
expense of transfer would be very great ; and that the
opinions of the most eminent scientific men were in favour

208 SIR WILLIAM GREGORY. [Ch.

of typical, and not indiscriminate representation. These opinions prevailed in the Committee, which reported in favour of an enlargement of the present site, much to the annoyance of the Government, who were anxious to have Prince Albert's Kensington scheme carried out, and to that of Panizzi, who was bent on getting rid of the scientific men, with whom he had no sympathy—of whom, indeed, he had expressed himself with sovereign contempt. The Committee made several other excellent recommendations —that the drawings should be transferred to the National Gallery whenever there was space for them in Trafalgar Square; that the ethnographical collections should be removed elsewhere; and that lectures should, when practicable, be given on the Museum collections. Not one of these recommendations was ever carried out, Mr. Gladstone having made up his mind that, though he could not oppose the appointment of the Committee, he could easily set at naught its report. I have been accused of being an Obstructionist, because I pertinaciously resisted the removal of the natural history collections; but if I was wrong I erred in company with the large majority of literary and scientific men of the time, and I certainly may take the credit to myself of having forced the Government to provide a proper structure for them, instead of stowing them away in the disused sheds of the Exhibition of 1862, to which Mr. Gladstone endeavoured to consign them. But I believe I never was adverse to a separate Natural History Museum. I had a grand idea of turning the present British Museum into what would have been the finest and most scientifically arranged Museum in the world. When I say, "I had the idea," I should have said that I adopted the grand idea of Mr. Layard to have one great Central Hall for Antiquities. The visitor would enter at the earliest period, the Egyptian, and then

proceed through Assyria and Greece to Rome.   In this
great hall the largest sculptures would be arranged, and
running out of it at right angles would have been rooms
for smaller objects.   The large hall would have been the
vertebræ of the building, the smaller rooms the bones
connected with the vertebræ.   The upper story would
have been exclusively devoted to the lighter objects of
natural history.   This grand idea might have been
carried out if extension on the present site had been
accepted by the Government.   As it was not, the next
best thing has been done, namely, the erection of the
present sightly, but by no means faultless, museum at
South Kensington, which would have had a far more
imposing appearance had it been raised, instead of
being sunk in a gravel-pit; but Mr. Ayrton, the then
First Commissioner of Works, for the sake of saving
£15,000, allowed this great wrong on posterity to be
perpetrated.

In May of this year, 1860, I made the first speech
which brought me to the front in Parliament.   It was on
"The Representation of the People Bill."   A new Reform
Bill had been introduced, in 1852, by Lord J. Russell, more
from electioneering motives, as was at that time un-
charitably supposed, than from any desire of the country
for fresh constitutional changes.   It was, however, revived,
and became, in spite of Lord Palmerston's ill-disguised
aversion to it, one of the "planks of the Liberal platform,"
to use an American expression recently adopted.   The
House of Commons was by no means well disposed to it,
and I, having recently returned from America, where I had
seen the evils of democracy, was as anxious as were the
majority, in their hearts, to delay the passing of the
measure, or, at all events, to make the change as little
violent as possible.   Much of my speech, which I had

P

carefully prepared, was illustrative of the evils resulting from the preponderating power of the masses in the United States.

1861.

I began the session with a short speech backing up General Peel in urging the Government to do all they could to clear up the uncertainty which prevailed as to the fate of Captain Brabazon. He was a young and most promising officer who was taken prisoner by the Chinese when we were advancing to Pekin. His father was a friend of mine, and was broken-hearted for his son, who was the pride of the family. Nothing authentic was ever heard of him, but rumour, which I fear was true, had it that he was first tortured and then decapitated by the Chinese. I also spoke on art questions, and at some length on the British Museum, advocating Professor Huxley's view of restricted exhibition against the scheme of Professor Owen, demanding a building large enough to cover ten acres. This speech was very well received.

I had the immense satisfaction of throwing open Glasnevin Gardens to the public on Sundays. These gardens were under the management and direction of the Royal Dublin Society, which received from the Government annually a sum of money for their sustentation. The members of the Royal Dublin Society availed themselves of the pleasant privacy of these gardens on Sunday, and thought it no sin to go there with their wives and their little ones, but they protested most vehemently against their being thrown open to the public, as a clear violation of the sabbath. They said the citizens of Dublin had many other pleasant walks, and specified the shady sides of the canals. They insisted on it that the gardens would be a scene of drunken riot, the flowers pulled up, and the flower-

beds trampled down. I presented a petition for opening
from 16,500 persons, including five judges, nine hundred
professional men, and 2740 voters. The corporation of
Dublin and the police magistrates were also favourable,
and I moved that the vote for Glasnevin should be struck
out of the estimates. The House was clearly with me, and
Mr. Lowe, to his credit be it said, on the part of the Government, pledged himself not to propose any money grant
till the gardens were thrown open after divine service on
Sundays. The Dublin Society had to yield, and I had the
gratification of running over to see the effects of my motion
a few Sundays afterwards. There was an immense crowd,
but the greatest order and good humour prevailed, and I
did not see one drunken man. At the end of the year I
wrote to the curator, Dr. Moore, as to the conduct of the
Sunday visitors. He said the attendance was immense,
and the conduct of the visitors most exemplary. No
flowers were stolen, the beds were not trampled on, and
only one flower-pot was broken by the voluminous crino-
line of a young lady. I also wrote to the police magistrate
of the district, asking him if the predicted increase of
drunkenness had taken place. He replied, sending me the
statistics of his court, showing that drunkenness had
greatly fallen off, and that the Dublin folks, instead of
resorting to the Glasnevin public-houses as they used to do,
went to the gardens and enjoyed themselves there together
with their families, and returned home in peace and quiet ;
and such, I am convinced, would be the tendency if all
our public museums and galleries were thrown open on
Sundays.

A matter arose in this session of much importance to
my constituents, and the part I took gave me general
popularity of a very legitimate character in the county,
and unbounded popularity in the town of Galway. In 1859,

under the *régime* of Lord Eglinton, a contract was sanctioned with the Atlantic Company, subsidizing a line of steamships direct to America. I do not remember any one act of any Government which was so well received. Although a Tory, Lord Eglinton's name has always since been held in honour in Ireland. It was considered, very rightly, that this was an attempt to improve the condition of the country, and to introduce capital, and that the Government, by its action, had brought down on it the wrath of Liverpool and Glasgow. Unfortunately, the company was got up by men of straw, and its ostensible principal was a Mr. Lever, who, on the strength of it, was elected member for Galway. The Galway constituency has been roundly abused for electing such a man as its member. I cannot join in that reproach. Galway was led to believe that the establishment of a company communicating directly with America would be the means of promoting extensive business and employment. They saw the ships ; they believed Father Peter Daly's panegyric on Mr. Lever, and, discarding abstract politics, they very wisely and properly voted for the man who would, as they thought, materially improve their condition ; and the town of Galway has always had a strong Tory tendency since Lord Eglinton's days. But, as I said before, the contract had fallen into the hands of men of straw, who did not possess the requisite capital. The ships were bad ; the terms of the contract were not observed ; fine after fine was imposed by the Post Office for delay in transport of mails, and at last Lord Stanley of Alderley, the Postmaster-General of Lord Palmerston, closed the contract.

The outcry on the part of the Irish members was loud, and Father Daly came over to London to rouse them to action. The vote on the paper duties was about to be taken, and it was supposed the division would be a close one.

With great want of judgment, and totally unauthorized, Father Peter Daly menaced the Government with the opposition of their Irish Liberal supporters, unless the subsidy to the Atlantic Company was restored. This took place at an interview with Lord Palmerston, which Lord Palmerston reported to Lord J. Russell, who in a speech made use of expressions extremely offensive to the Irish Liberal members. "Better," said he, "that a hundred ministries should be overthrown, better that a hundred dissolutions should take place, rather than that any Government should submit to such dictation." I made a very vigorous speech in reply to this accusation, showing that it was absolutely unfounded, that we had not made any endeavour to extort a promise from the Prime Minister in regard to a restoration of the subsidy, or, as it was hinted, that we had opened any negotiations with the Conservatives, and I appealed to Lord Naas, the previous Irish Secretary, to confirm my statement, which he did, and undoubtedly turned the tables on Lord J. Russell, whom I accused of "simulated indignation." A little later on in the session I moved for a Committee to inquire into the circumstances which had led to the discontinuance of the subsidy, in a speech on which I was warmly congratulated by William Forster, Cobden, and Bright. I was well backed up by the Irish members, and Lord Palmerston, with his usual good sense, gave way and sanctioned the Committee, much to the discomfiture of some of the Scotch members, who were bitterly opposed to it. The Committee, a very fair one, was appointed, and I was the chairman. The result of the Committee was very satisfactory to me. I carried my report, which, while it justified the action of the Postmaster-General, also recorded the opinion "that the Atlantic Packet Company was deserving of the favourable consideration of her Majesty's

Government." Upon this the subsidy was restored, and another trial was given; but so hopelessly insolvent was the company that it soon broke down, and poor Galway's last state was worse than the first. Still, the citizens were ever very grateful to me for having fought a good battle in their interest, and I am quite sure the mob would have broken the heads of any supporters of a rival candidate, should any such have presented himself during my Parliamentary career.

William Forster entered Parliament as member for Bradford in the preceding year. He was a strangely uncouth, large-limbed man, always reclining on his bench in the most grotesque attitudes. His manners, too, were as little cultivated as his appearance; but for all that he almost immediately made his way to the front. Though his speeches were rugged, and at first got out with hesitation, one recognized at once their strength and the honesty of his convictions. My friend Michael Morris, now Chief Justice of Ireland, came one evening and sat under the Gallery. "Look at that uncouth member," I said to him, "with his limbs stretched out all over the floor. Mark my words, he is going to be one of the foremost men ere long in the House of Commons." He has often reminded me of this prophecy. We were almost immediately in fierce antagonism to each other. The one great feeling uppermost in his mind was hatred of slavery. He had inherited it from his father and his Quaker surroundings, and when civil war broke out in America he threw himself heart and soul into the cause of the Northern side, and undoubtedly exercised a most potent influence in the House of Commons in resisting the tendency that prevailed to aid indirectly, if not directly, the Southern Confederacy. The feeling of the upper classes undoubtedly preponderated in favour of the South, so much so that when I said in a

speech that the adherents of the North in the House of
Commons might all be driven home in one omnibus, the
remark was received with much cheering. But, on the
other hand, dislike to slavery, and an impression that
the South represented an aristocracy, turned the balance
towards the North among the manufacturing classes, and
the Lancashire cotton-spinning operatives, though exposed
to terrible privations, and though tempted by the prospect
of abundant cotton if the South prevailed, never faltered
on this question. I took up the Southern side warmly.
I firmly believed that if the Southern Republic were
established slavery must within no long period disappear.
To hold slaves within even a considerable distance of the
frontier would have been impossible. The territory would
become populated by free settlers, and so again the slave
zone would be thrown back. Slave tillage, moreover, had
been always so careless and exhausting that fresh tracts
would have been constantly required, but that expansion
would have been denied to the slave-holding States.
There was, therefore, the certainty that arrangements
must have been made for the gradual manumission of the
slaves, if the Southern Confederacy was established. On
the other hand, the Democratic party in the North always
stood up for slavery, and I found no more resolute
defenders of the system than the New York merchants.
Lincoln's celebrated saying is well known: "The Union
must be preserved—if without slavery, well and good; if
with slavery, well and good also." It was not till a far
later period, when the North hoped to incite insurrection in
the South, that abolition was proclaimed. In short, had
a peace been made at the beginning of the war, slavery
would have been stereotyped in America without a hope
of future emancipation. This was the view taken by some
of the most humane men in England, Lord Shaftesbury

among them.   No man was more eager than he was
for the success of the South, and on the sole account of
slavery.   I have by me a slip of paper sent to me at Spa,
in the summer of 1862, by Lord Shaftesbury, in return for
the *Times*, giving an account of one of Lee's great victories.
" What glorious news ! " is written on it.   There were other
reasons, also, which influenced me.   The Southerners were,
as producers of the raw material, devoted Free-traders, and
entirely opposed to the Northern protective system.   Their
ardent desire was to establish unrestrained intercourse
with England, and a magnificent market would thus have
been opened to us.   Again, as we know to our cost, Irish
influence is so powerful in the North that we have been,
to secure the Irish vote, subjected to affronts which the
enormous power of the United States enabled them to
inflict with impunity.   But things would have been very
different with a Southern Republic on their frontier,
closely allied to us.   There would have been no raids on
Canada, no filibustering seizure of islands like that of
St. Juan, no insolent dismissal of our Ministers.   Such
were my reasons, and I never since have had a misgiving,
though I espoused the defeated cause, that I acted wrongly
in so doing.

1862.

The seizure of Messrs. Mason and Slidell from the
British steam packet *Trent* occurred after Parliament was
prorogued in the previous year.   It had caused considerable irritation in England, and had made the opinion of
the upper classes more than ever favourable to the South.
I thought the time was propitious to advert to the undoubted laxity of the blockade of the Southern ports.
The maxim of international law that "blockades to be
legitimate must be efficacious," was not, in my opinion,

maintained. I quoted a statement I had received from the Southern delegates that four hundred vessels had successfully run the blockade, and I cited M. de Hauptville, a well-known French writer who had recently denounced the inefficiency of the blockade as being notorious, and who informed his countrymen that our tolerance of this inefficiency was due to our usual perfidious conduct, that we might cite the laxity of this blockade if hereafter we were involved in hostilities and had resorted to this mode of warfare. The American view of blockades was quite as stringent, and in my opinion the law as laid down by Judge Kent exactly applied to this case. "The occasional absence of a squadron does not suspend a blockade, but if the blockade be raised by the enemy, or by the employment of the naval force or part of it, though only for a time, to other objects, or by the mere remissness of the cruisers, the commerce of neutrals ought to go free." Judge Kent described a state of things constantly occurring off the Southern ports. William Forster greatly distinguished himself by his reply. He fully admitted the correctness of the general principles I had laid down, but contended that the lists of successful blockade-runners furnished to me by the Southern delegates was entirely incorrect, and that the blockade was quite sufficiently stringent as to be in accordance with the demands of international law. I was supported by Lord Robert Cecil, now Lord Salisbury, and by other influential members, but it was not considered advisable to press the motion to a vote.

Later on I made a vehement speech on General Butler's infamous proclamation at New Orleans, that "any women calling themselves ladies in that city, and showing contempt by word or movement for a Northern soldier, should be held liable to be treated as a woman of the town pursuing her avocation." This proclamation, which has gained for the general the well-deserved sobriquet of "Black Butler," was denounced as heartily by Lord Palmerston as by myself, and did not find one apologist in the House of Commons.

Towards the close of the session the American question again came on. Mr. Lindsay, a large ship-owner, made a speech in favour of offering mediation between the Northern and Southern States. I spoke also at length, and amused the House by opening my speech with the remark that "Four months ago a prophet had arisen among us and had prophesied that within ninety days the Civil War would probably be at an end, and that the prophet was the Secretary for Foreign Affairs, Lord J. Russell. This proved that it was better to prophesy after events than before." It was clear the Government had quite underrated the pertinacity of the conflict, and they were bound to ascertain if no means of restoring peace could be devised. France was disposed to act cordially with us. She was suffering as much as we were from the cotton famine, and she had the additional disadvantage that not a bale of cotton could be obtained by her except from England. I then rather diverged to the question of recognition of the Southern Confederacy. I showed that the American principle was always to recognize any Government that had the semblance of stability. Mr. Buchanan, when Minister of Foreign Affairs, boasted, in 1848, that "so anxious were the United States to recognize *de facto* Governments, that the Pope, the Emperor Nicholas, and President Jackson were the only authorities on earth who recognized Don Miguel in Portugal."

In 1849 Mr. Clayton, Minister for Foreign Affairs at Washington, sent an emissary to Hungary to take the earliest opportunity of recognizing the insurgent Government wherever it could be found, and, in reply to Austrian

reclamations, Daniel Webster wrote his celebrated letter
in which he declared American policy: "It is not to be
required by neutral powers that they should await the
recognition of the new Government by the *parent State.*"
These words were a clear recognition of the right of
secession. I then cited our own action in the case of
Greece, Belgium, and the South American Republic, the
only difference being that there was no danger in recognizing them, as they had seceded from weak States of
whose anger we had no fear. But the strongest case was
that of Texas. We were in amity with Mexico, but we
did not hesitate to recognize the flag of the " Lone Star,"
though Texas had only a population of 60,000. The
South, however, had a population of 8,800,000, perfectly
consentient, an established government, and no hostile
force in their territory. Lord Palmerston opposed the
motion by taking a very sensible view of the matter—that
the South had not asked for mediation, and that the
North would undoubtedly reject it with indignation—and
Mr. Lindsay withdrew his motion.

On the Science and Art estimates, Lord Henry Lennox
made a very able and well-considered speech on the
confusion which existed as regards the responsibility
attached to the administration of our Science and Art
institutions. The Secretary of the Treasury was answerable for some estimates, the Commissioner of Works for
others ; the British Museum estimates were moved by a
Trustee. The Trustees of the British Museum were a
curious and cumbrous Board, some elected, some hereditary,
some *ex officio.* I seconded the motion, advocating that
one member of the Government should be responsible for
all these institutions, and commented strongly on the
unsatisfactory state of things at the British Museum,
where the official Trustees, who had not taken the slightest

part in the management, came down and overrode without
scruple the committees of the Board, who had carefully
studied and were perfectly cognizant of every question
brought before them.   I had a very great triumph over the
Government shortly after this discussion.   The Chancellor
of the Exchequer moved the transfer of the natural history
collection to Kensington, chiefly on the ground of economy.
It will be remembered that the report of my Committee
was unfavourable to this transfer.   I resisted the bill:
first, on the ground of the central position of the Museum;
second, on the popularity of the natural history collections
among the working classes, and the difficulty of access to
them at Kensington; third, that the change would only
result in the patchwork of the present building, instead of
in the acceptance of a complete and indelible plan for the
housing both of antiquities and of natural history collections; and, lastly, I went closely into the calculations of
expense, and proved that no saving would be effected by
the proposed measure.   The House went entirely with me,
and rejected the bill by the immense majority of ninety-
two.

I spoke also on the subject of iron-plated ships, and
on the lesson taught us by the recent encounter between
the *Minotaur* and *Merrimac*, and seconded a motion of Sir
F. Smith's against a large expenditure on fortifications
instead of on the far more useful defences of ironclad
vessels.   I did not forget my own country.   I spoke on
Irish distress, advocating loans for tramways and drainage,
but strongly deprecated almsgiving, which has always done
us serious mischief.   In the Poor Relief Bill I took the
opportunity of recommending that in all cases where it
was proposed to visit a Roman Catholic chaplain with
reprehension or punishment an application should first be
made to the bishop of his diocese who had virtually

appointed him. Nothing came of the proposal, but it gave much satisfaction to my ecclesiastical supporters, and I was really anxious for the recommendation being acted on. We owed something to them for the wanton affront and indignity of the Ecclesiastical Titles Act; it was eminently for the good of the State that their relations should, if possible, be made cordial with the Government.

1863.

Inspired by my success in obtaining the opening of the Irish, I made a similar foray on the Edinburgh Botanical Gardens, which was a far tougher job. I presented a petition of 35,000 working men of Edinburgh in favour of opening. My opponents produced a counter-petition signed by 63,000 against opening. I was furnished with statements that the mode of getting up this petition was scandalous, children in schools were obliged to sign it, and instances were sent to me of girls having been dismissed from their schools because they refused to sign in obedience to their parents. The Scottish clergy were all in a blaze, and did not mince matters. The Rev. Dr. Begg made a speech, saying, "It was a painful thing to have the Scotch sabbath interfered with by the representative of an Irish Papist constituency, one of the most degraded communities in the world." I quoted the good effects of opening Glasnevin—the general happiness it gave, the exemplary conduct of the visitors, and the statistics that proved the diminution of drunkenness in a great degree, and I was manfully supported by Wm. Stirling Maxwell and Mr. Grant Duff. Lord Palmerston stated that personally he was in favour of my motion, so far as its merits went; but, as he considered that the bulk of Scotch feeling was opposed to it, he could not support it, and it was beaten by only sixteen. There was a Queen's

ball that night, and on looking over the list of the members
present at it, I found that there were more than sixteen
who would have voted with me, for they told me so afterwards, and there were none of the opposite opinion.

Our unfortunate Galway contract was again on the
tapis. Mr. Baxter, the member for Montrose, moved a
resolution against the renewal of it, which was rather
shamelessly seconded by Mr. Horsfall, the member for
Liverpool. I did my best for the unfortunate contract,
which had been granted a new lease of life in consequence
of the report of my Committee, and Lord Palmerston
opposed Mr. Baxter, whose motion was defeated by a
majority of sixty-three.

I advocated a grant towards the monument of Prince
Albert, and paid an ample, though not over-strained,
tribute to the memory of that excellent prince. I heard
that her Majesty expressed herself greatly pleased with
these very honest remarks.

I made a speech on Irish distress, on Colonel Dunne's
motion for a Committee of Inquiry into the subject, and
commented, somewhat to his annoyance, on Mr. Gladstone's expression that the Government could not send
down a local shower of wealth on a particular part of the
community. " I did not ask for this," I said, " but I did
complain that Ireland, like the fleece in the Bible, remained
dry, while everything else around was saturated with the
dew of Government benevolence."

In this session Lord Palmerston made and carried a
proposal which ultimately led to a terrible humiliation of
the Government, and to a perfect rebellion of the House
of Commons. It was to purchase from the Commissioners
of the Exhibition of 1851 certain lands and buildings—
in fact, the site of the Exhibition of 1862. I opposed
the vote, as it was clearly intended, if it were successful,

to purchase the whole of the buildings from the contractors, and to patch up those hideous structures for
the reception of the natural history collections from
Bloomsbury. I gave a full account of the bad condition
of these buildings—their unfitness, unsightliness, unsuita-
bility, etc.—and I quoted, largely from the report of Mr.
Mallet, an extremely able civil engineer, a most unfavourable account of them. He showed that this part must
be pulled down and rebuilt, another part strengthened,
another added, and so on, and I excited much laughter
by saying, " Let us suppose I had a carriage of light and
delicate materials, for which some years ago I had given
£200, and that I said to a friend, going to travel on the
Continent, ' Here is my carriage, it will just suit you while
you are abroad ; you can have it for £50. It is the best
bargain in the world. It cost me four times that sum.'
But my friend might say, ' I want something more sub-
stantial for my purpose,' and to that remark, if I should
reply, ' Well, even so, if you put a new body to it, and
new wheels and new springs, you will find the pole in
capital order, and to do all these repairs will only cost
£150,' I think he would answer, ' It would be better for
me to have a new carriage altogether ;' and this would be
an exactly parallel case with these buildings."

Mr. Gladstone, in an angry speech, quite lost his
temper, abused Mr. Mallet, and denounced my opposition.
The House adopted Lord Palmerston's proposal, as the
bargain offered to the Government of the land by the
Commissioners was really an excellent one. However,
my turn had to come, and it came with a vengeance. Lord
Elcho and other members and myself determined to await
the proposals which must follow this purchase, and in July
Mr. Gladstone brought forward a motion that a sum, not
exceeding £105,000, to purchase existing buildings at

Kensington Gore from the contractors of the Exhibition of 1862, and for repairing and altering and eventually completing said buildings, be voted by the House of Commons. He began by an attack on Mr. Mallet, whom he not only made little of as a civil engineer, but whom he ridiculed as having written a book on earthquakes, and on having constructed a huge and useless mortar gun. He was unable to deny that a great part of the buildings were for merely temporary purposes, and would have to be entirely rebuilt. He made little of the Society of Architects, who had protested against the monstrous proposal of this huge range of ungainly stucco, and spoke of Mr. Fergusson as not being any authority, but a mere writer of an ingenious book on architecture. He then proceeded, amid general murmurs, to argue that there was no stipulation whatever, of a written or specific character, which bound the contractors to remove the building within a given time, or indeed to remove it at all. I vindicated Mr. Mallet, and proved him not only from general reputation, but from his well-known works, to be an engineer of authority. If he had written a work on earthquakes, it was one which by its ability had attracted general notice, and I did not criticize Mr. Gladstone because he had written three volumes on Homeric studies, and because he had delivered in Wales a lecture on the "Volunteer System and Military Tactics." I inveighed strongly against the use of stucco in our public buildings, as being mean and disreputable, though it might be the Credo of the Kensington School of Architecture. I then turned to Mr. Gladstone's statement as to the power of the contractors to leave the buildings on the land if they pleased. If the Government were ignorant of the position of the contractors when they recently purchased the land, great and culpable was their ignorance ; if they were aware of it, they had practised in the House of Commons a palpable deception, and, having beguiled it into a bad bargain, they then turned round and said, "'You have made your purchase and cannot get out of it. The best thing you can now do is to throw more good money after bad.' These are the horns of the dilemma on which I place the Right Honourable gentleman, and I wish him joy of them." Then broke loose the indignation of the House. Sir Stafford North-cote, usually so popular with both sides, tried to come to the aid of the Government, but could get no hearing. Mr. Lowe was instantly cried down. Mr. Disraeli attempted to allay the storm by proposing to submit the question to a Select Committee, which evoked a fresh outburst of fury. The *Times* thus describes what occurred :—

"The scene of confusion and uproar which followed Sir S. North-cote and Mr. Lowe was almost unexampled in Parliamentary experi-ence. Mr. Disraeli rose to address the House and was received with loud groans and cries of 'Divide' from the Opposition, not less than from the other side of the House. After endeavouring for two or three minutes to make himself heard, the Right Honourable gentleman resumed his seat."

Mr. Henley then got up, and was well received, for his opening sentences showed that he was opposed to the project, and his high character for independence and sagacity carried great weight with it. He condemned it sternly and emphatically. Mr. Gladstone wound up the debate, evidently cowed, in a very feeble speech, and the vote was then taken. Amid the most tumultuous cheering the tellers announced that the Government was beaten by the immense majority of 166. Directly after the division I went to the buffet in the lobby, and there met Mr. Glad-stone. He was in a state of compressed fury, and said to me, " I can tell you, you shall never have any other Natural History Museum." I replied, " That is a matter

for the country. It does not concern me." But we have
got a very fine one, and I take no small pride in the
prominent part I played in eventually securing it.

In this session I began the course of conduct which
I pursued unremittingly while in Parliament, of endeavouring to remove the Turkish yoke from the Christian nationalities of Eastern Europe. I advocated the strengthening
of Greece, the union of the Roumanian principalities, the
departure of the Turkish garrisons from Servia.* I always
held, and rightly held, that the misgovernment of Turkey
was the cause of the influence of Russia among the
Eastern Slavs. Their only hope of escaping from the
bondage of the Turk was to throw themselves into the arms
of Russia. She was apparently their only friend. English
policy had been stereotyped by always supporting what
our diplomatists called our "old natural allies" the Turks,
and every effort of these nationalities in favour of self-
government was looked upon by our Foreign Office as the
effect of Russian intrigues or of dangerous revolutionists.
My theory was that Russian preponderance could only
be met by our encouraging these efforts, and by inducing
the nationalities to place confidence in our honest desire
to raise them from the abject condition into which they
had fallen by the infamous misgovernment of Turkey.
I said, Give them independence and you will find them the
best breastwork against Russian domination; keep them
oppressed and miserable, and you will ever find them
zealous and powerful allies to Russia in her advance
towards Constantinople. As to Turkish promises of reform,
we had had plenty of experience of their futility. They
could not reform if they wished. They were ignorant,

---

* In 1884 he received the Grand Cross of the Order of Takovo
from the King of Servia, as a mark of gratitude for help to that
country in bygone days —A. G.

fanatical, corrupt to the heart's core, and their continuance as a sovereign power in Europe depended solely on the mutual jealousies of the European States. But, I added, it was not for us to prop up this state of rottenness by keeping in bondage to it young nations from whose energy and love of freedom we might expect fresh life in those regions ; and I think all my prognostications and the correctness of my views have been justified by the prosperity of Greece and Servia and the astonishing advance of Bulgaria. But I regret to say in these opinions I found in Mr. Layard, the then Under Secretary for Foreign Affairs, and a most able man, a most determined antagonism. He was for the Turks *à tout prix.* No words could be more contemptuous than his as regards these " mongrel " nationalities, as he called them. He denied them any elements of stability, attributed their discontent to agitators, and fearlessly maintained the traditions, now happily exploded, of the Foreign Office· The Turk was to be upheld, no matter at what cost, and the appeals of these suffering peoples were to be utterly disregarded, as it was for our interests that they should bear their oppressions without hope. In spite of our warm conflicts in the House, I am glad to state that there never arose a cloud over our intimate and friendly relations, happily maintained unchanged until this day.

Later on I made a very long speech on the condition of Turkey, and on the fatal effect of our policy in supporting its iniquitous government. The debate was extremely interesting, and the views I expressed received the cordial support of Mr. Cobden. When the debate was over he waited outside and said to me, " You have done well to open men's eyes to our unjust and dangerous policy. Do not lose sight of the subject. Return to it

again. Sooner or later the country will get hold of right
views. It may not be in my lifetime, but let my mantle
fall upon you."

The debate was well supported on my side by Grant
Duff, Alfred Seymour, Lord Henry Scott, and finally by
Cobden, who made a long and very powerful speech,
chiefly going into the question of Ottoman finance, of the
soundness of which he drew very different conclusions
from those of Layard, and certainly far more correct.
The debate was wound up by Mr. Gladstone, in the
absence of Lord Palmerston, who had a fit of the gout,
in about as curious a speech as I ever heard. I knew
that in his heart he was favourable to everything I had
advanced, but the old stereotyped policy of successive
English Governments was upheld by the Cabinet, and he
was bound to do his best for it. I remember at the time
listening to his speech, of considerable length, with much
attention and not deriving one idea from it, and on reading
it over again now I will defy any one to discover any
definite opinion.

In the autumn of this year I determined to pay a visit
to Servia, where I was promised a warm reception from
the Prince, and I had made all preparations for winter and
rough weather, but, happening to meet Mr. J. C. Robinson
of the Kensington Museum, he earnestly recommended
me to change my plans and to accompany him to Spain,
through which he was commissioned to travel and to
procure objects of art for the Kensington Museum. He
intended to visit every town of importance and thoroughly
to ransack each. I could not help closing with his
invitation, and we started for Spain. Our first experiences
began at Burgos, and were amusing enough. We could
neither of us at the time speak one word of Spanish,
and we had at first to employ the services of a girl, a

relation of the interpreter. She was a comely little lass, and had been brought up at a nunnery in France ; but, as her company and good looks were somewhat com-promising, we found a substitute in a Spanish smuggler who spoke French and did his business with zeal and efficiency. We went thence to Valladolid and on to Madrid, where I first learned to appreciate the unrivalled grandeur of Velasquez, and where we received unbounded kindness and assistance from my old friend Sir John Crampton. We thence went to Cordova, Seville, Cadiz, Malaga, and Granada, and returned to Malaga, where I took ship and went to Cartagena and on to Murcia ; Mr. Robinson, who hated the sea, went by land—a difficult, rough, and somewhat dangerous journey. From Murcia we made our way to Valencia, Barcelona, Saragoza, and again to Madrid ; and from Madrid we made a most interesting journey to Salamanca, Astorga, Zamora, and Leon, and thence returned home. At Salamanca I saw a great deal of the Irish College of young men being educated as priests under a most polished and kind superior, Dr. Macaulay, and I had an opportunity of settling down as proprietor of a large and thriving farm which the family had held since the days of Ferdinand and Isabella. Old Don Balthazar, the owner of it, a hale and hearty and opulent old gentleman, had taken under his special protection the Irish College, and loaded the students with good things from his farm. He thought, probably with reason, that there was no people to be compared to the Irish, and took a particular fancy to me when he heard I was from that country. One morning Dr. Macaulay came to me with a grave face, full of import. He said, " I have a proposal of marriage for you. Don Balthazar desires me to offer you the hand of his extremely pretty daughter Manuelita, and the reversion

of his farm with a large accumulation of cash in gold—
'be sure to say in gold.'" Dr. Macaulay objected that
I was a heretic. "Oh no," said Don Balthazar, "no
Irishman is a heretic, and, even if he were, Manuelita
will soon cure him of his heresy." But I was obliged
to refuse. Poor old Don Balthazar said no more, but
clasped my hand with tears in his eyes when I was
departing.

CHAPTER XII.

1864.

I BEGAN the session with a passage of arms encounter-
ing my friend Sir Robert Peel, then Secretary for Ireland.
I moved for a report of Dr. Brodie, the Poor Law
Inspector, on the condition of the estates of the Law Life
Company in Connemara. This was refused by Sir
Robert Peel, but on my threatening to state the contents
of the report, leaving my accuracy [to be impugned, Sir
George Grey, the Home Secretary, a director of the
society, gave way, and the papers were granted. I was
well acquainted with this part of the West of Ireland.
During the time it had belonged to the Martin family the
tenants on this vast estate had been treated with consideration and kindness. It was greatly encumbered, but
still Mr. Martin had always dealt with his tenants as
if they were all members of the same family, and he and
his daughter and heiress were much beloved by them.
But when the famine times came on Mr. Martin was
unable to keep down the interest of the large sum he owed
the Law Life Society, and the whole estate, which had
devolved into the hands of Miss Martin, was taken over
by the society for the debt, and Miss Martin was left
virtually a pauper. A new *régime* was established—the
rents raised ; the rights of pasture over large tracts of
mountain land were taken from the small tenants and

handed over to large farmers. The sale of turf was restricted by a rent being put upon the turbary, which had previously been free. I never missed an opportunity of attacking the management of these estates by the Law Life Company, and I believe I was mainly instrumental in forcing them at last to part with the property. But the same agent was continued, the same system pursued, though not so scandalously, and I much fear that the tenants gained but little by the change.

Mr. Herbert, the painter, was dissatisfied with the terms of payment for his celebrated picture of Moses coming down from Mount Sinai. His original agreement was to paint it in fresco, but, owing to the failures of other frescoes in the Houses of Parliament, it was considered advisable to try a new system, that of water glass, which it was supposed would be durable. Mr. Herbert having had his arrangements completely altered, and additional labour imposed on him, applied for some extra remuneration. After some discussion, which I brought on, and in which I expressed opinions of my great admiration of Mr. Herbert's work, expressions which I would not now repeat, Mr. Gladstone sanctioned a Commission to inquire into the matter. They reported favourably to Mr. Herbert, and he got his money.

In this session I moved for a Committee of Inquiry into the condition of the scientific societies of Dublin. A Treasury Committee had been appointed with the same object, and its tendency was to merge all Irish scientific institutions in the Royal Dublin Society. An extremely angry feeling sprang up in Dublin in consequence. The Royal Dublin Society was by no means popular ; it was exclusive, and had done very little for science. The Royal Irish Academy protested. Petitions from seventeen towns against the proposed change were received,

and, when it was found that there was an intention that
the Museum of Irish Industry was to be handed over to
South Kensington, great indignation was felt.   Sir Robert
Peel, as Chief Secretary, agreed in my representations.   A
Committee was granted, of which I was chairman, and
which occupied my time nearly the whole of the session.
We completely defeated, by means of my report, the
ambitious designs of the Royal Dublin Society and South
Kensington, and the inquiry was of much benefit to our
Irish institutions.

We had a very animated debate on the destruction of
the fortress of Corfu, and I mooted the subject by moving
for all papers connected with the cession of the Ionian
Islands to Greece, and especially of those connected with
the demolition of the fortresses.

" If there was one spot," I said, " in all Europe where the name of
England was cherished before, it was in these Ionian Islands.   Now
there are few places where it is regarded with greater distrust and
dislike.   Had these islands belonged to us, and had we ceded them,
or parted company with them in any way, it would have been an evil
thing to destroy their fortifications ; but we are actually blowing up
now that which never belonged to us, and against the destruction of
which the owners protest.   These islands were always independent,
even when under our protection.   The rights of the Ionians to their
fortresses were recognized in the sixth article of the Congress of Vienna.
When Lord Malmesbury made a proposal, on the 16th of April, 1863,
that these islands should be neutralized, and their fortresses destroyed,
Lord Russell reprimanded him, saying that the Ionian Islands were
independent states, and that if they were united to Greece it would be
for them to decide whether the fortresses of Corfu were to be kept up.
They have kept up these fortresses by heavy taxation since 1825, though
I am quite ready to admit that they have not paid up the full amount
of necessary contributions.   The Ionians were altogether ignorant of
the terms of the treaty of 1863, by which their fortresses were to be
destroyed.   The whole affair arose from Austrian misgivings lest these
islands should be seized by the Italians, and used as a basis of hostile
operations ; but, if so, let Austria take on herself the discredit of this
act.   Why should we be execrated, and our good faith impugned, to
allay Austria's apprehensions ?   When, on the 10th of December, the

Acroceraunian Mountains, opposite Corfu, were lit up with fires of joy in answer to the illuminations in the islands, they were as the lighting up of hope in the breasts of the oppressed at the deliverance of their brethren, and the people of the whole East believed in the generosity and disinterestedness of England. But sad indeed was their subsequent disappointment. If we had told them that there was no obstacle raised by us to their being connected with Greece, but that Austria had insisted on the destruction of their fortresses, they could then have decided for themselves; but even if they did accept Austria's demands, let them blow up their own fortresses, and not regard us as their executioners, and as bringing shame on the young king we had been prominent in obtaining for them."

Seymour Fitzgerald and Lord John Manners both made excellent speeches on my side, and Mr. Layard consented to give the papers I moved for, accusing me at the same time of being the mouthpiece of all the discontent in Eastern Europe, and insisting on it that the Ionians did not want the fortresses, could not keep them up, and had no reason to complain.

1865.

I opposed the second reading of the bill for lowering the borough franchise, and also a motion brought forward by Sir J. Pope Hennessy for the increase of public works in Ireland. I also made a speech on the condition of our Art and Science collections, which was much commented on in the Press.

I spoke in favour of the Roman Catholic Oaths Bill, to do away with the offensive oaths which every Catholic had to take—"that he did not believe that princes excommunicated by the Pope could be dethroned and murdered by their subjects." This bill was carried by a majority of sixty-seven, and this miserable and insulting formula was thereby abolished.

1866.

This was a session in which I did a good deal of work. I began by supporting the bill of James Clay, the member for Hull, to extend the elective franchise by conferring votes on all persons educated up to a certain standard. Although I had very little faith in the prospect of carrying the bill I allowed my name to be put upon it, as a protest against the attack made upon me for desiring to exclude the working classes from Parliamentary influence. This bill would admit the *élite* of the working classes, who were debarred from votes because they lived in houses rented at less than £10; it would also admit a most valuable class of voters, lawyers, attorneys, clerks, etc. The proposals were eminently liberal, and would add a large number of voters to the suffrage, and they were endeavouring at that very time to establish a similar system of franchise in the very democratic colony of Victoria. As I foresaw, after a dull debate, the bill was read a first time and then came to nothing.

In the autumn of this year I took another journey through Spain and Portugal with Mr. J. C. Robinson. I picked him up at Santiago, having travelled through a lovely country, a land flowing with milk and honey, very different from the grim, stern plains of Leon and Castille, which we had traversed. Mr. Robinson had had his time well occupied in negotiating with the cathedral authorities to have a cast taken of the famous "Punta della Gloria," a magnificent work in granite of the twelfth century, by a certain Master Matthias, of whom we know nothing. This splendid example of early sculpture has been set up at Kensington Museum. From Santiago we proceeded to Tuy, and there crossed the

Minho to Viana, where we hired a small and most comfortable omnibus, at ten francs a day, paying nothing but
the keep when we were out on a journey. It was to
accompany us all through Portugal, and the bargain was
faithfully kept. We had a good courier, a certain old
Don Mathias, who spoke English, having kept an hotel,
I believe at Gibraltar. We had found him at Madrid,
and employed him during our former trip. He was a
thoroughly honest man, but very grumpy and ill-tem-
pered. I must say, however, that he served us willingly
and faithfully, and insisted on our always speaking Spanish
to him in order that we might learn the language, and we
certainly picked up, through his agency, a good deal of
it, sufficient to get along and express our wants and
remonstrate vigorously against attempts to cheat. He
took an extraordinary interest in Robinson's acquisitions,
and, I believe, did a little business in *bric-à-brac* after we
left Spain. We enjoyed Braga much, in spite of the filthy
hotel, and still more enjoyed a clean, excellent hotel at
Oporto, after all the fleas we had endured, and the unsavoury food we had had to put up with in Gallicia.
From Oporto we went to Coimbra, a town full of interest,
and thence diverged to the old, stern town of Vizeu, which
had rarely been visited, but where we heard there were
some pictures of great merit, by a mysterious painter
called Gran Vasco. The merits of these pictures did not
belie their fame. Most of them had been ruined by the
injudicious restoration of an ignorant, silly local artist; but
one remained quite intact, St. Peter sitting in his chair,
with the papal triple crown on his head. It is a magnificent work, Flemish undoubtedly in its motive, but not
executed by a Flemish hand. Every archaic picture in
Portugal is attributed to the same Gran Vasco, whose
birth and parentage is absolutely unknown. I revisited

Vizeu with my wife and an American gentleman of much
taste, Mr. Lee Childe, in 1885, and they were as much
amazed at this wonderful picture as Mr. Robinson and
myself.   I   am   happy   to   say   I   prevailed   on   the
Arundel Society to send an Italian painter to copy it in
1887.   He was also as much struck with it as we were,
and spoke of it as a *"cosa stupenda."* *   I was much
amused the first time I visited Vizeu by the extraordinary
cheapness of living there.   On asking our host what
would be the cost of our daily sojourn, he mentioned some
thousands of reals per day.   While I was converting these
huge numbers into English money the host thought I was
doubting the reasonableness of his charges, which came
to 3s. 9d. a day each, comprising breakfast, lunch, dinner,
and beds, and he added quickly, "But I mean to give
you wax candles."   "Well," said I, gravely, having just
finished my calculations, "if you give wax candles, I
accept the arrangement."   In 1885 I found the board per
diem had risen to 4s. 5d., on which I expressed my surprise and grief.   "Ah," said the host, with a sigh, "the
railroad has advanced prices so terribly that I cannot
arrange with you for less."

We returned to Coimbra, passing by Busaco's battle-
field, and spent a very pleasant week or ten days at
Lisbon.   I there was presented, by Mr. Lytton, who was
Secretary of Legation, to the King-Consort Ferdinand of
Coburg.   He was a very charming man, highly cultivated,
and an enthusiastic lover of art.   He showed us his collection of gorgeous old Portuguese plate, which I fear
since his death has been dispersed.   He was extremely
grotesque in his manner of speaking, having apparently
no palate, so the words came up through his nose.   There
is a story told of him that, at the Exhibition of Oporto,

* The reproduction was published in 1890 by the Arundel Society.

he complimented a French exhibitor, who, hearing his strange voice, stared in amazement. "Pourquoi donc regardez vous mon nez?" said the King. "Pardon, sire," replied the Frenchman, "je l'écoute."

I returned to England, as I said before, by long sea after a visit to Elvas with Mr. Robinson, and to Alcobaça and Batalha with a clever witty Frenchman, M. de Bamville, who was a well-known *bon vivant*, and much astonished the maritornes of the posades where we slept by cooking an excellent dinner. On board the ship I found the officers and crew of a steamer from Brazil, which had been wrecked on an island, or rather sandbank, off their coast. They were a ludicrous sight, having been decked out in the clothes of the other passengers, some of the ladies' dresses trailing on the ground, others reaching but little below the knees. They had had a terrible time, having been nearly a fortnight on the sandbank, exposed to the sun and weather. What they complained of most were the legions of crabs constantly crawling over them, chiefly by night, and in fighting and crushing these wretches their clothes, when they were taken on board our ship, had become a nauseous spectacle.

In October of this year Lord Palmerston died, to the deep regret of both parties, as much almost of the Conservatives as of the Liberals. He had governed firmly, and with good sense. He left England flourishing, Ireland perfectly tranquil and advancing in rapid strides of prosperity. Abroad he was respected, and, though feared, had quite overcome the feeling of dislike with which he had been formerly regarded. As regards his Turkish policy, I was opposed to it, but I never failed to recognize that he had been the ardent supporter of the independence of Greece, and that if he did not take the same line which I was constantly recommending, it was not from being blind to the iniquities of Turkish rule, and to the grievances of the Christian nationalities, but because he was always afraid of any movement in Eastern Europe of which Russia, ever on the watch, might take advantage. And yet Lord Palmerston, with all his good sense, was mistaken. Time has proved that a more enlightened and generous policy would have strengthened him in resistance to Russian ambition. It gratifies me greatly to find how entirely every speech of mine has been confirmed by the authority of Lord Stratford de Redcliffe, who had ever his hand, if I may use the expression, on the pulse of Eastern Europe, and understood every throb. He saw clearly that the only barrier to Russian aggrandizement was in the formation of self-governed Christian states under the suzerainty of the Sultan. In vol. ii., p. 462, of "The Life of Stratford Canning," I find the following passage :—

"He had never been a Turcophile, as people supposed, but had always looked forward to a belt of practically autonomous Christian states, under the suzerainty of the Sultan, as the surest barrier against Russian aggression. He would have welcomed the formation of a Christian empire in the place of Turkey if he could have discovered any Eastern Christian fit to rule it. Failing this, he believed that the supreme authority of the Sultan was necessary to counteract the influence of Russia in the Christian provinces, and he hoped for a regenerate Turkey worthy to take a place amongst civilized nations."

We soon found out the loss of the clear head, the solid judgment, and the firm hand of Lord Palmerston when Lord Russell succeeded him, and Mr. Gladstone assumed the leadership of the House of Commons. Hitherto Lord Palmerston had always repressed Mr. Gladstone's exuberances quietly but irresistibly. Since then, except for brief intervals, Mr. Gladstone has had a free hand, and Egypt and Ireland can attest the consequences. A member of Lord Palmerston's Cabinet gave me an amusing description of their proceedings. At the beginning of the session, and after each holiday, Mr. Gladstone used to come in charged to the muzzle with all sorts of schemes of all sorts of reforms which were absolutely necessary in his opinion to be immediately undertaken. Lord Palmerston used to look fixedly at the paper before him, saying nothing until there was a lull in Gladstone's outpouring. He then rapped the table and said cheerfully, " Now, my lords and gentlemen, let us go to business."

On Lord Russell becoming Prime Minister he very kindly sent a special messenger out to Nice, where I was staying with my mother, offering me office as a Lord of the Admiralty. I use the words "very kindly" as on more than one occasion I had spoken very hastily of him, for I am bound to say I had the most profound distrust of him as a statesman.

I replied very courteously, declining the offered appointment on the ground of my mother's health, which might necessitate absence, of more or less duration, from my Admiralty duties.

Perhaps the most important speech in my Parliamentary career was one which I made on the exemption from capture of private goods by sea. I was not successful in carrying my point, but every year has since convinced me of the soundness of my views, and of the misfortune, for I can use no other term, which prevented our having this provision adopted as a maxim of international law at that time. I doubt much, if we now mooted the question, that we should obtain the adhesion of those countries which were then favourable to such a proposal.

I stated that I was reproached personally for bringing forward this motion in favour of exempting the capture of all private property by sea. I was told that I was the last person who should do so, as I had extolled the construction in England of cruisers for the purpose of destroying

American property during the war between North and
South.   To this I replied that, though I had always proclaimed my sympathies with the South, I never could bring
myself to vindicate a mode of warfare which was barbarous
as regards individuals, which increased the exasperation of
the combatants, and which was perfectly useless as to
the great issue to be determined.   I therefore had no
hesitation in moving an address to the Queen in the
following terms :—" That an humble address be presented
to Her Majesty, praying that she will be graciously
pleased to use her influence with foreign powers for the
purpose of making the principle that private property
should be free from capture by sea a maxim of international law."

My object was thoroughly logical, for on the acceptance of the Declaration of Paris in 1856, that the neutral
flag covers the belligerent's goods, it must follow as a
rational consequence that all private property should be
exempt from capture by sea.   This proposal had been
unanimously supported by a Committee of the House of
Commons on merchant shipping, one of the members
of which was the actual President of the Board of Trade
(Mr. Milner Gibson).   It was supported by memorials
from Chambers of Commerce of some of our greatest
commercial communities, and only the day before the
debate the opinion of the Shipowners' Society was conveyed to me officially.   It referred to a resolution in
favour of the principle passed in 1862, and said, " The
experience of the last five years has confirmed the Committee in the opinion then expressed, that it is essential
to the interests of British shipping that private property
at sea should be exempt from capture."   Lord Palmerston
had, at a meeting in Liverpool in 1856, expressed his
hope "that the principles of war which were applied to

R

hostilities by land might be extended without exception to hostilities at sea, and that private property should no longer be exposed to aggression on either side."

During the period of the debates on Servia in 1863 there arrived in London a very beautiful and accomplished woman, Julie Obrenovitch, the wife of Nicholas, Prince of Servia. She was a Hungarian by birth, of the very ancient family of the Hunyadi. We became extremely intimate, and my friends conferred on me, in consequence, the name of Gregorevitch ; but our intimacy was purely political, and I derived the most valuable information from her, for she was as intelligent as she was handsome. I remember a charming *mot* of Lord Palmerston one evening at a party at his own house. The Princess of Servia was going out, and her dress caught in the doorway. Lord Palmerston stooped and loosened it, and then, bowing and laughing, said, " Vous voyez, Princesse, c'est toujours la Porte qui vous incommode."

I have always said and felt that there was no question connected with Ireland to be compared with the importance of that of the position of the tenants. The perfect indifference with which it was regarded is curious. Lord Palmerston dismissed it with the expression that "tenant right was landlords' wrong." Mr. Gladstone was equally indifferent to it, and yet no man acquainted with Ireland but must have felt it as a burning question ready at any moment to burst into conflagration. Agricultural prosperity had retarded it, but I was convinced that if bad times for the farmers came on there would be a most serious, disastrous, and just agitation. How could it be otherwise ? The good landlords were no doubt fair in their dealings, and considerate, but there was a leaven of bad landlords to leaven the lump, and to produce feelings of general insecurity and general indignation. How could it be otherwise, with the fatal notice to quit ever suspended over the peasants' heads? These notices, as Mr. Gladstone subsequently illustrated them, fell like snowflakes. I quoted the proceedings of the largest landowners in Ireland, the Law Life Insurance Company, whereby a notice to quit was handed to every tenant, together with the receipt for the rent. Tenants' associations sprung into life, and they were very moderate in their demands. They demanded some measure which would guarantee increased stability of tenure. Sir Colman O'Loughlin, the thoroughly liberal and far-sighted member for Clare, took exactly the same view of the state of public feeling and the justice of it, and we determined to see if we could induce Parliament to apply a remedy. He framed a singularly moderate bill, of which we sent copies to the tenants' associations, and from all of them, I believe, we received assurances of their complete satisfaction with it. He brought it in on July 29, and I made a statement of its objects. It proposed to discourage annual lettings. Where there was no written contract, a lease of twenty-one years was presumed. Every discouragement, though no actual prohibition, was thrown in the way of annual tenancies. In all such cases the tenant was empowered to deduct county cess, and distraint was forbidden. Compensation in case of ejectment of a yearly tenant was enacted, except in case of non-payment of rent. These were the main provisions which would have resulted in the general granting of leases, and we should have had peace in the land for twenty-one years. Before I introduced the bill I met Mr. Gladstone going out of the House, and I besought him to stay and hear what I had to say, and to help me if he approved. He said, " Let me look at your bill," and he ran his eye over the headings of the clauses. "Why, you want," said he, "to interfere with the management of a man's own property. I will have nothing to do with it," ejaculating these words with the greatest emphasis. We failed in making any way with our bill.

In the course of this session I had another and rather an amusing difference with Mr. Gladstone, which I write down word for word from the notes I took at the time and preserved. On the 21st of April Mr. Gladstone made his magnificent speech on the second reading of the Reform Bill, and stigmatized that portion of the Liberal party who were about to vote for Lord Grosvenor's amendment as " depraved little men." "Yes," added he, laughingly, "and παρακεκομμένα ('crooked') also." The same evening, at Lady Waldegrave's party, he came up to me and said, " It quite gave me pleasure when we were dividing to think I had in the other lobby a sympathizer in one respect, in love and remembrance of Aristophanes." I replied, "I was so pleased at hearing an old friend quoted, that I did not mind the delinquencies you imputed to us; but I hardly think the word παρακεκομμένα is well expressed by 'crooked,' I believe it refers to coins 'badly struck.'" To this he assented, but insisted that "crooked" conveyed the meaning. On the following Monday, when coming out of the House of Commons, the doorkeeper put into my hand the following letter from Mr. Gladstone, written, be it remembered, in the middle of great excitement, with the Budget coming on immediately :—

"April 30, '66.

" DEAR MR. GREGORY,

" I thought a little about the proper mode of rendering the word παρακεκομμένα, and it appeared to me that the term best fitted to convey the meaning was 'misbegotten,' corresponding closely as it does with 'mis-struck' or 'struck awry,' the meaning of the Greek word in its first intention. But such a translation was evidently inadmissible, so I adopted one which was simple, and seemed near enough to the mark. I am open to your criticism, but I beg you to believe I did not proceed in the matter lightly, and that I am aware of the responsibility of attempting in any way to represent or render Aristophanes.

"Believe me very faithfully yours,
                    "W. E. GLADSTONE.

"I must thank you for the exceedingly kind terms of your speech. But for the extreme pressure of time I should have wished to refer to it as one of those which entirely deprived us of the right to say that all who supported the resolution (of Lord Grosvenor) were enemies to a real dealing with the question."

On the 18th of June of this year Lord Dunkellin defeated the Government on an amendment in the Committee on the Reform Bill to substitute rating for rental, and Lord Russell resigned. We who voted in the majority offered to move a vote of confidence in the Government, but all atonement was refused. The chief leaders in this movement, to which Mr. Bright gave the name of "the Cave of Adullam," were Mr. Lowe (afterwards Lord Sherbrooke), Lord Elcho (now Lord Wemyss), Lord Grosvenor, Lord Lansdowne, Lord Dunkellin, and I may include myself, as I was always invited to the councils held at Lansdowne House. When Lord Derby assumed office he offered to place several of these "Cavemen," as we called ourselves, in his Government, and to me he proposed the secretaryship of the Admiralty, a very important and responsible office, from which I might certainly have aspired to the Cabinet.

None of our "Cave" joined Lord Derby's Government, but for the rest of the session we treated them with great urbanity. Lord Naas was Irish Secretary, and I saw a great deal of him. I had previously a poor opinion of him, but closer acquaintance altogether changed that view. I found him clear-headed, able, and singularly liberal in his views, but tied hand and foot, as he said to me, almost

with tears in his eyes, by the bigotry and obstinacy of the
northern Tory members, who stood in the way of every
advance.   On more than one occasion he expressed himself very gratefully for the consideration I always showed
him.   When his party had gone out, and he had received
the appointment of Governor-General of India, there was
a movement on our side to defeat the appointment, and
there was a strong desire to move an address to the
Queen to cancel it.   I did all I could to prevent any such
step being taken, and I wrote to him to say that if
his appointment was attacked in the House of Commons
he might rely on me to take a part in the debate in his
behalf.   Fortunately, for the credit of Mr. Gladstone's
Government, the intention was not persevered in, and
no opposition took place to the appointment of one
of the ablest and most active Viceroys who has ever
ruled India.   It is a grateful recollection to recall the
course I then adopted, not only from personal regard, but
from belief in Lord Mayo's abilities, and I know that he
never forgot the incident.

The subject of the condition of Irish railroads had been
occupying much attention in Ireland.   The report of the
Commission to inquire into them proved that they were in
a most unsatisfactory state, and that the universal complaints were well founded.   I was in hopes that a Tory
Government, which had always put forward its claim to be
an advocate of practical improvement in Ireland, would
be willing to deal with this matter, more especially as
Mr. Gladstone had indicated, not ambiguously, that he
considered it would be desirable to do so.   I therefore
brought the subject before the House, having received
very valuable assistance from Lord Clanricarde, who
fully recognized the importance of it.

CHAPTER XIII

DURING the session of 1867 I made a speech advocating liberality on the part of the Government to the Royal Irish Academy. Since its foundation it had numbered among its members almost every Irishman distinguished in science, archæology, and general literature. It had illustrated the history and physical phenomena of Ireland by works of originality and research. In the twentieth volume of its transactions came out the famous treatise of Dr. Petrie, which settled the question of the Round Towers of Ireland. Its museum contains the most important collection of Celtic antiquities in the world. A catalogue was being formed by Sir William Wilde of this collection, but was at a standstill for want of funds to print it, though the manuscript was complete. The members of the society had acted with great liberality. By private subscription they had bought Dean Dawson's collection of antiquities for £1067. For the Tara torques they had raised £190; for Sir W. Betham's Irish Manuscripts, £600; for Hodge's and Smith's Irish Manuscripts, £723. The first requirement was to rearrange the present building, which would enable the museum to be properly exhibited. A responsible curator and an attendant were also necessary. A clerk was required for the library and assistance for the purchase of books and binding of them. I mentioned some of the treasures of the library—a copy of the Gospels, said to be of the time of St. Patrick ; a copy of the Psalms, said to have been the miraculous work of St. Colomba, who transcribed them by stealth at night by the lights which streamed from the tips of his fingers. There was the book of Ballymote, sold in 1512 for a hundred and fifty milch cows. Another manuscript was of such value that it was given in ransom for the chief of the O'Dogherties, and to recover it O'Donel laid siege to Sligo in 1470. A Parliamentary Committee had recommended that £1000 a year should be granted in addition to the £500 a year now received by the society. I also strongly recommended the purchase of the collection of Dr. Petrie, then in the market. The Secretary of the Treasury, Mr. Hunt, gave a favourable answer. The Petrie collection was bought, and the structure of the Royal Irish Academy remodelled internally and fitted for proper exhibition. I subsequently took a prominent, indeed the principal, part in the purchase of the famous Tara brooch, one of the most marvellous specimens of early enamelling in the world, and an inestimable treasure.

Later on I made a vehement onslaught on the Chief Commissioner of Works for the vacillations, delays, and changes of purpose in connection with the enlargement of the National Gallery. I also joined Sir Francis Goldsmid in his remonstrances as to the manner in which the Jews were treated by my friends the Servians.

The Irish Secretary, Lord Naas, in this session brought forward a bill which was to settle the discontent of the Irish tenants. I objected to it because it had three cardinal defects. It was inapplicable to a great portion of Irish tenancies, it utterly ignored the real causes of discontent, and it needlessly violated the laws of property. The main provisions were to allow tenants to borrow

money for the improvement of their farms, and to remove
their fixtures in case of failing to come to terms with the
landlord, or the incoming tenant refusing to remunerate
them for the outlay.   There were great objections to lend
public money, unless in case of a lease.   No bill could in
any way touch beneficially the existing state of things
which did not aim at remedying the condition of the
occupier, ninety-five out of every hundred of whom
existed on the soil solely at the will of the landlord.
There could be no attachment on the part of a peasantry
to the institutions of a country under such circumstances ;
compensation for improvements was mere moonshine.   It
was the uncertain and precarious tenure which caused
discontent.   It would not be inconsistent with conservative principles to try and remedy this evil.   There
was nothing conservative in a tenancy at will.   It was
essentially a revolutionary tenure.   I did not ask to force
leases indiscriminately down on every tenant, but I did ask
that they should be encouraged, for, as Lord Dufferin
said, "the refusal of a lease to a solvent, industrious
tenant is nothing less than a crime.   The prosperity of
agriculture depends on security of tenure, and the only
proper tenure is a liberal lease."   There had been a great
growth of late in this tenant question, and it may be
attributed to the fact that at the beginning of the century,
and up to a comparatively recent time, leases were the
rule.   On my own estate in 1840 almost every tenant had
a lease.   Twenty years afterwards there was hardly a
lease remaining ; so it was elsewhere.   For many reasons
the landlord had no particular desire to grant them ; they
were bound by their provisions, the tenants were not ; and
political power was more effectually exercised on tenants
at will than on leaseholders.   Then came the Encumbered
Estates Act, and as a rule those who purchased under

it looked on land as a mere investment, determined to get as much interest as they could for their money; and the peasants found themselves in the hands of harsh and unsympathetic landlords, who turned them out without compunction if it suited their purposes. But the extermination of the present landlords would not mend matters. Far better to try a moderate remedial measure, and none could be more moderate or efficacious in the opinion of the tenants themselves than to devise a measure doing away as far as possible with the present insecurity of tenure. I therefore moved, as an amendment to Lord Naas's bill, "that no enactment for the settlement of the landlord and tenant question in Ireland can be deemed satisfactory which does not provide for the increase of leases in that country." Moderate—weak, indeed—as was this amendment, I failed to carry it after the adjournment of the debate, not by a direct vote, but by a side issue raised by Mr. Sandford, which saved the Government from a defeat, for the House of Commons would have gone with me.

On looking over my speeches during this session I find one on the case of the *Tornado*, a vessel which had been fitted out during the exciting war between Spain and Chili to become a war vessel of the last-named power. There never was a more rascally transaction ; our laws were evaded, every subterfuge resorted to, and, when the *Tornado* was seized by the Spaniards, our Government was besieged by those scamps who owned her and their friends, who protested their innocence and loudly proclaimed the harmlessness of this peaceful vessel. I went into all the details of the transaction, followed these worthies in their tortuous courses, and proved to a certainty the guilty objects of their schemes. The affair was complicated by the incredible stupidity of the Spaniards and their ignorance of the very rudiments of international law; but the *Tornado* was ultimately condemned, much to my delight and to the confusion and pecuniary loss of those rogues whose character I thoroughly exposed. I exempted one person from the severe expressions I employed towards the rest, and that was Commander McKillop, an officer in the English navy, who had actually been appointed by the Chilian Government to command the vessel when she reached Valparaiso. He told the whole truth, like an honest, frank sailor.

In August of this year one of the heaviest sorrows I have ever felt came upon me by the unexpected death of my dear friend Lord Dunkellin. He had had severe fits of gout, and was at last carried away by a complication of disorders affecting the kidneys and the heart. He knew that his health was enfeebled, but none of us had the least fear of his being in a precarious state. Almost the last words he said to me when I was leaving London for Ireland were these: "I can't conceal from myself that I am not the man I was, and I cannot go racketing about to Paris and Les Eaux as formerly. I should like much to pass my autumn and winter quietly in Ireland, but my father and mother will not be home till winter sets in, and to live alone at Portumna without a soul to speak to would be dreary work." I said, "Why don't you come to Coole? I shall be at home till Parliament meets. You can have your own rooms reserved for you, and do precisely as you please." "Do you really mean it?" he answered. "Don't you think I should inconvenience your mother?" I replied, "Of course I mean it; and you could not possibly give me greater pleasure than by closing with the offer. As for my mother, I know no one whom she likes as much as yourself, and she would greet your sojourn with us as eagerly as I do." "Well, Greg," said he, "L'idée me

sourit énormément. I will drop in on you in August, and
you can see then if you can stand so much of my company."
On the 10th of August I received a telegram announcing
his death, at the early age of forty. There was an enormous
concourse of the peasantry at his funeral, at the Abbey of
Athenry, and scarcely a dry eye. His poor father directed
the proceedings, and it was a piteous sight to see him. He
appeared like a man dazed after a sunstroke. He never
recovered the shock. He had every reason to be proud of
and attached to him, for he had always loved Dunkellin,
and Dunkellin loved him with the whole strength of his
loving nature. He was proud, too, of the position Dunkellin had reached in public estimation ; for, had his health
permitted, he would rapidly have become one of our
foremost men. I, too, was perfectly stunned, and, though
more than twenty years have passed away, often and often
do I recall him who was more than a brother to me. He
was essentially open-hearted, open-minded, generous to a
degree, even to those whom he knew to be scarcely worthy
of his generosity. I never met a man of such extraordinary sweetness of temper, and, when he did dislike a
man, he had always good cause for doing so. Had he
lived, not one of the troubles which have so broken up
our county would have befallen us. He would have dealt
with his tenantry, whom he well knew individually, not
merely justly, but generously ; he would have resided at
home, the darling wish of his life ; would have encouraged
improvements, and made Loughrea a very different town
from its present declining, disreputable, and disaffected
condition. And yet, though the lower orders universally
mourned his death, both in the county and the town of
Galway, and though they were fully aware of his character,
yet it was actually necessary, within twelve years of his
death, for the Bishop of Galway to denounce those who

were plotting to destroy his statue by Foley, in the town of Galway, which had been erected with acclaim by the subscription of all classes, landlords, shopkeepers, and peasants!

I moved, in a long speech, for papers connected with Servia and Crete. This was another duel with Mr. Layard, the Under Secretary for Foreign Affairs.

1868.

The great feature in this session was the Reform Bill, on which I never could bring myself to speak, so great was my indignation at the course resorted to by the Government and resented by General Peel, Lord Cranborne (afterwards Lord Salisbury), Lord Carnarvon, and others, who resigned their places in the Ministry.

I spoke early in the session on Mr. Maguire's motion on the state of Ireland. I advocated Mr. Bright's plan in favour of establishing peasant proprietors. I said that if an Irish Parliament, composed of wise and moderate men of all interests and classes, were called into existence, it would undoubtedly demand a settlement of the land question, giving increased stability of tenure, denominational education, equality in the endowment of the Churches, and would remove from the Statute Book the needless and insulting Ecclesiastical Tithes Bill. It would also insist on such practical measures as the purchase of railways by the State, and the drainage of the Shannon. The Legislature had hitherto treated Irish demands as Bumble treated the paupers. He said, " I know what they want, and when they come and ask for anything I give them something else, and they don't come again." It would be better to do nothing than to nibble at these questions. Let the Government face them, and propose a full plan for dealing with them, and submit it to the House and to the constituencies.

Shortly afterwards, in hopes that a Tory Government might be prevailed on to do more for the British Museum than I had hitherto induced my Liberal friends to do, I made a long statement about the condition of that institution. I described the congested state of the collections for want of room ; and stated that the antiquities recently acquired had to be stored away in pent houses in front of the building ; that most valuable objects were consigned to the basement, in the regions of Nox and Erebus ; that the insect rooms were so dark as to render it impossible to inspect its specimens ; that the lighting was defective ; the composition of the trust too extensive and fluctuating ; that the heads of departments were not allowed to be present at the Board of Trustees, when the business of their departments was transacted ; that discontent, discouragement, and want of efficiency was the result. I acquiesced in the removal of the natural history collections to Kensington, but recommended, in accordance with the report of the Committee of 1860, that the drawings of the old masters should go to the National Gallery. Mr. Disraeli replied in a most admirable speech, and perfectly astonished me by his intimate knowledge of the details of every point on which I had spoken. He did not agree in all my views, especially those in reference to the Trustees, but in other respects his answer was most favourable, and it was made additionally palatable by many compliments he paid me, the first I had been greeted with from any official mouth on this subject. But in all these matters he took a high and enlightened view. Nothing was too good for England's reputation. She ought to stand pre-eminently forward in her art and science institutions ; and he never shrank from expenditure, as I have said before, in forwarding this object, and was always cordially supported by both sides of the House in so doing.

After the Reform Bill was passed, Parliament was dissolved, and Lord Burke and myself were returned for Galway county without opposition.

1869.

Mr. Gladstone lost no time when Parliament met in cutting down the branches, as he termed them, of the upas tree ; and immediately brought in a bill for the suppression of the Irish State Church.   I had always, being much moved by O'Connell's conversations with me in early life, looked on this institution as an intolerable grievance ; but I am bound to say that I do not think the masses in Ireland cared much about the matter.   My views were that the Irish Church as a State Church should be abolished, but that the revenues should be applied equally to the wants of the three great denominations.   I had almost made up my mind to move an amendment to the bill in that direction, but I was dissuaded by Lady Waldegrave, with whom for the last few years I had contracted a strong friendship, and whose advice much influenced me in every action of my life.   She was a most remarkable woman, one of the most remarkable I have ever known.   She was very pretty as a girl, and married first Mr. Waldegrave, who soon died, and then his brother, Lord Waldegrave,* who

* I have been asked by Lord Carlingford to omit a few lines which appeared in the first edition, relating to Lord Waldegrave. He informs me that they contain inaccuracies as to the strange incident of his imprisonment shared by Lady Waldegrave, and that they give a wrong impression of his character, and of her married life with him. The facts are as follows. Six months after her marriage, Lord Walde-grave and Captain Duff surrendered to take their trial for an assault committed upon a policeman at Hampton Court, nearly a year before (in June, 1840), by themselves and other young men, all of them

shortly afterwards died, and left her a title and fine income
—in fact, everything he had—and thirdly, a very different
man, Mr. Harcourt, who was all that was respectable.
She was an excellent wife to him, and neither during her
married life with him, nor previously, was there ever a
whisper of disparagement on her character. No great
lady held her head higher, or more vigorously ruled her
society. Her house was always gay, and her parties at
Nuncham were the liveliest of the time; but she never
suffered the slightest indecorum, nor tolerated improprieties.
When Mr. Harcourt died she married Fortescue, and was
the idol of his life; and no wonder, for all her energy was
centred in him. It was in 1867 when I first began to
know her well, and from that time till the day of her
death I was admitted into her unreserved friendship, and
received constant and unremitting kindness from her. I
often said to her how much I regretted I had not known
her well when I re-entered Parliament. Her admirable
judgment would have preserved me from many false steps,
and from the erratic course which I am well conscious I

the worse for wine, and were sentenced to six months' imprisonment in the Queen's Bench. There was no question of manslaughter,
as the policeman had not died. Lady Waldegrave was allowed to
accompany her husband to prison, and lived with him there in
two small rooms, which they furnished for themselves in the
governor's house. Lord Waldegrave, before his marriage, was one
of a set of racketing young men, addicted to foolish mischief and
practical jokes, which was sometimes called the Waterford set, but
he was a kindly and honourable gentleman, not "a debauched
rowdy," and not given to low company. He disliked society,
however, and during the six years of his life with Lady Waldegrave,
to whom he was entirely devoted, they lived quietly in the country,
seeing scarcely any one beyond a few relations. Thus Lady
Waldegrave was not "thrown into bad company" by her marriage;
nor did that misfortune ever befall her, as she knew nothing of
society of any kind until she married Mr. Harcourt.—A. G.

took on more than one occasion. Towards the close of my Parliamentary career I intimated to her that the darling object of my life was the Government of Ceylon, and she at once, and successfully, betook herself to obtain the promise of it from Lord Granville, who conceded readily her request ; nearly two years, however, elapsed from the date of the promise being given to its being fulfilled.

In the meanwhile I loyally and conscientiously supported the Government and Mr. Gladstone in cutting down the upas tree, and I have no reason to regret having taken that course. His measures in regard to the Church and reform of the land laws I cordially acquiesced in and still entirely approve.

It is sad enough nowadays (1889) to see of what little effect in Ireland have been this great measure of justice and the "tenant charter," if I may so term it, which Mr. Gladstone passed the following year. In my speech on the Irish Church Bill, I quoted the salutary effects of previous measures of conciliation—Catholic Emancipation, abolition of tithes, etc. I thought these instances good arguments, and so did the House of Commons. But these measures of Mr. Gladstone, so just and so beneficent, were received with thanklessness, suspicion, and upbraiding, and were so many stepping-stones for the wildest demands, culminating in that for the virtual separation of England and Ireland, and the subsequent ruin of both countries.

In this session I brought forward the subject of building the new Courts of Justice on the Thames Embankment, the magnificent plan of Mr. Layard, Commissioner of Works, offering space and outlook for a grand building. Sir Roundell Palmer opposed, the debate was adjourned, but subsequently the Thames Embankment was adopted. At a later period, however, the influence of Sir Roundell Palmer prevailed against that of Mr. Layard and of Mr. Lowe, Chancellor of the Exchequer, who was also enthusiastically in favour of the Embankment. A Committee was appointed, and the Strand was decided on instead by one vote. We know what the result has been—a frippery, broken-up, ill-arranged edifice, a discredit to the Victorian era ; whereas it might have been, and ought to have been, a glory to all time—if, indeed, Street was architect of sufficient calibre for so great a work.

1870.

Mr. Gladstone proceeded at once to attack another branch of the upas tree, and brought forward in March his Land Bill for Ireland. The main object was to give security to tenants in their holdings, and to enable them to purchase them. The first object was to be secured by giving compensation for disturbances, except in cases of non-payment of rent ; the second, by means of the Bright Clauses. I objected to the stringency of these clauses, which lent to the tenants to the extent of half or two-thirds of the purchase money at six per cent. for twenty-two years. I thought it would render the measure quite inoperative ; and so it turned out to be. A considerable opposition to the bill was threatened by some of the Irish members, on the grounds of its not going far enough ; and a certain amount of agitation was raised against it in Ireland for the same reason. I also thought that, if it were to be the future tenant charter, it was inadequate, and left many serious points, sure to be revived, unsettled. I was, however, determined to support it loyally, knowing the untoward fate which had beset previous land bills. I thought the bill was intricate in its provisions, and yet the subject demanded that it should be eminently simple, clear of doubts and points of litigation. The judges of the land complained that they were puzzled with its intricacies ; even the Solicitor-General for Ireland was, in his speech, in order to explain it, obliged to go backwards and forwards, mitigating, expanding, and colouring one clause by the aid of some other clause or clauses. I said I was reminded of Dean Swift's famous house, which was built on such fine mathematical principles of compensations and adjustments, that, when a sparrow perched on one of the gables, he overthrew the equilibrium and brought the whole fabric to the ground. It was important that the House should know the full extent of the demands of the Irish tenant farmers. Their delegates had recently met in London and they had agreed that certain proposals which I had formulated would be satisfactory, and, if adopted, that the land question would never be heard of again ; that a Land Court should be adopted, the present rents throughout Ireland should be accepted as the basis of the settlement ; that the landlord might go before the Court and allege reasons as a ground for raising these rents ; while the tenant might go before the same Court to impugn rents as exorbitant. The last and most important proposal was this—that a tenant should have power to sell his goodwill in all cases, whether of eviction or of voluntary departure from the farm.

Lord Portsmouth had allowed this principle to be established on his Wexford estates, and his agent stated that it had inspired with energy and confidence every tenant in them. I had made this concession the rule of my estate, and the consequence was a total absence of complaint and friction when hopeless and insolvent tenants had to leave. It would be said that it would be a great injustice to a landlord to give to the tenant a property in the estate without compensation. But by the present bill every landlord became more or less an annuitant. By the bill I proposed he would be at least an annuitant with an annuity. I hoped that Irish landlords would join in asking for this final settlement, accepted by the tenant delegates as final. It was far better to put down one's foot and find bottom, than to flounder about amid continuous agitation, continued discontent, and continued terrorism. I wound up my speech by strongly urging the Government to render the Purchase Clauses more acceptable and workable. It always seemed to me one of the greatest evils of Irish society that the great mass of the agricultural population should be divorced from all ownership in the soil. If there was one thing more conservative in its tendency than another, it was the possession of land by a number of proprietors ; while, if there was one thing more revolutionary than another, it was the concentration of land in the hands of a few great proprietors. I concluded by saying that, though I preferred my own way of dealing with the land question, yet that I would unhesitatingly support the bill of the Government.

In Committee, Sir John Gray embodied my suggestions in clauses, but was opposed on all of them by the Government. On one of these clauses Mr. Gladstone, though speaking unfavourably as regards our proposal, paid me the compliment of saying "that I was well known as a worthy representative of an admirable class of landlords."

It is curious enough that the second Land Bill of Mr. Gladstone in 1880 was founded entirely on the plan I suggested, but with many mischievous additions. It would have been a great blessing had the Government decided to legislate in 1871 on the basis of my suggestions. The bill would have been received with gratitude and acclamation ; it would have come direct and spontaneously from the English Government, and not as extorted by the Irish Nationalist leaders. The tenant right would have been working quietly and successfully, and whatever evictions there were would have been money transactions, satisfactorily arranged between the out-going and in-coming tenant, and without the scenes of bloodshed and disorganization which have since attended every final disruption of a tenancy. But, as usual, every dealing with Ireland is too late.

1871.

As this was my last session in Parliament I might have well sat quiet, and voted for the Government on all occasions; but I was to a certain degree pledged to a measure for increasing the number of decent labourers' dwellings, and giving inducements to landlords to build them. In the previous year the Government had opposed my proposals, not on their demerits, but on the plea that the subject was too large to be tacked on to the Land Bill. I regarded the improvement of the condition of the Irish labourer to be the corollary and complement of the Land Act. There was a report drawn up in the previous year by the Irish Poor Law inspectors on the condition of the Irish labourer. Their testimony was almost unanimous, and it was to this effect—that discontent was general among that class chiefly owing to the miserable habitations in which they were compelled to dwell; that the sense of their degraded condition and their constant privations made them hopeless, and in some cases reckless and desperate ; that, without exception, they despaired of attaining decent comfort in their own land ; and, consequently, that all their thoughts were turned to America. On the other hand, it was stated that when they held direct from the landlord, they were generally cheerful and contented.

I held that the first provision of any bill should be to encourage landlords to build cottages by liberal terms, in lending money for that purpose. A small portion of grazing land for a cow should be attached to the cottage. All rent-paying cottages should be periodically inspected, and no rent recoverable for any habitation unless it were pronounced fit for a dwelling.

I exhorted the Government to take up the subject on the terms I had indicated, or to appoint a small Committee of both parties to report on the lines which should be made the basis of legislation.

There was a short but very interesting debate on the purchase by the Government of the famous collection of Dutch pictures from the present Sir Robert Peel for £75,000. There was a strong and unanimous feeling in the House in favour of the purchase, and I was able to pay a warm compliment to my old friend Sir Robert Peel, who had been offered £80,000, but preferred to take the sum proposed by the Government, in order that these noble works, testifying to the taste and knowledge of his great father, should become national property. The purchase was, however, clouded by the unfortunate condition that for seven years the annual grant of £10,000 to the National Gallery should be suspended. There was, however, a promise on the part of the Treasury that any applications during that period for the purchase of pictures of special importance to the Gallery should be favourably considered. Our director, Sir William Boxall, was highly pleased with the arrangement, as it relieved him from the responsibility, which he abhorred, of making any purchase. The Treasury, however, showed no sign of illiberality. It willingly acceded to the one application made by Sir William Boxall, and bought at a high price ' The Triumph of Scipio," by Mantegna; and in 1875

Mr. Disraeli placed £20,000 at the disposition of Mr. Burton, the new director, to make extensive purchases at the Barker sale. I may mention in reference to the Peel pictures, to show what an excellent bargain was made by the Government, that in 1884, when the Trustees of the National Gallery were endeavouring to secure, but alas! in vain, some of the pre-eminently fine Rubenses from the Duke of Marlborough, Alfred Rothschild met me in St. James's Street, and said, "If you think the Blenheim Rubenses are more important than your Dutch pictures to the Gallery, and that you cannot get the money from the Government, I am prepared to give you £250,000 for the Peel pictures; and I will hold good to this offer till the day after to-morrow."

The time came at last, the session ended. I left the House of Commons, of which I had been fourteen years a member, and a popular member, both outside and within its walls. I had worked hard and successfully, and had taken a prominent place; and when I quitted West-minster Hall for the last time, it was not without certain feelings of dejection. At the same time I felt that I had acted wisely in resigning my seat. I was not blind to the signs of the times, and I clearly foresaw that I could not long look forward to hold the county of Galway without giving pledges which no inducement would have made me accept. I knew I was leaving my constituents in the full blaze of popularity. I also knew well that before a year elapsed, my reception by them might be of a very different description. And so I buried my dead, and turned from the West to the glowing horizon of the East, and to Ceylon, the object of my ambition and my day-dream for many a long year.

PART II.

CEYLON.

CHAPTER XIV.

In January, 1872, I married Elizabeth, third daughter of Sir William Clay, M.P. for Tower Hamlets, and a well-known public man in his day. She was the widow of Mr. James Temple Bowdoin. She was a woman of many accomplishments, a good linguist, extremely fond of art, and remarkably well read. I had been deeply attached to her for many years of trouble to her, and she amply rewarded that attachment by her own. Through her liberality I was freed at once from every liability, and went out to Ceylon with a comfortable private income besides my official salary. We were married by my dear old friend and schoolfellow Hugh Pearson, at St. George's, Hanover Square, and set out at once for Brindisi.

We reached Brindisi on the 22nd of January, and Alexandria very prosperously on the 23rd. The Khedive Ismail gave us a gracious reception; a troop of Dragoons escorted us to our hotel, where we gave the gratified captain a sovereign, and a special train conveyed us to Cairo. There we tarried, greatly enjoying ourselves, for over a fortnight. I found an old friend there, Professor Huxley, and he was our constant companion in the many excursions we made. I never met a man so completely under a spell as Huxley was with Egypt. We were often

at Boulak Museum together, and he took the deepest
interest in it.

Before I left England, one of the chief subjects discussed with me at the Colonial Office was that of improving
the harbour accommodation of Ceylon. There were two
plans to be considered—that of spending a considerable
sum on Galle, so as to render it more free from danger ;
the other that of making Colombo the port of call, involving a very heavy expenditure. The issue was virtually
left to my decision. The official mind at Downing Street
was evidently in favour of the former plan, as involving
comparatively a small outlay, and there was but little
expectation of the extraordinary increase of shipping
which would result from a capacious and safe port of call.
The then Under Secretary for the Colonies, Mr. Monsell,
now Lord Emly, in solemn tones adjured me not to lend
myself on any account to the wild scheme of constructing
a new harbour at Colombo, which was not required, would
probably not be resorted to, and the construction of which
would seriously embarrass the finances of the colony.
These sage admonitions had the effect of sending me
out a decided partisan for the maintenance and improvement of the port of Galle. But this opinion was considerably shaken by some conversations I had on board.
My informant, whose opinion I could depend on, expressed
his conviction that Galle could not be made safe, nor
sufficiently large, whatever might be the expenditure on
it ; that it was most dangerous to approach, and dangerous
when in it, from the nature of its rocky bottom, which
had no secure anchorage ; and that during the south-
western monsoon it was at the greatest risk that landing
could be effected, from the heavy rollers coming right
into it, and which no works could possibly keep out.
" I never enter it," he said, " without fear ; and I never

find myself out of it without a sense of deep relief." The
truth of one of his objections was soon brought home to
me, for the fine new P. and O. ship, the *Peshawar*, which
had brought out my carriages, arrived there a few days
after us, and bumped heavily against the rocky bottom.
Fortunately, steam was up, and the captain got her out
at once in safety. As we entered the port I was pointed
out the masts of a large vessel just above water, which
had lately foundered by striking on a rock in trying to
make the entrance.

I had subsequently good reason myself for appre-
ciating the remarks I had heard as to the heavy seas
which rolled into Galle during the "south-western," for, on
returning from England in August, 1874, I was nearly
drowned in landing at Galle, and most of my boxes were
broken, and some of the contents injured.

I shall never forget that first entrance into Galle. The
morning was beautiful, and the scenery absolutely enchanting. On our right were hills clothed with verdure ; on the
left was the fort of Galle, built by the Dutch, so neat and
pretty that it seemed ornamental work ; and in the back-
ground was a deep grove of cocoanut palms, just issuing
from the water as from a bath, and bending lithely under
the morning breeze. The shore under the fort was covered
with the bright, pale yellow foliage of a tree I had never
seen before, and which rendered the appearance of my new
dominion singularly attractive. We were immediately
greeted by the official world and by my secretary, Mr.
Cockburn Stewart, whom I had taken over from Sir
Hercules Robinson. He was an extremely handsome
man, with most pleasant manners, thoroughly acquainted
with his work ; and he informed me that, if I had no
.objection, it was arranged that I should pass that day,
Saturday, and Sunday, at Galle, and make my official

entry into Colombo in the cool of the evening on Monday, going there by the Colonial steamer, the *Serendib*. On landing, amid a salvo of artillery, we were driven to the Queen's House at Galle, a very comfortable dwelling, where everything was prepared for our reception, and where in the evening I was visited by the *élite* of the town, civil and military. What most struck me was the beauty of the hibiscus flowers in the little garden attached, and the enormous size of the State bed, handed down from the Dutch, and which was large enough to allow at least half a dozen folks to sleep in comfort. While on the subject of this Queen's House I may mention that it was the subject of my first, and indeed only, quarrel with the Colonial Office. On making inquiries as to its *raison d'être*, I was informed that it was maintained, at the expense of the colony, for the entertainment of illustrious visitors with orders for their reception from the Colonial Office, and for the occasional visits of the Governor; that the charge was exorbitant, and that, as there was a most admirable hotel in the town, it was entirely unnecessary, except to afford to the Downing Street officials the means of exercising hospitality at the expense of Ceylon. I registered a resolution that it should be short-lived, as a Government institution, and I carried this resolution into effect during the autumn by selling it for about £1500, and purchasing the present Queen's Cottage at Nuwara-Eliya, with a good deal of wooded land at the back, for about the same amount. I was warned by my Colonial Secretary, Mr. Irving (now Sir Henry), that the Colonial Office, tenacious of their privileges of exercising hospitality, would refuse their sanction to any such proposal, so I thought the best course was to act first—*cosa fatto capo ha*—and inform the Secretary of State when the deed was done. Great was the wrath in Downing Street, and

an angry despatch was sent to me, stating I was not
warranted in disposing of a public building of that kind.
I replied in a penitent, but somewhat sarcastic missive.
As matters turned out subsequently, I acted with much
prescience. When Galle was doomed as a port, the value
of Queen's House fell to about a third what I got for it,
whereas the house and grounds at Nuwara-Eliya have
immensely increased in value.

The next day we attended church, and had an excellent sermon from a clergyman of colour, the Rev. Mr.
Schrader, of mixed Dutch and Singalese extraction. It
was the sermon of a scholar and a polished gentleman,
and I heard that he had taken his degree at Cambridge.
In the evening we were driven out to a place called
Wakwalla, celebrated in the old days, when Galle was in
its glory, for the extraordinary beauty of the surrounding
landscape, and for its being the rendezvous of the worst
rogues, who sold false jewellery to the very gullible
passengers who visited it.   The landscape was enchanting
behind us, near the sea ; and in front, right over an unbroken extent of foliage, the great ridge of Ceylon's
mountains.   We returned home delighted, and our antici-
pations of the beauty of our new country were not disappointed.   On this occasion I saw, for the first and last
time during my sojourn in Ceylon of five years and a half,
a cobra. He crossed the road at large just in front of
me, and took refuge in a huge white ant hill.   Good folks
at home are terribly frightened by stories of poisonous
snakes, but we English rarely are troubled by them. None
of them commence an attack, and, at the noise of our
boots, they slip quietly away.   The grounds round the
Pavilion at Kandy had a very evil reputation for an
abundance of cobras, but I never saw one, although the
coolies often brought them in alive to do battle with a

famous fighting mongoose belonging to me, of which
valiant and island-famed animal more anon.

We were not much pestered by the would-be vendors
of mock gems, because of the official presence; but when
any of us wandered any distance from the ruck, we were
sure to be met by a native holding out a tempting sapphire
ring. I may here recall an amusing story I heard of the
doings of these worthies. On returning from the great
festivities at the opening of the Isthmus of Suez, I was
travelling from Marseilles to Nice in the carriage with a
gentleman whom I had met on the steamer. He was
wearing a very remarkable sapphire ring. I knew nothing
of gems at that time, but I was always attracted to them.
I suppose my eyes were fixed on the ring, for the gentleman said to me, "I see, sir, you are looking at my ring.
I bought it at Galle the other day. Pray look at it, and
tell me what you think is its value." I said I thought
it a very fine coloured and perfect stone, but that, not being
much of a lapidary, I could not put a value on it. "Well,
make a guess," said he. I remembered having had a
sapphire ring, an heirloom in our family, valued in
London, and, comparing the two, I came to the conclusion that this ring might be valued at £100, and said
so. "You are quite right, sir," said the gentleman; "that
was exactly the price demanded for it; but I got it more
reasonably. I was on deck when we were leaving Galle,
and a well-dressed native came up to me mysteriously,
and said, 'I have no false jewellery to offer you, sir, but I
have come aboard to sell a very fine ring, the property of
my brother, who, if he does not sell it to-day, will have to
go to jail.' With these words he asked me to step aside,
and then showed me this ring, after unrolling it from one
covering after another of rags. 'I want £100 for it,' said
he, 'and it is cheap.' I said I could not give so much.

He insisted on its cheapness. I said I would not give half
that price. Then, with sad tones, he said he would take
£50 to save his brother. I said I would not give £50;
and so we descended till we got to £10, when the screw
began to move, and the boatswain to cry 'All strangers
ashore!' He then turned to me, with a look of supplication, and said, 'Well, what will you give?' 'I will give you
what I have in my hand,' said I ; and this was half a crown.
'Take the ring,' said he. 'May it relieve your brother
from going to prison,' was my valedictory salute, as he
hurried away. This is the story of the ring I wear, sir,
and I have found my friend was no loser by the transaction, as the supposed stone is glass, the supposed gold
setting brass, the whole being worth about 8*d*. or 10*d*."

On another occasion, when returning from Australia,
I met a lady who was very proud of the purchases she
had made at Galle, amounting to about £50. She showed
them to me with great exultation, and asked me to value
them. Although at that time I thoroughly understood
the value of gems, I was rather reluctant to do so, for, on
looking at them in the most careless manner, I saw they
were the veriest rubbish. The sapphires were opaque,
the cat's-eyes colourless, and I was obliged to say that
the whole lot was not worth £5 ; in fact, no one would
buy them at any price. She said she heard the man
from whom she bought them praised as one of the best-
known jewellers in Galle, and she showed me the receipt.
I knew the man well, and I told the lady if she would
entrust her valuables to my aide-de-camp we might probably recover the money ; and so we did. The jeweller
blustered at first, but was told that he would be refused
entrance to every steam packet, and that, when a ship
arrived, a placard should be placed before his house,
warning passengers against entering his shop. These

T

high-handed measures soon brought him to reason, and we had the pleasure of forwarding to the injured lady the full amount of which she had been cheated; but I doubt if this restitution made up for the humiliation of having been so cheated, and of being proved to be so ignorant of precious stones.

On Monday morning we started betimes by the Colonial steamer *Serendib*, and had a delightful journey. The sea was calm, with a slight breeze. We steamed along pretty close to the land, and reached Colombo about four o'clock. We found the whole population in anxious expectation, and in their best attire. The innumerable fishing-boats were adorned, and skimmed to and fro like huge marine insects. Triumphal arches, in the formation of which the Singalese show remarkable taste, were erected at the landing-place. The battery thundered its salute, and the garrison received us with the clashing of firearms, and sackbut, psaltery, trumpets, and all kinds of music. The distance from the landing-place to Queen's House is short, but we were delayed by the immense crowd, oblivious of a dark cloud, slowly but surely coming up. The custom used to be for the new Governor to dismount from his carriage, and, entering the green in front of the official buildings, there to have his commission read to him by the Government agent of the province, and then adjourn to the council chamber and be sworn in. Mr. Layard (now Sir Charles) performed the ceremony; but, as the commission was long and he was slow, the cloud above opened on us, and down came a tremendous shower. The wet smudged the ink, and poor Mr. Layard was fairly nonplussed; so I determined to abandon all nonsense of etiquette, and made off, as hard as I could run, to the neighbouring building. Every one was aghast at such a harum-scarum breach of tradition, but all were delighted ; and I was sworn in dry and comfortable, instead of being wet to the skin. I may mention that, in my commission, I was appointed, not only Commander-in-Chief of the land force of Ceylon, but also Lord High Admiral. I can't say I ever made use of these great powers, but they served me on my return to England. I desired to become a member of the Army and Navy Co-operative Stores, but was met by the inquiry in what manner I could claim to belong to either service. "By having been Commander-in-Chief in the one, and Lord High Admiral in the other," was my reply. I need not say that the portals of the establishment were at once thrown open.

I was surprised and elated by the size and grandeur of the Government House when I reached it. The bedrooms large and airy, each with its own bath, large enough to swim in ; the drawing-room seventy-five feet long, looking out on the sea and on a garden, in which were growing trees all decked out with flowers, some of them most gorgeous, such as I had never seen before—Barringtonia, with its grand leaves and showers of white flowers ; the pandanus, a towering banian, and innumerable others. In the stables I found an excellent pair of Australian carriage horses and a Persian cob of great strength, all purchased for me at Sir H. Robinson's sale. The cob had belonged to Lord Mayo, who sent him to Sir Hercules. I rode him till I left the island, and he never made a false step. He was extremely savage in the stable, but I won him over to thorough gentleness by always bringing him a banana, which he dearly loved. I subsequently bought two ponies, another carriage horse, and another riding horse, and this made up my stud. I found everything on a very generous scale. The house was lighted up and furnished at Government expense.

Glass and crockery were also provided, on which I had
to pay five per cent. for the use.   Besides the private
servants paid by myself, there were twelve other servants
in uniform, kept up by the Government, as was also
the   garden.   The   same   arrangements   prevailed   at
Kandy, and, subsequently, at Queen's Cottage, Nuwara-
Eliya.

One thing, however, gave me a start.   Before I left
London I was requested by Mr. Robinson, of the Colonial
Office, to see him upon a financial matter connected with
Ceylon, and he said, in an off-hand manner, " By the way,
it is right to mention that your salary is counted in
rupees.   You will get Rs. 70,000 instead of £7000.   It
makes no difference to you ; indeed, I believe you will gain
a fraction on each pound."   In the softness of my heart I
said it was all very good ; but when I arrived at Galle
I found that the rupee had then fallen to 1s. 10d., so I
was thus mulcted of 210,000 halfpennies at once, which,
according to Cocker, amount to £437 12s.   The rupee
subsequently fell to 1s. 5½d., thus diminishing my income
by one-fourth.   In the communication from the Colonial
Office announcing my appointment, my salary was stated
to be £7000 a year, and, though I was subsequently informed it was to be changed to rupees, still I was at the
same time told that the change would probably be a gain
rather than a loss.   I made no complaint, however, and
I need hardly say that the Colonial Office did not volunteer to relieve me ; but my successor, Sir James Longden,
was not so mealy-mouthed, and he got his salary raised
to Rs. 80,000.   I have always regretted I had any delicacy,
and I strongly recommend any dear friend or relative who
may read these garrulities, never to have the least compunction in exacting to the last penny whatever is fairly
due by the State.   You can gain nothing, not even credit,

by fine feeling, and you lose your money and are
thought soft.

I had still more reason to complain of the curtail-
ment of my finances, by finding that the revenue was in
the most flourishing condition.   As we drove about
Colombo, during the next three days, I fully made up
my mind that many things might be done for its improvement.   On the whole, we were much pleased with it,
except when we had to drive through native quarters,
which were most unsavoury in sight and smell.   There are
pretty drives about it in every direction, and the private
houses, with their compounds full of plants and flowers,
rendered the drives very pleasant, to say nothing of the
excellence of the roads, which were like a bowling-green.

It was settled we were to go up at once to Nuwara-
Eliya, the Ceylon sanatorium, about 6400 feet above the
sea.   We remained, however, for a few days at Kandy,
to hold an official reception, and above all to make
acquaintance with the Kandian chiefs.   This first railway
journey in Ceylon was immensely interesting, and even the
low, flat country which we traversed to the foot of the
hills, with its bare, paddy fields, clumps of trees, plants of
gigantic foliage, and herds of wallowing buffaloes, and
little humped cattle, uttering an extraordinary noise, more
resembling an eructation than the loud, bold lowing of
our domestic oxen, was not without enjoyment.   The
distance from Colombo to Kandy was about seventy-four
miles, and at the station of Rambakkan we all at once
went up the ascent from the flat plain to the mountainous
region of the Kandy kingdom.   The city of Kandy is
about 1700 feet above the sea-level, and we rose that
height in a few miles.   The engine grunted and creaked
as it dragged us up over alarmingly sharp curves and
gradients between forty-five and fifty feet; but the

scenery was of entrancing beauty and grandeur. On each side of us were bold peaks, clothed with vegetation almost to the summit. Afar were other peaks, in the coffee-planted country, one of them, the so-called "Duke's Nose," resembling that well-known feature of the Duke of Wellington. Another was a bold peak rising abruptly with a square summit like a huge book, called the "Bible Rock." Below us we looked down to immense depths, with only a foot or two between the rails and the precipice. Terrible spots these were. One in particular, called "Sensation Rock," was on a flat projection cut out of the solid cliff; the rail was laid by workmen let down from above by ropes. It is a fearful place for a nervous novice, but no accident has ever happened at these dangerous-looking spots, and so old ladies do not implore the guard to let them get out to go on foot over these awful passages. If they were awful to look down, still they were most beautiful, for, though in certain places the fall is sheer and unbroken, still the mountain-side was generally clothed with trees of remarkable beauty. Grand talipots, the giants of the palms, stood up head and shoulders above the rest, in all their glory of flowering. But these grand and majestic crests are the symbols of death, and after flowering, which is their last effort, these grand trees decline and die. Then there were the brilliant scarlet (so-called gold) mohur tree, and the Lagerstrœmia, some with fruit, some with purple blossoms; and many others, of which I know not the names; and parrots and strange birds of many hues were darting among them to and fro, and all about us huge and gorgeous butterflies, so that there was not for an instant repose for the eyes.

We found a prodigious crowd awaiting our arrival, and made our way in solemn procession to the Pavilion, the Governor's residence, a short distance from the station.

This residence was built by the vigorous and enlightened Sir Edward Barnes. It is Italian in style of architecture, and it is said he traced it with his finger, dipped in claret, on the dinner-table. Be that as it may, it is a very seemly edifice ; but it is only half finished, as, while it was progressing, a hard-hearted commission was sent to report on the finances of Ceylon, which were in a most tangled condition, and one of their first recommendations was that the portion of the Pavilion not finished should be left uncompleted. Even as it is, it is imposing in appearance, but sadly deficient in rooms, which prevents (perhaps rather a blessing to the Governors) any profuse irruption of visitors. The grounds are perfectly lovely with numerous kinds of tropical plants treasured up with infinite solicitude in our English greenhouses. The dining-room was particularly handsome, with its white chunam columns, in the construction of which report said some millions of eggs were expended. My secretary had his own house in the grounds, and my aide-de-camp had another. The stables were spacious, and well arranged, so that, on the whole, I was well satisfied with the prospect of an annual four months' residence at Kandy ; for the Governor's year was divided equally between Colombo, Kandy, and Nuwara-Eliya.

In the afternoon the Kandian chiefs mustered in great force, and in great magnificence. Their costumes were very notable, quite different from anything I had ever seen. They were men of stately presence, and of far more character of countenance than the low-country natives ; but what struck me most was the prodigious expanse of their stomachs, which was not to be wondered at, as round them were rolled from thirty to forty yards of muslin. When our interview had lasted long enough, and compliments and polite inquiries were pretty well exhausted, I bid them good evening.   But we had not done with them, for after dinner we heard a prodigious disturbance outside, and were informed that the chiefs desired to honour us by what is called a "perahara," which is a procession of elephants and "devil-dancers."

I have seen many peraharas since, but nothing that approached this.   The finest elephants in the island were brought in by the chiefs and heads of the temples, who always keep some of these animals for pomp and cere-monies, even more than for utility.   Each chief or head man of the temple marched up the avenue at the head of his band, playing the most awful instruments.   Behind the chiefs, painted and bedizened with brass ornaments rattling and ringing, and throwing themselves into every kind of contortion, followed the devil-dancers ; and then slowly emerged from the profound darkness of the back-ground, dimly shown by torches, the enormous, stately elephants.   It was indeed a weird sight.   Had I been an Arab, I should have imagined it was in honour of Eblis, prince of darkness, the preliminary for some dreadful nameless nocturnal sacrifice.   However, nothing on this occasion was sacrificed, except some sugar-cane, which was thankfully received and munched by the array of elephants which environed the Pavilion, and behaved in the most exemplary manner.

The next morning I was brought out at early dawn for a constitutional round the hill, at the foot of which stands the Pavilion ; and still higher rose my admiration of the natural beauties of Ceylon.   Never had I taken such a walk.   The morning mists were rolling up from the valleys at the other side of the hill, the mountain peaks had emerged, and gradually a vast extent of country came into view.   Below us roared the Mahawelli-ganga, the largest river of the island, as it dashed along its rock-encumbered channel, and the sides of the hill down to it were clothed with trees all new to me in foliage. As we turned the hill homewards we came in view of other mountain peaks, and below us was the Temple of the Sacred Tooth of Buddha, his most venerated relic, which we were to visit in the evening. Beyond it was the beautiful little Kandy Lake, and the town of Kandy laid out at right angles, and the square, red-brick tower of the English church, with creepers making their way up it, and looking for all the world like one of our home village churches, peaceable and unobtrusive, and quite venerable. The walk is called after Lady Horton, who had it constructed most skilfully, and, as it is a good wide road, it is the favourite morning ride of the European young ladies of Kandy, and a favourite flirting-ground for both pedestrians and equestrians.

In the evening we were conducted with much gravity to the Temple of the Tooth, to see this relic of Gautama Buddha, for which it is said a million of money was offered by the King of Burmah. It is brought out and shown to the multitude once or twice a year, but on other occasions no one, unless of princely station, or a representative of royalty, such as governors or ambassadors, are permitted to behold it. We were led upstairs to a very small room on the upper floor, full of yellow-robed priests. The heat was terrible, and the odour of cocoanut oil and many perspiring human beings was detestable. In a portion of the room inside a glass case was a profusion of jewels, chiefly rubies, and, so far as I could judge, very bad ones. A huge silver-gilt dagoba * contained minor dagobas, it

---

* The dagoba is a bell-shaped erection. The greater dagobas are supposed to have some slight relic of Buddha in their foundations, but there are innumerable small dagobas erected as a kind of pious tribute of respect.

is said of pure gold, and within the last was the relic, which appeared to me like a crocodile's tooth. It was on a stand, supported by a narrow gold band, so the whole of it was to be seen. As to any human being ever having been able to hold in his head such a monstrous tooth, two inches long at least, and proportionately wide, it is simply impossible ; but whether it be a carved piece of ivory or the tooth of an animal, I cannot say, though I incline to the latter view of the case. We were shown, besides all manner of jewels and relics, among other things, a sitting image of Buddha, about three inches in height, said to be an emerald, but there is no doubt of its being glass. We were heartily glad to get out of the heat and smell, and walked for a cup of tea to the "Old Palace" which is quite close, formerly the residence of the kings of Kandy, now inhabited by the Government agents of the Central Province. It is rather an interesting building, though of no great age, with its distinctive Kandian features, its picturesque, so-called " broken - backed " roof—an architectural arrangement peculiar to Kandian buildings—its thick walls with representations on them in stucco. In short, it is a very curious residence, though, we should imagine, very much restricted in space for the accommodation of a monarch of such greatness as the King of Kandy believed himself to be. The Government agent then showed us the Hall of Audience, only a few yards from the palace. The most remarkable features about it are the roof and the wooden pillars of jack wood of very beautiful design, and rich in the colouring of age. Here the king sat, received foreign envoys and his chiefs, and decided questions of importance. Formerly there ran a moat from the lake in front of the temple to the end of the king's palace, but a barbarous Government agent, thinking it gave him rheumatism, not only filled it up, but filled it with the beautiful old Kandian

wall which flanked it all along, and which he ruthlessly
pulled down. Fortunately, a portion of it in front of the
temple remained intact, and I was thus enabled, year after
year, at great expense, and with some grumbling in the
Legislative Council, to replace, not only these walls, but
all other walls, especially those along the lake, which had
originally been built in the Kandian style of architecture.
The King of Kandy, whom we took prisoner and expelled
in 1815, a man of a thousand crimes, cruel and perfidious,
had still one redeeming quality, he was a man of excellent
taste, and undoubtedly made the royal part of Kandy full
of architectural beauty, to say nothing of the charm of the
lake, which is due to him. I speak of the *royal* part of
Kandy, for such was the overweening pride of Kandian
kings that no house could be erected by any private
person, except of the most humble description and thatched
with mats.

The next day we paid a visit to the famous botanic
garden of Peradeniya, said to be the most beautiful in
the world. This garden is included in a bend of the
Mahawelli-ganga, which forms its boundary on three sides.
It is about three miles from Kandy, a very pretty drive,
and you enter it by a row of indiarubber trees of great
height and size. Their huge roots spread widely above
the ground, looking like the intertwined limbs of prehistoric monsters, or uncanny tentacles of gigantic cuttle-
fish.

We drove down an avenue fringed on each side with
palms and diverse tropical trees. At the end of it was a
circle of palms from various countries, some of them fierce,
thorny, dangerous productions, others graceful, slender,
wide-spreading, and in the midst, far above all, rose up a
magnificent talipot. Turning to the left, we came to the
residence of Dr. Thwaites, or, as he much preferred being

called, Mr. Thwaites, a small, slight, elderly man, who had tea and excellent bread and butter for us. He was the author of a work of great celebrity on the plants of Ceylon, " Flora Zeylanica," and held the highest reputation in Europe as a scientific botanist. He took us over the garden and showed us his magnificent clusters of gigantic bamboos, growing by the river side, and the *Amherstia nobilis*, a tree from Burmah, with the most beautiful blossoms I had ever seen, and all kinds of other trees and plants. A great deal of the garden was neglected and in a state of jungle, and hanging on the trees, in a portion of it, were clusters of innumerable flying-foxes, a kind of huge fruit-eating bat, the pests of the neighbourhood, from the ravages they committed on the garden. As we passed near the trees we were assailed by a villainous sour smell from the colony above us, and on my expressing my surprise that he had not extirpated these wretches, he made some excuse for them, as also for the uncultured portion of the demesne, for the reclaiming of which I in vain offered him additional labour. I found out, when our acquaintance had ripened into intimacy, indeed into great friendship, that the working director had many fads, among them was the inviolabilty of the flying-foxes, the retention of a portion of the garden in a scrubby, disreputable state, and a determination not to label any of the plants, in spite of the supplications of visitors and the remonstrances of scientific men at home, specially Sir Joseph Hooker, his friend and constant correspondent.

There were few persons who had more influence with Mr. Thwaites than myself, but my constant hints at first as to the expediency of getting rid of these drawbacks to the beauty and usefulness of the garden had no effect whatever, and, as they evidently caused him pain, I ceased to interfere. There was no one with whom I lived on such terms of extreme intimacy as with him, during the whole period of my appointment. I learned much from him, as he was a man of general information and of deep research. I much wish I had attended to his wise admonitions as to the instability of coffee. Year after year he foretold its downfall, year after year he was subjected to obloquy and ridicule for his disloyalty to the great King Coffee. He argued that it was impossible that any plant could long survive such weakening of its system as that caused by leaf disease, a kind of fungus, by the attacks of which the leaves fall off, and with them the coffee berries, which the tree is unable to mature. He knew no remedy, and laughed to scorn the various nostrums which were to have exterminated the disease. He implored of me not to lend any money on mortgage upon coffee estates, telling me how he had called in all his own investments and had transferred them to land and houses in Colombo. I should have been a much richer and less worried man had I hearkened to his advice. I well remember going through the thriving coffee districts in the spring of 1877. The blossom was out, and they were as white as a table-cloth. I saw Mr. Thwaites on my return, and rather mocked him as a prophet of evil, since, although there had been disease for several years, coffee had still such a vigorous appearance. "Never mind," said he, "what you saw. Coffee must go out, and that before long." The following year the blow fell, and when in 1883 I visited these valleys, the former splendid plantations contained little more than dried sticks, except where tea had begun to show itself.

Besides his great knowledge of botany, Mr. Thwaites was deeply interested in entomology and in the special branch of the lepidoptera, and under his auspices was begun that fine work, "The Lepidoptera of Ceylon,"

published a few years ago by the colony at the expense of
£1500. I took up the subject very warmly, and it gave
me a great deal of enjoyment, and it showed me how wise
it is to encourage young lads in pursuits which are too
often ridiculed—such as collecting insects, shells, minerals,
coins, etc. When a schoolboy, entomology was the
fashion of the school I was at. Most of us had collections
of butterflies, which we caught and impaled with infinite
gusto; and, not only that, but we hunted out with keen
industry the abodes of caterpillars, and tended them with
care during their various stages. The result was that
when I came to Ceylon my early proclivities were re-
awakened, and my visits to Mr. Thwaites, who had always
batches of fresh and very curious caterpillars to show me,
which his botanical knowledge enabled him to nourish
with great effect, were full of interest. His quick-eyed
coolies were well rewarded for all they brought in. These
caterpillars, in all their stages, and the plants on which
they fed, the chrysalis, and the full-formed butterfly or
moth, were drawn by one of his Singalese assistants with
the strictest fidelity. This man had a brother almost as
perfect an artist as himself, and I employed him in the
same work. It was an expensive affair, costing me
£100, from beginning to end, but I was enabled to lend
it to Dr. Moore, who edited from it "The Lepidoptera of
Ceylon," as the brother copy, done by the Government
draughtsman could not be spared from the island. The
amusement of forming butterfly collections was quite
general during my time in Ceylon; elderly gentlemen and
young dashing officers being equally ardent, especially my
staff. I brought home a very fine collection, which I gave
to the Kildare-street Museum.

During my short stay at Kandy I had many State
visits from the great Kandian chiefs, and was much

pleased with their dignity and perfection of manner. Of course their object was to please, and, if possible, to find out my views before committing themselves. But, as I determined to give them no lead, I obtained much valuable instruction from them. My chief friend was Dunawilla, the dewa nillame or guardian of the Sacred Tooth of Buddha. He often came in to have a talk in the morning, and was always welcome, for he was full of information and very sensible, besides having a great deal of humour. He was taxed one evening at dinner by Captain Watt, a very old officer in the Department of Works, with having been a Christian in early days, and with having relapsed into Buddhism in order to obtain the important office which he held. He denied the fact. " But," said Captain Watt, " you have sat in my pew often." " And I am perfectly ready to sit in it again any Sunday, if you can find room for me," replied Dunawilla. " Our religion is not exclusive. We consider it no sin to attend Christian worship. All that I heard at your church was good. Probably I should go there often, but I could not do so in my present position without incurring the reproach from my countrymen, that I was a Christian and not a Buddhist, and therefore unfit for my office."

I found there had been two policies as regards the management of the Kandian province. By some it was upheld that as far as possible it should be ruled by means of the old Kandian families, that is, by appointing efficient men, when they could be obtained, representatives of these families. The Kandian population is intensely aristocratic, and the influence of the chiefs very great. Of course the Government had the power to carry out its views without their co-operation, and even against their wishes, but there was no doubt that matters went on far more smoothly and efficiently when the native officers were selected from families of ancient lineage rather than from men who, though of excellent character and of experience, had risen from the ranks. There were others, and chief among them Sir Charles, then Mr. Layard, who adopted a totally different system. He contended that the Kandian chiefs acted tyrannically, that conceding power to them was giving them illegitimate influence, and that it was unjust to the lowly-born Kandian that he should be prejudiced by reason of birth. He was a thorough advocate of centralization in this, but the refutation was in Mr. Layard's own district. He was Government agent of the Western Province, in which were included some Kandian districts of great extent. To some of these he appointed as native heads, clerks from his office in Colombo, well-trained officials, but they were undoubted failures. The proud Kandians despised them, and evaded, and unwillingly obeyed their orders. My policy was the first named ; in all the Kandian districts I tried to select men of illustrious birth, and was well served by them, and I was able thereby to persuade the Kandian chiefs to send their sons to English schools, at Kandy and Colombo, and receive a thorough education. I well remember the joy that was felt by my giving one of these appointments to a member of the great Nuwara Wewa family, at Anaradhapura, who can show unbroken lineage and unchanged territory since the planting of the bô tree, some centuries before Christ. The family pride of these chieftains is very great indeed, and in no way did I more win their hearts, which I flatter myself I did thoroughly, than by always receiving them, not with condescending civility, but as if they were in every way deserving of respect.

CHAPTER XV.

WE were all so enchanted with Kandy, with its rides and walks, and Peradeniya Gardens, that it was difficult to tear us away to our mountain residence, Nuwara-Eliya. But the weather was at the hottest, and so we departed and mounted to an elevation of 6400 feet, where we had been lent a house by a kind friend, the Governor having then no habitation in the Sanatorium. Every new excursion that we made enchanted us more and more with the varied beauty of Ceylon scenery. The drive, from Kandy to Nuwara-Eliya, of thirty-six miles was no exception. The scenery was very beautiful among peaks starting up boldly, some close, some at a distance. The road was trying enough, from its narrowness and the tremendous declivities along which it ran. We had heard of constant accidents from its being absolutely devoid of all protection, while heaps of broken metal, instead of being enclosed at proper spots, were heaped up constantly on the sides of the road, thereby narrowing it, and rendering it more dangerous than ever. When we consider that Ceylon seems to be the last resort of the kickers, jobbers, bolters, halt, lame, and blind horses which it is advisable to deport from Bombay and Australia, it is no wonder that every week we read of accidents, broken collar-bones and legs, and smashed vehicles along these mountain roads. The roads themselves were

U

admirable, but, for reasons of economy, far too narrow, and one of my first resolves was to obtain a vote of money to widen them, and erect protective embankments in all dangerous places throughout the island, and to establish depôts for the metal; and many a blessing I received from those whose lot it was to travel over them.

We halted at Rambodda, at the foot of the famous pass, by which we ascended something over 3500 feet in five miles, to reach the highest range of tableland above it. It was a spot of extraordinary beauty; from the veranda of the rest-house we saw eleven cascades tumbling from the mountain in every direction. Right above us a stream plunged from a rocky height, and became as it were a ribbon of mist as it fell. Tennyson's beautiful line, " Slow-dropping veil of thinnest lawn," exactly describes it. The ascent was one series of zigzags, and through a primeval forest of a totally different character from the tropical vegetation of the lower country. It was stern, severe, and apparently of immense extent, but, alas! before I left Ceylon most of it had fallen to the axe of the coffee-planter. At last we reached the top, and looked down on the plain of Nuwara-Eliya. It was then far from prepossessing, being a long, extended, dismal swamp. Now a very different sight presents itself to the few who come up the road we climbed, for the iron horse has reached Nuwara-Eliya by another route. The first sight that now catches the eye is a deep blue lake, called after me, which has covered the ungainly swamp, and is about a mile in length and half a mile in breadth. It was one of my early undertakings, and this wonderful improvement was carried out at a cost hardly exceeding £1200. A river ran tortuously through this morass, to and fro in a constant series of curves. Though the distance from where it entered the morass to where it fell over a rocky barrier into a valley below could not have been more than a mile, it was calculated that the length of its windings was over eight miles. Immediately on seeing it I suggested to an engineer that, by erecting a stone embankment at the point where the river left the plain, its water could be arrested and regulated by sluices, and the whole plain inundated to whatever depth was required. This proposal of mine was assailed by carping criticisms of all kinds in the newspapers, and letters appeared as thick as blackberries with objections. This lake, if made, some said, would change the climate of Nuwara-Eliya, and render it too cold; others declared it would breed fever, and others mosquitoes; while an engineering class of objectors maintained that there would not be enough fresh water coming into it to fill it during certain months; and another insisted that it would never hold water, owing to fissures in the geological condition of the soil. Even Mr. Bailey, the clever, long-headed local manager of the Peninsular and Oriental Company, declared he would be prepared to walk across it as soon as it was filled, so far as our constructive efforts would fill it. However, the stone embankment was finished, and the rain came. I was telegraphed for to come and see the wonderful effect. At the top of the pass I looked down on a blue expanse of water, which we can raise or let fall exactly as we wish. And now boats are on it, and a beautiful drive of three or four miles runs round it, and the climate is said to be much improved. I sent Mr. Bailey an invitation to come up and perform the feat of walking across it, which he declined.

We all enjoyed the climate of Nuwara-Eliya after the first few days, during which the rarity of the air was

much felt.   Afterwards we rejoiced in its briskness and
elasticity.   We rode and drove, and had long walks
through jungle, by the side of tumbling streams, where
we were liable to meet a leopard or an elephant at any
minute, and we gave breakfast-parties on the top of
Pedrotallagalla, the highest mountain of Ceylon, something over eight thousand feet, which stood straight above
us, and the crest of which we reached by an easy riding-
path.   And oh, how cold it used to be! and oh, how
good was the strong boiling coffee! and how cold was
the night when we made a picnic and slept at the bungalow of the Horton Plains, a tableland one thousand
feet higher still than Nuwara-Eliya, and about fifteen
miles from it.   It was a very pleasant time, interspersed
with little adventures.   One morning a leopard was
espied in the fork of a tree within the precincts of our
bungalow, but he escaped before a rifle could be brought to
punish his intrusion.   On another occasion we were visited
by an elephant, who, after eating whatever vegetables he
found in the garden, poked his nose, or trunk, through the
back window, in order, I presume, to see what was doing
inside.

The weather was lovely, and time flew quickly, until
the period arrived for me to commence a tour of inspection of my dominions.   It was settled that I should go
down to Colombo, there take the Colonial steamer, the
Serendib, and go to Jaffna, the extreme northern point
of the island ; thence to the coast of India, to see the
arrangements for the coolie immigration from the Madras
Presidency to Ceylon ; then round by sea to Batticaloa,
where I was to visit the irrigation works ; and return thence
by land, over the road, which was advancing to completion,
from Batticaloa to Badulla, a great work of my predecessor,
Sir Hercules Robinson.   We had a very pleasant voyage

to Jaffna, which I found a most remarkable place. It is
inhabited by a Tamil population, which had crossed from
India many hundreds of years ago and driven out the
Singalese. It is virtually an island, being only joined to
the mainland by a causeway. I was greatly struck with
the civilization of this peninsula, and with the industry of
its inhabitants, which had made the waste places so many
gardens. They are a singularly intellectual and astute
race ; too astute, perhaps, for in all the island there are
not so many villainous conspiracies, supported by hard
swearing and consummate art, as in Jaffna. The spread of
education among them is great, and the Tamil doctors,
brought up and trained by an American, Dr. Green, are
about the ablest in the island. There have also come
from Jaffna some eminent engineer officers, members of
the Department of Public Works. The story of the institution of the Medical College at Jaffna by Dr. Green is
very curious. Many years ago a number of pious folks
departed from America on missionary work intent, among
them Dr. Green, a very pious man, but very practical
withal, who thought that healing the heathen would add
much to the effects of preaching to them. They had
determined to land and settle somewhere in India, but
they were shipwrecked close to Jaffna. They accepted the
catastrophe as an interposition of Providence—*Dieu le veut.*
There they were to stay, and there they established themselves, opened schools for boys and for girls, and were
received with open arms. What conversions they made
I cannot say, for when a Hindoo gives up his gods he
has a suspicion of our Trinity, and generally becomes
pure Unitarian. There are certainly, nevertheless, Jaffna
Christians, and it is not the fault of Roman Catholics,
Wesleyans, Presbyterians, Baptists, and English Churchmen that there are not more, for they are all working

away at high pressure, and if they do not convert, they certainly civilize. The effect of school teaching on the girls is very remarkable. When they marry they become, from their education, the head of the house, they keep the money, make up the accounts ; and, as the missionaries insist on cleanliness being akin to godliness, the neatness and tidiness of the cottages presided over by a school-taught mistress were very notable. As I drove through the peninsula with the Government agent, Mr. Twynam, he called my attention to this very interesting fact ; and I was, without difficulty, able to pronounce at sight, whether the lady owner of the house we passed had received a school education or not. I found Mr. Twynam quite devoted to the place ; he had been there for several years, and might have looked to obtain one of the highest appointments in the colony, but he preferred staying where he was exercising a valuable autocracy. This district had enjoyed the singular advantage of having had, as Mr. Twynam's predecessor, a Government agent who had ruled it for, I believe, twenty years. Mr. H. Dyke was his name, a man of great ability, great force of character, and thoroughly understanding the people with whom he had to deal. He was incessant in stimulating them to improvement, and in encouraging their exertions, and had stamped, as it were, the industrial character on them, for which they are now distinguished. They seemed to regard him as a superior being, and " H. Dyke, Esq.," as they always called him, was in every one's mouth.

We occupied fine spacious rooms on the fort, but very hot ; so much so that the following year I had a couple of sleeping-rooms built on the ramparts, which had the advantage of a free current of air, and were a perfect godsend to the judges and subsequent visitors. One evening at dinner

we had a surprise. The subject of conversation was
snakes, and Mr. Twynam mentioned that the huge python
was not uncommon in the forests. I happened to say I
should like to see one. "That is easily managed," he
said ; and gave an order to his servant, who brought in a
box, opened it, and out glided a monstrous snake, at
least sixteen feet long. Every one, and the party was
large, sprung on table and chairs, but Mr. Twynam
exhorted us to dismiss our fears as the reptile was harmless, indeed very friendly. He amused himself by gliding
about the room till it was thought high time to get rid of
him, when a hen was brought in. He did not seem to
notice it at first. At last he turned suddenly on it, threw
all his coils round it with the rapidity of lightning, and
extended it, by this squeezing process, to at least a yard
in length. He slowly, very slowly, began to swallow it,
and was carried off with two long legs sticking out of
his mouth.

From Jaffna we crossed over to the mainland of India
to Deviapatam to obtain a thorough knowledge of the
working of the coolie system of immigration. We
touched at the island of Ramisseram, where stands the
finest of all Hindoo temples in the Madras Presidency ;
the length and size of its galleries are wonderful and
unequalled. We were met at the landing-place by the
high priest and his attendants, among whom were some
very pretty bayaderes, the prettiest women I have ever
seen in India. Three of them walked backwards, tossing
gold balls as we advanced, and preserving their gravity
with dignity, in spite of the admiring and significant
glances of my staff, the worst offenders of whom were
not the young men or the unmarried. We then proceeded
to Deripatana, where we found elephants and horses and
all kinds of music awaiting us, and we were conducted

in great state to the residence of the Rajah of Ramnar,
who was awaiting us with an excellent luncheon. He
was a very good-looking, intelligent, and well-educated
young man, speaking and writing English perfectly. He
was extremely given to photography, and presented me
with a collection of his works, which was interesting. He
very often wrote to me, considering himself to be my
established friend, until his death about two years after
our meeting, some said by poison administered by his
women, others by champagne and brandy administered by
himself.

We steamed round the north of the island, and came
down its east coast till we reached Trincomalee. I had
heard much of this fine harbour, but I was astonished at
its capabilities. Deep water runs up close to the shore;
there is ample space for navies; it is perfectly land-
locked, and ought to be almost impregnable, unless
attacked by a land force. I was warned by Lord Torrington, who had been Governor of Ceylon, on no account
to sleep ashore at Trincomalee, but always to return
to my ship, and that even then I should be lucky if I
escaped from a dangerous type of fever which was always
more or less prevalent. I found, however, a very airy,
spacious house, which appertained to the admiral of the
station, prepared for my reception, and the authorities at
Trincomalee were much scandalized at the evil reputation
their district had received from Lord Torrington, for
they said, and proved by figures, that it was as free from
disease as any other district. It used to be, they said,
notorious for its malaria arising from a swamp to the
west of the town. The swamp has been drained and
reclaimed, and sickness has quite ceased. They all,
however, acknowledged that the heat was tremendous,
and that there was some truth in the legend that

Trincomalee lay directly over the fires of the infernal regions, with an extremely thin crust above them. All the dwellers in the district besought me to put the main road to Dambula in order, in other words, to reconstruct it, as it was only passable during dry weather, being at other times like a quagmire, and without any bridges. I promised to take this work in hand, and kept my word, and now there is an excellent road to Trincomalee from Dambula, spanned by bridges, and rendered comfortable by the establishment of rest-houses along it. From Trincomalee we steered southwards to Batticaloa, the capital of the Eastern Province. It is a difficult and somewhat dangerous place to reach, as one has to pass over a bar leading into a long inland lagoon, by the side of which the pretty neat town is situated. There is generally a heavy surf running over this bar, and many have been the fatal accidents in consequence. I was desirous of seeing the great irrigation works in this province, which had been begun by Sir Henry Ward in 1857, and carried on, after a long interruption, by Sir Hercules Robinson. I was astonished with their remarkable success. These works are of two kinds, either by the storage of water in a large tank or artificial lake, which is effected by taking advantage of the ground and embanking a river, or by constructing what are called "anicuts," namely, stone embankments across rivers, which, by being blocked with closed sluices for a time, have their streams diverted into canals which flow into various tanks where the water is received and held for the cultivation of the rice-fields. The word "tank" gives a very erroneous idea of the size of these artificial lakes, which are of great extent, many of them being miles in circumference—that of Kalawewa, for instance, now restored, the original dimensions of which were over thirty-five miles in circumference, and are not much less at present; while Padawiya, in the Northern Province, constructed by the great Singalese monarch Prakrama Bahu, is said to be not less than fifty-four miles. Of course these gigantic tanks require gigantic embankments. That of Kalawewa is eighty feet high, and would permit six carriages to be driven abreast on the top of it. Many of the tanks have spacious roads running on the top of their banks. These that I now visited, being the first I had seen, greatly surprised me by their size and solidity; and the tanks themselves were extremely beautiful, from the profusion of aquatic plants on their surface. They were, moreover, frequented by innumerable water birds of every kind, whose weird cries made the scene still more striking, and I was warned, when going out to shoot some teal, to beware of the numerous and ferocious alligators with which the tanks abounded. Formerly the regions watered by the tanks were the abode of a miserable half-starving population. Now out of every village there rushed swarms of plump children to see the Governor, and the rice was being exported from it to other districts.

This grand lesson on the benefits of irrigation was not lost upon me, and the work which I began and completed, and its results, in other parts of Ceylon, will be narrated elsewhere.

Before leaving Batticaloa I was brought out to see and believe the great marvel of the place, namely, singing fish. I have already mentioned that Batticaloa is situated on a salt-water lagoon, and it is underneath its placid waters that these concerts take place. I believe the fish only perform when the weather is fine. Most undoubtedly I heard them quite distinctly under our boat in one or two spots as we drifted quietly along. I again heard them on a subsequent occasion, and almost every one who has visited

Batticaloa has been present at these concerts. The sound resembles an Æolian harp, rather plaintive, and perfectly distinct. It goes on for a quarter of an hour or twenty minutes, then ceases, and then goes on again. There is a controversy whether it is caused by a swimming or a shell fish. I was assured by the Government agent that the musician was a shell, a kind of large volute, of which he presented me a specimen, fished up from the spot where a concert was being held. Sir Emerson Tennent, in his most exhaustive, interesting, and accurate account of Ceylon, has been, like poor Mungo Park, accused of romancing, by stating that in this island fish sing, fish climb trees, and spiders spin a single cord capable of knocking a man's hat off. Now I have heard the performances of singing fish, I have often witnessed those of climbing fish, who worked up, by means of their scales, the rough bark of trees rising from the water in order to catch sea-lice and other insects, and my private secretary assured me that his helmet was knocked off his head as he was riding swiftly through the jungle near Badulla, that he turned back to pick it up, and found it was a spider's single cord which extended across the path.

At Batticaloa we mounted our horses, which had been sent down to meet us, and had a long ride for several days before reaching Badulla. We stayed a night at the great tank of Rugam, and were nearly devoured by mosquitoes, so much so that the venom actually got into my system, and it was some weeks before I recovered from the effects of the desperate biting I had endured. I see in my almanac a note of having ordered my London tailors to send me out a pair of the thinnest chamois leather trousers in order to withstand similar attacks, for against them ordinary trousers were quite unavailing. One of our halts was at a stage where a bridge was being constructed over a river which intersected the new road by which we were travelling. There was a large force of pioneers employed and two elephants. One was a female of great size, sagacity, and gentleness, who seemed able to do everything but speak, and was a general favourite of the camp. Of this elephant the officer in charge told me a curious story. Some two or three years previously she had a young one—a very rare occurrence among elephants in captivity. She was perfectly devoted to her calf, but it died, and she was inconsolable, and from being the gentlest creature she became irritable and even dangerous. One morning it was announced to this officer that she had broken the chain confining her, and had escaped into the forest. Trackers were sent out in every direction, but as wild elephants were numerous it was impossible to trace her. The loss of such an animal was a heavy one, the works were much retarded, and there was general tribulation in consequence. One night, about ten days after her escape, the officer in question went out to lie in wait for bears at a pond in the jungle some distance off. As he and his native attendant were returning early in the morning the native silently nudged him, and they saw in the dim grey light an elephant with her calf making her way along the newly-formed road towards the camp. They both sprang behind trees, and when the elephant passed the native insisted it was their old friend. They moved back as fast as they could, and found the camp in a ferment. Sure enough the truant had returned, and she seemed quite as joyful as the rest of the assembly, going from one to another and touching them with her trunk, as if exhibiting her adopted child. There was a very pretty little elephant in the camp which ran in and out of our hut, and which was pressed on me in vain, and I believe it

was the one she had begged, borrowed, or stolen during
her absence. Her good temper and docility had completely returned.

At a place called Bibile, some marches onward, I saw,
for the first and only time, some of that wild race called
Veddahs, of whom so much has been written. They did
not show any particular sign of barbarity, except that
they went nearly naked and did not look clean. The
type of features was by no means a low one, and one of
the girls was decidedly pretty. It is said they never
laugh, but I am inclined to refuse to believe this pecu-
liarity. They are supposed to support themselves with
their bows and arrows, and possibly they do so, creeping
noiselessly through the jungle till close to their object,
but their bows are poor and weak, and they made by no
means good shots at a mark about fifty paces distant.
It is a very remarkable fact that the highest caste of
Singalese recognize these Veddahs as of a caste higher
than their own, and a proud Wellela, who would consider
himself lowered by taking one of the fisher or cinnamon-
peeler caste into his carriage, would feel rather proud of
having a Veddah by his side. I asked a Kandian chief
the meaning of the recognized superior rank of these
savages. He said he did not know the origin of it, but
that the belief prevailed that when his countrymen
conquered Ceylon the Veddahs were kings and queens
of the country. This tradition, and, if I am not mistaken,
the structure of the Veddah language, has established the
belief that they were originally descendants of a very
remote Aryan immigration, and that they were swept
away before Wijayo and his invading army about 2400
years ago, and took refuge in the most inaccessible forests,
where they have become gradually but completely bar-
barized. That they were not so originally is clear from

the tradition that Wijayo the Conqueror married a Yakko princess, and subsequently repudiated her; and this Yakko princess was, I have no doubt, of the same primitive race as the Veddahs. Tennent describes them as the lowest specimens of humanity, and declares they have no language, only a few words; but I cannot say I saw any remarkable repulsiveness in them which soap and water would not remove, and modern investigation has proved that they have a language of their own, but whether it is connected with Sanskrit and Pali I cannot say. Had Dr. Goldschmit lived this point would have been cleared up, as he was bent on exploring and mastering the Veddah language. On one point every one is agreed, namely, in the perfect harmlessness of this poor tribe, and of their capability of improvement.

We at length reached Nuwara-Eliya, and found all things flourishing; breakfasts on top of Pedro, picnics to various romantic spots, and gemming afternoons in the Moon Plains, which had no result whatever, as every inch of the plain had long before been ransacked in the time of the Kandian kings. Plenty of crystals of various sorts, however, were found, and the gemming tea-parties were very pleasant. I now completed my arrangements for the purchase of a residence at Nuwara-Eliya, and bought from Mr. Duff, the late manager of the Oriental Bank, a cottage with a good deal of wood attached to it. My boundary ran up to the top of the mountain, at its back, and besides the chief residence there was another cottage, where my staff were to be established. It was all in a wretched state of dilapidation—the roof in holes, the floor honey-combed by rats; in short, it would really have been cheaper in the end to have pulled it down and built it up *de novo*. But the situation was beautiful, and I was additionally tempted by the luxuriance of the flowers, old friends from

Europe, which were growing in front of it in wild profusion, though almost untended.

And now the terrible south-west monsoon was impending, when Nuwara-Eliya became intolerable for several months from constant mist, rain, and gales. So intolerable is it that the military authorities had to give it up as a permanent sanatorium; for the soldiers actually deserted and surrendered as prisoners, declaring they would prefer to undergo any punishment rather than endure such misery.

The Queen's birthday was also impending on the 24th of May, when it was the time-honoured custom to give a ball to the planters at Kandy, and to hold a levée there and a reception of the Kandian chiefs. Our first ball was a great success; a prodigious amount of champagne was drunk, but, on the whole, it was accompanied by fewer exuberances than on former occasions. Several of the Kandian chiefs were present, and added greatly to the brilliancy of the entertainment by their costumes. The evening after the ball the wives and female relatives of the chiefs came to pay our ladies a visit. They were gorgeously dressed with a profusion of jewels, but were very shy and ill at ease. There was one exception, a young lady of the great family of Nuwara Wewa, near Anaradhapura, of the bluest blood in Ceylon, and dating her pedigree in unbroken line for two thousand years. She had either just been married or was going to be married to a high-born, handsome Kandian, Paranagama by name, whom I subsequently appointed a magistrate, and who behaved himself worthily of such a wife. She came into the room, tall, erect, stately, and without the slightest *mauvaise honte*. She was richly dressed, but without a profusion of jewellery. Her head was admirably set on, and I felt grieved at being unable to converse with such a noble creature, more especially as she seemed bright and intelligent and quite pleased at being addressed by any of the gentlemen who understood Singalese. The ladies all refused liqueurs and champagne, but stuffed themselves with cakes, sweet things, and tea without reluctance. I met, ten years afterwards, when revisiting Ceylon, some of the same then young ladies upon whom time had laid his fingers rather sternly, and they were kind enough to send my wife a very handsome gold bracelet as a remembrance of old days, but the handsome wife of Paranagama was no more when I last was in Ceylon (1890).

Our life at Kandy was very pleasant ; there were charming rides over a great extent of country, very good roads, and a variety of drives ; and then there were always the beautiful Peradeniya Gardens, and old Mr. Thwaites ready to greet us warmly, to show us some rare and beautiful butterfly recently captured and being portrayed, and to feed us with unrivalled bread and butter, and, what was then a rarity, Ceylon tea. Though this was the rainy season still there were always fine hours in the morning and evening, and everything went on smoothly and as happily as any one could wish. In September I made my first excursion to Anaradhapura, the once famous capital of Ceylon. This city was a considerable place when Wijayo, in the fifth century before Christ, the William the Conqueror of Ceylon, came over from India with his Aryan hordes and conquered the country. It became the capital about a century afterwards.

We had a drive of extraordinary beauty from Kandy to Dambulla, breakfasting at the very pretty town of Mátalé on the way, and visiting the remarkable rock temple of Alu Wihara, a short distance from the road some miles beyond it. In the afternoon we reached

Dambulla, which lies at the foot of an enormous round mass of gneiss, said to be five hundred feet high. About halfway up is an immense cavern, lined with statues of Buddha, a most solemn and striking, partly natural and partly artificial excavation. The walls and ceiling are painted with scenes from the life of Buddha, and there rises in it a well of the purest and coldest water, of which we took an ample supply to the rest-house for our evening meal. We had just light to clamber up to the top and thence see a mass of foliage all around as far as the eye could reach, and got down without any slips to our abode. Up to this, about forty-seven miles from Kandy, the road was very fairly good, but henceforward we were warned we must not trust to wheels, as the so-called Great Northern Road, extending to Jaffna, was a mere track running through jungle and paddy fields, and without a single bridge over the many, and at times dangerous, rivers which intersected it. We accordingly mounted our horses, and rode the rest of the way. Whenever we stopped the villagers flocked in numbers to see the Governor. They were all emaciated, miserable, half-starved, and dejected-looking wretches. Many of them were terribly mutilated, their faces nearly torn off by bears, which always go at the head. The same story was told by all, they were dying out by disease and starvation ; the embankment of their tanks had given way almost universally, and they had neither numbers nor co-operation nor vitality to repair them properly. The consequence was that the rice crops were most precarious, more often a failure than otherwise, and the wretched people lived on roots or cut down the forest, thereby doing enormous injury, burning the trees, and obtaining a crop of what is called kourakan or fine grain, by scraping the ashes and sowing the surface of the ground. Vast forests have disappeared by this ruinous mode of cultivation, in spite of severe punishments when the culprit was discovered; but, as every one was interested in keeping this destruction secret, in the greater number of cases the offenders escaped detection, and indeed the authorities had hardly the heart to proceed against breakers of the law who pleaded starvation as their excuse, though in many, perhaps in the majority of cases, this lazy mode of raising a crop had more attraction than rice cultivation, which requires care and labour.

Our journey was auspicious enough. We safely forded the rivers, and, if rough enough, the track was dry. On the second day after leaving Dambulla we reached Anaradhapura. I was immensely struck with its picturesque appearance. The huge dagobas rose above the forest, and as we advanced the remains of its former magnificence were apparent. The ground was strewn with broken pillars; in some places the columns stood erect, with richly carved capitals. The so-called Brazen Palace of the great and chivalrous King Datugammenu, who reigned about 160 B.C., was, according to the Maha-wanso, supported by sixteen hundred columns of rock, and these still stand, though shorn in number. Everywhere were seen the entrances to private dwellings, decorated either by dancing dwarfs graven on stone or by vases of flowers, also graven. Everywhere are gigantic stones forming portions of these structures. The jungle, wherever one penetrates, is full of these remains, and, in the thick of it, where a clearance is made, appear here and there all alone sitting statues of Buddha. We were brought to see the bathing-places of the king and another of the queen, lined with stone, and gigantic stone troughs in which the royal elephants are said to have been given their rice, and the stone couch in which the dying King Datugammenu

lay watching for the completion of the great Ruanwellé
Dagoba, which, if finished, would render his end a happy
one, and last, not least, some small stone figures of animals
to which women, desirous of children and failing to be
blessed with them, resorted.   By sitting on them and
turning them round they were sure of obtaining their desire.
The village was much improved since 1848, when Sir E.
Tennent wrote his description of it.   Large and extensive
cuttings had been made, by order of Sir Hercules Robinson, in the jungle from north-east to south-west, and the
jungle itself had been cleared in the immediate vicinity.
There were a few extremely bad houses of officials and
one small street of a few hovels.   All the tanks and
washing-places were dry ; the tank of Bassawakulam, close
to the town, which should have supplied it with water, was
dry land, owing to its embankment having been breached,
and the fine tank of Tissawewa, about a mile off, the
overflow of which used to fill Bassawakulam, had itself
shrank by a large portion of its dimensions, owing to
the canal that fed it having been filled up.   There was
a wretched hospital filled with miserable sufferers from
the disease called parangi, which no one had understood,
or properly suggested a cure for, till the present principal
medical officer, Dr. Kynsey, boldly pronounced it to be
simply disease by which the population was literally
rotting away, arising from bad food and bad water.
" You are the proper doctor," said he to me ; " give these
poor wretches good water, good air, by clearing the
jungle round the villages, and good food by abundant
rice crops, and you will perform a greater cure than all
the doctors and hospitals in Ceylon can ever effect."   I
took his advice, and he was perfectly right.   It was not
a kind of syphilitic form, as some medicos wrote treatises
to prove it to be, nor was it akin to the West Indian

yams, as some other equally learned leeches maintained. It derived its origin and virulence solely from the causes indicated by Dr. Kynsey, and exactly as these causes were removed so did the disease decline, until at present (1890) it is almost a thing of the past, unless provoked by the same causes.

CHAPTER XVI

THE great sight at Anaradhapura was, of course, the celebrated bô tree, said to be an offshoot of the *Ficus religiosa* under which Gautama Buddha reclined just before his death. If so, and there seems no reason to disbelieve the story, it must, having been planted 288 B.C., be now 2178 years old. It is regarded with the greatest reverence; to lop a twig would be sacrilege, even to pick up a leaf is forbidden, as the priests make a good thing of the sale of the sacred foliage. A part of the trunk is gilt with gold leaf, and there are some healthy offshoots from it.

Before leaving Anaradhapura I had thoroughly made up my mind that the great Kandian district of Nuwara-kaláwiya, of which that village is the capital, and which formed a large portion of the Northern Province, should be removed from it and formed into a separate province. I gave my reasons to the Secretary of State, Lord Kimberley—the wretched state of this huge extent of country; its totally neglected condition; the impossibility of a Government agent residing at Jaffna, the northern point of the island, being able to supervise the immediate improvements necessary; and last, but not least, the fact that this portion of the Northern Province was Kandian in its population, whereas to the north it was Tamil, and generally ruled by a Government agent who was more conversant with Tamils than with Singalese. Lord Kimberley gave his immediate sanction to the proposal, and I placed Mr. Dickson, a civil servant of high standing, at the head of the new province. I immediately set to work to carry out to Anaradhapura the present excellent roads, to build bridges and culverts the whole way to Jaffna, along what I may call the chine of the island. I announced that I should never be satisfied till I had driven a coach and four from Colombo to Jaffna, and I was virtually as good as my word, for I drove four horses from the railway station at Mátalé to Jaffna, over what had been a mere unbridged track. To Mr. Dickson I left the management of the irrigation works which were to be immediately undertaken. He was, like myself, a thorough believer in the efficacy of good water, good air, and good food to restore this wretched decaying race to health and strength, and to bring back wealth to this fine country. As regards the large store tanks, some hundreds of acres of extent, they were taken in hand by the Department of Works ; the cost was not heavy, as generally their embankments only required clearing and shaping and the filling up of some breaches, which were occasionally formidable. But the restoration of the small village tanks, on which everything immediately depended, was no light affair. For at least two centuries these tanks, owing to apathy and want of co-operation, had been gradually falling into decay. The unfortunate villagers patched them up as best they could, and badly was the best. Sickness and constant failure of their crops had driven them to despair, and there was very little desire on their part to join in the work of restoration ; in fact, unless coercion were to be resorted to, there was no hope of some thousands of tanks being rendered available for cultivation. It was absolutely necessary that each village should expend a certain number of days' labour in the year upon its tanks, but the peasants were unwilling to work, some to work at all, others at the time judged most convenient by their fellows. In former days the difficulty would have been easily met by resorting to rajacaria, or forced labour for the rajah ; but that power was formally abandoned by our Government in, I think, the year 1832. Mr. Dickson was, however, equal to the occasion. He established village councils throughout the new province, and, as these councils had power to enforce labour for the general good of the community, he persuaded a large number of villages to enforce and to call out labourers on fine, in proportion to their amount of land. They had then to labour for a certain number of days, according to the instructions of irrigation officers appointed by Government. In return he promised that the cultivators should have a masonry sluice put into each tank, when a certain degree of restoration was reached. A large number of villages set to work, encouraged and stimulated by Mr. Dickson, and, as well as I recollect, work was going on at some nine hundred tanks within the first year. Never was a great social experiment more speedily and entirely successful. Crops were obtained where they had failed for years. The revenue rose immensely. Sickness gradually declined. An eminently listless and lazy population, being compelled to work, resumed habits of industry ; and on occasions of my subsequent visits to this district, I was supplicated by various villages to inspect their tanks and see what good work they had done. I had not long been at work at my revival of this fine province before I perceived that the restoration of the great tank of Kalawewa was the first point on which the success of the scheme turned. It had been constructed by King Datu Sen, in the year A.D. 459. I shall never forget my astonishment on

visiting it.   It was the great reservoir on which the whole
water-supply of that district depended.   The river ran
into it, and was dammed up, forming an inland sea, thirty-
five miles in circumference.   The bund was from sixty to
eighty feet high, and was several miles long.   From it
there used to run a canal, called the Yodi Ella, or Giant's
Canal, to Anaradhapura, about sixty miles in length.
This canal supplied all the great store tanks *en route*, and
supplied Anaradhapura and its bathing-places.   It was
clear to me that this great work must be restored, if we
meant to be, for the future, throughout this extensive district, free from periodical famines ; but careful surveying
was required, and the rough estimate for the repair of the
tank and of the Yodi Ella was about £40,000, so I began
with the Yodi Ella, and had completed a good deal of it
when I left.   My successor did nothing towards advancing
this useful work.   I cannot blame him, as the financial
condition of the colony during his rule was a subject of
anxiety to him, and there was no margin for any but the
most necessary expenditure.   Better days, however, came
with the next Governor, Sir A. Gordon, and I had the
gratification of driving over the completed bund in 1890,
and visiting this magnificent work, this monument of real
kings, in perfect order.   It is contemplated to raise the
spill five feet, and to divert another river into it.   This
will enable it to hold up a vast body of water, amply
sufficient to supply the tanks beneath it as far as Anaradhapura, in times of exceptional drought.

In September we went down to Colombo to open the
Legislative Council, and to show what metal we were
made of in the way of entertainments ; and I must say
that, as regards our kitchen and cellar and general hospitality, my conscience has nothing to reproach me.   It
was said that, in the case of certain Governors, there

was one kind of wine for his Excellency and another, and a very bad one, for his guests. *A propos* of that, the tradition of such proceedings seems to have lingered ; for, on giving a large ball at Colombo, the following amusing occurrence took place. I need hardly say that on such occasions the consumption of champagne was enormous, and I had written for a supply of fifty dozen at 54s. a dozen, exclusive of duty. I mention the price to show that the wine should have been, and was, good. It only arrived about half an hour before the ball began, and so afraid was I that it might not be up to my standard, that I ordered half a dozen to be at once placed in ice and sent up to the supper-room. This wine, be it noted, was covered with gold foil. In the meantime, rather than run the least risk of giving bad champagne, I ordered the finest of Cunningham's, at 84s. a dozen, to be supplied. This wine was covered with silver foil. Shortly after I had tried the newly-arrived and comparatively cheap wine, my butler came and said there were a number of gentlemen very much dissatisfied with getting the silver-covered champagne while his Excellency was drinking the gold. I need hardly say I joyfully ordered the more expensive silver-corked to be shut up, and gave them as much of the gold foil as was good for them.

We had not been long in Colombo before we had very serious troubles to encounter from inundations. A long continuance of rain had flooded the eastern and lower part of the city. The consequences were terrible. Most of the houses were composed of mud and sunburnt bricks, and they were swept away with all their contents. The inhabitants were saved in boats. I felt it my duty, not only to subscribe liberally for the relief of the sufferers, and to sanction the purchase of food for the distressed, but also to be on several occasions on the spot, almost, as it were, directing the men engaged in the work of relief.

In September the Legislative Council met, and my speech was long and exhaustive ; in fact, more of an essay on all matters concerning the colony and of my intentions rather than a dry enumeration of past events and of future measures. It was much approved of, both by the colony and Colonial Office. The flourishing condition of the Exchequer enabled me to begin in good earnest on the northern roads, and to construct two buildings greatly wanted ; the one, a new Custom House, the other a Museum. They were both designed by the Government architect, Mr. Smither, a man of great taste and refinement, and they are both an honour to the colony. The Museum is a singularly beautiful building —light, bright, and well ventilated. It was strange that nothing of the kind had been previously attempted, and yet all our other colonies united could not furnish such a collection of objects of such varied interest as Ceylon. I may here quote a short passage of my address in reference to this subject :—

" The want of a museum, in which may be represented the natural history, antiquities, and industrial products of the island, has been forcibly urged on me. During the period when the revenue of the island did not suffice for its most imperative wants, it would have been inexpedient to have sanctioned an institution which it was better to leave untouched rather than establish it on an inadequate and unsatisfactory footing. For a comparatively small sum, considering the object in view, a museum may be constructed which shall not be a mere random collection of miscellaneous objects, but a scientific, teaching exhibition, which, while ministering to the amusement of many, may convey instruction to all who seek it.

" I propose, in connection with this museum, to obtain reproductions of the inscriptions throughout the island, by means of photography, casts, and hand-copying. These inscriptions, varying in character and dialect, will be of deep interest to the philologist, and throw light on the ancient usages, religious customs, and early history of Ceylon. I purpose to affix a limit to our collections. They should be strictly confined to the productions of Ceylon."

Considerable space within the Museum was devoted to a library, open to all readers. A large accession of books was obtained from the Royal Asiatic Society; but it has increased so rapidly that plans had been prepared, when I was recently in Ceylon, for a large extension of the building to house books and inscriptions which were awaiting acceptance.

Another measure which will be imputed to me for righteousness was vigorously and successfully urged by me this year, namely, the reduction of drinking-shops. During the whole of my government I never lost sight of this object, and I quote the words of my first address to the Legislative Council, which may be interesting to advocates of temperance :—

" There is one subject more on which I cannot be silent, and that is the extension of drunkenness throughout the island. English rule has given to Ceylon many blessings which the inhabitants are ever ready to acknowledge—security of life and property, equality before the law, just tribunals, the abolition of serfdom, and excellent roads to promote intercourse and facilitate the conveyance of produce ; but we have at the same time extended a curse throughout the island which weighs heavily in the other scale, namely, drunkenness. Some years ago a drunken Kandian would have been disgraced in the eyes of his fellows. Now the occurrence is so common that the disgrace has passed away. Drunkenness is extending itself into villages where it was before unheard of, and even the women are accustoming them-selves to intoxicating drinks. I have had some remarkable petitions on this subject, first from the Roman Catholics of Jaffna, and other parts of the Northern Province, numerously signed by Europeans and natives alike. Another petition was recently presented to me by the Rev. Mr. Scott, signed by no less than 32,396 persons ; 7382 English, 16,419 Singalese, 8595 Tamils. These petitions are characterized by moderation and good sense. They do not go the length of advocating the total prohibition of the sale of spirituous liquors. The petitioners are aware that such an attempt would be impossible. But they say,

'*Restrict the places of sale, and thus discourage intoxication and diminish the great moral and social evils which flow from it.*'

"In these recommendations I warmly concurred. In restricting the sale of intoxicating liquor, some diminution of revenue was to be expected ; but, in the words of the petitioners, any decrease under that head would be more than compensated by an improvement in the general well-being of the community, and in the reduced cost of establishments for the suppression and punishment of crime."

In order the more emphatically to enforce the policy of my government in regard to the gradual reduction of drinking-shops, I ordered a map to be placed in the Legislative Council room. On this map, in red crosses, was marked every tavern in the island, and coloured marks indicated suppressions and additions throughout the year. Thus, at a glance, a Governor could see if his views were carried out in regard to suppression of arrack taverns, in the rural districts at all events.

I was extremely glad, in the course of this session, to be able to announce to the Legislative Council that Sir John Coode, whom we had consulted as to the possibility of constructing a breakwater at Colombo, had expressed himself most favourably towards the project. He foresaw no difficulty in the way of its completion for a sum not exceeding £630,000, which comprised the erection of two jetties of a thousand feet long, and the dredging of the bar. Sir Hercules Robinson, in his concluding address in 1871, said to the Legislative Council :—" The question of improving harbour accommodation for Colombo has been discussed with so much practical good sense that I trust some definite move may now soon be made towards supplying this great and pressing want." I can claim the merit of taking this " definite move," which was left to me to accept or refuse, and of pressing it on the Home Government, of obtaining their consent, and of immediately commencing the work.

It was during this summer that I instituted the custom of an annual gathering of the Government agents as my guests before the preparation of the estimates. This was called the durbar and was productive of much satisfaction and good temper among them. I had remarked, in the course of my travels through the island, that a great deal of soreness prevailed among these very intelligent and zealous officials. They all seemed hurt at their appeals being ignored, at works being conducted in their provinces without their being consulted, and at their being unable to bring their ideas and objects fairly before the Governor, from the few opportunities they had of seeing him. The durbar altered all this. Each agent was enjoined to bring a list of the works he required, and each had full time to give all necessary explanations, and to be comforted if the future budget could not include all his claims. After lunch we had a general meeting to discuss various subjects of public interest on which the agents had been invited to prepare themselves. These parties were very pleasant and instructive, they were greatly appreciated by the Government agents, and they gave the Governor ample opportunity to judge of the resources of each man. I believe they were omitted by Sir James Longden, but Sir Arthur Gordon and Sir A. Havelock have wisely continued them.

Amongst our notable visitors this year were the two Coburg princes, Augustus and Philip of Saxe-Weimar, the latter the son-in-law of the Emperor of Brazil. They were both charming young men, very intelligent, easily and greatly pleased, and I flatter myself that they carried away grateful recollections of the warm reception they met with in Ceylon.*

* Our writing-set in crocodile skin and ivory, with their monogram and coronet, was a present sent by them.

Two things equally struck them—one the working of elephants and their extraordinary sagacity, the other a battle between a cobra and a mongoose. I had been given a mongoose which had been running about as a pet at Galle Face Hotel, and, as cobras abounded in the grounds of Kandy, I offered a reward of a rupee to the coolies for every cobra brought in uninjured. I soon found my Mungo, as I called him, to be a desperate fighter, and absolutely fearless, whereas an Indian companion of his, which I bought from some jugglers, was extremely averse to any battle with a snake, and would generally not face even one round. The battle-field was a small bedroom inside my study. The snake was brought in noosed to the end of a long bamboo. The noose was cut by a pen-knife tied to the end of another bamboo, and then the snake was free. He glided all round the room, raising himself aloft and examining every part, but the moment his antagonist appeared he used to draw himself up, with hood expanded and ready to strike, in the open part of the room, as if he were afraid of being attacked from behind. The mongoose, too, adopted similar tactics. On being brought in he always appeared unconscious of the presence of his foe, except that every hair stood erect on his body. He also ran round the room and examined every corner. At last the battle began, and it was intensely interesting. The attack of the mongoose was a series of feints, evidently to wear out the snake, who struck continual blows at him, but all fruitless. The extraordinary activity of the mongoose saved him. He kept his bright eyes constantly fixed on the dull, expressionless eyes of the cobra, and seemed to get warnings from them of the coming blow. As the snake grew wearier the mongoose became more audacious, and would actually stand up on his hind legs, with his head only a few inches from the cobra's, who in vain struck often and fiercely. The end of the battle was now near. Foam ran down from the lips of Mungo, who showed at last a row of snow white teeth as sharp as needles. In an instant he seized the cobra, always by one spot, the side of the mouth, and whisked him round and round till he had fairly knocked the breath out of him. He then laid himself down by his side for rest, and when the snake gave signs of returning animation he attacked and killed him, and generally ate his head off as a trophy of victory. I never saw a braver animal than "my Mungo, hero of a thousand fights," as we called him, and with bravery was combined consummate skill and patience, never attacking *à l'outrance* until sure of success. He was only beaten three times, twice by cobras of remarkable endurance, which fairly wore him out, and once by another terrible snake, a ticpolonga, who curled himself tightly like a turban, and left no means for the mongoose to attack him without coming to imme-diate close quarters, involving sudden death. Owing to his hind legs slipping on the smooth matting he was once bitten by a cobra, and ran round the room on three legs, lying down at last. I said in grief, "This is poor Mungo's last battle." But after a time he rose up, and again fought and conquered. He must have been engaged in at least fifty single combats, and it is a curious fact that, though generally very gentle and attached, he was abso-lutely ferocious, even to those he loved best, for nearly an hour after every fight. He then became as pleasant as ever. Besides his exploits with snakes he was an extraordinary ratter, and I have seen him kill a dozen rats let loose at the same time as quickly as any famous terrier. I am glad to add that, unlike the generality of pets, he died peaceably and happily in the fulness of years and honours. When I left Ceylon I gave him to Lady

Elphinstone, who treated him with great kindness, appreciated his good qualities and overlooked his love of mischief, particularly his hatred of natives, whom he always attacked. He was found dead one morning in his cage, having lived his full term of years.

The working of elephants also greatly excited their Serene Highnesses. There were no elephants belonging to the Department of Public Works at Kandy, where we were staying, but the Guardian of the Temple lent a couple belonging to it. I much regretted the absence of my dear, affectionate Bombera, who would have astonished them by his sagacity; but he was at work at Nuwara-Eliya. These temple elephants, however, did everything they were ordered to do with their usual intelligence, carrying large stones wherever they were told to place them, fixing the chains to the stones and unfixing them. One of them, a tusker, on that occasion, performed an act, apparently of his own accord, which greatly struck all of us. He was carrying a long and very heavy stone down a steep declivity. The stone was suspended from his neck by a chain, and as the chain was too long the stone struck his knee repeatedly. He stopped, made what sailors call a bight of the chain, gave it a roll round his tusk, and, having thus shortened it, carried the stone to its destination without further discomfort to his knees. What the mahout said to him, or whether he said anything, I do not know, but it is difficult to imagine that out of the eighty phrases which a very highly educated elephant is supposed to understand, there would have been one framed to meet such an emergency as this, and if there was not, it was the clearest exercise of the reasoning faculty, pure and simple, which prompted this act.

In the course of this session I abolished the Ceylon Rifles, and with very great regret. It was an excellent

regiment, in a high state of discipline, most creditable to
its officers, and had done excellent service during the so-
called rebellion of 1848.   It was composed of Malays,
small, active, and extremely brave men, and would have
been quite sufficient to keep the colony free from any
internal disturbances, for the natives greatly feared them,
and remembered their ruthlessness at the time I mention.
But they had become a luxury and no longer useful for
any purpose, and cost the colony a large annual sum
which could be far better employed.   It would have been
dangerous to have left Ceylon without white troops, as
this Malay and Mahommedan regiment might have
revolted and made themselves masters of it.   Still I
regretted being the author of the overthrow of an institution long connected with the colony, and of which it was
justly proud, and I regretted losing a team of such excellent cricketers ; but we took over their admirable band,
trained by a first-rate German bandmaster, Herr Pape.
He was extremely irritable, and it was impossible to keep
one's countenance within earshot of his remarks.   He
had a very great dislike to his musicians indulging in
betel-chewing during the performance, which was natural
enough, and one night at Queen's House he was heard to
shout, "Oh, you Goddam rascals, you take your Goddam
beetles out of your mout."

Early next year I paid a visit to the gem-producing
district of Ceylon, in the neighbourhood of Ratnapura.   I
was invited by one of the leading gem merchants to assist
at the opening of a pit from which he expected good
results.   Deer-stalking and salmon-fishing are considered
highly exciting amusements, but I doubt if either of them
can be compared to gemming at a really good pit.   You
are always in expectation, you have infinite variety, you
may light on a stone of extraordinary value or you may

find—nothing. The region about Ratnapura abounds in gems of many descriptions, but has no emeralds or diamonds. Sapphires and star sapphires, rubies and star rubies, amethysts, topazes, cat's-eyes, aquamarines, are all constantly being found. They have been worked from their matrix in the mountains ages ago, and now lie at the bottom of what once were streams, but which became filled with sand and gravel. Over this sand and gravel has since spread a fresh stratum of soil which has to be cleared away before each vein can be reached. At six o'clock we were at our diggings. We found a nice square tent and tea ready for our reception. We sat at the mouth of the tent with a glass of clear water on a table by our side in which were cast all stones of any shade of colouring to be examined afterwards. The workmen had cleared off the surface soil, and had reached what is called the "illam," a gemmiferous stratum of gravel. There was plenty of water in adjacent pits, and as soon as the workmen had swept off superficial stones, and had washed away earthy particles, the baskets full of gravel were handed up to us, and we examined every grain. Nothing could be more delightful; at one moment a red glint denoted a ruby, at another a gleam of blue indicated a sapphire. All these were deposited in the tumbler, that the vivid tints should be maintained by moisture, and when we had done our work they were poured out on a sheet of blotting-paper. My collection was miscellaneous, but of no great value, though I willingly gave £10 for it, which was the price fixed by the owner of the pit. There were several nice small sapphires, and a cat's-eye which I sold in London for £10, besides other stones of mineralogical interest. The occupation was so delightful that, though we began our work at about 6.30, and intended to return to breakfast at 9.30, we could not tear ourselves away before twelve o'clock.

I was invited the next day to the wedding of the only child, a daughter, of Iddawalgoda, the great chief of the district, and one of the most extensive and wealthiest of the Kandian landed proprietors. His abode was about twelve miles from Ratnapura, and we did the journey on horseback. As I rode along I was accosted by a miserable-looking man, with scarcely anything on save a crupper. Out of this crupper he pulled a rag, and out of the rag he produced four uncut rough sapphires. I took up one of them, and, as it appeared a fine colour, I asked how much he wanted for it. He said a hundred rupees. I said that was an absurd price for an uncut stone, which might not be worth a hundred cents. He answered, "Yes, but it may be worth five hundred rupees." I liked the look of the stone, and thought it *infra dig.* of a Governor to bargain with the poor creature, so I ordered the sum asked for to be paid, and pocketed the sapphire. On returning to Colombo I had it cut, and it turned out to be the most perfect stone as regards colour that was found that year, so much so that my friends the gem dealers used constantly to come to Queen's House and ask permission to compare their stones with it. I eventually sold it to Mr. Hill, of Oxford Street, for £50, at which price he took it eagerly, though it was a small stone, about the size of the little finger-nail.

On going up to Nuwara-Eliya we found our cottage done up, and fairly comfortable, though very different from what it is at present. Nothing could be more brilliant and genial than the weather. The place was crowded, and there were walking parties in the forest and rides everywhere, and breakfasts on the top of Pedro, and races and picnics.

But all these happy days were over at the latter end of May. As usual we went down to Kandy, held our Birthday Ball, and received the Government agents at the durbar. I had resolved on paying a visit to Anaradhapura at this time, and on making a *détour* homewards through the North-eastern Province, to go over the track of a very important road connecting those towns, and to become acquainted with the nature of the rivers that had to be bridged.

And now came upon me the greatest sorrow of my life, the death of my wife. On my return from my journey I found her suffering from illness brought on by too much exposure to the heat of the sun. After a few days, first of anxious, then of hopeless watching, she passed away, conscious to the last.

> " Anfangs wollt' ich fast verzagen
> Und ich glaubt' ich trüg' es nie ;
> Und ich hab' es doch getragen,—
> Aber fragt mich nur nicht : wie ? "

My life was terrible for some time in the deserted, mournful Queen's House at Colombo. My dear kind friend Dr. Thwaites came down and stayed with me for some time, and was my companion in my daily walk. Much do I owe to his tender sympathy then, and to his infinite tact when so little seemed to open the wound. Work, however—incessant, slogging work, far harder than I would otherwise have undertaken—restored my strength of mind ; then various expeditions were necessary, and then came the preparation of my address for the meeting of the Legislative Council.

I was able to announce to the Council a most flourishing revenue, and a large surplus to be employed on useful public works, among them the northern road and the road to Trincomalee, which were pushed on with great vigour. One of my favourite projects was a sea line of railway to Galle ultimately to be extended to Mátara, a charming town in the south of the

island. This I proposed to construct solely out of surplus
revenue, without incurring any debt. The chief item of
expense was the construction of a very wide bridge over
the broad river, the Kalu-ganga, and, as I anticipated
opposition from the Colonial Office to my ambitious
project, I obtained first of all their consent to the bridge
which I had so designed as to be available for ordinary
traffic as well as for a railway. This being provided, the
remaining cost of the line was comparatively small, and
I had the satisfaction of completing half of it. I regret
to say it has hung fire, and has only been extended some
twenty miles further by Sir A. Gordon, but I hear the
present Governor talks of finishing it.

My flourishing exchequer also enabled me to devote
considerable sums to the improvement of jails, both in
regard to discipline and to their sanitary condition.
Hitherto, in most of the jails, the prisoners were herded
together at night, the worst characters with men convicted
of trivial offences. Of course each man went out taking
with him seven devils worse than himself. I assured the
Council that before the opening of next session the money
spent on jails since my assumption of the government,
and the attention paid to their improvement, would enable
the jails of Ceylon to stand comparison with those of any
one of her Majesty's possessions. I at once began five
new jails, and set on foot the work of improvement in all
the others. The pivot point on which everything turned
was separation. My ultimate aim was that every prisoner
convicted of a crime should be segregated at night from
his fellows. One man, one cell, was my prison motto.
To carry out that object I largely increased cellular accommodation in the existing jails, and built the fine convict
prison at Kandy, ultimately intended to hold 500 con-
victs. I had the satisfaction, on resigning my appointment,

of informing the Secretary of State that, whereas the annual prison population averaged 2200, I had provided cellular accommodation, if the works laid out and actually begun were finished, for 1700 prisoners, which virtually gave a separate cell to every criminal, the balance being made of debtors, road-defaulters, and women, very few of whom, I am happy to say, enter prison precincts in Ceylon. Nothing could have been better than our prison system when I left Ceylon. A large number of long-sentenced men were drafted into temporary prisons to work on the breakwater, by no means a pleasant occupation, and the strictest discipline was kept up in the jails, which became by no means pleasant retreats for idleness and high feeding. The civil servants were strictly forbidden to employ prisoners about their compounds. They were only to be employed, after the first penal stage was over, on public works.

Besides this improvement of the colonial prisons, my fine income allowed me to expend a considerable amount on the medical department, and with the most excellent effect, in building, enlarging, and improving our hospitals, so that I could in this respect have challenged competition with the hospital system of any country in the world. On my arrival I had, during my various and extensive journeys, been painfully struck with the want of a proper system of medical relief for the great bulk of the people. Most liberal provision had been secured for the European stations and the medical institutions connected with them, but, as regards the mass of the population in outlying stations, they were still at the mercy of ignorant quacks and devil-dancers. This state of things reflected discredit on our Government, more especially as it was well known that the natives, formerly suspicious of European treatment, were becoming anxious to avail themselves of it, whenever they had the opportunity. To remedy this, I went on the admirable lines of the Irish medical relief system, the establishment of small dispensaries in rural districts, where a doctor, connected with the central hospital of the district, is bound to attend on certain days of the week.

When recently in Ceylon I heard from the principal medical officer that this dispensary system had been working admirably, that it had gradually overcome native suspicion, and one of the items of the budget involved a considerable increase under the head of local dispensaries.

In the autumn of this year I paid one of my inspection visits to the Southern Province, and was greatly pleased with its prosperity and the high character and position of the native officials, well born and generally well to do. I passed through the salt district of Hambantota, and went on to the *ultima Thule* of civilization, Tissamaharama, where are the remains of one of the oldest cities in Ceylon. It was from this place, in which his family had taken refuge for many years, while foreign invaders ruled at Anaradhapura, that the great and good Dutugammenu, about 204 B.C., the King Arthur of Ceylon, started, in spite of the remonstrances of his parents, to combat the Tamil usurper, Elara, and to recover his lost kingdom. He possessed not only bravery but vigour and foresight, and having got round him large bodies of his countrymen, and thoroughly trained them in martial exercises and tactics, he made his great march right through the island on his famous elephant Kandalu, fought several battles, and the decisive one at Anaradhapura, in which he utterly routed the forces of his opponent Elara, and killed him in hand-to-hand fight. All the district seemed teeming with remains of ancient civilization, but there was no population except the priests of a temple, who guarded a celebrated and fine dagoba of very early origin. The stone pillar to which young Prince Dutugammenu used to fasten his horse is still shown, and is probably authentic. Sir Hercules Robinson had begun the somewhat expensive repair of a very fine tank at this place; but, as there was no population to cultivate the lands to be watered by it, the reflections of the local press became still more adverse when it was discovered that the water of the tank was not nearly sufficient to irrigate the land sold. My visit was to see how this difficulty could best be supplied, and it was found easy enough to divert some of the water of the fine river Magam into the tank by a channel, which involved no great difficulty or expense. This has been done, and a most flourishing colony has been established on the splendid land of this district, at the time of my visit under the dominion of wild beasts. I may mention, in illustration, that we remained quiet during the day which followed my arrival, being Sunday. A small and very rickety canoe belonging to the tank had been brought to the Magam river, and we took an excursion of a few miles, the first time it is supposed that a boat was ever on it. In coming into a large reach of shallow, smooth water we found it occupied by a herd of wild buffaloes, which we thought would take to flight immediately. But not a bit of it. They not only stood their ground but advanced to attack, and we had not a chance. The water was shallow, and we had not taken a gun. We threw stones, which they received with tosses and snorts. Matters were very serious, and escape was impossible; but fortunately there was no old bull among them, or I should not be writing this account of their doings. We at last, three of us, raised a united howl and roar, they bolted, and we were saved.

In 1874 my brother-in-law, Major George Clay, came out to me as aide-de-camp. We took a tour through the North Central Province to visit the famous tank, or rather inland sea of Kalawewa. It was then the wildest jungle, and I do not believe that half a dozen Europeans had visited it. We encamped on the bund, which was from sixty to eighty feet high, and, while I was exploring, George Clay went forth to get some venison. I had returned in the afternoon to our tent, when I heard a double shot, and said, " I suppose we may put down venison on our bill of fare this evening ; " but not so, for shortly after, George Clay came galloping in, in the wildest excitement, the reins on his pony's neck, and holding in each hand an elephant's tail. He had shot two, right and left, the first time he had ever seen them, an exploit worthy of the oldest shikar.

We went through a wild country thence, and through a wretched, half-starved, dying-out population, now, however, plump, well fed, sleek and healthy, and well to do, from the spread of irrigation through this miserable district. We passed the celebrated and remarkable image of Buddha, of which Sir Emerson Tennent thus writes :—

"A few years previous to my tour through this part of Ceylon, a gentleman who accompanied me on this part of my present journey chanced to follow the track of a herd of wild elephants near the tank of Kalawewa, when he suddenly found himself in front of a gigantic statue in the forest, the existence of which had been previously unknown to Europeans. He led us to the spot, and our surprise was extreme on beholding a figure of Buddha, nearly fifty feet high, carved from the face of a rock, and so detached that only two slender ties had been left unhewn at the back to support the colossus by maintaining its attachment with the living stone."

The scene was most remarkable. As usual, advantage had been taken of a group of enormous rocks to form temples and pansclas in the fissures between, and prodigious labour had been expended in hewing steps, hollowing niches, and excavating baths. There had previously been a pandal to shelter the statue, and holes still remain in the rock which had served for the insertion of the columns which supported it. The place was deserted and silent. Close by dwelt one solitary priest, with no attendant save a neophyte, his pupil ; he told us that the statue had been made by order of Prakrama Bahu, and that the temple in its prosperity was called Magampeka Istane, but since it fell into ruins it has been known as the Aukana Wihara.

I mounted the rock from which the image was carved, and found it to be about three or four feet above the top of the head of the statue. I was told by Mr. Adams, still living, a man remarkable for his extraordinary activity and nerve, of a feat he had performed in regard to this statue many years previously, when assistant agent in that district. He actually took it into his head to jump from the top of the rock to the head of the statue, on which there would have been only the smallest standing ground, even if the head had been of ordinary construction. But the legend of Buddha gives him a somewhat sloping head with a sharp top-knot. On this slope Mr. Adams alighted ; he had then to turn round without any support, and to jump up two or three feet to reach the rock again. He found his nerve failing, but at last made a desperate effort, and just reached the ledge from which he had sprung, when he was seized and pulled up by his attendant. The very thought of such a desperate feat makes me giddy. There is not the least doubt of the truth of the story.

We went on to Anaradhapura, and thence to Mullaittivu, a station on the east coast, to the north of Trincomalee, the most God-abandoned spot I had seen in the island. It was low and sandy, with only a few scrubby trees, and with small, shallow lagoons and reaches of swamp. On these were lying the most enormous crocodiles in great numbers. They were shown to me twenty feet long, and are most ferocious and daring. At the river, which runs past the town, I was warned not to go too near the banks, where I was shown a house in which a Tamil man and his wife and family had resided. Unfortunately, a huge male and female crocodile also took up their residence in the same spot. They gradually carried off all the children, then the wife. The bereaved husband still remained, and nothing would induce him to leave, more especially as the female crocodile had been shot. But the male still dwelt in the deep pool beneath the hut, and one day the man was missing. The male crocodile had avenged his mate, and the whole Tamil family had been quietly devoured in some hole beneath the bank.

We returned thence to the main northern road from which we had struck off, and on reaching a place called Chavakacherri, the last halting-place before the end of my journey at Jaffna, I was called on by the priest, a Frenchman, the only European in the district. He was a remarkably good-looking man of about forty, tall and erect, and I was greatly struck by his well-bred manner and conversation. I asked him to take a walk and to dine, both which invitations he readily accepted. During the walk he made use of some expression which caused me to turn round, and, looking him full in the face, I said, "Mon pere, vous avez été militaire?" He coloured and was silent, and then, after a long pause, as we walked on, he said, "Yes, I have been a soldier, a French officer, and I fought side by side with your countrymen throughout the Crimea. I had a strong liking for them. Look here, see what I wear, and shall wear till I die." And he opened his *soutane*, and underneath, next to the skin, was our Crimean medal. "What made you abandon the military life?" I asked. "Ah!" said he, "there are some misfortunes that it is pleasant to recount, for there is comfort in doing so, if one meets with sympathy. But there are other misfortunes, too great to touch on." I asked him if he was happy. "Perfectly so," he said. He had made himself the guide and friend and doctor of the people about him, he never intended to leave them till it was the will of God to take him. I asked him to come and visit me in Colombo. No, he could not leave his people, by whom I heard that he was perfectly adored from his kindness and gentleness. The archbishop told me recently that he had offered him advancement, but to no purpose, and that he is now dead. He would not leave his solitary post, he held it to the last, a true soldier of the Cross. I asked the archbishop if he knew his history. He did not, but he believed his whole life had been changed by some terrible event.

CHAPTER XVII

On returning to Colombo I made up my mind that I could not recover my spirits if I remained in Ceylon. Even my usual hard work became distasteful, and I longed most earnestly for a complete change of every-thing—men, scenery, thought, and associations. I had no right to leave until after five years' residence abroad, but Lord Carnarvon in the kindest manner gave me three months' leave of absence to see my mother and some friends I much valued, and my home.

On reaching Egypt we found we had four spare days, so we made off for Cairo, and had a very pleasant time. We visited the Pyramids, and witnessed that which I had never, in all my experience of that country, witnessed before, a simoon. Our driver foresaw it, and our horses foresaw it also, for they strove with might and main to reach shelter, and rushed to the opposite side of the empty shed at the base of the Pyramids. The air was filled with dust, a furious blast of wind was raging, a dim circle of light showed where the sun was. At last it blew over with a slight shower, and all was bright and cool. It is an event worth recalling.

I found my mother wonderfully well at Coole, and while there I gave a dinner and a dance to my tenants, by whom I was most cordially received. Coming events had not then cast their shadows before. The country was prosperous and rents were well paid, and the general feeling of the peasantry was contented and peaceable. The Roman Catholic clergymen attended the dinner, and were very complimentary; and I took occasion, in responding to the toast of my health, to refer to the effects of the Land Act of 1870, of which I was a strong supporter. Although its provisions had effected a great amelioration in the condition of the Irish peasantry, I asked them if, in any single instance during the time that Coole had been in my possession, the necessity of the bill had been shown by my conduct as a landlord, as had too often been the case on other properties. The spokesman of the tenants replied that no such instance had ever occurred, that no one had a case of injustice to allege, and we parted with expressions, which I believe to have been thoroughly sincere, of good will and regret on both sides.

Nothing could exceed the civility of the Colonial Office. They offered me any more leave I might require; but I felt myself so revived and strengthened by the mere sight of home and of old friends and of topics of interest, till of late strange to me, that I could not conscientiously extend my departure; so on the day three months from the date of leaving Ceylon, the 16th of July, I embarked at Southampton, and after having enjoyed the Red Sea, so pleasant was it, I reached Galle on the 14th, and was nearly drowned in landing, owing to the tremendous sea that was rolling into the harbour. I received thereby a practical proof of my wisdom in abandoning Galle and forming a breakwater at Colombo, for no artificial works could have given security to the former port during the south-west monsoon.

In September I opened the Legislative Council, under the most favourable auspices. I was able to congratulate

our members on the flourishing condition of the finances.
The revenue of the past year was the largest hitherto
received, and a very large excess of receipts over expenditure was at my disposal.   I had plenty of calls to dispose
of it—the construction of the seaside railway, and of
the great Kalutara bridge, and a splendid new gaol at
Kandy, with separate accommodation for five hundred
prisoners ; the pressing on of the great arterial roads to
Trincomalee and Jaffna ;   irrigation in every province ;
increase of telegraphic communication ;   the establishment
of fountains and pure water-supply to towns ;   improvements at Nuwara-Eliya, to render it attractive to all
comers ;   forest preservation, where abuses and roguery
and wholesale destruction were rife, by which those vast
tracts, which should have been of immense value, had
been almost denuded of the most valuable trees.   I took
the opportunity, in alluding to the increase of education
through the mis sionary schools, thus to express myself on
missionary efforts :—

" I need hardly assure you that I have received this announcement
of the vigour with which the missionaries are progressing with unfeigned satisfaction.   I have visited the schools of various denominations, and have generally found them conducted with efficiency and
judgment.   By judgment I mean that the object of the missionaries
is to give a sound education, so as to influence the reasoning powers
of their pupils, and thence to direct them to highest truths, rather
than to aim at filling their register with lists of nominal conversions.
I know of no country where missionary work is doing better than
here, or where there is less apparent *odium theologicum.*   All are
working with conscientious rivalry, and by the thoroughly impartial
action of the Government, each denomination is made aware that, so
far as Government assistance is concerned, it is to be obtained solely
by results."

I may here quote another passage from my closing
address to the Legislative Council on a subject in which
I took the greatest interest, and which had previously

been sadly neglected ; I mean the preservation of the ancient literature of the country, and the scientific exploration, copying, and translation of the inscriptions with which, on rocks and slabs, Ceylon abounded :—

"I am confident you will agree with me that it is highly expedient to make an effort to preserve the ancient literature of Ceylon. It is a duty which we owe, not merely to the large and annually increasing number of students of Oriental history and of Oriental philology, but to the natives of this island, many of whom have already widely distinguished themselves by antiquarian research, many more of whom will devote themselves to it if facilities for study be afforded. With this object, for some time past the Government has annually spent a small sum in procuring copies of all books of interest which are still in existence in the temple libraries. But, in addition to this, I have thought it advisable to take immediate steps to obtain reproductions of all the other records which are to be found on rocks and detached stones, and which are gradually perishing by the action of time and weather and the ravages of man."

During this year I had a most important correspondence with the Duke of Buckingham, Governor of Madras. The absence of all safe ports in the Presidency rendered the shipment of goods precarious, and even dangerous ; and he very wisely considered that the erection of a breakwater at Madras would cost an enormous sum, and probably turn out, as it has done, an enormous failure. His proposal to me was that the Madras Government should run a railway to the nearest point of junction with Ceylon, and that the Ceylon Government should then join it by a railway, and, by that junction, Colombo would become the port and great emporium of South India. I was greatly taken with the proposal, and deeply regret that I was unable to adopt measures to bring it to effect. But, in the first place, I was hampered by the great expense of the imminent extension of our then railway system into Elva, a question of a million of money, and by consideration of the cost of constructing a railway over

Adam's Bridge, a work of great magnitude. This ridge of rocks almost connects India with Ceylon, and is passed through by the Panuban Channel. These rocks are erroneously supposed to be the remains of a junction with India, and to have been worn away by the action of the sea. Geological investigation has, however, proved that they are of a comparatively modern formation of conglomerate and sandstone, which have been widened and enlarged by deposits of sand.

The scheme of the Duke of Buckingham was looked coldly on by the Government of India, and the local opinion of Madras was in favour of the expenditure on a home harbour, so that the matter fell through. But in conversation, subsequently, with Mr. Kyle, the extremely able engineer of our breakwater, he produced a plan, with every detail carefully worked out, whereby the sea-passage from Colombo to India would be accomplished at a mere trifle of expense. He proposed that the trains should be run down into a long raft, and be ferried across by steam, leaving the locomotive on each side, and picking up another on landing. There would be no fear of the perils of the sea, as Adam's Bridge served as a perfect natural breakwater. It might be rough enough during the south-west monsoon at the south of the bridge, but it would be perfectly smooth water to the north, and *vice versâ*; during the north-east monsoon the raft would travel by the south of the bridge. Had this simple and perfectly practical suggestion been made to me at the time I cannot but think that something would have come out of the Duke of Buckingham's proposal. It, at all events, redounds to his credit, and will possibly be carried out eventually.

In the course of this year we had the good fortune of a pearl-fishery, and I went in the Government steamer to see this remarkable sight. A pearl-fishery being announced, the divers flocked in, most from India and some from Ceylon, all Tamils, in their own sailing-boats. The number of vessels, each manned by about six men, generally averages a hundred and fifty. These are divided into three fleets, each fleet being distinguished by a red, blue, or white flag. The ground, or rather that part of the sea, had been carefully mapped out by Captain Dounan, the master attendant. He knew accurately where every deposit of oysters was to be looked for. In the afternoon this particular spot was marked by a buoy, and in the morning, at gun-fire, one of the detachments of the fleet scudded off and took its moorings round the buoy. The breeze blew from the land from an early hour, and later from the sea, landward. When another gun was fired, the vessels seemed to fly homewards. They quite ran away from our steamer. We were up and about at cockcrow, and round from one fishing-boat to another, taking toll of one oyster from each. Out of the fifty oysters thus obtained I did not secure even one pearl. It was a very amusing sight. The divers sat on the side of the vessel like so many cormorants on a ledge of rocks. When ready they went down with one foot in the hollow of a heavy stone, something like a sugar-loaf, and attached to a rope, and threw themselves on the oysters, which they scrambled into a net fastened to the waist. At one moment the surface of the sea was perfectly smooth, then, all at once, bob, bob, bob, would come up a series of black heads, puffing and blowing. No one remained under the water as long as a minute, and I was informed that very few divers could exceed or even reach that time. When the gun was again fired the sports of the day were over, and the financial business began. On landing, the crews of the various boats carried up their spoils to the Government sheds. The oysters were then divided into four heaps, and the crew were ordered to take their choice. This was their payment. It was a gambling affair. Sometimes they got high prices for their lots, sometimes low ; but this gambling is a great attraction. In former days there was a special heap assigned to the shark-charmer, who, by his incantations, was supposed to banish these monsters. During the latter fisheries this appendage was got rid of, much to the terror of the divers, who now laugh at their super-stition. The noise and splashing keep off the sharks, which are numerous enough, and no accident has occurred since the discontinuance of the charmer till this year (1890), when a diver was attacked and carried away by one.

When the oysters were divided the Government agent put them up to auction, and my aide-de-camp, Major Clay, and secretary, Mr. Stewart, each bought a thousand at £3 10s. Mr. Stewart opened his on the way back, and found nothing. Major Clay buried his in a barrel in Queen's House garden, and when he dug it up, two or three months afterwards, he got several good pearls, cer-tainly worth £12. Such is the uncertainty. At Aripo there were great fluctuations in price, from £10, and even £12 per thousand, to £3, just as reports came in from various deposits where the oysters were left to rot, and where they impregnated the atmosphere with a stench exceeding all other stenches which have ever affected my nostrils. A number of speculators were in attendance at the auction—merchants from India, from China, and many from Colombo, who bought wholesale to retail unopened with very high profits. All the coolies about the harbour, and every loafer about the streets, who had a few pence in his pocket, bought oysters. A little Tamil boy had been given sixpence by some traveller. He ran down and parted with it for one oyster, but in it was found a pearl for which he was immediately given £10, and which the purchaser sold the same day for £50. The story of such ventures spread like wildfire, and the oyster-sellers drove a roaring trade. I refrained from any speculation, remembering Mr. Hill's (the Oxford-street jeweller) advice : " Never buy pearls ; you have always the Indian rajahs to outbid you."

The beginning of this year was not signalized by any remarkable events, except that I was as near killed as a man could be by a fall from my horse when visiting the North Central Province. I had made an excursion of some distance from the northern road to visit some newly restored village tanks, which the cultivators were very proud of, and had begged me to inspect. I remained in the village for a day, to please the people, and because of the excellent snipe-shooting. On mounting my horse, a fine grey Australian, belonging to one of the escort, he plunged, and bolted along the very narrow jungle path, twisting in and out through trees. Although I had only one foot in the stirrup I contrived to steer him some short distance, when I was struck under the chin by a branch of a tree and flung with the greatest violence to the ground. I was not stunned, but grievously hurt, and was carried on a bed to the station, some six miles off, in desperate pain. There was, fortunately, an excellent surgeon with us, who pronounced that no injuries, external and internal, were discoverable, and he was right ; but the whole of my back became as black as my hat, and, though I was able to finish the trip in a carriage, I was unable for a month to mount my horse.

In September I opened the Legislative Assembly, and had again the satisfaction of announcing an ever-increasing revenue, leaving an excess of nearly a million and a half of rupees over expenditure. Again I was able to pour forth from my full cornucopia all manner of good things. More improvements at Nuwara-Eliya, including the construction of the beautiful road from the Moon Plains to the Barrack Plains, an esplanade which was to be the fashionable walk of North Colombo, and which was perfectly delightful till it was entirely washed away by the sea a few years later. Irrigation was continued everywhere at high pressure, especially in the uncontested benefit of repairing the village tanks. The breakwater was begun under most favourable auspices. The arterial roads were bridged and nearly finished, which enabled me to begin others, not so ambitious but of great usefulness. I set going a scheme, which I longed to see executed, of giving Colombo an ample supply of pure water. So far back as 1862, in the days of Sir H. Robinson, the subject was mooted, but nothing was done till 1866, when a special committee was appointed to report on the water-supply and drainage of the town. Nothing could have been stronger than that report. The water was pronounced insufficient and utterly unfit for use. It proceeded from wells, many of them close to cess-pits, hence yielding impure and coloured water, often brackish. They recommended a supply from the river Kelani. Various negotiations were then entered into with companies, but they all broke down, and after eleven years' procrastination I took up the matter in 1873, and referred the subject to Mr. Bateman, the well-known water engineer, who reported in 1874 there was nothing to prevent it from being carried out. But first of all arose delays at the Colonial Office as to the manner of payment; then Mr. Bateman was taken ill and neglected the business; then he quarrelled with the Colonial Office authorities, so that this, my favourite project, lingered on until a considerable time after my retirement, and my successor had the credit and satisfaction of completing this undertaking, which I had determined to culminate by the erection of a magnificent fountain just opposite the Town Hall, which should be a glory to Colombo, and a monument of my good taste.

In 1879 it was determined not to make use of Kelavi river, and the determination was a very proper one. In 1882 the works were begun, but not completed till 1889. At a place called Labugama, about eight miles from Colombo, and 360 feet above the sea-level, a mountain river, flowing between two hills, has been blocked up and converted into a lake about 80 feet deep. This is the very purest water, coming from a perfectly uncontaminated stream ; it is conveyed to Colombo in pipes, and every drop passes through a screen of woven wire which intercepts the smallest extraneous substance. The supply of water is so large that it is calculated even if not a drop of rain fell for 200 days, there would still be a supply of 600,000,000 gallons, about 3,000,000 being the ordinary consumption. This great reservoir is one of the most lovely spots in Ceylon. It reminds one of Scottish scenery, the wild woods coming down to the mountain tarn, and the bright blue glittering water reflecting the clear sky. There is a capital rest-house at the reservoir which I am surprised is not more frequented by the *jeunesse dorée* of Colombo ; and also excellent boats, though I believe the stern law which forbids access of all domestic animals to the water is extended to tourists, who cannot obtain boats without leave from the superintendent. The only large animal which gets access to the water is the elephant, a herd of wild ones being somewhere in the neighbourhood, and paying it periodical visits. I

see by the Ceylon papers of September, 1890, that this
herd is to be captured forthwith in a kraal.

I much regret I cannot lay my hand on the letter of
Mr. MacBride,* giving the account of the transport of a
famous lion from its original site in the Council Hall of
King Nusanka Malla, at Polannarua. This is the ruined
city of greatest interest after Anaradhapura. It is of
much later origin. The lion in question is a fine object,
quite as spirited as his Cnidian brother in the British
Museum. There is an inscription on it to this effect : "On
this lion King Nusanka Malla sat and administered
justice." A capital caricature was done of me by a Mr.
Van Dort, a native. I was portrayed as King Nusanka,
dressed up in royal Kandian robes and seated on the
lion, with the title, "The modern Nusanka Malla." But
to return to the journey. Every mishap attended the
transfer of this huge stone beast. Its first dray fell to
pieces beneath its weight. On descending from the
elevated ground where it stood the two elephants attached
to it pulled over-vigorously, and the dray and the lion and
the elephants flew apart in different directions. It had
then to be drawn over a difficult jungle path, a distance of
fifteen miles from the main road ; but the elephants had
now learned their business, and these obstacles were
surmounted. But when it reached the high road the
worst of all remained. The wooden bridges, constructed
to sustain a moderate load, were quite unable to bear the
combined weight of the lion and the dray, and the banks
of the river were precipitous and deep. But this, too, was
overcome by digging out a sloping passage to the bed
of the river, and another on the opposite side. The
elephants with their immense strength and sagacity
sustained the strain of letting down the lion, and easily

* Director of Public Works, Ceylon.;

drew it up again. Much of this took place in the solitary jungle, but when the inhabited regions were approached, the whole country turned out in amazement. MacBride on horseback in front, the procession of elephants, the lion decked with wreaths and flowers, was a magnificent sight. The tom-tommer from each village joined the *cortége*. The head man of the district asked permission for his little boy to ride the monster into Mátalé, whence he was to be conveyed by rail to Colombo. This gay, populous town was wild with excitement and delight, and MacBride as elated as Paulus Emilius or Metellus, when they marched in triumph through Rome, and exhibited their spoils to the wondering citizens. No further adventures occurred. The lion now stands calmly in the Museum, and few know, or could understand if told, all the cares it caused, and the excitement it created. It is a most valuable archæological record, and would have been undoubtedly destroyed ere this had it not been removed. How the artist who carved this fierce majestic beast got the notion of him it is difficult to say, as there is no record of there having been lions in Ceylon at that period.

Among other measures which I proposed to the Legislative Council was one to provide a Widows' Fund, and I quote the words of my address :—

"I have every expectation of being able to lay before you a measure for making provision for the widows of public servants of all classes in the colony. No one but members of the Executive Council can form an idea of the sad cases, which perpetually come before them, of widows of trustworthy and deserving public servants, who have by their husbands' deaths been left on the verge of destitution. Sad, too, is the position of the Government, which is obliged to meet their appeals for assistance by refusal."

Here, again, I was fated to meet with disappointment. It was coldly received by the Colonial Office, who had

some scheme of its own for a universal Colonial Widows'
Fund, an impossibility on the face of it.   Who could frame
a scale to meet the deadly climate of our West African
colonies, and of those which are notably healthy?   The
Legislative Council had returned a cordial reply of assent.
We were prepared to vote a liberal sum as the basis of the
scheme.   At last the Colonial Office, finding its own plan
impracticable, gave way.   The Auditor-General, who was
going home, was commissioned to confer with competent
actuaries.   This he did, but of course much delay ensued.
At last all was being got ready when he lost every paper
connected with the subject, and all had to be done again.
The scheme did not come into operation for several years
after I had first proposed it, and it grieved me much that
many cases, very sad ones, occurred which I could not
relieve, and I am deeply sorry not to have seen in my
day the fulfilment of this most valuable boon to the
public servants of the colony.   It should be sufficient to
me that it is now in full working order, and conferring
immense good.

Early in the spring rumour was rife that the Prince of
Wales was about to visit his Mother's Eastern possessions.
In the autumn I received the official announcement that
Ceylon was to be included.

On the morning of December 1, the royal fleet
steamed into the roads at Colombo, and, in due time, I
had to go off in full dress to pay my respects.   It was
rough and wet, and I had great difficulty in clamber-
ing into the *Serapis* with a sword between my legs,
much to the amusement of Lord Charles Beresford,
the commander.   Nothing could be more gracious and
pleasant than the Prince.   He seemed gratified with our
programme, the first part of which was to land, after his
luncheon, to drive through Colombo and admire the

arches and decorations erected in his honour. The land-ing was auspiciously conducted, and so was the drive, except that, at starting, the two imported Australian leaders were so fractious that they had to be removed. The multitude thought this a bad omen, that the Prince should have to take his round with two rather than four horses. My Malay mounted body-guard was greatly admired.

The following day the sun rose bright and clear, and we made an early start for Kandy. The Prince rode on the engine up the famous incline, and we halted at the top of the pass to enable him to lunch and to change his dress, so as to enter Kandy in grand attire. On reaching Kandy we drove very slowly to the Pavilion, and the sight was very beautiful. All the population was out in holiday costume ; the steep bank from the railway station was a close mass of human beings, who rose simultane-ously when the Prince's carriage reached them, and then at once sat down again. It was a curious and brilliant sight.

In the evening, after dinner, we had a perahara of the finest elephants belonging to the temples, headed by the Kandian chiefs, together with devil-dancers, torch-bearers, and other appurtenances of these functions. But the most important of the Kandian ceremonies was reserved till the following evening, when, after dinner, we adjourned to the Audience Hall, now the Hall of the Supreme Court, formerly that of the Kandian kings. Here were assembled all the great Kandian chiefs, each of whom was introduced to the Prince, and received most graciously. Moreover, the wives of these chiefs were also assembled, in a blaze of jewellery. Among them was a celebrated old lady, one of the largest landowners in Ceylon. She was a woman of the highest rank and bluest blood, and had been lady-in-waiting to the Queen of Kandy. To the memory of her ancient mistress she had remained unswervingly faithful, stubbornly refusing to pay her respects to the Governors or their wives—a good, honest rebel in heart. She, however, had the strongest regard for Mr. Parsons, the Government agent of the Central Province, and placed the most unhesitating confidence in him. He had persuaded her that she could not avoid, as a great landowner, paying her respects to the son of her sovereign. Mr. Parsons pointed her out to the Prince, and told him her story. He at once descended from the raised daïs, went to the old lady and took her by the hand. He said, "I have heard of your unshaken fidelity to your former mistress, and I admire you for it. But she is gone and dead. I ask you now to show the same fidelity to my Mother and your Queen, and to accept and wear this ornament,* which is one of the symbols of the English crown, in remembrance of me." These few words were said with singular kindness. The old lady was silent for a minute, and then burst into tears. " I will always wear it," she said, "in memory of you and your Mother, who will henceforth have no more devoted servant than myself." And a devoted loyalist she became, and remained till the end of her life.

It was on this occasion that I was invested by the Prince with the Order of St. Michael and St. George.

The weather all that afternoon was terrible, a continual downpour. The temple was brilliantly lighted, so far as it could be managed, but the rain soon extinguished the illuminations. In the afternoon the Prince visited it, inspected the tooth, and then went and showed himself to the multitude from the octagon in front of it. The poor multitude presented the appearance of a sea of umbrellas,

* A gold brooch representing the Tudor Rose.

and was thoroughly drenched. The morning had been bright, and we had visited Peradeniya Gardens ; and the Prince was delighted with Mr. Thwaites, who was not equally delighted with him, for, on seeing the flying foxes, the Prince cried aloud, " Oh, if I only had a gun ! " I remarked that there were two or three in one of the carriages, together with ammunition, which I had with forethought provided, feeling quite sure of a *battue*, and of the destruction of numbers of these odious beasts, the special favourites of Mr. Thwaites. The party went to work with a will, and poor old Thwaites retired groaning and sighing when he saw the huge heap of the bodies of these hitherto protected robbers. This was the first attack in force on their fortress, and since then, I am glad to say, they have been utterly banished.

The following morning the sun was bright, and the appearance of the weather promising, so we started on our journey of about sixty miles to Ruanwellé. The quantity of baggage carried by the party was inconceivable. We had every cart and car we could press into the service, but they were utterly inadequate, and a large body of coolies was told off to carry the effects.

Part of the journey was effected by train, and we had hardly entered our carriages when the rain, persistent and remorseless, came down. The unfortunate coolies, wet and cold, were unable to carry their heavy loads, so they threw them down, and bolted into the jungle. Several of the carts also came to grief, and some of the carriages also broke down, from the terrible condition of the road. These luckily contained the servants, and we colonists were by no means sorry to see such great magnificoes crawling in, wet to the skin, and very sorry for themselves, after walking several miles in the slush. However, we made the best of it, and had a very pleasant dinner, enlivened by the extraordinary stories of Mr. ——, the assistant agent, some of which Baron Munchausen might have enrolled among his own.

Sunday the 5th we halted at Ruanwellé, and the Prince, having due regard to sabbath observance, refrained from all manner of sports.

Favourable reports arrived of the elephants having been driven in at no great distance, and I detached two of our most famous hunters, Messrs. Varian and Fisher, to keep a watchful eye on the Prince, and not to scruple to lose their own lives in saving his. I must confess I watched him and his companions off the next morning to the scene of action with unmitigated apprehension. Telegram after telegram was being forwarded, that, under no circumstance, was I to permit the Prince to incur danger. But to try and stop him would have been as futile as the Pope's bull against a comet. We had provided against danger as far as we could, by placing the guns on rocks above the jungle, and towards these points the elephants were driven. But they absolutely refused to advance in these directions; they rushed madly about in terror; the jungle was about fifteen feet high, so that only their motion could be seen. At last, after waiting till their patience was exhausted, the sportsmen determined to leave their posts and go down into this jungle, which was impassable, save by the elephant tracks. It was a most reckless undertaking, and such as no experienced hunter would have dreamed of. Fortunate was it for them that a notoriously fierce elephant, with one tusk, had broken away from the herd the day before, or there would have been some dreadful work. Mr. Fisher described to me the scene in the evening. He could not tell where the elephants were going, as he could see nothing save the waving of the bamboos. All at

once one came right down upon, and, as it were, over the
Prince, who was as cool as a cucumber, and brought him
down, literally at his feet.   He shot another, and jumped
on his carcase in triumph to possess himself of his tail.
When this was effected they say that the courtier-like
elephant got up and made his way to his friends tailless.

All's well that ends well.   They got out of the jungle
without injury, and, providentially, without fever afterwards, which I much feared.   We had shifted our quarters
some eighteen or twenty miles nearer Colombo, to Ramula,
during the day ; and when the shooting was over the
royal party was driven there by a by-road, as fast as the
poor jaded horses could go.   Lord Aylesford was on
the box, and took the reins from the Tamil coachman
and began to flog the horses, who, having had enough of
it already, swerved and upset the party into the ditch.
No one was hurt, and the Prince's sole care was not to
lose his elephants' tails.   The Malay escort soon put the
carriage to rights, Lord Aylesford was removed from the
box, and all was ready for a start, when Lord Charles
Beresford, pointing to the coachman who was mounting
to his seat, said to the Malay sergeant, in a solemn tone
of command, "Cut that man's head off!"   In an instant
out flashed the Malay's sword, and in an instant the
command would have been obeyed, for a Malay is ever
ready and willing for a fierce deed ; but, fortunately, the
coachman understood English, and sprang up on the other
side of the road to a ledge of rocks, where he was safe.
Lord Charles, seeing how nearly his joke had caused a
serious catastrophe, now called out in stately tones, "The
Prince has graciously pardoned him, let him come down."
And so he descended, and, though frightened out of his
wits, brought us safely to Colombo on the afternoon of
the 6th.   Then came all sorts of doings—a levée, a ball,

inspection of the coffee-mills, the laying the first stone of the breakwater, a visit to the celebrated enormous tortoise, who is, by tradition, reputed to have been of great size and good age when the Dutch ceded the island, and him with it, in 1796. He is still alive (1890). He is said to have been imported from the Seychelles. His strength is prodigious, as he is able to carry several persons on his back, but he is very lethargic, and, to quicken his movements, some inhuman person has bored a hole through his carapace, wherein to insert a sharp stick ; but this amusement is not sanctioned.

The ball was a most splendid affair. A large iron building was erected on Galle Face, and most tastefully decorated. In spite of all sinister forebodings, everything was completed, and the Prince and his suite danced till all hours of the morning.

All things, however, have an end ; and it was with the most heartfelt feelings of relief that I watched, the following morning, the departure of the royal squadron, and telegraphed to her Majesty that all had passed off well.

I cannot conclude this episode without stating that no one could have been more kind, courteous, and considerate than his Royal Highness, and I must pay the same tribute to all his retinue. The effect of the visit was certainly good among the Europeans, among whom loyalty was a passion ; but even on the natives it has had a strong effect. Hitherto their ideas of royalty had been confined to the image and superscription of her Majesty on their coin. Now they saw its visible representation in the person of one who would in all probability be their future king.

The Prince had expressed a strong wish that I should follow him to Calcutta, and Lord Northbrook had sent me a cordial invitation, so I telegraphed for the necessary leave of a month, which was immediately accorded by Lord Carnarvon. So, ten days after the departure of the royal party, I proceeded, on the 20th, to Calcutta, visiting for a few hours the Duke of Buckingham, at Madras, and arrived on the 27th at Calcutta, which was in a state of ferment. All the great natives (except the Nizam) were flocking in, or had arrived, and the constant salutes of cannon announced the arrival of each potentate. I was duly introduced to all—the sullen and repulsive Holkar; the somewhat insolent Scindia; Rewa, an excellent fellow with a painted face, owing to some eruption; the dear, kindly disposed Maharajah of Benares; the little Begum of Bhopal, who, being in "purdah," as it is called, was always veiled, but whose bright eyes shone merrily through the veil when we shook hands; the charming Maharanee of Cooch Behar; the Burmese ambassadors; the brother of Jung Behauder, of Nepaul; and last, but not least, that most remarkable man, Sir Salar Jung, the powerful minister of the Nizam. Many of them visited me, among others Salar Jung, who remained with me for over an hour, discussing English subjects and giving me most valuable information. From all I had most pressing invitations to visit them. There were successions of balls, levées, native entertainments, races, tent-pegging, and feats of swordmanship; a delightful Sunday at Barrackpore, where Miss Baring (now Lady Emma) did the honours.

But the durbar, at which all these famous people attended, was the greatest spectacle ever seen in India since the days of British rule, if, indeed, even the great Akbar had ever such a *cortège* at Delhi. It is impossible to describe the brilliancy of colouring, the variety of dresses of the great chiefs from Cape Comorin to the

Himalayas, and the magnificence of the jewellery. Some of the Maharajahs seemed oppressed by the weight of diamonds, emeralds, and pearls which covered their breasts and head-dresses. Eight of these great natives were to be invested by the Prince with the highest Indian Order, the Grand Cross of the Star of India. A large piece of ground on the Maidan was enclosed, and from the immense tent, which was occupied by the Prince, Viceroy, and officials, myself included, in the place of honour after the two first-named personages, a long strip of red cloth was extended to the end of the enclosure. On each side of it were four tents, one for each of the knights, and up to each ran a narrower strip of red cloth. Not a soul was in the enclosure, save two attendants with silver trumpets. At the sound of these trumpets each advanced to the royal tent, his long, sky-blue train being held up by two boys in most brilliant attire. There he was received by his Royal Highness with a few courteous words, and the star was duly fastened on his breast. One was almost dazed with the gleam of the diamonds of these illustrious persons; but, at the last note of the trumpet, the last tent opened, and a tall, commanding figure, all in white, and absolutely devoid of ornament, save one magnificent diamond in his turban, stalked forth, and all recognized the man of men, Sir Salar Jung.

At earliest morning, before the sun had risen, the Duke of Sutherland and I used to visit all things which did not usually attract visitors—the jails, hospitals, sewerage system, jute factories, etc., and a capital companion he was, from his knowledge and determination to be fully informed.

We were much interested at Calcutta with the experiments on the poison of serpents, instituted by Sir Joseph Fayrer, the author of the fine work on the Thanotophidia

of India (the death-bringing snakes). We were brought
to a house where a large number of various species of
these reptiles were confined. An extremely intelligent
young medical officer, the assistant of Sir J. Fayrer,
attended, and explained to us the experiments which
were being conducted. He informed us that the most
deadly of all snakes was the cobra, and its gigantic
relative the hamadryad, whose food was small snakes of
other species. The next in order of virulence was the
Daboia elegans, called in Ceylon, where it is common,
the "ticpolonga," a very beautiful reptile, whose bite
was nearly as deadly, the poison operating some minutes
more slowly. The Australian black snake and the rattle-
snake were far less deadly. I was much amused, but
rather alarmed, at the cool way in which the English
doctor and his native attendants thrust their hands into
the baskets and pulled out the reptiles for exhibition.
The doctor took out a large cobra, grey with age, I
presume, and, on my remarking the danger of their handling it, he remarked very coolly, "Oh, this is a very good
old fellow; he never tries to bite." They were made to
bite a leaf placed in a spoon, and the venom was copious.
My alarm came to its height when two huge hamadryads,
about ten or twelve feet long, were taken out of their
boxes, and made to exhibit themselves on the floor.
They sat up with expanded hoods, and I did not forget
that Sir J. Fayrer had mentioned in his book that these
were the fiercest of the serpent race, and that they alone
did not scruple to attack, and, if enraged, to follow in
pursuit for a considerable distance. I was at the far end
of the small room, away from the door, and at their mercy,
as I must have passed close to them to escape. I was
assured that there was no danger, and they returned
peaceably into their boxes. It is strange that all these

investigations and experiments have not had for their
result the discovery of any cure for snakebites.   They
have found that the venom is akin to albumen, the white
of eggs, but nothing more.   It is a reproach to science
that it has failed in its researches, and that there is absolutely no remedy, save immediate cautery and excision
round the wound, and that twenty thousand persons
annually die of snakebites in Hindustan.

At last the revels came to an end, and we bade farewell to the Prince and his party, who, one and all, assured
me that they had been right well entertained in Ceylon,
and enjoyed their visit there.

The last days of my stay at Calcutta were clouded
over by sad affliction.   I received a telegram to the effect
that my dear mother was in a precarious state at Coole,
and two days afterwards another followed to say she had
died.   She passed away without pain, aged seventy-six,
and in her hand was my telegram, just arrived, announcing
that all had gone well during the royal visit, and that I
had been invested with the Order of St. Michael and
St. George.

It was a terrible blow to me, for I had looked forward,
in spite of her failing health, to passing some years in
happiness with her at home.   All her letters had breathed
that hope, and were full of joy and pride at the success
which was attending my government.   This more than
made up to her, she constantly said, for all the sorrows
and disappointments which the follies of my early life
had caused her.   I was indeed left lonely.

She was a woman full of affection, and of great natural
ability, well read, well educated, witty in conversation, of
high spirits, and essentially a lady.   Few people had
more devoted friends, and the tenants and country
people adored her for her constant acts of kindness and

generosity.   In all her troubles, which, alas! I had too often caused her, she was sustained by a strong religious belief, and by her confidence that her prayers would ultimately be granted by God, in whose infinite mercy she had unswerving trust.   Deeply as religion coloured her life, she never obtruded her thoughts and opinions on any one, unless they desired the discussion, and I never knew any one more free from unjust dislikes of other persuasions.   If I was cast down by her death, I was cheered by the thought that she died so happily and so comforted.   She lies by my father's side in our burial-place at Coole.

CONCLUSION.

THOSE who have been interested in the account of my husband's life recorded in the preceding chapters will like to know something of its last fifteen years. It would have been a sad task for me, to whom his loss is still so fresh, to write a sketch of these. But it has been spared me. His friend of many years, Sir Henry Layard, has given me a number of his letters written during this period, and I have chosen from them a passage here and there, a thread of connection from one year to another till the end. I am glad his own vivid words should tell of the interests of these last years. It is pleasant also to be able to witness, as it were, his happiness and pleasure at the success of his work in Ceylon, and to be present with him when he revisited his dear island. I will not give a list of all the addresses he received there of gratitude for material benefits, for encouragement of learning, for wide-minded toleration. It is enough to say that all creeds and classes joined to do him honour by putting up a statue to his memory at Colombo.

He has written so frankly and candidly of the errors and mistakes of his youth, that it is only just that this great success of his later days should be dwelt on. His old friend Frank Lawley, writing of his early days on the turf,* applies to him the saying, "On ne revient pas de si loin pour peu de chose."

* "Racing Life of Lord George Bentinck."

He went back to Ceylon three times as a visitor. The account of the first visit is given in the letters to Sir Henry Layard. The second time he took me, after a winter in India, to see the wonderful beauty of his "old raj," and to make the acquaintance of his many friends out there. He went again, for a little time, in 1890, and said his farewells, feeling that it was his last look at the East and his enchanted isle. I had been a little jealous for our own "disconsolate island," our poor Ireland, and was pleased when he wrote at last, "much as I like Ceylon, and much as the people like me, I have begun to yearn greatly for home."

The groundwork, if I may so call it, of his letters to Sir H. Layard is of affairs connected with the National Gallery, but in this there is so much of detail, and so much that is confidential, that I have given but little of it. The four pictures he bequeathed to the Gallery testify to the great interest he, as one of the trustees, took in it to the end.

Other subjects often dwelt on, and in which he took a vigorous part, are the Arundel Society, the Hellenic Society, and the exploration of Egypt and of Cyprus. The event that gave him the keenest pleasure of his last year was witnessing the unveiling of the bust of Sir Henry Layard in the Hall of the British Museum.

I was very glad to find among the letters so clear an exposition of the part he had taken, and the views he held, in Egyptian affairs. These have been remembered vaguely, and distorted through the haze of the war. He kept up his warm friendship for the Egyptian exiles in Ceylon to the last.

He took no part in Irish politics of late, but they were none the less near his heart. He had been, when in Parliament, so earnest and advanced an advocate of the tenants that he grieved that at the end of life, while their well-being was as warmly desired by him as before, he was cut away from the possibility of serving them. He felt that landlords ought not to live in a fool's paradise, with their eyes shut, and not marking the signs of the times, and was ready to welcome any reform which he could recognize as such. But he could not ally himself with either "the rebel or the sacerdotal party," and he was indignant at the long and demoralizing continuance of unchecked crime. His real hope for Ireland lay in the extension of land purchase, I may almost say in its introduction, for he held and pressed the idea when others had given it but little attention. His theory, founded on experience, was, that every tenant who becomes the owner of his holding, becomes as it were a special constable sworn in on the side of law and order. He held that once the majority of tenants had become landowners, Home Rule might safely be given, if indeed it was still desired. Practically, he wished Government to advance so much as a million for the purpose, allowing the loans as soon as repaid to be lent out again. He would in no case have made it compulsory on the tenant to buy, as this might eventually be used as an excuse for repudiation, but trusted to the gradual effect of example. He was anxious to put it into practice at Coole, but the tenants, one and all, refused to make any alteration in the relations between us.

He was very fond of his people. In a letter he wrote me just before our marriage he says—

"I am very glad indeed that the country people are pleased. Whatever naughty deeds I may have done I always felt the strongest sense of duty towards my tenants, and I have had a great affection for them. They have never in a single instance caused me displeasure, and I know you can and will do everything in your power to make them love and value us."

We are too near the borders of Clare to have got

through the bad years quite free of trouble, but the trouble was very little, and its memory had soon passed away. We spent our summers and autumns very happily at Coole. Though a Nationalist farmer had been elected in his place as Chairman of the Board of Guardians, Sir William bore no malice. He attended whenever difficult or important subjects arose, and would come back pleased and surprised at the deference shown to his views, and the welcome given him by the " frieze-coated men." They would have been hard to win if they had not been won by his courteous cordial manner and the " genius for kindness " that was his characteristic.

He was glad at the last to think that, having held the estate through the old days of the Famine and the later days of agitation, he had never once evicted a tenant.

Now that he has put his harness off I may boast this on his behalf. And, in the upheaval and the changing of old landmarks, of which we in Ireland have borne the first brunt, I feel it worth boasting that amongst the first words of sympathy that reached me after his death were messages from the children of the National School at Coole, from the Bishops and Priests of the diocese, from the Board of Guardians, the workhouse, the convent, and the townspeople of Gort.

His letters to Sir Henry Layard show that he saw and did not fear the approach of death. He had no dread of it, but a great dread of the infirmities of old age, and these, in spite of his years, had not yet touched him. His last acts were acts of kindness. His last conscious words to me were the embodiment of his religion—" We are all God's children. We must do our best to help one another." He died, in London, on the 6th of March, 1892.

He had always disliked the idea of the decking of

the dead with flowers, and I had told his near friends of this. But just at the last three wreaths came that I knew would have pleased him. One was from a poor London parish, one from a Ceylon native, and the third from the Greek community in England, in gratitude for his help to their country many years ago. These went with him to Coole, where his people laid him beside his mother, who had devoted her life to him, and his father, who had died in their service in the Famine years.

AUGUSTA GREGORY.

LETTERS, 1875–1892.

CHIEFLY TO THE RIGHT HON. SIR A. HENRY LAYARD, G.C.B.

"*October*, 1875.—I am pretty nearly as anxious to get away from Ceylon as you are from Madrid. The loneliness of my life is unbearable. When I have a piece of business it is all very well, but as I know pretty well all about every paper before it comes up to me, the ordinary work I can always despatch in a few hours. After that I turn to Homer or Tacitus, and another hour or two of them go a long way."

"*July* 4, 1876.—My letter of resignation goes by this mail, that is, resignation in February next. Herbert, the Secretary, wrote to me a short time ago, to say that there were rumours that I was not going to remain, and that he hoped I should *long* continue Governor. This expectation frightened me, so I am determined to give them plenty of time, and no excuse for not having some one ready to step into my shoes. I shall regret the glorious climate and scenery and the occupation, but I cannot stay, nostalgia is too strong for me. Besides, I have done my work ; I have set on foot all the great material improvements on which my heart was bent, and have thoroughly reorganized, or at least shall have, every department. A man with new ideas should now come, and ladies would do much to popularize the government. I say to myself daily, when I struggle to entertain, ' *Tempus abire tibi*,' but I hope to live and be strong enough to come here once more, and see what my successor has done at the close of his reign. I am a little nervous about my estimated revenue, but I am creeping up month by month, and, in spite of a very bad coffee year and general depression at home, I am still in hopes of not only fulfilling my budget expectations, but of closing my government with a large surplus. Inshallah!"

" *September* 26, 1876.—All that I have done has been approved of at home, and no Governor could have had a more complimentary letter than the reply of Lord Carnarvon to my resignation. They want me to stay on, but even if I had not other pressing reasons for returning, it would be impossible for me to remain and maintain the position of Governor, as it should be maintained, on £5600 a year, to which my income has fallen by the depreciation of the rupee."

" *On board s.s. 'Assam,' April* 10, 1877.—Your letter of November 30 reached me the morning I was about to embark for a three months' run through the Australian colonies. I am now near Ceylon once again, and am able to answer it in peace and quiet.

" I am so cheered and revived by my 'outing' to Australia that I now regret having resigned my appointment. I am sure I shall not be so happy, or in such health, at home, nor shall I ever again have such work to do, with ample means and no restraint. Latterly, however, I was so dispirited by the loneliness of my life that I could bear it no longer, and though I had well weighed the consequences, yet I felt I could not remain, and so I sent off my letter. With a companion, a wife, a sister, or even a very intimate friend, I should prefer the government of Ceylon to anything that could be offered to me. It is such a comfort when you find things going wrong to be able to set them right with the strong hand, and it is such a gratification to see great public works begun and finished according to your own plans, and not marred by vexatious interference. The people, moreover, are pleasant to govern ; they are quick witted and intellectual, and the higher classes singularly well-bred and taking in their deportment. I think, too, there are indications, in a faint way, no doubt, of the quality of gratitude, in the existence of which, in the East, I had long disbelieved. I am sure much may be done with them by kindness, courtesy, and respectful treatment. I have known some whom I would trust as implicitly as I would Englishmen, and I am as confident as one can ever be of human conduct, that if future rulers of Ceylon will endeavour to induce the natives to trust them and rely on them, much more of the administration of the country may be vested in them. Weakness and moral and physical timidity are their main faults, and, as you well know, cowardice is a difficult defect to cure. The way to deal with such a race is to give them confidence and en- couragement, to reward even ostentatiously good conduct, fidelity, and strength, but to be down on offenders with relentless severity. I have pursued this course, and without egotism I can say that I believe no Governor ever before succeeded in inspiring such a universal trust in his motives.

" My trip to Australia has been one of great interest, and I much wish that some of our most prominent public men, such as Wm. Forster, could visit these splendid colonies. There they would see the working of democracy in its most extreme form, for there is no controlling power such as that which is vested in the President of the United States. The Governor is a mere pageant, and the Secretary of State absolutely powerless. The whole power is in the

Assembly, elected by Universal Suffrage, and if half the
stories be true of the jobbing of public men, probity is
not of much account. Still the jobbing is of a far less
gross and palpable description than that in the United
States. I believe money bribery of and by ministers is
rare, it takes the form of granting of expenditure on
localities, the members of which support the Government,
while the opposition remains out in the cold. Appointments of value are also a constant ingredient in securing
party allegiance. On the whole I am inclined to think
that, in spite of faults and blunders, they have contrived
to manage their affairs well, and that no other form of
Government would have been equally successful. I thought
the speaking execrable ; voluble and weak and violent. I
expected strong untutored eloquence, but I only heard
one man above par, the present Prime Minister of New
South Wales, Mr. Parkes, who was excellent. One thing
is very remarkable in these democracies, and that is their
extraordinary liberality in everything which conduces to
the health and improvement and recreation of the people.
Their hospitals for every disease are princely buildings,
so are their museums, public libraries, botanical gardens,
public parks, etc. This is especially the case in Victoria,
and the same prominent idea is seen uppermost in the
laying out of their smaller towns. Another striking feature
of Australian society is the extreme civility of every one
you speak to, no matter how low may be his occupation.
It is a manly, honest country, they respect themselves and
respect others, and education is universal. It is marvellous
to think that Melbourne, the fourth largest city of the
British dominions was an unexplored scrub when I was
a big boy at Harrow, and it is strange to meet many men
who remember the fires and corrobborees of the natives
in the grand streets now studded with palatial buildings.

Free trade and protection are the burning questions of the hour. New South Wales has flung off protection, and so has South Australia, but Victoria, the most extreme of all in its political views, still clings to it, and remorselessly piles duty on duty, avowedly not for revenue, but for protection. The evil results of this vicious system have become already manifest, and the rapid advance of New South Wales under her financial system has alarmed the jealousy of her neighbour, and a change is confidently expected. I know no place where the most interesting social problems can be studied with more advantage than in these colonies, and it is pleasant to think that you may speak out your own opinion as frankly as you like without ever giving offence, which is far from being the case in America. As for loyalty, it is simply at fever heat, a perfect passion, and the man who would nowadays publicly advocate a separation from England would be simply ruined as a politician, and would probably receive rough treatment into the bargain."

"*London, September* 27, 1877.—It is quite true, all that Hankey writes as to my intentions. I have no wish to enter Parliament again, though no doubt I should enter it with far greater authority and experience than when I left it. Five years of despotic government have removed all interest in our wretched Irish squabbles, into which, however, I could not fail to be drawn."

"*October* 6, 1878.—I shall look out for a pleasant companion, and I hope to pay you a visit in the spring (at Constantinople), seeing Athens, and probably Elis, by the way. I have no particular desire to see Cyprus. I entirely disapprove of our connection with it, as I do emphatically of our Turkish obligations in all other respects. The notion of our being able to induce the Turks to establish decent government in any portion of

their dominions is too preposterous. It is, with this hopeless and incurable race, the old story of trying to wash
the blackamoor white. I dare say that even you, with all
your energy and good will, have begun to despair of
effecting anything. I shall be curious to hear the discussions at the beginning of next session, for already some
of the most staunch Conservatives have not hesitated to
express their convictions to me that they are not by any
means happy about our position in the East, and that they
fear there has been a good deal of charlatanism in the
bunkum of 'peace with honour' of Lord B——. These
irreverent ideas are freely expressed, but I doubt if the
feeling has pervaded the low class of voters in the constituencies, and if we should gain much by a dissolution."

"*February* 15, 1880.—I am not yet off, as I am impeded
by lawyers, who are drawing up my marriage settlements.
I hope they will finish their task shortly, and that I shall
have changed my condition, and be, like Lars Porsena, 'on
the way to Rome.' . . . I think you and Lady Layard
will like my wife, and I hope I do not ask too much in
requesting you to receive her as well as me at Constantinople.

"I agree with you, and I think most persons of my
opinions would agree with you, as to the excellence of the
Turkish population, but what can be done with such a
Government? And the worst of it all is that these sober,
hospitable, honest people instantly take seven devils to
themselves the moment they obtain situations and advancement."

"*March*, 9, 1880.—I received your most kind letter last
night, and I can assure you my wife actually jumped for
joy at the delightful prospect of nightingales, roses, and
boats on the Bosphorus. We shall certainly pay you a
visit when you go to Therapia.

"I am hardly recovered as yet from the surprise which my marriage * has caused me. My wife, who was quite a student, is now plunged among *chiffons* and *modistes*, and I am bound to admit that she bears the infliction with a resignation which is rather alarming and ominous, excusing her new-fangled interest in dress on the grounds of pleasing me."

"*Rome, April* 5, 1880.—I see that the Tories are hopelessly routed, for which of course I am thankful, but two things I dread in regard to the incomers are, first, the domination of Gladstone, and second, a truckling to the Home Rulers. I never can overlook Gladstone's wanton and most unpatriotic speech about Austria. She has been carrying out our policy, and has made herself a bulwark against a Russian advance to Constantinople, and Gladstone denounces her for this. The mischief he has done in Italy by his words is more than you can conceive; it has given strength to the disturbing element of Italia Irredenta, which is, in fact, the revolutionary element. Even sober Italians are excited."

"*Coole, August* 27, 1880.—We have been here now for a month, and are likely to remain till the end of November, after which time we shall be free as air, and ready for Egypt or any other warm place.

"I have been doing my duty as a country gentleman—attending petty sessions, presiding as chairman over our Poor Law Union weekly meetings, and giving a dinner to our tenants. I made them a speech, reprobating the evil doings of agitators and communists, which was well received. After the dinner the wives and daughters had

* "On the 4th of March, at St. Matthias, Dublin, by the Rev. Canon Wynne, the Right Hon. Sir William Gregory to Augusta, youngest daughter of the late Dudley Persse, Esq., D.L. of Roxborough, co. Galway."

tea, cake, and plum-pudding, and then they danced till
five in the morning. Nothing can be better than the
spirit apparently of the people about here, but I dread
that all may be changed in a day by some of these violent
agitators, who lash the tenant classes into fury even
against the best landlords."

" *Coole, September* 3, 1881.—We have had a charming
tour. Fortunately Lady G—— is as fond of pictures and
architecture and works of art as myself. We have had a
week in Holland ; Cologne, with its Masters Stephan and
Wilhelm ; Cassel, and its Rembrandts; Brunswick, and
its Jan Steens; Hildesheim, a delightful old-world place,
with a rose tree a thousand years old. What would your
roses of Therapia say to such a patriarch as that ? Would
they not burst out and blush ? Then Berlin, Dresden,
Leipsic, Brussels, and the beautiful Aremberg Gallery,
and so home, without any *contretemps*, although having
eaten much veal and plum sauce."

" *London, October* 10, 1881.—I have very little to write
to you of interest, though it may be of interest to you to
know that as yet I am in the land of the living, albeit the
landlord shooting season has set in with great briskness
in my county. Personally I believe I am quite as safe at
Coole as I am here, but all around me there prevails an
absolute reign of terror. We rate the Turks and the
Italians for the insecurity of life and property which
prevails in their respective countries, but a state of things
is now prevalent in her Majesty's dominions, and within
sixteen hours of London, which would astonish the
dwellers in Sicily and even in Asia Minor. Besides assassinations successful and assassinations incomplete, there
is cutting off ears, and desperate assaults, and mutilation
of cattle, and orders, which dare not be resisted, to
servants to leave their masters' houses, and to shepherds

and herds to leave their flocks. Tenants are told to abandon their holdings and restore them to some one else and a single emissary of the Land League exercises more terror and authority over a whole district than all the magistrates, police, and *priests* put together. The priests, hitherto all-powerful, are utterly disregarded when they inculcate obedience to the law, and one of them, a friend of mine, who had refused to attend a Land League meeting, nearly lost his life, as he returned from dining with Col. ——, by the trunks of trees so placed as to upset his car. The car was not upset, thanks to the sagacity of the horse. The perpetrators were quite anxious that the priest's neck should be broken, though they would not shoot him, or shed the blood of God's anointed. But this is not all. Threatening notices of murders are flying like snowflakes, and in every house you visit terror prevails, lest the corpse of one of its inmates be brought back in the evening. For all this I hold the Government responsible.

"I presume you have heard of the purchase of Lord Suffolk's picture for £9000. It is a great acquisition, but you and Burton are more competent than I am to form an opinion whether it is worth the cost. As a general rule I am all for getting what ought to be got, regardless of price, and I am well aware that the day has gone by when one can get great pictures for small sums. I have full confidence in Burton, and the more so because he has the courage to buy cheap pictures at Christie's and elsewhere which Boxall had not, and I am sure he would not give this great sum except for a very great picture."

"*Coole, December* 5, 1881.—My tenants have behaved splendidly; they have paid all their rents, and I have not £100 arrears. So I gave them back ten per cent. They said they did not belong to the League, and would not belong to it. Since then they have been so persecuted and abused they have almost all joined within one week. The combination is creeping on like lava, filling every cranny."

"*Helouan, November* 27, 1881.—I caught a cold at Alexandria, so have come on here for change of air, and am now quite well again. This place is about fifteen miles from Cairo, and quite in the desert. The air is most enchanting. All we want are horses to have the most famous galloping in the desert, so instead of horse we have donkey exercise, and made a very long expedition, and a very pleasant one, to Sakkara yesterday, and Lady G—— talks of nothing since except Thothmes, and Rameses, and Kneph, and Shoofoo. We return on Tuesday to Cairo, which is so spoilt that I detest it. It has become a tenth-rate French provincial town. Old houses are being daily pulled down to make huge wide streets, and the charm of the cool narrow thoroughfares and of the beautiful lattices and stone-work is entirely disappearing. Most of the lattices are sold to *bric-à-brac* dealers, and will be found in various capacities in England, looking very dingy and out of place. Even the one thing you would have thought unchangeable has changed for the worse, namely, the climate. It rained three days out of the five we were there, and is raining there now. It has become damp and very treacherous. In former days a shower was a portent, now heavy rain and long continuing is not unusual. Last week it rained all night, and the mud was over your ankles, to say nothing of the smell.

"Egyptian politics are extremely interesting at this moment. There are several movements at work. First, the Arab, headed by Arabi Bey; secondly, the Turkish; and thirdly, that of Ismail, the late Khedive. His operations may be summarily dismissed. He has no party except a few of the old *régime*, who profited by his extortions, and would wish to profit again. Arabi Bey, whom the *Times* treats with little ceremony, describing him as a 'heavy fellah,' and as the mere mouthpiece of a turbulent soldiery, is a very different man. He has clearly defined views, the main object being the reign of law as against the reign of pure despotism. He insists on it that his countrymen shall be taken by Turkish Governors before impartial courts, and tried in the open day for their alleged offences, and not sent off by mere word of mouth to Fazagh and the White Nile. He is reported to be a fanatic in religion, and to aim at removing all Europeans from their posts. He is not a fanatic, but, like the Arabs, a very liberal man in matters of religion, and he looks on the Europeans as the friends and protectors of his countrymen against the Turks, whom he hates with a just and holy hatred.

"Lastly, there is the Turkish party, constantly receiving their instructions from Constantinople. They are the ruling class, and they see their power and rascality kept in check by Europeans on one side, and by the growing Arab movement on the other, and they are reviving everywhere religious fanaticism. To this party the Viceroy now altogether inclines. The soldiers have behaved extremely well, and so have the colonels hitherto. They have got their men in hand, and say they will guarantee to maintain tranquiility, unless, indeed, an armed intervention occurs to crush the Arab movement, and to maintain the despotism of the Pashas, in which case they will not be answerable for what may occur."

"*Cairo, January* 2, 1882.— I think you would be deeply interested in all that is going on in this country. So far as I can see, the National party are proceeding with great good sense and moderation. They are intent on remedying abuses, and, God knows, they have a fine crop to mow down ! Nothing can be more scandalous than the privileges which the Europeans claim under the Capitulations. I refer specially to immunity from taxation. The unfortunate blue-shirted fellah pays, through the nose, taxation for his house, while the Greek Jew, Levantine usurer and extortioner, dwells in magnificent palaces untaxed, and drives over flagged streets not one shilling of the expense of which he contributes. I hear we are ready to abandon our rights *on this point*, but that nothing of concession can be obtained from the French, who are in all these countries the foremost agents in maintaining every corruption, if they think its abolition can in any way interfere with their gains and speculations. I remember Tunis perfectly well in 1858. M. Roche was then Consul-General, notoriously corrupt, notoriously extracting presents for his wife, notoriously wresting from the Bey concessions for his countrymen in which he shared. In 1856 the same game was going on here, and M. Sabatier was feathering his nest at the expense of Said Pasha, out of whom he made a fortune by cards. The place is still swarming with French adventurers, who used to amass fortunes by the recklessness of the ladies of the different harems, who ran up enormous debts, which were ultimately paid by the Khedive. Now debts have run up fast and far enough, but the Khedive has neither the inclination nor the means to pay, and so all these freebooters are united in the one object of disturbing existing arrangements, and getting rid of European frugality and control. The same spirit prevails in many other quarters. The old vultures still remember the happy days when they preyed on the land, and the European population have not forgotten the great and glorious days of the Oppenheims *et hoc genus omne*, and sigh for their return. All these classes are doing their best to try and get the National party to make exorbitant demands, and to kick up a row when they are refused, in hopes of Turkish intervention, and a return to the old state of things and the government of baksheesh and the kurbaj. You will have read ere this my letter in the *Times*. I follow it up with another by next mail. I think you may rely on the truth of what I write, as it all comes from head-quarters, and *I trust Arabi*, perhaps unwisely.

"I have not at all a bad opinion of the Khedive. Every one abuses him on some ground. One says he is stingy ; another that he has no go in him ; a third, that he is a coward ; a fourth, that he is a fanatic ; a fifth, that he is a fool ; a sixth, that he is a deep intriguer. I believe, as regards the first charge, that he is very hard pressed, owing to the *gaspillage* of Egyptian palaces, to make both ends meet, but that he does so honestly, and is consequently frugal. He has 'no go in him' because he is an excellent husband, deeply attached to his pretty, fat wife. Colvin describes him as being anything but a coward on the 9th of December, and that he was acting bravely till his own aide-de-camp told him all was up, and that he must give way. He is certainly not fanatical, judging from his conversation, and we have no grounds for calling him either a fool or an intriguer. I have no doubt he is in communication with Constantinople, and that he longs, by means of Turkish troops, to regain the absolute power of his predecessors, and probably to avenge the indignities to which he has been subjected. This is natural enough, more especially as he has no pledge or promise from us or France against the army in case its insubordination increases, but I think he will act loyally with the Control and the European powers, if he can do so and they will support him. He is a far better man to be on the throne here at present, while the country is in tutelage, than a man of strong will and determination, or than a desperate intriguer like the Sultan. *He* has been busy enough here, but he has failed to gain the slightest support among the people. They know too well what the Turks are; even the religious bodies are altogether opposed to his influence in this country. . . . Colvin is very able and far-seeing, and, as far as I can judge, he views things as I do, and thinks that much may be done by guiding and moderating this movement. Blunt is here, quite in the thick of it all, and entirely in the confidence of the army and the sheikhs of Azar, and he seems to have the fullest reliance on their assurance of remaining quiet. This I always preach. The burden of my song is, 'There can be only one Governor. Parliamentary government, in the European sense, is impossible at present. You have neither strength enough nor education enough for it. Your work is to do away patiently and carefully the manifold abuses which afflict you.' So much for Egyptian politics."

" *Cairo, February* 6.—We have both been longing for you and Lady Layard during the last three weeks at Luxor. Nothing could have been pleasanter, in spite of the coldness of the weather. Fancy cold at Luxor! But so it was, and a deal of sneezing and coughing was the result. On the other hand, the extreme coolness permitted all kinds of long excursions to be constantly performed without the least fatigue. We had agreeable society in the evening, for there were a number of learned men, such as Professor Sayce, M. Maspero, M. Rhoné, M. de Naville, Mr. Villiers Stuart, and, last but not least, a young German, Dr. Wiederman, a perfect prodigy of learning, who charmed every one by his modesty, gaiety, and good looks. All these Egyptologists occupied their mornings in various excursions, clearing up points of difference, copying inscriptions, Egyptian, Coptic, and Greek, and in the evening bringing back to the common stock accounts of their adventures. I think you would have been amused, and if Lady L—— had taken to the purchase of blue beads with the avidity of Lady G—— and her friend Mrs. Lee Childe (*née* De Triqueti), she would have had plenty of occupation. These ladies were always running after these objects, to make necklaces, I believe, and what with their exertions and those of Lady Galway last year, blue beads, previously a drug, have risen to a fabulous price. I have picked up two very curious objects, both from Karnak, Greek glass heads, very well done, one of Pan and one of Serapis ; but my purchases have been few and unobtrusive, as I have only bought a few scarabæi, acknowledged forgeries, to make bracelets for young ladies who will care very little whether they were made in the days of Rameses or Thothmes, or in these of Sheikh Ali, the present fabricator."

" *Cairo, March* 13.—I wrote recently to the *Times* about the state of affairs here, but my letter was shamelessly long, and I doubt if it will be inserted, considering the great press of matter at present.

"I am quite satisfied that our policy at present is to support the present Egyptian Government. They are trying their best to do what is right, and Arabi (now Minister of War) is a thoroughly honest, patriotic man. No doubt they are ignorant, but they are governing according to the light that is in them, and everything is going on very fairly, though in parts of the country the mudirs are timid, being afraid to use energy lest they may be attacked in the Assembly, but all that will come right.

"Our position is this. The present Government hates France, and is well-inclined to England. If we treat them benevolently, they will cling to us and our counsels.

"It is impossible for us to have a clear and honest

understanding with France on the Egyptian question. Our policy and our objects are different. You see De Freycinet claims to have 'preponderating' influence in Egypt, which we cannot admit.

"It is inconvenient to admit the great powers into the Egyptian administration and to allow Russia any voice in it.

"*Ergo*, try and work on with the Egyptian native Government, and see if, by degrees, we cannot make them stand alone.

"I can see no better mode of proceeding than, using an Irishism, to stand still and to abandon menaces and misrepresentations."

"*Aci Reale, April* 16, 1882.—We have been for some time on the east coast of Sicily. The first two days were cold and bleak at Catania, but since then the weather has taken up, and we have enjoyed our excursions immensely. As for Taormina, it cannot be beaten for beauty, and there is a most charming hotel there, clean and good, at eight francs per head per day!!! I think I shall have to stay there when I get no rents either from Ireland or from Ceylon. We went to Messina on purpose to see the Antonellos. They are hopelessly ruined, and it is melancholy to look on such wrecks, while the Cartellino, with the beautiful neat writing of Antonello, is intact."

"*Palermo, April* 20.—We have arrived here after a most pleasant excursion to Girgenti. I thought Taormina must be unrivalled, but I was inclined to change my mind on looking down, from the heights of Girgenti, on the fine plain and the temples standing so grandly above it. The town, also, seems to be very prosperous, and it is most pleasant to witness everywhere the efforts of the municipalities to establish museums for the various objects

—Greek, Roman, Saracenic, and mediæval—which are constantly being found. At Syracuse they are building a new and apparently a very pretty museum, and they have many good things to be installed in it, among others, a most beautiful Greek Venus, though, alas! headless. At Girgenti they have also their museum, with a very interesting collection of coins, only begun within the last three years. The keeper of it said there were remarkably fine and complete collections in the town, but the owners would give nothing, and the municipality was hard set to pay the price demanded for valuable articles. I think, when I return to London, I shall ask Poole to get the coins of Acragus electrotyped, and send them as a present, with a neat and appropriate letter.

"We had a specimen of Sicilian doings on our nearing Palermo the day before yesterday. A huge and excited crowd surrounded the train at Termini, every one shouting and weeping with joy, and patting the back of a respectable middle-aged man, who entered the compartment next to ours. I asked a Sicilian gentleman who got into our carriage, what it was all about. He said, 'It is Signor Notar Bartolo who has just returned.' I, imagining him to be a Sicilian Parnell, or a relative of Garibaldi, requested to know who he was, and my friend informed me that he is a man of high position in Palermo—director, I think, of the Sicilian Bank—who, on returning a week ago from his country house near Termini, was seized by brigands and carried off. He had been released that morning, on payment of fifty thousand francs, and was so weak from starvation, or, rather, from bad food, stale bread and cheese, that he could hardly walk. At each stage there were the same demonstrations, and at Palermo the whole town seemed to have turned out. Every one was kissing the poor prisoner and each other, and the kisses were like the popping of soda-water bottles. I never kissed any one so loudly in all my life. The strange part of the business was the mode of capture. Shortly after Notar Bartolo left home, he saw on the road four bersaglieri and a carabiniere. They advanced to him, and desired to see the permits of his two servants, who were armed, and who are said to have been in the plot. They made him go into a near grove to examine the papers, and when there they informed him that he was their prisoner. They were admirably dressed, and are perfectly well known. Another case has recently occurred at Caltanisetta. It would be far safer to be under the rule of Arabi Pasha. But we Irishmen had best hold our tongues."

"*Palermo, May* 4.—Now as to Egypt. I have given the subject much thought. I had no preconceived ideas when I reached land at Alexandria. Like the rest of the world, I regarded Arabi as a mutinous rascal, who ought to be sent to the Soudan, though not blown from a gun, according to the prescription of that blood-thirsty old ass B——. I looked on the so-called National movement pretty much as we look on the Land League, and I took for granted that intervention would be employed with great propriety forthwith to maintain Sherif Pasha, and to glorify Malet. But, a little experience, and, I trust, an honest desire to reach the truth, proved to me that I was completely on the wrong track. It seems to me that my view of the character of the man is now universally accepted—that he is honest, patriotic, indus-trious, and intelligent, but without much education, and with no experience of public affairs. As to the cock-and-bull stories of his fierceness and threats, nothing can be more unfounded. He has far too little of 'the brute' in him. The danger lies much more in the gentleness of his disposition, which is essentially that of the fellah.

Whatever be his fortune, I believe hereafter it will be allowed that I gave to Englishmen a true insight into the character of the man who was about to be the virtual dictator of Egypt. I next asserted that there was a National party. In this you do not agree, and it is much disputed. I am quite ready to go thus far with you. There is no National party of any strength, such as there was, and is, in Servia and Greece, but there was a prevalent desire for a change in the administration of the country. That desire extended from the Cataracts to the Mediterranean, and was entertained, from various reasons, by every man of influence and education in the country and in the villages. It was a mixed feeling. There were a few of the best educated who wished for 'Egypt for the Egyptians'—these were the National party pure and simple—and to them were joined others in large numbers, some hoping to get redress of grievances, some influenced by envy at the salaries of Europeans, others chafing at being under European supervision, believing themselves to be as capable, others, again, and these the least numerous, affected by religious feelings. It was difficult to draw clear lines among these persons, as the different shades of opinion so ran into and tinted each other. It is enough to say that the great mass of the people who thought and read (and bear in mind that recently newspapers are circulated throughout the length and breadth of Egypt) were of one opinion. They wished to get the government as much as possible out of the grasp of France and England, and to govern themselves according to their own ideas.

"Now, I beg of you to acquit me of sentimental notions in all I have said, done, and written. I have backed up the present Egyptian Government all along, not from thinking it the best that Egypt could get, for undoubtedly,

so far as the material prosperity of the country is concerned, it would have flourished far more in the hands
of the Control, but because I thought the Egyptians, however degraded they may be from centuries of oppression,
ought to have a voice as to the government of their
country ; and, secondly, because the interests of England
would be far better served by a National Government, if
it can be kept on its legs, than by a joint Government
of England and France. You concur with me in viewing
with extreme dissatisfaction all solidarity with France in
this matter, if it can be avoided. We are certain to suffer
in our material interests if we ally ourselves with them,
and to be tarred with the same brush, in the estimation
of Europe and of Egypt, for their misdeeds. But how
are we to escape from this entanglement, except by the
success of Arabi and his government? Surely the wise
step would have been for us to have recognized the
importance of the revolution that had occurred, to have
abstained from foolish menaces, which at first caused
panic, suspicion, and irritation, and afterwards contempt,
and to have endeavoured to get hold of Arabi by offering
him the hand of friendship, and the promise of support,
so long as he and his friends behaved with prudence. I
am confident he would have warmly accepted the hand
thus held out, and would have been ready to be guided
by us in all serious matters, if left to deal with minor
matters according to his own views. We could have, in
return, given him a great position, by taking the lead
in examining and helping him to remedy the flagrant
abuses which exist, and which will continue to exist
without European help—the inequality of taxation, and
the inordinate salaries and sinecures of foreign employees.

"Now, in the present emergency, if we had had in
Egypt a man of far-seeing views and strength of mind,

I feel confident he would have recommended the Government to let him deal with the present men in the most cordial spirit. He would have seen that favouring intervention was neither more nor less than tying ourselves to the car of France, and being dragged through the mud in doing so. He would have seen that if he could prop up these people and establish them he would gain time, which is a great matter, and they have done absolutely nothing as yet which justifies intervention. He would have seen that a Turkish descent on Egypt, if France would have allowed it, would be playing the Sultan's most dangerous game. It is undoubtedly better than European intervention, but it is more easy to get the Turk in than to get him out, and, besides, who is to pay the expense of the expedition?

"I view all these matters differently from Blunt, who pushes things to first principles, but I think that Blunt deserves great credit for the bold and indefatigable manner in which he has fought this battle almost single-handed. He has fought for Egypt alone. I have fought for England first, and for Egypt also. Looking back now many years, I can well remember how I stood alone, or very much alone, in Parliament on many similar cases, which were called my 'crazes'—the union of the Roumanian provinces, the complete liberation of Servia, the increase of Greek territory; and I still think I was right in my advocacy of the South against the North in America, firstly, as regards English interests; secondly, as regards the interests and rights of the Southern States."

"*London, October* 12, 1882.—After having been the cockshy of London society during the summer, and been heartily abused on all sides, I find myself greeted as a prophet. This will please you, as you always stuck to me during evil report. Even Chenery, whom I met in Paris, told me he thought I ought to be highly gratified at having opened men's eyes to the iniquities perpetrated in Egypt with our connivance."

"*London, December 6*, 1882.—We went to the opening of the Courts of Justice. It was a fine sight, and the going there well arranged and easy. Not so the return; the confusion was frightful. The barriers all but gave way to the surging mob, as no police kept them back. A number of boys and girls got over, which added to the desperate pressure inside.

"I am sorry to say that I fear these Law Courts will not add credit to the Victorian era. The great hall is not a great hall at all, and it is hard that it should be eclipsed by the hall of Rufus, built all but seven hundred years ago, when England was very poor. It is, in fact, a passage, a gallery, an arcade, rather than a great hall. It could not be otherwise, with the stone roof which Street insisted on. Had he condescended to a wooden roof, he might have made a magnificent hall, and the effect of the roof might also have been made very fine. But no, he must have a French stone roof, and a great opportunity has been lost. We have had three great chances, besides the new Houses of Parliament, during our epoch, and have failed in all—the Law Courts, the new Whitehall blocks, by Scott, and the Natural History Museum—the last the best."

"*London, December* 30, 1882.—This day we have been to the Old Masters. I was aghast when I first entered the Rossetti room, with the strange-lipped, long-jawed, weird, disconsolate women which met my eye, but I soon passed from them among most remarkable pictures, remarkable from grandeur of conception and rich gorgeous colouring. They are different from anything I have ever seen, and, before I left the room, I was quite won over.

I can think of nothing else, and now no longer wonder at the inordinate admiration, approaching idolatry, of some men for Rossetti's works. I shall go again on Monday, to see if first impressions are correct. I wish we had a fine specimen of him ; but there is Rossetti and Rossetti—the one sublime, the other ridiculous, or, rather, appalling."

" *January* 5, 1883.—X—— (a member of the Government) said to me yesterday, ' There ought never to have been a war. We all feel it now. It is clear that Arabi had the whole country with him,' and it is equally clear to me that he would have pulled as steadily with you, or with Dufferin, as an old wheeler.* I have written to friends in Ceylon to be kind to him, and I think they will be so, for my sake, though they are much exercised in their minds whether he is *ange ou démon*."

" *London, September* 21, 1883.—I left A—— happy enough with your godson,† who is in a state of beatitude with the horse-chestnuts. It is a never-failing pleasure to him to break the green husk and fish out the bright brown nut inside. He returns home daily with his wheelbarrow filled. I wish that in future years he may be able to take out a patent for a cheap mode of divesting the horse-chestnut of acidity, and making it wholesome human, or even pig food. What a grand invention !"

" *Coole, November* 25, 1883.—I have been for the last week sitting on a Committee in Dublin (very far from a strong one), appointed by the Treasury, to report on the designs for a new museum and library, to be built by

---

* " *Aldermaston, June* 2, 1884.—I am gradually assuming all the airs and impudence of a prophet, as every one now comes up and says, ' Well, so it seems you were right after all.' I think I shall write a fierce letter to the *Times*, such a one as Elijah would have written, reproving the nation for its blindness and following of false idols."

† William Robert Gregory, born 1881.

Government in Dublin. We were told to select five designs, and there were thirty-three competitors. One of the designs is of remarkable beauty,* in harmony with the best architecture of Dublin, which is really very fine, far better than anything in London, except the Banqueting Hall. Some of the others are good *per se*, but are objectionable in many respects. I should greatly like you to see the one I so much approve of. Our former labours at the National Gallery, and the Committee on the British Museum, and my own work in building a museum at Colombo, gave me a good deal of practical knowledge which was of use to my associates."

To *the* COUNTESS OF DARTREY.

"*Coole, December*, 1883.—I have just read a most delightful book, which I think every man, woman, and child ought to be condemned to read twice a year—Dean Bradley's 'Recollections of Arthur Penrhyn Stanley.' The tone of it is most impressive, and the English very beautiful. Moreover, the scope of Stanley's life so harmonizes with all my own views on Church matters, that I have felt this little book very deeply, and thought much of the enormous loss we have sustained by the untimely death of such a brilliant example."

To SIR H. LAYARD.

"*Anaradhapura, Ceylon, February* 22, 1884.—My head is so turned by the fuss the good people of this island are making about me, both the English and the natives, especially the latter, that if I write conceitedly and egotistically, you will understand that it is only a temporary aberration, and that I shall subside very soon into my habitual humility on returning to England. But you must

---

* That by Deane, afterwards adopted.

2 C

bear with my conceit in this letter. On my arrival at
Colombo the first thing I saw was fourteen large steamers,
all riding undisturbed within the magnificent breakwater,
over four thousand feet in length, which I began, and
which is now finished. Many a bad half hour has it given
me. Since I returned to England I was told repeatedly
that I had saddled the colony with a debt approaching a
million for a work which would be forthwith washed away,
and which would be but of little use. The result is, not a
stone has stirred during the worst gales, and the engineer
is willing to stake his life that not a stone will stir for the
next hundred years. So far from saddling the colony
with a debt, the harbour dues in the first year have paid
all the interest and a part of the sinking fund, and it is
confidently expected that next year it will pay a surplus to
the revenue, and in fifty years the colony will be free from
all debt on account of it, and have some £50,000 a year
added to its income, besides an annual surplus all the time.

"I am at this moment at the old city of Anaradhapura,
the capital of the Kandian kings. The district round was,
about a thousand years ago, the granary of Ceylon, all
owing to the magnificent system of irrigation maintained
by the native monarchs. The district had fallen into
decay. When I came to Ceylon there were not sixty
thousand people in it, the rest had perished from starvation and from a dreadful disease, called 'parangi,' by which
whole families and villages literally rotted away. All
their food depended on the very precarious chance of
storing whatever rain fell, and they had to cut the bunds
of their tanks to let the water into their fields. The result
was that, if additional rain fell, the part of the bund which
had been opened gave way, all the stored water was lost,
and the cultivators starved, or burnt the fine Crown forest
to raise a crop of grain. There was no road to the centre

of the island and to this city. The city itself was hid in jungle, and so pestilential that for several months it was actually deserted. I at once made the huge district a separate province. I made a series of magnificent roads, connecting it to the east with Trincomalee, to the west with Puttalami, the salt emporium, and made a road running by it from Kandy to Jaffna, 184 miles, the most northern point of the island. You could now drive a coach and four from the extreme south to the extreme north of the island. I then set to work to restore the tanks and their feeders, and passed an ordinance, whereby the villagers received, and had put in gratuitously, a masonry sluice for each of their village tanks, on condition of their all turning out and repairing their wretched broken-down bunds. Thanks to the energy and tact of the officer, Mr. Dickson, to whom I entrusted the new province, the plan succeeded. The villagers were inspired with confidence, and have worked bravely at their tanks, some hundreds of which have been, and are being supplied with sluices, the large catchment tanks have been placed in thorough order, and now Sir Arthur Gordon is so thoroughly impressed with the astonishing results of what has been done, that he is going to restore the huge inland tank, almost a sea, which will render the district absolutely independent of dearth. And what are the results? The produce of the last five years is five times greater than of the previous five. Rice used to be five, six, and eight shillings a bushel; it is now one and eightpence. There is ample food for every one, and now they are exporting large quantities from the district. The hospitals, which had been crammed with 'parangi' patients, are almost deserted, for the disease has generally given way to plentiful food and good water. The revenue is paying hand over head the expenditure, and the old city, once so deadly, is now

one of the most healthy in the island.   It is the loveliest
spot I have ever seen.   The forest all round the town has
been cleared, and it is now a beautiful park, full of ruins
of great interest, and the drives are lovely, some of them
constructed on the bunds of the large tanks, and looking
over the vast sheets of water below, one in particular
running round the town for several miles, and touching
every architectural monument of interest.   How I do
wish we were all here together for, at least, a week !   You
would enjoy yourself beyond measure.   I believe there is
nothing in India which can approach this place in antiquity
and beauty combined ; and then we have the old native
history, giving the full account of the different monuments,
and written about the time when the finest were constructed, between 300 B.C. and 150 A.D.

   " Nothing can equal Sir A. Gordon's nobility of hospitality—for that is the only word I can use—putting me
forward on all occasions, adopting my plans and policy,
and treating me, and ordering me to be treated, as if I
were a second Governor.   There are few men who could
have divested themselves so totally of all jealousy of a
very popular predecessor."

   " *Nuwara-Eliya, March* 15, 1884.—I went to the
elephant kraal on the 5th, under the full impression that
the elephants were close at hand, and sure to be driven
in within a couple of days, but we waited there till the
following Wednesday.   My patience and that of the
Governor were then exhausted, and my carriage was
actually at the door when the news arrived that a great
and combined effort had been made during the night, and
that the beasts were at the very mouth of the kraal ; and
so they were.   So the horses were sent back, and up we
went, and, amid a storm of shouts and volley of shots, in
they rushed, twenty-six in number, several of them of

large size and some small calves. While this was going on the tame elephants were sent in to beat down the jungle, about two acres in extent, and it was a curious sight the clever way in which they worked, trampling down everything, even good-sized trees. We were all in the stand directly over them, a large number of ladies present, when a frightful scene occurred. An attendant of one of the elephants was on foot by his side, and was handing up to the mahout either a spear or a goad which he had dropped, when the brute turned on him as quick as thought, dashed him to the ground with his trunk, drove his tusk through his body, and then absolutely kneaded him with his head and knees. Of course the poor wretch was dead in a second, but it was horrible, as it all took place within a few yards of us. They say the man had ill-treated the elephant, who had three times before tried to kill him. After the murder the elephant seemed to show no sign of excitement or ferocity, but was driven by his rider quite quietly out of the enclosure and was tied up. The animal was notoriously in 'must,' and consequently very dangerous, and ought never to have been allowed inside the stockade Everything was suspended for an hour or two, and then the noosing began. It was very exciting work, and the bravery of the noosers was marvellous. When the tame elephants had driven the wild ones into a lump, the noosers actually crawled among the legs of the wild ones, and before evening six were caught and tied up. The tame elephants behaved like heroes, except just at the beginning they never flinched, and when a wild one was noosed they dragged him by main force, one pulling the rope, and two others pushing behind. They always placed themselves in a position that the captives should not be able to strike the men who were tying them up, and gave the ropes a turn and a tug round the tree whenever it was necessary.

There was one very fierce male solitary elephant who kept away from the rest, and who made several demonstrations of a charge. At last he screwed up his courage, and made at the foremost tame elephant, rather a small one, but a splendid worker, and always to the front in a row. The wild champion with a scream made at him, and struck him a desperate blow with his trunk; the little fellow never moved at the blow, but met his antagonist with his forehead and drove him right down a slippery bank, utterly discomfited. He never charged again. I left in the evening after six had been caught; the last was a very large cow with a calf. She had been the *bête noire* of the drive, always charging back and fighting, but she seemed quite resigned to her fate, and thinking only of her little child, who followed her very quietly into captivity. The whole thing was a wonderful affair. It was got up in the middle of a wild jungle about two months ago, when the driving began with about two thousand beaters. There had not been previously a living soul near the spot, and when I arrived I drove through a wide street of native shops, and up by a row of beautiful and spacious bungalows, all made of cocoa-nut matting. The Governor had declined going, but changed his mind, as Lady Gordon wished to see the function, and a house was placed at his disposition and mine by the Kandian chiefs, containing nine bedrooms, all of good size and very comfortable. They had previously assigned it to me, requesting me to fill it with my friends, which fortunately I did not do. They were going to have supplied everything, but the Governor relieved them of this very generous hospitality, brought his own cook and champagne, and had dinner-parties every evening. There were actually between four thousand and five thousand persons in Kraaltown, and not a policeman! Next week the wild beasts will have the

soda-water bottles and sardine tins to themselves. Before
leaving elephant tales I must tell you a touching story
of the former kraal, in February, in the Western Province.
A calf was noosed and caught and tied up in a corner
of the enclosure, close to the great crowd of spectators.
The poor mother had done her best to save him, but in
vain. When she saw it was all over, and that no hope
remained of his escape, she quietly left the main body of
her uncaptured friends, walked down to the tree where the
calf was tied, and remained with it there all day, comfort-
ing it and caressing it with her trunk, and not taking the
slightest notice of the crowd.

"And now for the National Gallery. I sincerely trust
that whatever be the result of our dealings as regards the
Marlborough pictures, Burton will not hesitate to buy the
Gaudenzio Ferrari and the Paris Bordone, and I am very
glad he has got the Matteo da Siena. As for the Luinis,
I should be *cast down* at the thought of losing such a
treasure as nine pictures by that master; but if the
Government is to aid us we must try and aid them in
making their grant as small as possible to obtain the
Marlborough pictures. Of course the Raphael ought to be
secured at any price, but there are one or two Rubenses
which are magnificent, I think unrivalled, but it is many
years since I saw them. I am afraid if we bought the
whole collection, took our pick, and sold them again, the
rejected pictures would fetch much less than their value.
Fancy, if we had picked out of the Hamilton lot our
thirteen, how much the value of the others would have
sunk!

"I do not think the House will sanction just yet the
nocturnal lighting of the Gallery. Fancy the electric
light striking work all of a sudden, and the mischief that
might be done by the soldiers and their 'Polls' in the

dark! If Gladstone resists, and I think Howard could thoroughly insense him, Cope would not have a chance of carrying the measure, and one defeat would set it at rest for years. I think our course is clear to give our reasons for objecting to the measure, and then to place the whole responsibility on the Government. It would be most unwise for Burton and the Trustees to resign, because if we were to be replaced by a set of ignorant toadies, God help these fine collections, for which we have worked so earnestly! and we may be left power to enforce such regulations as will render the measure as little dangerous as possible.

"I came up here to cool myself after the terrible heat of the kraal. It is far too cold. I had a fire of huge logs in a huge chimney last night in my bedroom. There never was anything like the affection and kindness of the people ; fancy their coming from the extreme north of the island, two hundred and eighty miles off, a journey of many days, merely to salaam their old Rajah and be off again !" *

To LADY GREGORY.

" *Colombo, February* 14.—Arabi has paid me a visit, and I sat with him and Abd-el-al (a fine honest soldier) last night. You have no idea how he is liked and re-spected by every one. The colonel in command here, and his wife, a clever and charming woman, think him one of the finest, most modest, and truthful men they have ever met. Mr. Campbell the head of the police, who has a good deal to say to him (more than Arabi thinks) speaks of him in the highest possible terms. The same impression

* "A gentleman told me that, two days before my arrival, the old nurse in his family at Nuwara-Eliya asked for her wages and leave to go to Colombo, a hundred and fifteen miles away, to see Sir William arrive, 'for,' said she, 'he is our God. He is the God of my people.'"—*Letter to Lady Gregory, March* 22.

I find prevalent everywhere. . . . I regret to say that some things take place which must mar the contentment of the exiles. They are subjected at every hour to intrusions, without introductions, from all the vulgar riff-raff which lands at Colombo, and which goes to see the large tortoise, and then to see Arabi. While Lord Rosebery (whom I had introduced to Arabi) was speaking very seriously to him, a Melbourne betting bookmaker forced himself in, and hailed Arabi in the most familiar manner."

To LADY GREGORY.

"*Kandy, February* 24.—There was not an hour of my stay at Anaradhapura in which I was not longing for you. We did the journey with the greatest ease, starting at first light in the morning. It was perfectly cool, and not a mosquito or tick to annoy one, and ample room for us all, and you would have now been very proud of me. I have never seen anything so beautiful as this child of mine —this North Central Province. . . . It is a splendid success. I hope I may have merit put to my credit side for having thus rescued tens of thousands of poor helpless wretches from gradual extinction. You never saw anything more grateful than they were. Every soul came, if only to see their deliverer, as they said, once more. It is balm of Gilead to me that Sir Arthur goes on gallantly with this great and good work. I really think, whatever happens henceforth, that my life will be serene, from my present fulness of happiness. Thank God I have seen this great success, and now I may depart in peace."

To SIR H. LAYARD.

" *Coole, September* 15, 1884.—Let me strongly press on you to read every word of Rosebery's address at the Trades Union meeting, Aberdeen, on the great coming question of the day, the incorporation of the colonies into the imperial system. It is a subject in which I take the very deepest interest. Of course you will naturally say that the question is so vast and so crude that it is still a long way off. So it is ; but it is entering into the field of practical politics, and it has fortunately been taken up by the foremost young statesman of the day—a man of far-seeing views, great industry and energy, combined with caution. It is pretty clear to me that the first step must be the establishment of something like an Imperial Con-sultative Parliament, in which the representatives of great colonies might attend, and express their opinions on strictly defined questions of imperial policy. The mere discussion of such subjects at present would be a material strengthening of the link which binds the colonies to the mother country. At a future period, when the colonies expand still further in wealth and population, it is pro-bable they will claim something more than the mere discussion of imperial policy ; but these things grow of themselves, and mould fresh combinations which will have to be dealt with by those who come after us. I do not shrink from acknowledging the difficulties in the path, and the objections which can be raised, but they will have to be faced, discussed, and overcome. These speculations, and the form which the movement will take at first, are entirely my own ; I have not seen them mooted elsewhere, nor do I in the least insist on the correctness of my ideas. But it is clear, from the way the whole press of England has taken up Rosebery's speech, that men's minds are rapidly awakening to the necessity of working out the question. All I dread is that it may be made the 'fad' of those who, disheartened by the break-down of our Parliamentary system at present, are for resorting to a new system of governing by local Parliaments, one for

Ireland, one for Scotland, and probably one for Wales, besides one for England, with a central Parliament for imperial questions. A brave and combined effort by both parties to level all obstructions which impede our present system, and to make this obstruction a personal affair, a crime of ' *lèse-majesté*' against Parliament, to be visited on the offender by expulsion would be far better than to lower the dignity of our country by turning Parliament into a set of vestries, and to the same level of public spirit."

"*London, December* 4, 1886.—I beg of you to read my article in the *Nineteenth Century* on our Indian Mussulmans. I think you will approve of it. My well-known friendship with Arabi had reached India, and made his co-religionists far more effusive and confidential than they would otherwise have been."

"*Coole, October* 20, 1890.—I send you the *Pall Mall Gazette*, with an account of our recent acquisitions. The cost of them makes me blush when I think of it. I have had many letters from good judges, praising the Velasquez portrait as one of his finest works, but no one says much for the Moroni. For the life of me I can't make out the skull in the Holbein, though A—— says it is as plain as the nose on my face, and that is plain enough.

"We are all very flourishing. I am busy planting, and the rabbits destroy during the night my work of the day before, and nearly drive me mad. The woods are redolent of tar, with which we anoint the trees, and the walks are dangerous from traps. I think I shall win in the end, and exterminate my enemies, but how many of my young trees will be alive this day year is another matter. Robert is growing and learning. He gained half a sovereign from me yesterday, by repeating the twenty-two stanzas of Wilfrid Blunt's fine ballad of

'Sancho Sanchez' without a fault. He would do very well if he would only think a little more. He is really an excellent boy, full of go, but obedient and strictly truthful.

"I have nothing to tell you of our country. Generally it is as orderly as Venice. The higher order of Roman Catholic priests are undoubtedly seriously alarmed by the defiant attitude of the Parnellites towards them, and are turning towards his Holiness. I have been fighting for them in the *Times*, solely on one point—that they do not hate Protes*tants*. Of course they are bound to hate Protestantism."

"*London, December* 12, 1890.—I do not know if I should inflict another letter on you so soon, but you may like to hear my notions of the present astounding state of affairs.* A—— thinks Parnell will win, and she is supported by the great authority of Lord ——, who was here yesterday evening, and discussed the situation with much wit and good sense. They rely on Parnell's ability, audacity, and resolution, his power of the purse, his possession of the press, and the immense wave of popular enthusiasm, more especially among the young and formidable portion of the population.

"I am quite of the contrary opinion. I believe, in spite of his successes in Dublin and Cork, that he will be beaten, and is beaten already. With all their folly, the haters of England must see that the rift in their ranks will infallibly defeat that separation which they have at heart, and are sure to gain, if they once get Home Rule. Reflection will make this clear.

"Then, in every parish in Ireland you have powerful spiritual agencies at work. The Roman Catholic hierarchy

* Written after the O'Shea divorce case and the split in the Irish party.

see that this is their supreme chance of regaining the power that has been slipping from them. They know that if Parnell wins this battle they are virtually annihilated, so far as their political and social influence goes, and they will bring to bear a solid mass of opposition to him, which I am confident will crush him.

"I have, in a letter to ——, thus described the situation. 'Parnell suggests to me the idea of an avalanche, which at first carries everything before it, and then melts away. The Catholic hierarchy that of a glacier, which slowly, imperceptibly almost, but irresistibly forces its way, by its enormous bulk and weight, and its steady, continuous motion.'

"I was sorry to hear of Drake's death. I am sorry to hear of any death, even of an acquaintance. There are too few leaves left on my old tree, and I grieve to see them falling one by one ; and I shall not repine when my time comes, except to leave my wife and child unguarded."

"*London, March* 18, 1891.—You will have read, in this day's *Times*, Plunket's extremely unsatisfactory reply to Dr. Farquharson about the National Gallery. When you return to England, the subject of space and danger of fire should again be taken up by the Trustees ; in fact, we are challenged by Plunket to do so. His argument, that because we had an increase of space given us in 1887, therefore we do not require more in 1891, is pretty much on a par with my objections to give Robert fresh clothes, he having grown out of his last suit, which was too tight when he got it. The expansion of the Gallery by the accession of most notable works seems to be looked on by the Treasury as a national calamity, and that we are a pestilent set of fellows."

"*Coole, September* 8, 1891.—I am at present reading

Herodotus, whom I have not opened since Oxford, where I knew him well. I am reading his work critically, that is, as a Greek scholar, rather than as an inquirer into history. I obtained a second-hand copy of Rawlinson's edition, and am disappointed with the translation. Difficulties of expression are evaded and slurred over in a slovenly manner. I have just finished the first book, but have not ventured on the long and intricate lucubrations concerning the Median, Assyrian, and Babylonian dynasties, which, I dare say, have been modified ere this. The style is very pleasing, the stories delightful, and the Greek peculiarly easy. I mean, if I can summon up courage, to tackle, during the winter, the recently discovered works of Herodas, with new words, new grammatical inflections, new everything. I shudder at the thought.

"Robert has not gone back yet. He is anxious to get on in Greek, to beat a boy above him, and to move over him into the top class. He is really beginning to master the very great difficulties of Greek grammar, and I wish I was as sure of Common winning the St. Leger on Wednesday as I am of Robert passing his antagonist. His outdoor thoughts are cricket and caterpillars, both harmless and cheap amusements.

"We have had several visitors, among others Sir A. Lyall, a most delightful visitor. I believe Robert Meade and his most taking daughter meditate coming here. I hope so, as I like them both so much ; and when I like guests I am an excellent and attentive host, when I don't like them their departure is a relief."

"*London, October* 1, 1891.—Congratulate me on a real *trouvaille*. The picture* I bought at G. Bentinck's sale for £12 10s. has come out splendidly, and is in first-rate condition. Burton is greatly struck with it, and has no

* Now in the National Gallery.

doubt of its being by Savoldo, it having all his characteristics. The accessories and landscape have a great
charm. The subject, the 'Adoration of the Shepherds,'
seems to have been a favourite with the painter. It is a
wonderful bit of luck to have picked up so fine a picture
from among so many of the *cognoscenti*."

" *London, November* 22, 1891.—I have seen no one, for I
am hardly able to get about. I must tell you, as my oldest
friend, the whole truth—I am extremely ill. As you are
aware, I suffered from what seemed to be palpitation of
the heart when I was with you in the summer, and I also
had a severe, almost dangerous, attack of bronchitis. Both
of these ailments have disappeared, but they have been
succeeded, ever since my return to England, by constantly
increasing diarrhœa. I am getting weaker and weaker,
and thinner and thinner, having lost seven pounds in
weight since September, and eleven pounds since June.
I have been under Andrew Clarke and my own village
Æsculapius (an exceedingly clever man), but the disease
beats them. To-morrow I am going to consult Maclagan.
I have very little care for life, but I should like a few years
more, to help poor A—— and Robert, for these are critical
times for them."

" *London, January* 10, 1892.—I have plenty of time on
hand to intrude on your occupations, for I am, and have
been, a fast prisoner in my bedroom since Thursday. I
am a good deal cast down by this, for, although I knew
I had not conquered my disease, I thought I had so far sub-
dued it as to be on the way to convalescence ; and I must
try to live, for the sake of my boy and my dear good wife."

" I send you two letters—one referring to the Arundel,
the other to the National Gallery. . . . The great *de-
sideratum* now is another Dutch room. It is, as we say
in Ireland, 'Millia murther' to see a number of charming

Dutch pictures so huddled and incongruously placed that no justice can be done to our Dutch collection, now almost unrivalled. If you had seen the delicate Habich pictures brought near to the light before being placed in the Octagon, you would be grieved, as I am, by the contrast."

"*Bournemouth, January* 29, 1892.—I was very ill again last week, and Maclagan bundled me out of London. This is a delightful place, very mild, and the hotel looking out on the sea. I am now on different treatment, and am certainly better, but, having been here only two days, it would be premature to express an opinion. I know I take a deal of the twenty-four hours in sleep, which is pleasant and harmless. Robert is here for his Sunday, and has just lodged a flotilla of paper boats in one of the garden basins. I believe they are to resist a Spanish Armada."

"3, *St. George's Place, London, February* 15, 1892.— Although there were only Lord Hardinge, Burton, and myself at the Board on Tuesday, yet the matter was so important that I must go into it in full. I ought to have done so before, but I have really been too ill to give much thought to anything. The subjects considered were— first, extension of space; secondly, finance; thirdly, the purchase of the 'Gates of Calais.' . . .

"I am about to present to the Gallery my two Velas-quez—'Sketch of a Duel in the Prado,' and 'Christ at the House of Mary and Martha.' They are, at least such is the judgment of *cognoscenti*, two excellent specimens of the master at two extreme periods. I think I mentioned that I meant to present my Jan Steen in monochrome, for which the French dealer, M. Ganchez, offered me £250, the day after I bought it for £2 3*s.* I also give my Savoldo, a very fine picture of large size. . . .

"We determined, ultimately, not to come to any decision till you return, when MAY all of us meet again."

INDEX.

LONDON : PRINTED BY WILLIAM CLOWES AND SONS, LIMITED,
STAMFORD STREET AND CHARING CROSS.

ALBEMARLE STREET, LONDON,
June, 1894.

MR. MURRAY'S
GENERAL LIST OF WORKS.

ALBERT MEMORIAL. A Descriptive and Illustrated Account of the National Monument at Kensington. Illustrated by numerous Engravings. By DOYNE C. BELL. With 24 Plates. Folio. 10*l*.10*s*.
———————— HANDBOOK. 16mo. 1*s*.; Illustrated, 2*s*.6*d*.

ABBOTT (REV. J.). Memoirs of a Church of England Missionary in the North American Colonies. Post 8vo. 2*s*.

ABERCROMBIE (JOHN). Enquiries concerning the Intellectual Powers and the Investigation of Truth. Fcap. 8vo. 3*s*. 6*d*.

ACLAND (REV. C.). Manners and Customs of India. Post 8vo. 2*s*.

ACWORTH (W. M.) The Railways of England. With 56 Illustrations. 8vo. 14*s*.
———————— The Railways of Scotland. Map. Crown 8vo. 5*s*.
———————— The Railways and the Traders. The Railway Rates Question in Theory and Practice. Crown 8vo. 6*s*., or *Popular Edit*. 1*s*.

ÆSOP'S FABLES. A New Version. By REV. THOMAS JAMES. With 100 Woodcuts, by TENNIEL and WOLFE. Crown 8vo. 2*s*. 6*d*.

AGRICULTURAL (ROYAL) JOURNAL. 8vo. Quarterly. 3*s*. 6*d*.

AINGER (A. C.). Latin Grammar. [See ETON.]
———————— An English-Latin Gradus, or Verse Dictionary. On a New Plan, with carefully Selected Epithets and Synonyms. Crown 8vo. (450 pp.) 9*s*.

ALICE (PRINCESS): GRAND DUCHESS OF HESSE. Letters to H.M. THE QUEEN. With a Memoir by H.R.H. Princess Christian. Portrait. Crown 8vo. 7*s*. 6*d*.

AMBER-WITCH (THE). A most interesting Trial for Witchcraft. Translated by LADY DUFF GORDON. Post 8vo. 2*s*.

AMERICA (THE RAILWAYS OF). Their Construction, Development, Management, and Appliances. By Various Writers. With an Introduction by T. M. COOLEY. With 200 Illustrations. Large 8vo. 31*s*.6*d*.
———————— [See BATES, NADAILLAC, RUMBOLD, VILLIERS STUART.]

APOCRYPHA : With a Commentary Explanatory and Critical. By Dr. Salmon, Prof. Fuller, Archdeacon Farrar, Archdeacon Gifford, Canon Rawlinson, Dr. Edersheim, Rev. J. H. Lupton, Rev. C. J. Ball. Edited by HENRY WACE, D.D. 2 vols. Medium 8vo. 50*s*.

ARCHITECTURE : A Profession or an Art. Thirteen short Essays on the qualifications and training of Architects. Edited by R. NORMAN SHAW, R.A., and T. G. JACKSON, A.R.A. 8vo. 9*s*.

ARGYLL (DUKE OF). THE UNSEEN FOUNDATIONS OF SOCIETY: An Examination of the Fallacies and Failures of Economic Science due to Neglected Elements. 8vo. 18*s*.
———————— Unity of Nature. 8vo. 12*s*.
———————— Reign of Law. Crown 8vo. 5*s*.
———————— Irish Nationalism. Crown 8vo. 3*s*. 6*d*.
———————— The Burdens of Belief, and other Poems. Crown 8vo. 6*s*.

ARISTOTLE. [See GROTE.]

ARTHUR'S (LITTLE) History of England. By LADY CALLCOTT. *New Edition, continued to* 1878. With Woodcuts. Fcap. 8vo. 1*s*. 6*d*.
———————— HISTORY OF FRANCE, from the Earliest Times to the Fall of the Second Empire. With Woodcuts. Fcp. 8vo. 2*s*. 6*d*.

B

AUSTIN (John). General Jurisprudence; or, The Philosophy of Positive Law. Edited by Robert Campbell. 2 Vols. 8vo. 32s.

———— Student's Edition, compiled from the above work, by by Robert Campbell. Post 8vo. 12s.

———— Analysis of. By Gordon Campbell. Post 8vo. 6s.

AUSTRALIA. [See Lumholtz.]

BAINES (Thomas). Greenhouse and Stove Plants, Flowering and Fine-Leaved. Palms, Ferns, and Lycopodiums. With full details of the Propagation and Cultivation. 8vo. 8s. 6d.

BALDWIN BROWN (Prof. G.). The Fine Arts. With Illustrations. Crown 8vo. 3s. 6d. (University Extension Series.)

BARKLEY (H. C.). Bulgaria Before the War. Post 8vo. 10s. 6d.

———— Studies in the Art of Rat-catching. 3s. 6d.

———— Ride through Asia Minor and Armenia. Crown 8vo. 10s. 6d.

BARNCRAIG. [See Setoun.]

BARROW (John). Life of Sir Francis Drake. Post 8vo. 2s.

BATES (H. W.). Records of a Naturalist on the Amazons during Eleven Years' Adventure and Travel. A new Edition of the unabridged work. With a Memoir of the Author by Edward Clodd. With Portrait, Coloured Plates, Illustrations, and Map. Medium 8vo. 18s.

———— Abridged Edition without Memoir. Crown 8vo. 7s. 6d.

BATTLE ABBEY ROLL. [See Cleveland.]

BEACONSFIELD'S (Lord) Letters, and "Correspondence with his Sister," 1830—1852. Portrait. Crown 8vo. 2s.

BEATRICE, H.R.H. Princess. Adventures in the Life of Count George Albert of Erbach. A True Story. Translated from the German. Portrait and Woodcuts. Crown 8vo. 10s. 6d.

BECKETT (Sir Edmund), (Lord Grimthorpe). "Should the Revised New Testament be Authorised?" Post 8vo. 6s.

BENJAMIN (Dr. G. W.). Persia and the Persians. Illustrations. 8vo. 24s.

BENSON (Archbishop). The Cathedral; its necessary place in the Life and Work of the Church. Post 8vo. 6s.

BERKELEY (Hastings). Japanese Letters; Eastern Impressions of Western Men and Manners. Post 8vo. 6s.

BERTHELOT (M.). Explosives and their Powers. Translated and condensed from the French by C. Napier Hake and William Macnab, F.I.C.E. With Preface by Lt.-Colonel J. P. Cundill, R.A., H.M. Inspector of Explosives. With Illustrations. 8vo. 24s.

BERTRAM (Jas. G.). Harvest of the Sea: an Account of British Food Fishes, Fisheries and Fisher Folk. Illustrations. Post 8vo. 9s.

BIBLE COMMENTARY. Explanatory and Critical. With a Revision of the Translation. By Bishops and Clergy of the Anglican Church. Edited by Canon F. C. Cook, M.A.

The Old Testament. 6 Vols. Medium 8vo. 6l. 15s.

Vol. I. Genesis—Deuteronomy. 30s.	Vol. IV. Job—Song of Solomon. 24s.
Vol. II. Joshua—Kings. 20s.	Vol. V. Isaiah—Jeremiah. 20s.
ol. III. Kings ii.—Esther. 16s.	Vol. VI. Ezekiel—Malachi. 25s.

The New Testament. 4 Vols. Medium 8vo. 4l. 14s.

Vol. I. St. Matthew—St. Luke. 18s.	Vol. III. Romans—Philemon. 28s.
Vol. II. St. John. — Acts of the Postles. 20s.	Vol. IV. Hebrews — Revelation. 28s.

BIBLE COMMENTARY. THE APOCRYPHA. By Various Writers. Edited by HENRY WACE, D.D. 2 vols. Medium 8vo. 50s.

THE STUDENT'S EDITION. Abridged and Edited by REV. J. M. FULLER, M.A. 6 Vols. Crown 8vo. 7s. 6d. each. OLD TESTAMENT. 4 Vols. NEW TESTAMENT. 2 Vols.

BIRD (ISABELLA). Hawaiian Archipelago; or Six Months among the Palm Groves, Coral Reefs, and Volcanoes of the Sandwich islands. Illustrations. Crown 8vo. 7s. 6d.

———— A Lady's Life in the Rocky Mountains. Illustrations. Post 8vo. 7s. 6d.

———— The Golden Chersonese and the Way Thither. Illustrations. Post 8vo. 14s.

———— Unbeaten Tracks in Japan: Including Visits to the Aborigines of Yezo and the Shrines of Nikko and Isé. Illustrations. Crown 8vo. 7s. 6d.

———— Journeys in Persia and Kurdistan: with a Summer in the Upper Karun Region, and a Visit to the Nestorian Rayahs. Maps and 36 Illustrations. 2 vols. Crown 8vo. 24s.

BISHOP (MRS.). [See BIRD (ISABELLA).]

BLACKIE (C.). Geographical Etymology; or, Dictionary of Place Names. Third Edition. Crown 8vo. 7s.

BLUNT (REV. J. J.). Undesigned Coincidences in the Writings of the Old and New Testaments, an Argument of their Veracity. Post 8vo. 6s.

———— History of the Christian Church in the First Three Centuries. Post 8vo. 6s.

———— The Parish Priest; His Duties, Acquirements, and Obligations. Post 8vo. 6s.

BOOK OF COMMON PRAYER. Illustrated with Coloured Borders, Initial Letters, and Woodcuts. 8vo. 18s.

BORROW (GEORGE). The Bible in Spain; or, the Journeys and Imprisonments of an Englishman in an attempt to circulate the Scriptures in the Peninsula. Portrait. Post 8vo. 2s. 6d.

———— The Zincali. An Account of the Gypsies of Spain; Their Manners, Customs, Religion, and Language. 2s. 6d.

———— Lavengro; Scholar—Gypsy—and Priest. 2s. 6d.

———— Romany Rye. A Sequel to Lavengro. Post 8vo. 2s. 6d.

———— WILD WALES: its People, Language, and Scenery. Post 8vo. 2s. 6d.

———— Romano Lavo-Lil. With Illustrations of the English Gypsies; their Poetry and Habitations. Post 8vo. 5s.

BOSWELL'S Life of Samuel Johnson, LL.D. Including the Tour to the Hebrides. Edited by Mr. CROKER. Seventh Edition. Portraits. 1 vol. Medium 8vo. 12s.

BOWEN (LORD). Virgil in English Verse, Eclogues and Æneid, Books I.—VI. Map and Frontispiece. 8vo. 12s.

BRADLEY (DEAN). Arthur Penrhyn Stanley; Biographical Lectures. Crown 8vo. 3s. 6d.

BREWER (REV. J. S.). The Endowments and Establishment of the Church of England. Edited by L. T. DIBDIN, M.A. Post 8vo. 6s.

BRIDGES (MRS. F. D.). A Lady's Travels in Japan, Thibet, Yarkand, Kashmir, Java, the Straits of Malacca, Vancouver's Island, &c. With Map and Illustrations from Sketches by the Author. Crown 8vo. 15s.

B 2

BRITISH ASSOCIATION REPORTS. 8vo.

, The Reports for the years 1831 to 1875 may be obtained at the Offices
of the British Association.

Glasgow, 1876, 25s.	Southampton, 1882, 24s.	Bath, 1888, 24s.
Plymouth, 1877, 24s.	Southport, 1883, 24s.	Newcastle, 1889, 24s.
Dublin, 1878, 24s.	Canada, 1884, 24s.	Leeds, 1890, 24s.
Sheffield, 1879, 24s.	Aberdeen, 1885, 24s.	Cardiff, 1891, 24s.
Swansea, 1880, 24s.	Birmingham, 1886, 24s.	Edinburgh, 1892, 24s.
York, 1881, 24s.	Manchester, 1887, 24s.	Nottingham, 1893, 24s.

BROCKLEHURST (T. U.). Mexico To-day: A Country with a
Great Future. Plates and Woodcuts. Medium 8vo. 21s.

BRODRICK (Miss). Outlines of Egyptian History: Based on the
Work of Mariette Bey. Translated and Edited by MARY BRODRICK.
A new and Revised Edition. With Maps. Crown 8vo. 5s.

BRUCE (Hon. W. N.). Life of Sir Charles Napier. [See NAPIER.]

BRUGSCH (PROFESSOR). A History of Egypt under the
Pharaohs. Derived entirely from Monuments. A New and thoroughly
Revised Edition. Edited by M. BRODRICK. Maps. 1 Vol. 8vo. 18s.

BUCKINGHAM AND CHANDOS (DUCHESS OF). Glimpses of
Four Continents. Letters written during a tour in Australia, New
Zealand and North America in 1893. Crown 8vo. 8s. net.

BUNBURY (SIR E. H.). A History of Ancient Geography, among
the Greeks and Romans, from the Earliest Ages till the Fall of the
Roman Empire. Maps. 2 Vols. 8vo. 21s.

BURBIDGE (F. W.). The Gardens of the Sun: or A Naturalist's
Journal in Borneo and the Sulu Archipelago. Illustrations. Cr. 8vo. 14s.

BURGHERSH'S (LADY) LETTERS from Germany and France
during the Campaign of 1813—14. Edited by her daughter. LADY
ROSE WEIGALL. Portraits. Crown 8vo. 6s.

BURGON (DEAN). A Biography. Illustrated by Extracts from
his Letters and Early Journals. By E. MEYRICK GOULBURN, D.D.
Portraits. 2 Vols. 8vo. 24s.

———— ———— The Revision Revised: (1.) The New Greek
Text; (2.) The New English Version; (3.) Westcott and Hort's Textual
Theory. Second Edition. 8vo. 14s.

———————— Lives of Twelve Good Men. Martin J. Routh,
H. J. Rose, Chas. Marriott, Edward Hawkins, Saml. Wilberforce,
R. L. Cotton, Richard Greswell, H. O. Coxe, H. L. Mansel, Wm.
Jacobson, C. P. Eden, C. L. Higgins. New Edition. With Portraits.
1 Vol. 8vo. 16s.

BURN (COL.). Dictionary of Naval and Military Technical
Terms, English and French—French and English. Crown 8vo. 15s.

BUTTMANN'S LEXILOGUS; a Critical Examination of the
Meaning of numerous Greek Words, chiefly in Homer and Hesiod.
By Rev. J. R. FISHLAKE. 8vo. 12s.

BUXTON (CHARLES). Memoirs of Sir Thomas Fowell Buxton,
Bart. Portrait. 8vo. 16s. *Popular Edition.* Fcap. 8vo. 5s.

———————— Notes of Thought. With a Biographical Notice.
Second Edition. Post 8vo. 5s.

———————— (SYDNEY C.). A Handbook to the Political Questions
of the Day; with the Arguments on Either Side. 8vo. 10s. 6d.

———————— Finance and Politics. 1783—1885. 2 Vols. 26s.

———————— Handbook to the Death Duties. Post 8vo. 3s. 6d.

BYRON'S (LORD) LIFE AND WORKS :—
 LIFE, LETTERS, AND JOURNALS. By THOMAS MOORE. One
  Volume, Portraits. Royal 8vo. 7s. 6d.
 LIFE AND POETICAL WORKS. *Popular Edition.* Portraits.
  2 Vols. Royal 8vo. 15s.
 POETICAL WORKS. *Library Edition.* Portrait. 6 Vols. 8vo. 45s.
 POETICAL WORKS. *Cabinet Edition.* Plates. 10 Vols. 12mo. 30s.
 POETICAL WORKS. *Pocket Ed.* 8 Vols. 16mo. In a case. 21s.
 POETICAL WORKS. *Popular Edition.* Plates. Royal 8vo. 7s. 6d.
 POETICAL WORKS. *Pearl Edition.* 2s. 6d. Cloth, 3s. 6d.
 CHILDE HAROLD. 16mo. 2s. 6d. Vignettes. 16mo. 1s.
  Portrait. 16mo. 6d.
 TALES AND POEMS. 16mo. 2s. 6d.
 MISCELLANEOUS. 2 Vols. 16mo. 5s.
 DRAMAS AND PLAYS. 2 Vols. 16mo. 5s.
 DON JUAN AND BEPPO. 2 Vols. 16mo. 5s.

CAILLARD (E. M.). Electricity. A Sketch for General Readers.
 With Illustrations. Crown 8vo. 7s. 6d.
——— ——— ——— - The Invisible Powers of Nature. Some
 Elementary Lessons in Physical Science for Beginners. Post 8vo. 6s.

CALDECOTT (ALFRED). English Colonization and Empire.
 Coloured Maps and Plans. Crown 8vo. 3s. 6d. (Univ. Extension Series.)

CAMPBELL (LORD). Autobiography, Journals and Correspon-
 dence. By Mrs. Hardcastle. Portrait. 2 Vols. 8vo. 30s.
——— ——— Lord Chancellors and Keepers of the Great
 Seal of England. From the Earliest Times to the Death of Lord Eldon
 in 1838. 10 Vols. Crown 8vo. 6s. each.
——— - Chief Justices of England. From the Norman
 Conquest to the Death of Lord Tenterden. 4 Vols. Crown 8vo. 6s. each.
——————— (THOS.) Essay on English Poetry. With Short
 Lives of the British Poets. Post 8vo. 3s. 6d.

CAREY (Life of). [See GEORGE SMITH.]

CARLISLE (BISHOP OF). The Foundations of the Creed. Being
 a Discussion of the Grounds upon which the Articles of the Apostles
 Creed may be held by Earnest and Thoughtful Minds in the 19th
 Century. 8vo. 14s.

CARNARVON (LORD). Portugal, Gallicia, and the Basque
 Provinces. Post 8vo. 3s. 6d.
——————— (Fourth Earl of). Prometheus Bound, translated
 into English Verse. Crown 8vo. 6s.

CAVALCASELLE'S WORKS. [See CROWE.]

CESNOLA (GEN.). Cyprus; its Ancient Cities, Tombs, and Temples. With 400 Illustrations. Medium 8vo. 50s.

CHAMBERS (G. F.). A Practical and Conversational Pocket
 Dictionary of the English, French, and German Languages. Designed
 for Travellers and Students generally. Small 8vo. 6s.

CHILD-CHAPLIN (Dr.). Benedicite; or, Song of the Three Children;
 being Illustrations of the Power, Beneficence, and Design manifested
 by the Creator in his Works. Post 8vo. 6s.

CHISHOLM (Mrs.). Perils of the Polar Seas; True Stories of
 Arctic Discovery and Adventure. Illustrations. Post 8vo. 6s.

CHURTON (ARCHDEACON). Poetical Remains. Post 8vo. 7s. 6d.

CLARKE (MAJOR SIR G. SYDENHAM), R.E. Fortification; Its Past Achievements, Recent Development, and Future Progress. With Illustrations. Medium 8vo. 21s.

CLARENCE (H.R.H. THE LATE DUKE OF). A Memoir written with the sanction of H.R.H. the Prince of Wales. By JAMES EDWARD VINCENT. With Portraits and Illustrations. Crown 8vo. 9s.

CLASSIC PREACHERS OF THE ENGLISH CHURCH. Lectures delivered at St. James'. 2 Vols. Post 8vo. 7s. 6d. each.

CLEVELAND (DUCHESS OF). The Battle Abbey Roll. With some account of the Norman Lineages. 3 Vols. Sm. 4to. 48s.

CLIVE'S (LORD) Life. By REV. G. R. GLEIG. Post 8vo. 3s. 6d.

CLODE (C. M.). Military Forces of the Crown; their Administration and Government. 2 Vols. 8vo. 21s. each.

———— Administration of Justice under Military and Martial Law, as applicable to the Army, Navy, and Auxiliary Forces. 8vo. 12s.

COLEBROOKE (SIR EDWARD, BART.). Life of the Hon. Mountstuart Elphinstone. With Portrait and Plans. 2 Vols. 8vo. 26s.

COLERIDGE (SAMUEL TAYLOR), and the English Romantic School. By PROF. BRANDL. With Portrait, Crown 8vo. 12s.

———— Table-Talk. Portrait. 12mo. 3s. 6d.

COLES (JOHN). Summer Travelling in Iceland. With a Chapter on Askja by E. D. MORGAN. Map and Illustrations. 18s.

COLLINS (J. CHURTON). Bolingbroke: an Historical Study. With an Essay on Voltaire in England. Crown 8vo. 7s. 6d.

COLONIAL LIBRARY. [See Home and Colonial Library.]

COOK (Canon F. C.). The Revised Version of the Three First Gospels, considered in its Bearings upon the Record of Our Lord' Words and Incidents in His Life. 8vo. 9s.

———— The Origins of Language and Religion. 8vo. 15s.

COOKE (W. H.). History and Antiquities of the County of Hereford. Vol. III. In continuation of Duncumb's History. 4to. £2 12s. 6d.

———— Additions to Duncumb's History. Vol. II. 4to. 15s.

———— The Hundred of Grimsworth. Part I., 17s. 6d., Pt. II., 25s. 4to.

COOKERY (MODERN DOMESTIC). Adapted for Private Families. By a Lady. Woodcuts. Fcap. 8vo. 5s.

COOLEY (THOMAS M.). [See AMERICA, RAILWAYS OF.

CORNEY GRAIN. By Himself. Post 8vo. 1s.

COURTHOPE (W. J.). Life and Works of Alexander Pope. With Portraits. 10 Vols. 8vo. 10s. 6d. each.

CRAIK (HENRY). Life of Jonathan Swift. Portrait. 8vo. 18s.

CRIPPS (WILFRED). Old English Plate : Ecclesiastical, Decorative, and Domestic, Its Makers and Marks. Fourth Edition. Revised and enlarged. With 70 Illustrations and 2010 facsimile Plate Marks. Medium 8vo. 21s.
. Tables of the Date Letters and Marks sold separately. 5s.

———— Old French Plate : Its Makers and Marks. A New and Revised Edition. With Tables of Makers' Marks, in addition to the Plate Marks. 8vo. 10s. 6d.

CROKER (RT. HON. J. W.). Correspondence and Journals. Edited by the late LOUIS J. JENNINGS. Portrait. 3 Vols. 8vo. 45s.

———— Boswell's Life of Johnson. [See BOSWELL.]

———— Historical Essay on the Guillotine. Fcap. 8vo. 1s.

CROWE AND CAVALCASELLE. Life and Times of Titian, with some account of his Family. Illustrations. 2 Vols. 8vo. 21s.

———— Raphael; His Life and Works. 2 Vols. 8vo. 33s.

CUMMING (R. GORDON). Five Years of a Hunter's Life in the Far Interior of South Africa. Woodcuts. Post 8vo. 6s.

CUNNINGHAM (PROF.W.), D.D. The Use and Abuse of Money. Crown 8vo. 2s. (University Extension Series.)

CURTIUS' (PROFESSOR) Student's Greek Grammar, for the Upper Forms. Edited by SIR WM. SMITH. Post 8vo. 6s.

————Elucidations of the above Grammar. Translated by EVELYN ABBOT. Post 8vo. 7s. 6d.

———— Smaller Greek Grammar for the Middle and Lower Forms. Abridged from the larger work. 12mo. 3s. 6d.

———— Accidence of the Greek Language. Extracted from the above work. 12mo. 2s. 6d.

———— Principles of Greek Etymology. Translated by A. S. WILKINS and E. B. ENGLAND. New Edition. 2 Vols. 8vo. 28s.

———— The Greek Verb, its Structure and Development. Translated by A. S. WILKINS, and E. B. ENGLAND. 8vo. 12s.

CURZON (HON. ROBERT). Visits to the Monasteries of the Levant. Illustrations. Post 8vo. 7s. 6d.

CUST (GENERAL). Warriors of the 17th Century—Civil Wars of France and England. 2 Vols. 16s. Commanders of Fleets and Armies. 2 Vols. 18s.

———— Annals of the Wars—18th & 19th Century. With Maps. 9 Vols. Post 8vo. 5s. each.

DARWIN'S (CHARLES) Life and Letters, with an autobiographical Chapter. Edited by his Son, FRANCIS DARWIN, F.R.S. Portraits. 3 Vols. 8vo. 36s. Or popular Edition, condensed in 1 Vol., crown 8vo. 7s. 6d.

———— An Illustrated Edition of the Voyage of a Naturalist Round the World in H.M.S. Beagle. With Views of Places Visited and Described. By R. T. PRITCHETT. 100 Illustrations. Medium 8vo. 21s.

JOURNAL OF A NATURALIST DURING A VOYAGE ROUND THE WORLD. Popular Edition. With Portrait. 3s. 6d.

ORIGIN OF SPECIES BY MEANS OF NATURAL SELECTION. Library Edition. 2 vols. 12s.; or popular Edition. 6s.

DESCENT OF MAN, AND SELECTION IN RELATION TO SEX. Woodcuts. Library Ed. 2 vols. 15s.; or popular Ed. 7s. 6d.

VARIATION OF ANIMALS AND PLANTS UNDER DOMESTICATION. Woodcuts. 2 Vols. 15s.

EXPRESSIONS OF THE EMOTIONS IN MAN AND ANIMALS. With Illustrations. 12s.

VARIOUS CONTRIVANCES BY WHICH ORCHIDS ARE FERTILIZED BY INSECTS. Woodcuts. 7s. 6d.

MOVEMENTS AND HABITS OF CLIMBING PLANTS. Woodcuts. 6s.

INSECTIVOROUS PLANTS. Woodcuts. 9s.

CROSS AND SELF-FERTILIZATION IN THE VEGETABLE KINGDOM. 9s.

DIFFERENT FORMS OF FLOWERS ON PLANTS OF THE SAME SPECIES. 7s. 6d.

POWER OF MOVEMENT IN PLANTS. Woodcuts.

THE FORMATION OF VEGETABLE MOULD THROUGH THE ACTION OF WORMS. Illustrations. Post 8vo. 6s.

DAVY (Sir Humphry). Consolations in Travel; or, Last Days of a Philosopher. Woodcuts. Fcap. 8vo. 3s. 6d.
———— Salmonia; or, Days of Fly Fishing. Woodcuts. Fcap. 8vo. 3s. 6d.

DE COSSON (Major E. A.). The Cradle of the Blue Nile; a Journey through Abyssinia and Soudan. Map and Illustrations. 2 Vols. Post 8vo. 21s.
———— Days and Nights of Service with Sir Gerald Graham's Field Force at Suakim. Plan and Illustrations. Crown 8vo. 14s.

DENNIS (George). The Cities and Cemeteries of Etruria. 20 Plans and 200 Illustrations. 2 Vols. Medium 8vo. 21s.
———— (Robert). Industrial Ireland. Suggestions for a Practical Policy of "Ireland for the Irish." Crown 8vo. 6s.

DERBY (Earl of). Iliad of Homer rendered into English Blank Verse. With Portrait. 2 Vols. Post 8vo. 10s.

DE ROS (Georgiana Lady). A Sketch of the Life of: With some Reminiscences of her Family and Friends, including the Duke of Wellington, by her Daughter, the Hon. Mrs. Swinton. With Portrait and Illustrations. Crown 8vo 7s. 6d.

DERRY (Bishop of). Witness of the Psalms to Christ and Christianity. Crown 8vo. 9s.

DICEY (Prof. A. V.). Why England Maintains the Union. Fcap. 8vo. 1s.
———— A Leap in the Dark. Crown 8vo. 3s. 6d.

DOG-BREAKING. [See Hutchinson.]

DÖLLINGER (Dr.). Studies in European History, being Academical Addresses. Translated by Margaret Warre. Portrait. 8vo. 14s.
———— Essays on Historical and Literary Subjects, translated by Margaret Warre. 8vo.

DRAKE'S (Sir Francis) Life, Voyages, and Exploits, by Sea and Land. By John Barrow. Post 8vo. 2s.

DRINKWATER (John). History of the Siege of Gibraltar, 1779-1783. With a Description of that Garrison. Post 8vo. 2s.

DU CHAILLU (Paul B.). Land of the Midnight Sun; Illustrations. 2 Vols. 8vo. 36s.
———— The Viking Age. The Early History, Manners, and Customs of the Ancestors of the English-speaking Nations. With 1,300 Illustrations. 2 Vols. 8vo. 42s.
———— Equatorial Africa and Ashango Land. Adventures in the Great Forest of Equatorial Africa, and the Country of the Dwarfs. Popular Edition. With Illustrations. Post 8vo. 7s. 6d.
———— Ivar the Viking. A Romantic History based on authentic facts of III. and IV. Centuries. 8vo. 6s.

DUFFERIN (Lord). Letters from High Latitudes; a Yacht Voyage to Iceland. Woodcuts. Crown 8vo. 7s. 6d.
———— Speeches in India, 1884—8. 8vo. 9s.
———— (Lady). Our Viceregal Life in India, 1884—1888. Portrait. Crown 8vo. 7s. 6d. Also 2 Vols., large crown 8vo, 24s.
———— My Canadian Journal, 1872—78. Extracts from Home Letters written while Ld. Dufferin was Gov.-Gen. Portraits, Map, and Illustrations. Crown 8vo. 12s.

DUNCAN (Col.). English in Spain; or, The Story of the War of Succession, 1834-1840. 8vo. 16s.

DUNMORE (Lord). The Pamirs: a Narrative of a Year's Expedition on Horseback through Kashmir, Western Tibet, Chinese Tartary, &c. With Maps and Illustrations. 2 Vols. Crown 8vo. 24s.

DÜRER (Albert); his Life and Work. By Dr. Thausino. Edited by F. A. Eaton. Illustrations. 2 Vols. Medium 8vo. 42s.

EARLE (Professor John). The Psalter of 1539: A Landmark of English Literature. Comprising the Text, in Black Letter Type. With Notes. 8vo. 16s.

EASTLAKE (Sir C.). Contributions to the Literature of the Fine Arts. With Memoir by Lady Eastlake. 2 Vols. 8vo. 24s.

EDWARDS (W. H.). Voyage up the River Amazon, including a Visit to Para. Post 8vo. 2s.

ELLESMERE (Lord). Two Sieges of Vienna by the Turke. Post 8vo. 2s.

ELLIOT (Mrs. Minto). The Diary of an Idle Woman in Constantinople. With Plan and Illustrations. Crown 8vo. 14s.

ELLIS (Robinson). Poems and Fragments of Catullus. 16mo. 5s.

ELPHINSTONE (Hon. M.). History of India—the Hindoo and Mahommedan Periods. Edited by Professor Cowell. Map. 8vo. 18s.

———————— Rise of the British Power in the East. A Continuation of his History of India in the Hindoo and Mahommedan Periods. Maps. 8vo. 16s.

———————— Life of. [See Colebrooke.]

ELTON (Capt.). Adventures among the Lakes and Mountains of Eastern and Central Africa. Illustrations. 8vo. 21s.

ELWIN (Rev. Warwick). The Minister of Baptism. A History of Church Opinion from the time of the Apostles, especially with reference to Heretical and Lay Administration. 8vo. 12s.

ENGLAND. [See Arthur—Croker—Hume—Markham—Smith —and Stanhope.]

ESSAYS ON CATHEDRALS. Edited by Dean Howson. 8vo. 12s.

ETON LATIN GRAMMAR. For use in the Upper Forms. By F. H. Rawlins, M.A., and W. R. Inge, M.A. Crown 8vo. 6s.

———————— ELEMENTARY LATIN GRAMMAR. For use in the Lower Forms. Compiled by A. C. Ainger M.A., and H. G. Wintle, M.A. Crown 8vo. 3s. 6d.

———————— PREPARATORY ETON GRAMMAR. Abridged from the above Work. By the same Editors. Crown 8vo. 2s.

———————— FIRST LATIN EXERCISE BOOK, adapted to the Elementary and Preparatory Grammars. By the same Editors. Crown 8vo. 2s. 6d.

———————— FOURTH FORM OVID. Selections from Ovid and Tibullus. With Notes by H. G. Wintle. Post 8vo. 2s. 6d.

———————— HORACE. The Odes, Epodes, and Carmen Sæculare. With Notes. By F. W. Cornish, M.A. Maps. Crown 8vo. 6s.

———————— EXERCISES IN ALGEBRA. by E. P. Rouse, M.A., and Arthur Cockshott, M.A. Crown 8vo. 3s.

———————— ARITHMETIC. By Rev. T. Dalton, M.A. Crown 8vo. 3s.

FERGUSSON (James). History of Architecture in all Countries from the Earliest Times. A New and thoroughly Revised Edition. With 1,700 Illustrations. 5 Vols. Medium 8vo.
Vols. I. & II. Ancient and Medieval. 2 Vols. 63s. New Edition. Edited by Phené Spiers.
III. Indian & Eastern. 31s. 6d. IV. Modern. 2 Vols. 31s. 6d.

FITZPATRICK (William J.). The Correspondence of Daniel O'Connell, the Liberator. With Portrait. 2 Vols. 8vo. 36s.

FLEMING (Professor). Student's Manual of Moral Philosophy. With Quotations and References. Post 8vo. 7s. 6d.

FLOWER GARDEN. By Rev. Thos. James. Fcap. 8vo. 1s.

FORD (ISABELLA O.). Miss Blake of Monkshalton. A Novel. Crown 8vo. 5s.

FORD (RICHARD). Gatherings from Spain. Post 8vo. 3s. 6d.

FORSYTH (WILLIAM). Hortensius; an Historical Essay on the Office and Duties of an Advocate. Illustrations. 8vo, 7s. 6d.

FORTIFICATION. [See CLARKE.]

FRANCE (HISTORY OF). [See ARTHUR—MARKHAM—SMITH— STUDENTS'—TOCQUEVILLE.]

FREAM (W.), LL.D. Elements of Agriculture; a text-book prepared under the authority of the Royal Agricultural Society of England. Enlarged Edition. With 256 Illustrations. Crown 8vo. 3s. 6d.

FRENCH IN ALGIERS; The Soldier of the Foreign Legion— and the Prisoners of Abd-el-Kadir. Post 8vo. 2s.

FRERE (MARY). Old Deccan Days, or Hindoo Fairy Legends current in Southern India, with Introduction by Sir BARTLE FRERE. With Illustrations. Post 8vo. 5s.

GALTON (F.). Art of Travel; or, Hints on the Shifts and Contrivances available in Wild Countries. Woodcuts. Post 8vo. 7s. 6d.

GAMBIER PARRY (T.). The Ministry of Fine Art to the Happiness of Life. Revised Edition, with an Index. 8vo. 14s.

———— (MAJOR). The Combat with Suffering. Fcap. 8vo. 3s. 6d.

GARDNER (PROF. PERCY). New Chapters in Greek History. Historical results of recent excavations in Greece and Asia Minor. With Illustrations. 8vo. 15s.

GEDDES (PROF. P.). Outlines of Modern Botany. With Illustrations. (Univ. Extension Series.) 3s. 6d.

GEOGRAPHY. [See BUNBURY—CROKER—RAMSAY—RICHARDSON —SMITH—STUDENTS'.]

GEOGRAPHICAL SOCIETY'S JOURNAL. (1846 to 1881.) SUPPLEMENTARY PAPERS. Royal 8vo.
Vol. I., Part i. Travels and Researches in Western China. By E. COLBORNE BABER. Maps. 5s.
 Part ii.—1. Recent Geography of Central Asia; from Russian Sources. By E. DELMAR MORGAN. 2. Progress of Discovery on the Coasts of New Guinea. By C. B. MARKHAM. Bibliographical Appendix, by E. C. Rye. Maps. 5s.
 Part iii.—1. Report on Part of the Ghilzi Country, &c. By Lieut. J. S. BROADFOOT. 2. Journey from Shiraz to Jashk. By J. R. PREECE. 2s. 6d.
 Part iv.—Geographical Education. By J. S. KELTIE. 2s. 6d.
Vol. II., Part i.—1. Exploration in S. and S.W. China. By A. R. COLQUHOUN. 2. Bibliography and Cartography of Hispaniola. By H. LING ROTH. 3. Explorations in Zanzibar Dominions by Lieut. C. STEWART SMITH, R.N. 2s. 6d.
 Part ii.—A Bibliography of Algeria, from the Expedition of Charles V. in 1541 to 1887. By SIR R. L. PLAYFAIR. 4s.
 Part iii.—1. On the Measurement of Heights by the Barometer. By JOHN BALL, F.R.S. 2. River Entrances. By H. ROBERT MILL. 3. Mr. Needham's Journey in South Eastern Tibet. 2s. 6d.
 Part iv.—1. The Bibliography of the Barbary States. Part i. By SIR R. L. PLAYFAIR. 2. Hudson's Bay and Strait. By Commodore A. H. MARKHAM, R.N. 3s.
Vol. III., Part i.—Journey of Carey and Dalgleish in Chinese Turkestan and Northern Tibet; and General Prejevalsky on the Orography of Northern Tibet. 4s.
 Part ii.—Vaughan's Persia, &c. 4s.
 Part iii.—Playfair's Bibliography of Morocco. 5s.
 Part iv. Milne's Jezo, &c.
 Part v.—Hogarth's Asia Minor.
Vol. IV.—Ramsay's Asia Minor. 18s.

GEORGE (Ernest). Loire and South of France; 20 Etchings. Folio. 42s.

GERMANY (History of). [See Markham.]

GIBBON'S History of the Decline and Fall of the Roman Empire. Edited with notes by Milman, Guizot, and Dr. Wm. Smith. Maps. 8 Vols. 8vo. 60s. Student's Edition. 7s. 6d. (See Student's.)

GIFFARD (Edward). Deeds of Naval Daring; or, Anecdotes of the British Navy. Fcap. 8vo. 3s. 6d.

GILBERT (Josiah). Landscape in Art: before the days of Claude and Salvator. With 150 Illustrations. Medium 8vo. 50s.

GILL (Capt.). The River of Golden Sand. A Journey through China to Burmah. Edited by E. C. Baber. With Memoir by Col. Yule, C.B. Portrait, Map, and Illustrations. Post 8vo. 7s. 6d.

—— (Mrs.). Six Months in Ascension. An Unscientific Account of a Scientific Expedition. Map. Crown 8vo. 9s.

GLADSTONE (W. E.). Gleanings of Past Years, 1843-78. 7 Vols. Small 8vo. 2s. 6d. each. I. The Throne, the Prince Consort, the Cabinet and Constitution. II. Personal and Literary. III. Historical and Speculative. IV. Foreign. V. and VI. Ecclesiastical. VII. Miscellaneous.

—— - Special Aspects of the Irish Question; A Series of Reflections in and since 1886. Collected from various Sources and Reprinted. Crown 8vo. 3s. 6d.

GLEIG (G. R.). Campaigns of the British Army at Washington and New Orleans. Post 8vo. 2s.

—— Story of the Battle of Waterloo. Post 8vo. 3s. 6d.

—— — Narrative of Sale's Brigade in Affghanistan. Post 8vo. 2s.

—— Life of Lord Clive. Post 8vo. 3s. 6d.

—— Sir Thomas Munro. Post 8vo. 3s. 6d.

GOLDSMITH'S (Oliver) Works. Edited with Notes by Peter Cunningham. Vignettes. 4 Vols. 8vo. 30s.

GORDON (Sir Alex.). Sketches of German Life, and Scenes from the War of Liberation. Post 8vo. 3s. 6d.

—— (Lady Duff). The Amber-Witch. Post 8vo. 2s. See also Ross.

—— The French in Algiers. Post 8vo. 2s.

GORE, Rev. Charles (Edited by). Lux Mundi. A Series of Studies in the Religion of the Incarnation. By various Writers. Popular Edition, Crown 8vo. 6s.

—— The Bampton Lectures, 1891; The Incarnation of the Son of God. 8vo. 7s. 6d.

—— The Mission of the Church. Four Lectures delivered in the Cathedral Church of St. Asaph. Crown 8vo. 2s. 6d.

GOSSE (Edmund W.). The Jacobean Poets. Crown 8vo. 3s. 6d. (University Extension Series).

GOULBURN (Dean). Three Counsels of the Divine Master for the conduct of the Spiritual Life:—The Commencement; The Virtues; The Conflict. Crown 8vo. 9s. (See also Burgon.)

GRAMMARS. [See Curtius — Eton—Hall — Hutton—King Edward—Leathes—Matthiæ—Smith.]

GRANT (A. J.). Greece in the Age of Pericles. Crown 8vo. (University Extension Series.) 3s. 6d.

GREECE (History of). [See Grote—Smith—Students'.]

GRIFFITH (Rev. Charles). A History of Strathfieldsaye. With Illustrations. 4to. 10s. 6d.

GROTE'S (George) WORKS:—

    History of Greece. From the Earliest Times to the Death of Alexander the Great. *New Edition.* Portrait, Map, and Plans. 10 Vols. Post 8vo. 5s. each. (*The Volumes may be had Separately.*)

    Plato, and other Companions of Socrates. 3 Vols. 8vo. 45s.; or, New Edition, Edited by Alex. Bain. 4 Vols. Crown 8vo. 5s. each.

    Aristotle. 8vo. 12s.

    Minor Works. Portrait. 8vo. 14s.

—— (Mrs.). A Sketch. By Lady Eastlake. Crown 8vo. 6s.

GRUNDY (G. B.) The Topography of the Battle of Platæa. With Maps and Plans. 8vo. 7s. 6d.

GUILLEMARD (F. H.), M.D. The Voyage of the Marchesa to Kamschatka and New Guinea. With Notices of Formosa and the Islands of the Malay Archipelago. New Edition. With Maps and 150 Illustrations. One volume. Medium 8vo. 21s.

HAKE (G. Napier) on Explosives. [See Berthelot.]

HALL'S (T. D.) School Manual of English Grammar. With Illustrations and Practical Exercises. 12mo. 3s. 6d.

—— Primary English Grammar for Elementary Schools. With numerous Exercises, and graduated Parsing Lessons. 16mo. 1s.

—— Manual of English Composition. With Copious Illustrations and Practical Exercises. 12mo. 3s. 6d.

—— Child's First Latin Book, comprising a full Practice of Nouns, Pronouns, and Adjectives, with the Verbs. 16mo. 2s.

—— Introduction to the Study of the Greek Testament, comprising a connected Narrative of our Lord's Life from the Synoptic Gospels in the original Greek, with concise grammar, notes, &c. With facsimiles of texts. Crown 8vo. 2s. 6d.

HALLAM'S (Henry) WORKS:—

    The Constitutional History of England. *Library Edition,* 3 Vols. 8vo. 30s. *Cabinet Edition,* 3 Vols. Post 8vo. 12s. *Student's Edition,* Post 8vo. 7s. 6d.

    History of Europe during the Middle Ages. *Cabinet Edition,* 3 Vols. Post 8vo. 12s. *Student's Edition,* Post 8vo. 7s. 6d.

    Literary History of Europe during the 15th, 16th, and 17th Centuries. *Library Edition,* 3 Vols. 8vo. 36s. *Cabinet Edition,* 4 Vols. Post 8vo. 16s.

HART'S ARMY LIST. (*Published Quarterly and Annually.*)

HAY (Sir J. H. Drummond). Western Barbary, its Wild Tribes and Savage Animals. Post 8vo. 2s.

HAYWARD (A.). Sketches of Eminent Statesmen and Writers, 2 Vols. 8vo. 28s.

—— The Art of Dining. Post 8vo. 2s.

    A Selection from his Correspondence. By H. E. Carlisle. 2 vols. Crown 8vo. 24s.

HEAD'S (Sir Francis) WORKS:—

    The Royal Engineer. Illustrations. 8vo. 12s.

    Rapid Journeys across the Pampas. Post 8vo. 2s.

    Stokers and Pokers; or, the L. and N. W. R. Post 8vo. 2s.

HEBER'S (Bishop) Journals in India. 2 Vols. Post 8vo. 7s.

—— Poetical Works. Portrait. Fcap. 8vo. 3s. 6d.

HERODOTUS. A New English Version. Edited, with Notes and Essays by Canon Rawlinson, Sir H. Rawlinson and Sir J. G. Wilkinson. Maps and Woodcuts. 4 Vols. 8vo. 48s.

HERRIES (Rt. Hon. John). Memoir of his Public Life. By his Son, Edward Herries, C.B. 2 Vols. 8vo. 24s.

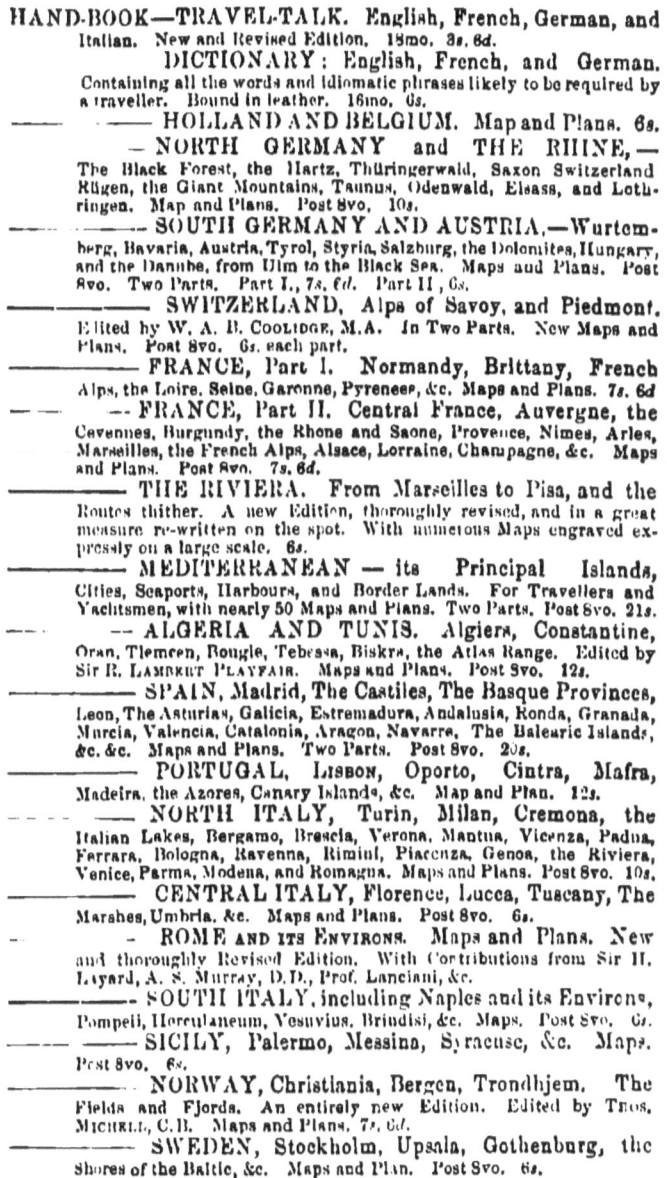

FOREIGN HAND·BOOKS.

HAND-BOOK—TRAVEL-TALK. English, French, German, and Italian. New and Revised Edition. 18mo. 3s. 6d.

DICTIONARY : English, French, and German. Containing all the words and idiomatic phrases likely to be required by a traveller. Bound in leather. 16mo. 6s.

————— HOLLAND AND BELGIUM. Map and Plans. 6s.

— NORTH GERMANY and THE RHINE, — The Black Forest, the Hartz, Thüringerwald, Saxon Switzerland Rügen, the Giant Mountains, Taunus, Odenwald, Elsass, and Lothringen. Map and Plans. Post 8vo, 10s.

————— SOUTH GERMANY AND AUSTRIA.—Wurtemberg, Bavaria, Austria, Tyrol, Styria, Salzburg, the Dolomites, Hungary, and the Danube, from Ulm to the Black Sea. Maps and Plans. Post 8vo. Two Parts. Part I., 7s. 6d. Part II , 6s.

————— SWITZERLAND, Alps of Savoy, and Piedmont. Edited by W. A. B. COOLIDGE, M.A. In Two Parts. New Maps and Plans. Post 8vo. 6s. each part.

————— FRANCE, Part I. Normandy, Brittany, French Alps, the Loire, Seine, Garonne, Pyrenees, &c. Maps and Plans. 7s. 6d

——— --FRANCE, Part II. Central France, Auvergne, the Cevennes, Burgundy, the Rhone and Saone, Provence, Nimes, Arles, Marseilles, the French Alps, Alsace, Lorraine, Champagne, &c. Maps and Plans. Post 8vo. 7s. 6d.

————— THE RIVIERA. From Marseilles to Pisa, and the Routes thither. A new Edition, thoroughly revised, and in a great measure re-written on the spot. With numerous Maps engraved expressly on a large scale. 6s.

————— MEDITERRANEAN — its Principal Islands, Cities, Seaports, Harbours, and Border Lands. For Travellers and Yachtsmen, with nearly 50 Maps and Plans. Two Parts. Post 8vo. 21s.

————— --ALGERIA AND TUNIS. Algiers, Constantine, Oran, Tlemcen, Bougie, Tebessa, Biskra, the Atlas Range. Edited by Sir R. LAMBERT PLAYFAIR. Maps and Plans. Post 8vo. 12s.

————— SPAIN, Madrid, The Castiles, The Basque Provinces, Leon, The Asturias, Galicia, Estremadura, Andalusia, Ronda, Granada, Murcia, Valencia, Catalonia, Aragon, Navarre, The Balearic Islands, &c. &c. Maps and Plans. Two Parts. Post 8vo. 20s.

————— PORTUGAL, Lisbon, Oporto, Cintra, Mafra, Madeira, the Azores, Canary Islands, &c. Map and Plan. 12s.

————— NORTH ITALY, Turin, Milan, Cremona, the Italian Lakes, Bergamo, Brescia, Verona, Mantua, Vicenza, Padua, Ferrara, Bologna, Ravenna, Rimini, Piacenza, Genoa, the Riviera, Venice, Parma, Modena, and Romagna. Maps and Plans. Post 8vo. 10s.

————— CENTRAL ITALY, Florence, Lucca, Tuscany, The Marshes, Umbria. &c. Maps and Plans. Post 8vo. 6s.

————— ROME AND ITS ENVIRONS. Maps and Plans. New and thoroughly Revised Edition. With Contributions from Sir H. Layard, A. S. Murray, D.D., Prof. Lanciani, &c.

————— SOUTH ITALY, including Naples and its Environs, Pompeii, Herculaneum, Vesuvius, Brindisi, &c. Maps. Post 8vo. 6s.

————— SICILY, Palermo, Messina, Syracuse, &c. Maps. Post 8vo. 6s.

————— NORWAY, Christiania, Bergen, Trondhjem. The Fields and Fjords. An entirely new Edition. Edited by THOS. MICHELL, C.B. Maps and Plans. 7s. 6d.

————— SWEDEN, Stockholm, Upsala, Gothenburg, the Shores of the Baltic, &c. Maps and Plan. Post 8vo. 6s.

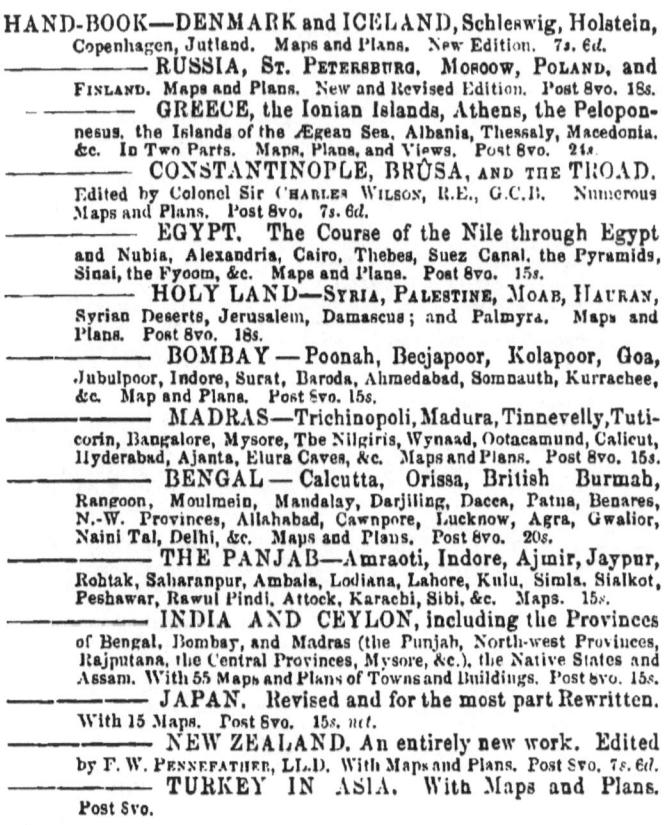

HAND-BOOK—DENMARK and ICELAND, Schleswig, Holstein,
Copenhagen, Jutland. Maps and Plans. New Edition. 7s. 6d.
——————— RUSSIA, St. Petersburg, Moscow, Poland, and
Finland. Maps and Plans. New and Revised Edition. Post 8vo. 18s.
——————— GREECE, the Ionian Islands, Athens, the Pelopon-
nesus, the Islands of the Ægean Sea, Albania, Thessaly, Macedonia,
&c. In Two Parts. Maps, Plans, and Views. Post 8vo. 24s.
——————— CONSTANTINOPLE, BRÜSA, AND THE TROAD.
Edited by Colonel Sir Charles Wilson, R.E., G.C.B. Numerous
Maps and Plans. Post 8vo. 7s. 6d.
——————— EGYPT. The Course of the Nile through Egypt
and Nubia, Alexandria, Cairo, Thebes, Suez Canal, the Pyramids,
Sinai, the Fyoom, &c. Maps and Plans. Post 8vo. 15s.
——————— HOLY LAND—Syria, Palestine, Moab, Hauran,
Syrian Deserts, Jerusalem, Damascus; and Palmyra. Maps and
Plans. Post 8vo. 18s.
——————— BOMBAY — Poonah, Beejapoor, Kolapoor, Goa,
Jubulpoor, Indore, Surat, Baroda, Ahmedabad, Somnauth, Kurrachee,
&c. Map and Plans. Post 8vo. 15s.
——————— MADRAS—Trichinopoli, Madura, Tinnevelly, Tuti-
corin, Bangalore, Mysore, The Nilgiris, Wynaad, Ootacamund, Calicut,
Hyderabad, Ajanta, Elura Caves, &c. Maps and Plans. Post 8vo. 15s.
——————— BENGAL — Calcutta, Orissa, British Burmah,
Rangoon, Moulmein, Mandalay, Darjiling, Dacca, Patna, Benares,
N.-W. Provinces, Allahabad, Cawnpore, Lucknow, Agra, Gwalior,
Naini Tal, Delhi, &c. Maps and Plans. Post 8vo. 20s.
——————— THE PANJAB—Amraoti, Indore, Ajmir, Jaypur,
Rohtak, Saharanpur, Ambala, Lodiana, Lahore, Kulu, Simla, Sialkot,
Peshawar, Rawul Pindi, Attock, Karachi, Sibi, &c. Maps. 15s.
——————— INDIA AND CEYLON, including the Provinces
of Bengal, Bombay, and Madras (the Punjab, North-west Provinces,
Rajputana, the Central Provinces, Mysore, &c.), the Native States and
Assam. With 55 Maps and Plans of Towns and Buildings. Post 8vo. 15s.
——————— JAPAN. Revised and for the most part Rewritten.
With 15 Maps. Post 8vo. 15s. net.
——————— NEW ZEALAND. An entirely new work. Edited
by F. W. Pennefather, LL.D. With Maps and Plans. Post 8vo. 7s. 6d.
——————— TURKEY IN ASIA. With Maps and Plans.
Post 8vo.

ENGLISH HAND-BOOKS.

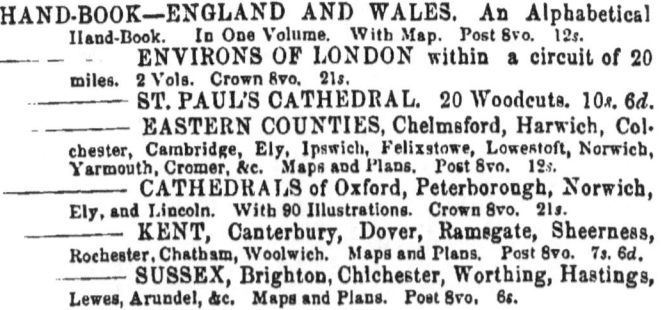

HAND-BOOK—ENGLAND AND WALES. An Alphabetical
Hand-Book. In One Volume. With Map. Post 8vo. 12s.
——————— ENVIRONS OF LONDON within a circuit of 20
miles. 2 Vols. Crown 8vo. 21s.
——————— ST. PAUL'S CATHEDRAL. 20 Woodcuts. 10s. 6d.
——————— EASTERN COUNTIES, Chelmsford, Harwich, Col-
chester, Cambridge, Ely, Ipswich, Felixstowe, Lowestoft, Norwich,
Yarmouth, Cromer, &c. Maps and Plans. Post 8vo. 12s.
——————— CATHEDRALS of Oxford, Peterborough, Norwich,
Ely, and Lincoln. With 90 Illustrations. Crown 8vo. 21s.
——————— KENT, Canterbury, Dover, Ramsgate, Sheerness,
Rochester, Chatham, Woolwich. Maps and Plans. Post 8vo. 7s. 6d.
——————— SUSSEX, Brighton, Chichester, Worthing, Hastings,
Lewes, Arundel, &c. Maps and Plans. Post 8vo. 6s.

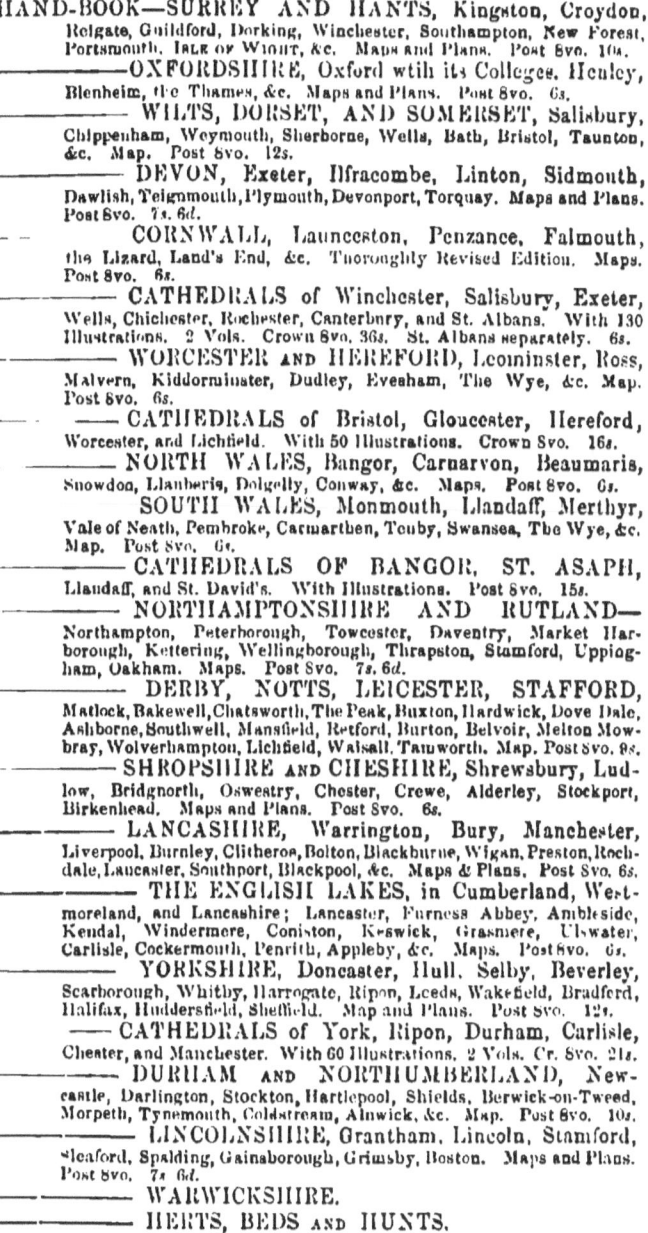

HAND-BOOK—SURREY AND HANTS, Kingston, Croydon, Reigate, Guildford, Dorking, Winchester, Southampton, New Forest, Portsmouth, Isle of Wight, &c. Maps and Plans. Post 8vo. 10s.

————OXFORDSHIRE, Oxford wtih its Colleges, Henley, Blenheim, the Thames, &c. Maps and Plans. Post 8vo. 6s.

———— WILTS, DORSET, AND SOMERSET, Salisbury, Chippenham, Weymouth, Sherborne, Wells, Bath, Bristol, Taunton, &c. Map. Post 8vo. 12s.

———— DEVON, Exeter, Ilfracombe, Linton, Sidmouth, Dawlish, Teignmouth, Plymouth, Devonport, Torquay. Maps and Plans. Post 8vo. 7s. 6d.

———— CORNWALL, Launceston, Penzance, Falmouth, the Lizard, Land's End, &c. Thoroughly Revised Edition. Maps. Post 8vo. 6s.

———— CATHEDRALS of Winchester, Salisbury, Exeter, Wells, Chichester, Rochester, Canterbury, and St. Albans. With 130 Illustrations. 2 Vols. Crown 8vo. 36s. St. Albans separately. 6s.

———— WORCESTER AND HEREFORD, Leominster, Ross, Malvern, Kidderminster, Dudley, Evesham, The Wye, &c. Map. Post 8vo. 6s.

———— CATHEDRALS of Bristol, Gloucester, Hereford, Worcester, and Lichfield. With 50 Illustrations. Crown 8vo. 16s.

———— NORTH WALES, Bangor, Carnarvon, Beaumaris, Snowdon, Llanberis, Dolgelly, Conway, &c. Maps. Post 8vo. 6s.

———— SOUTH WALES, Monmouth, Llandaff, Merthyr, Vale of Neath, Pembroke, Carmarthen, Tenby, Swansea, The Wye, &c. Map. Post 8vo. 6s.

———— CATHEDRALS OF BANGOR, ST. ASAPH, Llandaff, and St. David's. With Illustrations. Post 8vo. 15s.

———— NORTHAMPTONSHIRE AND RUTLAND— Northampton, Peterborough, Towcester, Daventry, Market Harborough, Kettering, Wellingborough, Thrapston, Stamford, Uppingham, Oakham. Maps. Post 8vo. 7s. 6d.

———— DERBY, NOTTS, LEICESTER, STAFFORD, Matlock, Bakewell, Chatsworth, The Peak, Buxton, Hardwick, Dove Dale, Ashborne, Southwell, Mansfield, Retford, Burton, Belvoir, Melton Mowbray, Wolverhampton, Lichfield, Walsall, Tamworth. Map. Post 8vo. 9s.

———— SHROPSHIRE AND CHESHIRE, Shrewsbury, Ludlow, Bridgnorth, Oswestry, Chester, Crewe, Alderley, Stockport, Birkenhead. Maps and Plans. Post 8vo. 6s.

———— LANCASHIRE, Warrington, Bury, Manchester, Liverpool, Burnley, Clitheroe, Bolton, Blackburne, Wigan, Preston, Rochdale, Lancaster, Southport, Blackpool, &c. Maps & Plans. Post 8vo. 6s.

———— THE ENGLISH LAKES, in Cumberland, Westmoreland, and Lancashire; Lancaster, Furness Abbey, Ambleside, Kendal, Windermere, Coniston, Keswick, Grasmere, Ulswater, Carlisle, Cockermouth, Penrith, Appleby, &c. Maps. Post 8vo. 6s.

———— YORKSHIRE, Doncaster, Hull, Selby, Beverley, Scarborough, Whitby, Harrogate, Ripon, Leeds, Wakefield, Bradford, Halifax, Huddersfield, Sheffield. Map and Plans. Post 8vo. 12s.

———— CATHEDRALS of York, Ripon, Durham, Carlisle, Chester, and Manchester. With 60 Illustrations. 2 Vols. Cr. 8vo. 21s.

———— DURHAM AND NORTHUMBERLAND, Newcastle, Darlington, Stockton, Hartlepool, Shields, Berwick-on-Tweed, Morpeth, Tynemouth, Coldstream, Alnwick, &c. Map. Post 8vo. 10s.

———— LINCOLNSHIRE, Grantham, Lincoln, Stamford, Sleaford, Spalding, Gainsborough, Grimsby, Boston. Maps and Plans. Post 8vo. 7s. 6d.

———— WARWICKSHIRE.

———— HERTS, BEDS AND HUNTS.

HAND-BOOK—SCOTLAND, Edinburgh, Melrose, Kelso, Glasgow, Dumfries, Ayr, Stirling, Arran, The Clyde, Oban, Inverary, Loch Lomond, Loch Katrine and Trossachs, Caledonian Canal, Inverness, Perth, Dundee, Aberdeen, Braemar, Skye, Caithness, Ross, Sutherland, &c. Maps and Plans. Post 8vo.

———————— IRELAND, Dublin, Belfast, the Giant's Causeway, Donegal, Galway, Wexford, Cork, Limerick, Waterford, Killarney, Bantry, Glengariff, &c. Maps and Plans. Post 8vo. 10s.

HICKSON (Dr. Sydney J.). A Naturalist in North Celebes; a Narrative of Travels in Minahassa, the Sangir and Talaut Islands, with Notices of the Fauna, Flora, and Ethnology of the Districts visited. Map and Illustrations. 8vo. 16s.

HISLOP (Stephen). [See Smith, George.]

HOBSON (J. A.). [See Mummery.]

HOLLWAY (J. G.). A Month in Norway. Fcap. 8vo. 2s.

HONEY BEE. By Rev. Thomas James. Fcap. 8vo. 1s.

HOOK (Dean). Church Dictionary. A Manual of Reference for Clergymen and Students. New Edition, thoroughly revised. Edited by Walter Hook, M.A., and W. R. W. Stephens, M.A. Med. 8vo. 21s.

———————— (Theodore) Life. By J. G. Lockhart. Fcap. 8vo. 1s.

HOPE (A. J. Beresford). Worship in the Church of England. 8vo, 9s.; or, Popular Selections from, 8vo, 2s. 6d.

——— - Worship and Order. 8vo. 9s.

HOPE-SCOTT (James), Memoir. [See Ornsby.]

HORACE; a New Edition of the Text. Edited by Dean Milman. With 100 Woodcuts. Crown 8vo. 7s. 6d.

———————— [See Eton.]

HOUGHTON'S (Lord) Monographs. Portraits. 10s. 6d.

——————— (Robert Lord) Stray Verses, 1889-90. Second Edition, fcap. 8vo. 5s.

HOME AND COLONIAL LIBRARY. A Series of Works adapted for all circles and classes of Readers, having been selected for their acknowledged interest, and ability of the Authors. Post 8vo. Published at 2s. and 3s. 6d. each, and arranged under two distinctive heads as follows:—

CLASS A.

HISTORY, BIOGRAPHY, AND HISTORIC TALES.

SIEGE OF GIBRALTAR. By John Drinkwater. 2s.

THE AMBER-WITCH. By Lady Duff Gordon. 2s.

CROMWELL AND BUNYAN. By Robert Southey. 2s.

LIFE of Sir FRANCIS DRAKE. By John Barrow. 2s.

CAMPAIGNS AT WASHINGTON. By Rev. G. R. Gleig. 2s.

THE FRENCH IN ALGIERS. By Lady Duff Gordon. 2s.

THE FALL OF THE JESUITS. 2s.

LIVONIAN TALES 2s.

LIFE OF CONDE. By Lord Mahon. 3s. 6d.

SALE'S BRIGADE. By Rev. G. R. Gleig. 2s.

THE SIEGES OF VIENNA. By Lord Ellesmere. 2s.

THE WAYSIDE CROSS. By Capt. Milman. 2s.

SKETCHES of GERMAN LIFE. By Sir A. Gordon. 3s. 6d.

THE BATTLE of WATERLOO. By Rev. G. R. Gleig. 3s. 6d.

AUTOBIOGRAPHY OF STEFFENS. 2s.

THE BRITISH POETS. By Thomas Campbell. 3s. 6d.

HISTORICAL ESSAYS. By Lord Mahon. 3s. 6d.

LIFE OF LORD CLIVE. By Rev. G. R. Gleig. 3s. 6d.

NORTH WESTERN RAILWAY. By Sir F. B. Head. 2s.

LIFE OF MUNRO. By Rev. G. R. Gleig. 3s. 6d.

CLASS B.
VOYAGES, TRAVELS, AND ADVENTURES.

JOURNALS IN INDIA. By
BISHOP HEBER. 2 Vols. 7s.
TRAVELS IN THE HOLY LAND.
By IRBY and MANGLES. 2s.
MOROCCO AND THE MOORS.
By J. DRUMMOND HAY. 2s.
LETTERS FROM THE BALTIC.
By A LADY. 2s.
NEW SOUTH WALES. By MRS.
MEREDITH. 2s.
THE WEST INDIES. By M. G.
LEWIS. 2s.
SKETCHES OF PERSIA. By
SIR JOHN MALCOLM. 3s. 6d.
MEMOIRS OF FATHER RIPA.
2s.
MISSIONARY LIFE IN CAN-
ADA. By REV. J. ABBOTT. 2s.
LETTERS FROM MADRAS. By
A LADY. 2s.

HIGHLAND SPORTS. By
CHARLES ST. JOHN. 3s. 6d.
PAMPAS JOURNEYS. By
F. B. HEAD. 2s.
GATHERINGS FROM SPAIN.
By RICHARD FORD. 3s. 6d.
THE RIVER AMAZON. By
W. H. EDWARDS. 2s.
MANNERS & CUSTOMS OF
INDIA. By REV. C. ACLAND. 2s.
ADVENTURES IN MEXICO.
By G. F. RUXTON. 3s. 6d.
PORTUGAL AND GALICIA.
By LORD CARNARVON. 3s. 6d.
BUSH LIFE IN AUSTRALIA.
By REV. H. W. HAYGARTH. 2s.
THE LIBYAN DESERT. By
BAYLE ST. JOHN. 2s.
SIERRA LEONE. By A LADY.
3s. 6d.

*** Each work may be had separately.

HUME (The Student's). A History of England, from the Invasion of Julius Cæsar to the Revolution of 1688. New Edition, revised,
corrected, and continued to the Treaty of Berlin, 1878. By J. S.
BREWER, M.A. With 7 Coloured Maps & 70 Woodcuts. Crown 8vo. 7s. 6d.
*** Sold also in 3 parts. Price 2s. 6d. each.

HUTCHINSON (GEN.). Dog Breaking, with Odds and Ends for
those who love the Dog and the Gun. With 40 Illustrations. Crown
8vo. 7s. 6d. *** A Summary of the Rules for Gamekeepers. 1s.

HUTTON (H. E.). Principia Græca; an Introduction to the Study
of Greek. Comprehending Grammar, Delectus, and Exercise-book,
with Vocabularies. Sixth Edition. 12mo. 3s. 6d.

HYMNOLOGY, DICTIONARY OF. [See JULIAN.]

ICELAND. [See COLES—DUFFERIN.]

IMPERIAL INSTITUTE YEAR BOOK for 1893. Royal 8vo.
10s. net.

INDIA. [See BROADFOOT—DUFFERIN—ELPHINSTONE—HAND-BOOK
—LYALL—SMITH—TEMPLE—MONIER WILLIAMS.]

IRBY AND MANGLES' Travels in Egypt, Nubia, Syria, and
the Holy Land. Post 8vo. 2s.

JAMES (F. L.). The Wild Tribes of the Soudan : with an account
of the route from Wady Halfa to Dongola and Berber. With
Chapter on the Soudan, by SIR S. BAKER. Illustrations. Crown 8vo.
7s. 6d.

JAMESON (MRS.). Lives of the Early Italian Painters—
and the Progress of Painting in Italy—Cimabue to Bassano. With
50 Portraits. Post 8vo. 12s.

JANNARIS (PROF. A. N.). A Pocket Dictionary of the Modern
Greek and English Languages, as actually Written and Spoken. Being
a Copious Vocabulary of all Words and Expressions Current in Ordinary
Reading and in Everyday Talk, with Especial Illustration by means of
Distinctive Signs, of the Colloquial and Popular Greek Language, for
the Guidance of Students and Travellers. Fcap. 8vo.

o

JAPAN. [See BIRD—HANDBOOK.]

JEKYLL (JOSEPH). Correspondence with his Sister-in-Law, Lady
Gertrude Sloane Stanley, 1818—1828. Edited by the Hon. ALGERNON
BOURKE. 8vo. 16s.

JENNINGS (L. J.). Field Paths and Green Lanes : or Walks in
Surrey and Sussex. Popular Edition. With Illustrations. Cr. 8vo. 6s.
[See also CROKER.]

JESSE (EDWARD). Gleanings in Natural History. Fcp. 8vo. 3s. 6d.

JOHNSON'S (DR. SAMUEL) Life. [See BOSWELL.]

JOWETT (B.). The Epistles of St. Paul to the Thessalonians,
Galatians and Romans. With Notes and Dissertations. Edited and
condensed by Lewis Campbell, M.A., LL.D. 2 vols. Crown 8vo.
7s. 6d. net, each vol.

JULIAN (REV. JOHN J.). A Dictionary of Hymnology. A
Companion to Existing Hymn Books. Setting forth the Origin and
History of the Hymns contained in the Principal Hymnals, with
Notices of their Authors, &c., &c. Medium 8vo. (1626 pp.) 42s.

JUNIUS' HANDWRITING Professionally investigated. Edited by the
Hon. E. TWISLETON. With Facsimiles. Woodcuts, &c. 4to. £3 3s.

KEENE (H. G.). The Literature of France. 220 pp. Crown
8vo. 3s. (University Extension Manuals.)

KENDAL (MRS.) Dramatic Opinions. Post 8vo. 1s.

KERR (ROBT.). The Consulting Architect : Practical Notes on
Administrative Difficulties. Crown 8vo. 9s.

KIRKES' Handbook of Physiology. Edited by W. MORRANT
BAKER and V. D. HARRIS. With 500 Illustrations. Post 8vo. 14s.

KNIGHT (PROF.). The Philosophy of the Beautiful. Two Parts.
Crown 8vo. 3s. 6d. each. (University Extension Series.)

———— The Christian Ethic. Crown 8vo. 3s. 6d.

KUGLER'S HANDBOOK OF PAINTING.—The Italian Schools.
A New Edition, revised. By Sir HENRY LAYARD. With 200 Illustrations. 2 vols. Crown 8vo. 30s.

———————————————— The German, Flemish, and
Dutch Schools. New Edition revised. By Sir J. A. CROWE. With
60 Illustrations. 2 Vols. Crown 8vo. 24s.

LANDOR (A. H. SAVAGE). Alone with the Hairy Ainu, or 3,800
Miles on a Pack Saddle in Yezo, and a Cruise to the Kurile Islands.
With Map, and many Illustrations by the Author. Medium 8vo. 18s.

LANE (E. W.). Account of the Manners and Customs of Modern
Egyptians. With Illustrations. 2 Vols. Post 8vo. 12s.

LAWLESS (HON. EMILY). Major Lawrence. F.L.S. : a Novel.
3 Vols. Crown 8vo. 31s. 6d. Cheap Edition, 6s.

———————— Plain Frances Mowbray, etc. Crown 8vo. 6s.

LAYARD (Sir A. H.). Nineveh and its Remains. With Illustrations. Post 8vo. 7s. 6d.

———————— Nineveh and Babylon. Illusts. Post 8vo. 7s. 6d.

———————— Early Adventures in Persia, Babylonia, and Susiana,
including a residence among the Bakhtiyari and other wild tribes.
Portrait, Illustrations and Maps. 2 Vols. Crown 8vo. 24s.

LEATHES (STANLEY). Practical Hebrew Grammar. With the
Hebrew Text of Genesis i.—vi., and Psalms i.—vi. Grammatical.
Analysis and Vocabulary. Post 8vo. 7s. 6d.

LESLIE (C. R.). Handbook for Young Painters. Illustrations.
Post 8vo. 7s. 6d.

LETTERS FROM THE BALTIC. By LADY EASTLAKE. Post 8vo. 2s.

———— MADRAS. By MRS. MAITLAND. Post 8vo. 2s.

LEVI (Leone). History of British Commerce; and Economic Progress of the Nation, from 1763 to 1878. 8vo. 15s.

LEWIS (T. Hayter). The Holy Places of Jerusalem. Illustrations. 8vo. 10s. 6d.

LEX SALICA; the Ten Texts with the Glosses and the Lex Emendata. Synoptically edited by J. H. Hessels. 4to. 42s.

LIDDELL (Dean). Student's History of Rome, from the earliest Times to the establishment of the Empire. Woodcuts. Post 8vo. 7s. 6d.

LILLY (W. S.). The Great Enigma. 1. The Twilight of the Gods. 2. Atheism. 3. Critical Agnosticism. 4. Scientific Agnosticism. 5. Rational Theism. 6. The Inner Light. 7. The Christian Synthesis. 8vo. 14s.

LIND (Jenny), The Artist, 1820—1851. Her early Art-life and Dramatic Career. From Original Documents, Letters, Diaries, &c. in the possession of Mr. Goldschmidt. By Canon H. Scott Holland M.A., and W. S. Rockstro. Popular Edition. With Portraits and Illustrations. Crown 8vo. 6s.

LINDSAY (Lord). Sketches of the History of Christian Art. 2 Vols. Crown 8vo. 21s.

LISPINGS from LOW LATITUDES; or, the Journal of the Hon. Impulsia Gushington. Edited by Lord Dufferin. With 24 Plates. 4to. 21s.

LIVINGSTONE (Dr.). First Expedition to Africa, 1840–56. Illustrations. Crown 8vo. 7s. 6d.

—————— Second Expedition to Africa, 1858-64. Illustrations. Crown 8vo. 7s. 6d.

—————— Last Journals in Central Africa, to his Death. By Rev. Horace Waller. Maps and Illustrations. 2 Vols. 8vo. 15s.

—————— Personal Life. By Wm. G. Blaikie, D.D. With Map and Portrait. Crown 8vo. 6s.

LOCKHART (J. G.). Ancient Spanish Ballads. Historical and Romantic. Translated, with Notes. Illustrations. Crown 8vo. 5s.

—————— Life of Theodore Hook. Fcap. 8vo. 1s.

LONDON: Past and Present; its History, Associations, and Traditions. By Henry B. Wheatley, F.S.A. Based on Cunningham's Handbook. Library Edition, on Laid Paper 3 Vols. Medium 8vo. 3l. 3s.

LOUDON (Mrs.). Gardening for Ladies. With Directions and Calendar of Operations for Every Month. Woodcuts. Fcap. 8vo. 3s. 6d.

LUMHOLTZ (Dr. C.). Among Cannibals; An Account of Four Years' Travels in Australia, and of Camp Life among the Aborigines of Queensland. With Maps and 120 Illustrations. Medium 8vo. 21s.

LUTHER (Martin). The First Principles of the Reformation, or the Three Primary Works of Dr. Martin Luther. Portrait. 8vo. 12s.

LYALL (Sir Alfred C.), K.C.B. Asiatic Studies; Religious and Social. 8vo. 12s.

—————————— The Rise of the British Dominion in India. From the Early Days of the East India Company. University Extension Series. With coloured Maps. Crown 8vo. 4s. 6d. Also Library Edition with considerable additions. 8vo. 12s. net.

LYELL (Sir Charles). Student's Elements of Geology. A new Edition, entirely revised by Professor P. M. Duncan, F.R.S. With 600 Illustrations. Post 8vo. 9s.

—————————— Life, Letters, and Journals. Edited by his sister-in-law, Mrs. Lyell. With Portraits. 2 Vols. 8vo. 30s.

LYNDHURST (Lord). [See Martin.]

c 2

McCLINTOCK (Sir L.). Narrative of the Discovery of the
Fate of Sir John Franklin and his Companions in the Arctic Seas.
With Illustrations. Crown 8vo. 7s. 6d.

McKENDRICK (Prof.) and Dr. Snodgrass. The Physiology of the
Senses. With Illustrations. (Univ. Extension Series). Crown 8vo. 4s. 6d.

MACDONALD (A.). Too Late for Gordon and Khartoum.
With Maps and Plans. 8vo. 12s.

MACGREGOR (J.). Rob Roy on the Jordan, Nile, Red Sea, Gen-
nesareth, &c. A Canoe Cruise in Palestine and Egypt and the Waters
of Damascus. With 70 Illustrations. Crown 8vo. 7s. 6d.

MACKAY (Thomas). The English Poor. A Sketch of their
Social and Economic History; and an attempt to estimate the influence of private property on character and habit. Crown 8vo. 7s. 6d.

———— A Plea for Liberty : an Argument against Socialism and
Socialistic Legislation. Essays by various Writers. Introduction by
Herbert Spencer. Third and Popular Edition. Post 8vo. 2s.

———— A Policy of Free Exchange. Essays by various Writers
on the Economical and Social Aspects of Free Exchange and various
matters. 8vo. 12s.

MACPHERSON (Wm. Charteris). The Baronage and the Senate,
or the House of Lords in the Past, the Present, and the Future. 8vo. 16s.

MAHON (Lord). [See Stanhope.]

MAINE (Sir H. Sumner). A brief Memoir of his Life. By the
Right Hon. Sir M. E. Grant Duff, G.C.S.I. With some of his Indian
Speeches and Minutes. Selected and Edited by Whitley Stokes,
D.C.L. With Portrait. 8vo. 14s.

———— Ancient Law : its Connection with the Early History
of Society, and Its Relation to Modern Ideas. 8vo. 9s.

———— Village Communities in the East and West. 8vo. 9s.

———— Early History of Institutions. 8vo. 9s.

———— Dissertations on Early Law and Custom. 8vo. 9s.

———— Popular Government. 8vo. 7s. 6d.

———— International Law. 8vo. 7s. 6d.

MALCOLM (Sir John). Sketches of Persia. Post 8vo. 3s. 6d.

MALLET (C. E.). The French Revolution. Crown 8vo. 3s. 6d.
(Univ. Extension Series.)

MARKHAM (Mrs.). History of England. From the First Invasion by the Romans, continued down to 1880. Woodcuts. 12mo. 3s. 6d.

———— History of France. From the Conquest of Gaul by
Julius Cæsar, continued down to 1878. Woodcuts. 12mo. 3s. 6d.

———— History of Germany. From its Invasion by Marius
to the completion of Cologne Cathedral. Woodcuts. 12mo. 3s. 6d.

MARLBOROUGH COLLEGE. A History of, during Fifty
Years. By A. G. Bradley, A. C. Champneys, and J. W. Baines.
With numerous illustrations. Crown 8vo. 7s. 6d. net.

MARSH (G. P.). Student's Manual of the English Language.
Edited with Additions. By Dr. Wm. Smith. Post 8vo. 7s. 6d.

MARTIN (Sir Theodore). Life of Lord Lyndhurst. With
Portraits. 8vo. 16s.

MASTERS in English Theology. Lectures by Eminent Divines.
With Introduction by Canon Barry. Post 8vo. 7s. 6d.

MATTHIÆ'S Greek Grammar. Abridged by Blomfield.
Revised by E. S. Crooke. 12mo. 4s.

MAUREL'S Character, Actions, &c., of Wellington. 1s. 6d.

MELVILLE (Hermann). Typee : or the Marquesas Islanders.
With Memoir, Maps and Illustrations. Crown 8vo. 3s. 6d.

———— Omoo : Adventures in the South Seas. With Memoir,
Maps and Illustrations. Crown 8vo. 2s. 6d.

MEREDITH (Mrs. C.). Notes & Sketches of N. S. Wales. Post 8vo. 2s.

MEXICO. [See Brocklehurst—Ruxton.]

MICHAEL ANGELO, Sculptor, Painter, and Architect. His Life and Works. By C. Heath Wilson. Illustrations. 8vo. 15s.

MILL (Dr. H. R.). The Realm of Nature: An Outline of Physiography. With 19 Coloured Maps and 68 Illustrations and Diagrams (380 pp.). Crown 8vo. 5s. (University Extension Manuals.)

MILLER (Wm.). A Dictionary of English Names of Plants applied among English-speaking People to Plants, Trees, and Shrubs. In in-English and English-Latin. Medium 8vo. 12s.

MILMAN'S (Dean) WORKS:—

History of the Jews, from the earliest Period down to Modern Times. 3 Vols. Post 8vo. 12s.

Early Christianity, from the Birth of Christ to the Abolition of Paganism in the Roman Empire. 3 Vols. Post 8vo. 12s.

Latin Christianity, including that of the Popes to the Pontificate of Nicholas V. 9 Vols. Post 8vo. 36s.

Handbook to St. Paul's Cathedral. Woodcuts. 10s. 6d.

Quinti Horatii Flacci Opera. Woodcuts. Sm. 8vo. 7s. 6d.

Fall of Jerusalem. Fcap. 8vo. 1s.

———— (Bishop, D.D.) Life. With a Selection from his Correspondence and Journals. By his Sister. Map. 8vo. 12s.

MILNE (David, M.A.). A Readable Dictionary of the English Language. Etymologically arranged. Crown 8vo. 7s. 6d.

MINCHIN (J. G.). The Growth of Freedom in the Balkan Peninsula. With a Map. Crown 8vo. 10s. 6d.

MINTO (Wm.). Logic, Inductive and Deductive. With Diagrams. Crown 8vo. 4s. 6d. (University Extension Series.)

MISS BLAKE OF MONKSHALTON. By Isabella Ford. A New Novel. Crown 8vo. 6s.

MIVART (St. George). The Cat. An Introduction to the Study of Backboned Animals, especially Mammals. With 200 Illustrations. Medium 8vo. 30s.

MOORE (Thomas). Life and Letters of Lord Byron. [See Byron.]

MORELLI (Giovanni). Italian Painters. Critical Studies of their Works. Translated from the German by Constance Jocelyn Ffoulkes, with an Introductory Notice by Sir Henry Layard, G.C.B. With numerous Illustrations. 8vo.

Vol. I.—The Borghese & Doria Pamphili Galleries. 15s.

Vol. II.—The Galleries of Munich and Dresden. 15s.

MOSELEY (Prof. H. N.). Notes by a Naturalist during the voyage of H.M.S. "Challenger" round the World in the years 1872-76. A New and Cheaper Edit., with a Memoir of the Author. Portrait, Map, and numerous Woodcuts. Crown 8vo. 9s.

MOTLEY (John Lothrop). The Correspondence of. With Portrait. 2 Vols. 8vo. 30s.

—— History of the United Netherlands: from the Death of William the Silent to the Twelve Years' Truce, 1609. Portraits. 4 Vols. Post 8vo. 6s. each.

———— Life and Death of John of Barneveld. Illustrations. 2 Vols. Post 8vo. 12s.

MUIRHEAD (John H.). The Elements of Ethics. Crown 8vo. 3s. (University Extension Series.)

MUMMERY (A. F.) and J. A. HOBSON. The Physiology of Industry: Being an Exposure of certain Fallacies in existing Theories of Political Economy. Crown 8vo. 6s.

MUNRO'S (General) Life. By Rev. G. R. Gleig. 3s. 6d.

MUNTHE (Axel). Letters from a Mourning City. Naples during the Autumn of 1884. Translated by Maude Valerie White. With a Frontispiece. Crown 8vo. 6s.

MURRAY (John). A Publisher and his Friends : Memoir and Correspondence of the second John Murray, with an Account of the Origin and Progress of the House, 1768—1843. By Samuel Smiles, LL.D. With Portraits. 2 Vols. 8vo. 32s.

MURRAY (A. S.). A History of Greek Sculpture from the Earliest Times. With 130 Illustrations. 2 Vols. Medium 8vo. 36s.

———————— Handbook of Greek Archæology. Sculpture, Vases, Bronzes, Gems, Terra-cottas, Architecture, Mural Paintings, &c. Many Illustrations. Crown 8vo. 18s.

MURRAY'S MAGAZINE. Vols. I. to X. 7s. 6d. each.

NADAILLAC (Marquis de). Prehistoric America. Translated by N. D'Anvers. With Illustrations. 8vo. 16s.

NAPIER (General Sir Charles). His Life. By the Hon. Wm. Napier Bruce. With Portrait and Maps. Crown 8vo. 12s.

———————— (General Sir George T.). Passages in his Early Military Life written by himself. Edited by his Son, General Wm. C. E. Napier. With Portrait. Crown 8vo. 7s. 6d.

———————— (Sir Wm.). English Battles and Sieges of the Peninsular War. Portrait. Post 8vo. 5s.

NASMYTH (James). An Autobiography. Edited by Samuel Smiles, LL.D., with Portrait, and 70 Illustrations. Post 8vo, 6s. ; or Large Paper, 16s.

———————— The Moon : Considered as a Planet, a World, and a Satellite. With 26 Plates and numerous Woodcuts. Medium 8vo. 21s.

NEWMAN (Mrs.). Begun in Jest. 3 vols. 31s. 6d.

NEW TESTAMENT. With Short Explanatory Commentary. By Archdeacon Churton, M.A., and the Bishop of St. David's. With 110 authentic Views, &c. 2 Vols. Crown 8vo. 21s. bound.

NEWTH (Samuel). First Book of Natural Philosophy ; an Introduction to the Study of Statics, Dynamics, Hydrostatics, Light, Heat, and Sound, with numerous Examples. Crown 8vo. 3s. 6d.

———————— Elements of Mechanics, including Hydrostatics, with numerous Examples. Crown 8vo. 8s. 6d.

———————— Mathematical Examples. A Graduated Series of Elementary Examples in Arithmetic, Algebra, Logarithms, Trigonometry, and Mechanics. Crown 8vo. 8s. 6d.

NIMROD, On the Chace—Turf—and Road. With Portrait and Plates. Crown 8vo. 5s. Or with Coloured Plates, 7s. 6d.

NORRIS (W. E.). Marcia. A Novel. Crown 8vo. 6s.

NORTHCOTE'S (Sir John) Notebook in the Long Parliament. Containing Proceedings during its First Session, 1640. Edited, with a Memoir, by A. H. A. Hamilton. Crown 8vo. 9s.

O'CONNELL (Daniel). [See Fitzpatrick.]

ORNSBY (Prof. R.). Memoirs of J. Hope Scott, Q.C. (of Abbotsford). 2 vols. 8vo. 24s.

OVID LESSONS. [See Eton.]

OWEN (Lieut.-Col.). Principles and Practice of Modern Artillery. With Illustrations. 8vo. 15s.

OWEN (Professor). Life and Correspondence, Edited by his Grandson. Rev. R. Owen. With Portraits and Illustrations. 2 vols. 8vo.

OXENHAM (Rev. W.). English Notes for Latin Elegiacs ; with Prefatory Rules of Composition in Elegiac Metre. 12mo. 3s. 6d.

PAGET (LORD GEORGE). The Light Cavalry Brigade in the Crimea. Map. Crown 8vo. 10s. 6d.

PALGRAVE (R. H. I.). Local Taxation of Great Britain and Ireland. 8vo. 5s.

PALLISER (MRS.). Mottoes for Monuments, or Epitaphs selected for General Use and Study. With Illustrations. Crown 8vo. 7s. 6d.

PARKER (C. S.), M.P. [See PEEL.]

PEEL'S (SIR ROBERT) Memoirs. 2 Vols. Post 8vo. 15s.

―――― Life of: Early years; as Secretary for Ireland, 1812–18, and Secretary of State, 1822–27. Edited by CHARLES STUART PARKER, M.P. With Portrait. 8vo. 16s.

PENN (RICHARD). Maxims and Hints for an Angler and Chessplayer. Woodcuts. Fcap. 8vo. 1s.

PERCY (JOHN, M.D.). METALLURGY. Fuel, Wood, Peat, Coal, Charcoal, Coke, Fire-Clays. Illustrations. 8vo. 30s.

―――― Lead, including part of Silver. Illustrations. 8vo. 30s.

―――― Silver and Gold. Part I. Illustrations. 8vo. 30s.

―――― Iron and Steel. A New and Revised Edition, with the Author's Latest Corrections, and brought down to the present time. By H. BAUERMAN, F.G.S. Illustrations. 8vo.

PERRY (J. TAVENOR). The Chronology of Medieval Architecture. A Date Book of Architectural Art. Illustrations. 8vo. 16s.

PERRY (REV. CANON). History of the English Church. See STUDENT'S Manuals.

PHILLIPS (SAMUEL). Literary Essays from "The Times." With Portrait. 2 Vols. Fcap. 8vo. 7s.

PLEA FOR LIBERTY. See MACKAY.

POLICY OF FREE EXCHANGE. See MACKAY.

POLLOCK (C. E.). A Book of Family Prayers. Selected from the Liturgy of the Church of England. 16mo. 3s. 6d.

POPE'S (ALEXANDER) Life and Works. With Introductions and Notes, by J. W. CROKER, REV. W. ELWIN, and W. J. COURTHOPE. 10 Vols. With Portraits. 8vo. 10s. 6d. each.

PORTER (REV. J. L.). Damascus, Palmyra, and Lebanon. Map and Woodcuts. Post 8vo. 7s. 6d.

PRAYER-BOOK (BEAUTIFULLY ILLUSTRATED). With Notes, by REV. THOS. JAMES. Medium 8vo. 18s. cloth.

PRINCESS CHARLOTTE OF WALES. Memoir and Correspondence. By LADY ROSE WEIGALL. With Portrait. 8vo. 8s. 6d.

PRITCHARD (CHARLES, D.D.). Occasional Thoughts of an Astronomer on Nature and Revelation. 8vo. 7s. 6d.

PROTHERO (ROWLAND E.). Life and Correspondence of Arthur Penrhyn Stanley, late Dean of Westminster. With Portraits and Illustrations. 2 vols. 8vo. 32s.

PSALMS OF DAVID. With Notes Explanatory and Critical by Dean Johnson, Canon Elliott, and Canon Cook. Medium 8vo. 10s. 6d.

PSALTER OF 1539. [See EARLE (Professor John.)]

PUSS IN BOOTS. With 12 Illustrations. By OTTO SPECKTER. 16mo. 1s. 6d. Or coloured, 2s. 6d.

QUARTERLY REVIEW (THE). 8vo. 6s.

QUILL (ALBERT W.). History of P. Cornelius Tacitus. Books I. and II. Translated into English, with Introduction and Notes Critical and Explanatory. 8vo. 7s. 6d.

RAE (EDWARD). Country of the Moors. A Journey from Tripoli to the Holy City of Kairwan. Etchings. Crown 8vo. 12s.

―――― The White Sea Peninsula. Journey to the White Sea, and the Kola Peninsula. Illustrations. Crown 8vo. 15s.

RAE (GEORGE). The Country Banker; His Clients, Cares, and Work, from the Experience of Forty Years. Crown 8vo. 7s. 6d.

RAMSAY (PROF. W. M.). The Historical Geography of Asia Minor. With 6 Maps, Tables, &c. 8vo. 18s.

RASSAM (HORMUZD). British Mission to Abyssinia. Illustrations. 2 Vols. 8vo. 28s.

RAWLINSON'S (CANON) Five Great Monarchies of Chaldæa, Assyria, Media, Babylonia, and Persia. With Maps and Illustrations. 3 Vols. 8vo. 42s.

———— Herodotus, a new English Version. *See* page 12.

RAWLINSON'S (SIR HENRY) England and Russia in the East; a Series of Papers on the Condition of Central Asia. Map. 8vo. 12s.

REJECTED ADDRESSES (THE). BY JAMES AND HORACE SMITH. Woodcuts. Post 8vo. 3s. 6d.; or *Popular Edition*, Fcap. 8vo. 1s.

RENTON (W.). Outlines of English Literature. With Illustrative Diagrams. Crown 8vo. 3s. 6d. (Univ. Extension Series.)

RICARDO'S (DAVID) Works. With a Notice of his Life and Writings. By J. R. M'CULLOCH. 8vo. 16s.

RIPA (FATHER). Residence at the Court of Peking. Post 8vo. 2s.

ROBERTS (DR. R. D.). An Introduction to Modern Geology. With Coloured Maps and Illustrations. Crown 8vo. 6s. (Univ. Extension Series.)

ROBERTSON (CANON). History of the Christian Church, from the Apostolic Age to the Reformation, 1517. 8 Vols. Post 8vo. 6s. each.

ROBINSON (W.). English Flower Garden. An Illustrated Dictionary of all the Plants used, and Directions for their Culture and Arrangement. With numerous Illustrations. Medium 8vo. 15s.

———— The Vegetable Garden; or, the Edible Vegetables, Salads, and Herbs cultivated in Europe and America. By M. VILMORIN-ANDRIEUX. With 750 Illustrations. 8vo. 15s.

———— Sub-Tropical Garden. Illustrations. Crown 8vo. 5s.

———— Parks and Gardens of Paris, considered in Relation to other Cities. 350 Illustrations. 8vo. 18s.

———— God's Acre Beautiful; or, the Cemeteries of the Future. With 8 Illustrations. 8vo. 7s. 6d.

———— Garden Design. Illustrations. 8vo. 5s.

ROMANS, St. Paul's Epistle to the. With Notes and Commentary by E. H. GIFFORD, D.D. Medium 8vo. 7s. 6d.

ROME. [See GIBBON—LIDDELL—SMITH—STUDENTS'.]

ROMILLY (HUGH H.). The Western Pacific and New Guinea. 2nd Edition. With a Map. Crown 8vo. 7s. 6d.

ROSS (MRS.) The Land of Manfred, Prince of Tarentum and King of Sicily. Illustrations. Crown 8vo. 10s. 6d.

RUMBOLD (SIR HORACE). The Great Silver River: Notes of a Residence in the Argentine Republic. Second Edition, with Additional Chapter. With Illustrations. 8vo. 12s.

RUXTON (GEO. F.). Travels in Mexico; with Adventures among Wild Tribes and Animals of the Prairies and Rocky Mountains. Post 8vo. 3s. 6d.

ST. JOHN (CHARLES). St. John's Wild Sports and Natural History of the Highlands of Scotland. A New Edition, thoroughly revised. With hitherto unpublished Notes by the Author. Edited, with a Memoir of the Author, by the Rev. M. G. WATKINS. With Portrait of Mr. St John and several new Illustrations. Medium 8vo. 17s.

———— (BAYLE). Adventures in the Libyan Desert. 2s.

ST. MAUR (Mrs. Algernon), Lady Seymour. Impressions of a Tenderfoot, during a Journey in search of Sport in the Far West. With Map and Illustrations. Crown 8vo. 12s.

SALE'S (Sir Robert) Brigade in Affghanistan. With an Account of the Defence of Jellalabad. By Rev. G. R. Gleig. Post 8vo. 2s.

SALMON (Prof. Geo., D.D.). An Introduction to the Study of the New Testament, and an Investigation Into Modern Biblical Criticism, based on the most recent Sources of Information. Crown 8vo. 9s.

———— Lectures on the Infallibility of the Church. Post 8vo. 9s.

SCEPTICISM IN GEOLOGY; and the Reasons for it. An assemblage of facts from Nature combining to refute the theory of "Causes now in Action." By Verifier. Woodcuts. Crown 8vo. 6s.

SCHLIEMANN (Dr. Henry). Ilios; the City and Country of the Trojans. With an Autobiography. Illustrations. Imperial 8vo. 50s.

———— Tiryns: A Prehistoric Palace of the Kings of Tiryns, discovered by excavations in 1884-5. With Illustrations. Medium 8vo. 42s.

SCHREIBER (Lady Charlotte). English Fans and Fan Leaves. Collected and Described. With 160 Plates. Folio. 7l. 7s. Net.

———— Foreign Fans and Fan Leaves. French, Italian, and German, chiefly relating to the French Revolution, Collected and Described. 150 Plates. Folio. 7l. 7s. Net.

———— Playing Cards of Various Ages and Countries. Vol. I., English and Scottish; Dutch and Flemish. With 141 Plates. Folio. 3l. 13s. 6d. Net. Vol. II., French and German. With 180 Plates. Folio. 3l. 18s. 6d. Net.

SETOUN (Gabriel). Barncraig. Episodes in the life of a Scottish Village. Crown 8vo. 5s.

SHAIRP (Principal) and his Friends. By Professor Wm. Knight, of St. Andrews. With Portrait. 8vo. 15s.

SHAW (T. B.). Manual of English Literature. Post 8vo. 7s. 6d.

———— Specimens of English Literature. Post 8vo. 5s.

SHAW (R. Norman). [See Architecture.]

SMILES' (Samuel, LL.D.) WORKS:—

British Engineers; from the Earliest Period to the Death of the Stephensons. Illustrations. 5 Vols. Crown 8vo. 7s. 6d. each.

George Stephenson. Post 8vo. 2s. 6d.

James Nasmyth. Portrait and Illustrations. Post 8vo. 6s.

Jasmin: Barber, Poet, Philanthropist. Post 8vo. 6s.

Scotch Naturalist (Thos. Edward). Illustrations. Post 8vo. 6s.

Scotch Geologist (Robert Dick). Illustrations. 8vo. 12s.

Self-Help. With Illustrations of Conduct and Perseverance. Post 8vo. 6s. In French. 5s.

Character. A Book of Noble Characteristics. Post 8vo. 6s.

Thrift. A Book of Domestic Counsel. Post 8vo. 6s.

Duty. With Illustrations of Courage, Patience, and Endurance. Post 8vo. 6s.

Industrial Biography. Iron-Workers and Tool-Makers. 6s.

Men of Invention. Post 8vo. 6s.

Life and Labour. Post 8vo. 6s.

SMILES' (Samuel, LL.D.) Works—*continued.*

THE HUGUENOTS; Their Settlements, Churches, and Industries in England and Ireland. Crown 8vo. 7*s.* 6*d.*

BOY'S VOYAGE ROUND THE WORLD. Illustrations. Post 8vo. 6*s.*

SIEMENS (Sir Wm.). The Scientific Works of: a Collection of Papers and Discourses. Edited by E. F. Bamber, C.E. Vol. i.—Heat and Metallurgy; ii. — Electricity, &c.; iii. — Addresses and Lectures. Plates. 3 Vols. 8vo. 12*s.* each.

———— (Dr. Werner von). Collected Works of. Translated by E. F. Bamber. Vol. i.—Scientific Papers and Addresses. ii.—Applied Science. With Illustrations. 8vo. 14*s.*

SIMMONS' Constitution and Practice of Courts-Martial. 15*s.*

SMEDES (Susan Dabney). A Southern Planter. Memoirs of Thomas Dabney. Preface by Mr. Gladstone. Post 8vo. 7*s.* 6*d.*

SMITH (Dr. George) Student's Manual of the Geography of British India, Physical and Political. Maps. Post 8vo. 7*s.* 6*d.*

———— Life of Wm. Carey, D.D., 1761—1834. Shoemaker and Missionary. Professor of Sanscrit, Bengalee and Marathee at the College of Fort William, Calcutta. Illustrations. Post 8vo. 7*s.* 6*d.*

———— Life of Stephen Hislop, Pioneer, Missionary, and Naturalist in Central India, 1844—1863. Portrait. Post 8vo. 7*s.* 6*d.*

———— The Conversion of India, from Pantænus to the present time, 193—1893. With Illustrations. Crown 8vo. 9*s.*

———— (Philip). History of the Ancient World, from the Creation to the Fall of the Roman Empire, A.D. 476. 3 Vols. 8vo. 31*s.* 6*d.*

———— (R. Bosworth). Mohammed and Mohammedanism. Crown 8vo. 7*s.* 6*d.*

SMITH'S (Sir Wm.) DICTIONARIES :—

DICTIONARY OF THE BIBLE; its Antiquities, Biography, Geography, and Natural History. Illustrations. 3 Vols. 8vo. £4 4*s.* The New and Revised Edition of Vol. I. sold separately, 2*l.* 2*s.*; Vols. II. and III., 2*l.* 2*s.*

CONCISE BIBLE DICTIONARY. Illustrations. 8vo. 21*s.*

SMALLER BIBLE DICTIONARY. Illustrations. Post 8vo. 7*s.* 6*d.*

CHRISTIAN ANTIQUITIES. Comprising the History, Institutions, and Antiquities of the Christian Church. Illustrations. 2 Vols. Medium 8vo. 3*l.* 13*s.* 6*d.*

CHRISTIAN BIOGRAPHY, LITERATURE, SECTS, AND DOCTRINES; from the Times of the Apostles to the Age of Charlemagne. Medium 8vo. Now complete in 4 Vols. 6*l.* 16*s.* 6*d.*

GREEK AND ROMAN ANTIQUITIES. Including the Laws, Institutions, Domestic Usages, Painting. Sculpture, Music, the Drama, &c. Third Edition, Revised and Enlarged. 2 Vols. Med. 8vo. 31*s.* 6*d.* each.

GREEK AND ROMAN BIOGRAPHY AND MYTHOLOGY. Illustrations. 3 Vols. Medium 8vo. 4*l.* 4*s.*

GREEK AND ROMAN GEOGRAPHY. 2 Vols. Illustrations. Medium 8vo. 56*s.*

ATLAS OF ANCIENT GEOGRAPHY—BIBLICAL AND CLASSICAL. Folio. 6*l.* 6*s.*

CLASSICAL DICTIONARY OF MYTHOLOGY, BIOGRAPHY, AND GEOGRAPHY. 1 Vol. 800 Woodcuts. New Edition. 8vo. 18*s.*

SMALLER CLASSICAL DICT. Woodcuts. Crown 8vo. 7*s.* 6*d.*

SMALLER DICTIONARY OF GREEK AND ROMAN ANTIQUITIES. Woodcuts. Crown 8vo. 7*s.* 6*d.*

SMALLER LATIN-ENGLISH DICTIONARY. 12mo. 7*s.* 6*d.*

SMITH'S (Sir Wm.) Dictionaries—*continued.*
>COMPLETE LATIN-ENGLISH DICTIONARY. With Tables of the Roman Calendar, Measures, Weights, Money, and a Dictionary of Proper Names. 8vo. 16s.
>COPIOUS AND CRITICAL ENGLISH-LATIN DICT. 8vo. 16s.
>SMALLER ENGLISH-LATIN DICTIONARY. 12mo. 7s. 6d.

SMITH'S (Sir Wm.) ENGLISH COURSE:—
>SCHOOL MANUAL OF ENGLISH GRAMMAR, WITH COPIOUS EXERCISES, Appendices and Index. Post 8vo. 3s. 6d.
>PRIMARY ENGLISH GRAMMAR, for Elementary Schools, with carefully graduated Parsing Lessons. 16mo. 1s.
>MANUAL OF ENGLISH COMPOSITION. With Copious Illustrations and Practical Exercises. 12mo. 3s. 6d.
>PRIMARY HISTORY OF BRITAIN. 12mo. 2s. 6d.
>A SMALLER MANUAL OF MODERN GEOGRAPHY. 16mo. 2s. 6d.

SMITH'S (Sir Wm.) FRENCH COURSE:—
>FRENCH PRINCIPIA. Part I. A First Course, containing a Grammar, Delectus, Exercises, and Vocabularies. 12mo. 3s. 6d.
>APPENDIX TO FRENCH PRINCIPIA. Part I. Containing additional Exercises, with Examination Papers. 12mo. 2s. 6d.
>FRENCH PRINCIPIA. Part II. A Reading Book, containing Fables, Stories, and Anecdotes, Natural History, and Scenes from the History of France. With Grammatical Questions, Notes and copious Etymological Dictionary. 12mo. 4s. 6d.
>FRENCH PRINCIPIA. Part III. Prose Composition, containing Hints on Translation of English into French, the Principal Rules of the French Syntax compared with the English, and a Systematic Course of Exercises on the Syntax. 12mo. 4s. 6d. [Post 8vo. 6s.
>STUDENT'S FRENCH GRAMMAR. With Introduction by M. Littré.
>SMALLER GRAMMAR OF THE FRENCH LANGUAGE. Abridged from the above. 12mo. 3s. 6d.

SMITH'S (Sir Wm.) GERMAN COURSE:—
>GERMAN PRINCIPIA. Part I. A First German Course, containing a Grammar, Delectus, Exercise Book, and Vocabularies. 12mo. 3s. 6d.
>GERMAN PRINCIPIA. Part II. A Reading Book; containing Fables, Anecdotes, Natural History, and Scenes from the History of Germany. With Questions, Notes, and Dictionary. 12mo. 3s. 6d.
>PRACTICAL GERMAN GRAMMAR. Post 8vo. 3s. 6d.

SMITH'S (Sir Wm.) ITALIAN COURSE:—
>ITALIAN PRINCIPIA. Part I. An Italian Course, containing a Grammar, Delectus, Exercise Book, with Vocabularies, and Materials for Italian Conversation. 12mo. 3s. 6d.
>ITALIAN PRINCIPIA. Part II. A First Italian Reading Book, containing Fables, Anecdotes, History, and Passages from the best Italian Authors, with Grammatical Questions, Notes, and a Copious Etymological Dictionary. 12mo. 3s. 6d.

SMITH'S (Sir Wm.) YOUNG BEGINNER'S FIRST LATIN COURSE.
>I. A FIRST LATIN BOOK. The Rudiments of Grammar. Easy Grammatical Questions and Exercises, with Vocabularies. 12mo. 2s.
>II. A SECOND LATIN BOOK. An Easy Latin Reading Book, with an Analysis of the Sentences, Notes, and a Dictionary. 12mo. 2s.
>III. A THIRD LATIN BOOK. The Principal Rules of Syntax, with Easy Exercises, Questions, Vocabularies, and an English-Latin Dictionary. 2s.
>IV. A FOURTH LATIN BOOK. A Latin Vocabulary for Beginners. Arranged according to Subjects and Etymologies. 12mo. 2s.

SMITH'S (Sir Wm.) LATIN COURSE.

PRINCIPIA LATINA. Part I. First Latin Course, containing a Grammar, Delectus, and Exercise Book, with Vocabularies. 12mo. 3s. 6d.

. In this Edition the Cases of the Nouns, Adjectives, and Pronouns are arranged both as in the ORDINARY GRAMMARS and as in the PUBLIC SCHOOL PRIMER, together with the corresponding Exercises.

APPENDIX TO PRINCIPIA LATINA. Part I.; being Additional Exercises, with Examination Papers. 12mo. 2s. 6d.

PRINCIPIA LATINA. Part II. A Reading-book of Mythology, Geography, Roman Antiquities, and History. With Notes and Dictionary. 12mo. 3s. 6d.

PRINCIPIA LATINA. Part III. A Poetry Book. Hexameters and Pentameters; Eclog. Ovidianæ; Latin Prosody. 12mo. 3s. 6d.

PRINCIPIA LATINA. Part IV. Prose Composition. Rules of Syntax, with Examples, Explanations of Synonyms, and Exercises on the Syntax. 12mo. 3s. 6d.

PRINCIPIA LATINA. Part V. Short Tales and Anecdotes for Translation into Latin. A New and Enlarged Edition. 12mo. 3s. 6d.

LATIN-ENGLISH VOCABULARY AND FIRST LATIN-ENGLISH DICTIONARY FOR PHÆDRUS, CORNELIUS NEPOS, AND CÆSAR. 12mo. 3s. 6d.

STUDENT'S LATIN GRAMMAR. For the Higher Forms. A new and thoroughly revised Edition. Post 8vo. 6s.

SMALLER LATIN GRAMMAR. New Edition. 12mo. 3s. 6d.

SMITH'S (Sir Wm.) GREEK COURSE:—

INITIA GRÆCA. Part I. A First Greek Course, containing a Grammar, Delectus, and Exercise-book. With Vocabularies. 12mo. 3s. 6d.

APPENDIX TO INITIA GRÆCA. Part I. Containing additional Exercises. With Examination Papers. Post 8vo. 2s. 6d.

INITIA GRÆCA. Part II. A Reading Book. Containing Short Tales, Anecdotes, Fables, Mythology, and Grecian History. 12mo. 3s. 6d.

INITIA GRÆCA. Part III. Prose Composition. Containing the Rules of Syntax, with copious Examples and Exercises. 12mo. 3s. 6d.

STUDENT'S GREEK GRAMMAR. For the Higher Forms. Post 8vo. 6s.

SMALLER GREEK GRAMMAR. 12mo. 3s. 6d.

GREEK ACCIDENCE. 12mo. 2s. 6d.

PLATO, Apology of Socrates, &c. With Notes. 12mo. 3s. 6d.

SMITH'S (Sir Wm.) SMALLER HISTORIES:—

SCRIPTURE HISTORY. Maps and Woodcuts. 16mo. 3s. 6d.

ANCIENT HISTORY. Woodcuts. 16mo. 3s. 6d.

ANCIENT GEOGRAPHY. Woodcuts. 16mo. 3s. 6d.

MODERN GEOGRAPHY. 16mo. 2s. 6d.

GREECE. With Coloured Map and Woodcuts. 16mo. 3s. 6d.

ROME. With Coloured Maps and Woodcuts. 16mo. 3s. 6d.

CLASSICAL MYTHOLOGY. Woodcuts. 16mo. 3s. 6d.

ENGLAND. With Coloured Maps and Woodcuts. 16mo. 3s. 6d.

ENGLISH LITERATURE. 16mo. 3s. 6d.

SPECIMENS OF ENGLISH LITERATURE. 16mo. 3s. 6d.

SOMERVILLE (MARY). Physical Geography. Post 8vo. 9s.

———— Connexion of the Physical Sciences. Post 8vo. 9s.

SOUTH (JOHN F.). Household Surgery; or, Hints for Emergencies. With Woodcuts. Fcap. 8vo. 3s. 6d.

SOUTHEY (ROBT.). Lives of Bunyan and Cromwell. Post 8vo. 2s.

STANHOPE'S (Earl) WORKS :—

History of England from the Reign of Queen Anne to the Peace of Versailles, 1701-83. 9 Vols. Post 8vo. 5s. each.

Notes of Conversations with the Duke of Wellington. Crown 8vo. 7s. 6d.

Miscellanies. 2 Vols. Post 8vo. 13s.

British India, from its Origin to 1783. Post 8vo. 3s. 6d.

History of "Forty-Five." Post 8vo. 3s.

Historical and Critical Essays. Post 8vo. 3s. 6d.

Retreat from Moscow, and other Essays. Post 8vo. 7s. 6d.

Life of Condé. Post 8vo. 3s. 6d.

Story of Joan of Arc. Fcap. 8vo. 1s.

Addresses on Various Occasions. 16mo. 1s.

STANLEY'S (Dean) WORKS :—

Sinai and Palestine. Coloured Maps. 8vo. 12s.

Bible in the Holy Land; Extracts from the above Work. Woodcuts. Post 8vo. 3s. 6d.

Eastern Church. Plans. Crown 8vo. 6s.

Jewish Church. From the Earliest Times to the Christian Era. Portrait and Maps. 3 Vols. Crown 8vo. 18s.

Church of Scotland. 8vo. 7s. 6d.

Epistles of St. Paul to the Corinthians. 8vo. 18s.

Life of Dr. Arnold. Portrait. 2 Vols. Cr. 8vo. 12s.

Canterbury. Illustrations. Crown 8vo. 6s.

Westminster Abbey. Illustrations. 8vo. 15s.

Sermons Preached in Westminster Abbey. 8vo. 12s.

Memoir of Edward, Catherine, and Mary Stanley. Cr. 8vo. 9s.

Christian Institutions. Crown 8vo. 6s.

Essays on Church and State; 1850—1870. Crown 8vo. 6s.

Sermons to Children, including the Beatitudes, the Faithful Servant. Post 8vo. 3s. 6d.

STANLEY (Dean) Life of. [See Bradley and Prothero.]

STEPHENS (Rev. W. R. W.). Life and Times of St. John Chrysostom. A Sketch of the Church and the Empire in the Fourth Century. Portrait. 8vo. 7s. 6d.

STREET (G. E.), R.A. Gothic Architecture in Brick and Marble. With Notes on North of Italy. Illustrations. Royal 8vo. 26s.

———— Memoir of. By Arthur E. Street. Portrait. 8vo. 15s.

STUART (Villiers). Egypt after the War. With Descriptions of the Homes and Habits of the Natives, &c. Coloured Illustrations and Woodcuts. Royal 8vo. 31s. 6d.

———————— Adventures Amidst the Equatorial Forests and Rivers of South America, also in the West Indies and the Wilds of Florida; to which is added " Jamaica Revisited." With Map and Illustrations. Royal 8vo. 21s.

STUDENTS' MANUALS. Crown 8vo. 7s. 6d. each Volume :—

Hume's History of England from the Invasion of Julius Cæsar to the Revolution in 1688. Revised, and continued to the Treaty of Berlin, 1878. By J. S. Brewer, M.A. Coloured Maps and Woodcuts. Or in 3 parts, price 2s. 6d. each.

. Questions on the above Work. 12mo. 2s.

History of Modern Europe, from the Fall of Constantinople to the Treaty of Berlin, 1878. By R. Lodge, M.A.

STUDENTS' MANUALS. 7s. 6d. EACH VOLUME :—*continued.*

OLD TESTAMENT HISTORY ; from the Creation to the Return of
'the Jews from Captivity. Woodcuts.

NEW TESTAMENT HISTORY. With an Introduction connecting
the History of the Old and New Testaments. Woodcuts.

ECCLESIASTICAL HISTORY ; a History of the Christian Church.
By PHILIP SMITH, B.A. With numerous Woodcuts. 2 Vols. PART I.
A.D. 30—1003. PART II., 1003—1614.

ENGLISH CHURCH HISTORY. By CANON PERRY. 3 Vols.
First Period, A.D. 596—1509. Second Period, 1509—1717. Third Period.
1717—1884.

ANCIENT HISTORY OF THE EAST ; Egypt, Assyria, Babylonia,
Media, Persia, Asia Minor, and Phœnicia. By PHILIP SMITH, B.A.

————— GEOGRAPHY. By CANON BEVAN. Woodcuts.

MODERN GEOGRAPHY ; Mathematical, Physical and Descriptive.
By CANON BEVAN, M.A. Woodcuts.

HISTORY OF GREECE ; from the Earliest Times to the Roman
Conquest. By WM. SMITH, D.C.L. Woodcuts.
*** Questions on the above Work, 12mo. 2s.

HISTORY OF ROME; from the Earliest Times to the Establishment of the Empire. By DEAN LIDDELL. Woodcuts.

HISTORY OF THE ROMAN EMPIRE ; from the Establishment of
the Empire to the reign of Commodus. By J. B. BURY. With Coloured
Maps and many Illustrations.

GIBBON'S DECLINE AND FALL OF THE ROMAN EMPIRE. Woodcuts.

HALLAM'S HISTORY OF EUROPE during the Middle Ages.

HALLAM'S HISTORY OF ENGLAND ; from the Accession of
Henry VII. to the Death of George II.

HISTORY OF FRANCE ; from the Earliest Times to the Fall
of the Second Empire. By H. W. JERVIS. With Coloured Maps and
Woodcuts.

ENGLISH LANGUAGE. By GEO P. MARSH.

ENGLISH LITERATURE. By T. B. SHAW, M.A.

SPECIMENS OF ENGLISH LITERATURE. By T. B. SHAW. 5s.

GEOGRAPHY OF BRITISH INDIA. Political and Physical. By
GEORGE SMITH, LL.D. Maps.

MORAL PHILOSOPHY. By WM. FLEMING.

STURGIS (JULIAN). Comedy of a Country House. 6s.

————— Count Julian. A Tragedy. Crown 8vo. 2s.

SWAINSON (CANON). Nicene and Apostles' Creeds ; Their
Literary History ; together with some Account of "The Creed of St.
Athanasius." 8vo. 16s.

TACITUS. [See QUILL.]

TEMPLE (SIR RICHARD). India in 1880. With Maps. 8vo. 16s.

————— Men and Events of My Time in India. 8vo. 16s.

————— Oriental Experience. Essays and Addresses delivered
on Various Occasions. With Maps and Woodcuts. 8vo. 16s.

————— Life in Parliament. From 1862 to 1892 inclusive.
Crown 8vo. 7s. 6d.

THOMAS (SIDNEY GILCHRIST), Inventor ; Memoir and Letters.
Edited by R. W. BURNIE. Portraits. Crown 8vo. 9s.

THOMSON (J. ARTHUR). The Study of Animal Life. With many
Illustrations. Crown 8vo. 5s. (University Extension Manuals.)

THORNHILL (MARK). The Personal Adventures and Experiences
of a Magistrate during the Indian Mutiny. Crown 8vo. 12s.

TITIAN'S LIFE AND TIMES. By Crowe and Cavalcaselle.
Illustrations. 2 Vols. 8vo. 21s.

TOCQUEVILLE'S State of Society in France before the Revolution,
1789, and on the Causes which led to that Event. 8vo. 12s.

TOZER (Rev. H. F.). Highlands of Turkey, with Visits to Mounts
Ida, Athos, Olympus, and Pelion. 2 Vols. Crown 8vo. 24s.

———— Lectures on the Geography of Greece. Post 8vo. 9s.

TRISTRAM (Canon). Great Sahara. Illustrations. Crown 8vo. 15s.

———— Land of Moab : Travels and Discoveries on the East
Side of the Dead Sea and the Jordan. Illustrations. Crown 8vo. 15s.

TWINING (Louisa). Symbols and Emblems of Early and
Mediæval Christian Art. With 500 Illustrations. Crown 8vo. 6s.

TYLOR (E. B.). Researches into the Early History of Mankind,
and Development of Civilization. 3rd Edition. 8vo. 12s.

———— Primitive Culture : the Development of Mythology,
Philosophy, Religion, Art, and Custom 2 Vols. 8vo. 3rd Edit. 21s.

UNIVERSITY EXTENSION MANUALS. Edited by Professor Wm. Knight (St. Andrew's). A series of Manuals dealing
with Literature, Science, Philosophy, History, Art, &c. Crown 8vo.
Prospectus with full particulars will be forwarded on application.

An Introduction to Modern Geology. [See Roberts.]

The Realm of Nature. [See Mill.]

The Study of Animal Life. [See Thomson.]

The Elements of Ethics. [See Muirhead]

English Colonization and Empire. [See Caldecott.]

The Fine Arts. [See Baldwin Brown.]

The Use and Abuse of Money. [See Cunningham.]

The Philosophy of the Beautiful. [See Knight.]

French Literature. [See Keene.]

The Rise of the British Dominion in India. [See Lyall.

The Physiology of the Senses. [See McKendrick.]

Chapters in Modern Botany. [See Geddes.]

The French Revolution. [See Mallet.]

English Literature. [See Renton.]

Logic, Inductive and Deductive. [See Minto.]

Greece in the Age of Pericles. [See Grant.]

Jacobean Poets. [See Gosse.]

VINCENT (James Edmund). [See Clarence, Duke of.]

WACE (Rev. Henry), D.D. The Principal Facts in the Life of
our Lord, and the Authority of the Evangelical Narratives. Post 8vo. 6s.

———— Christianity and Morality. Boyle Lectures for 1874 and
1875. Seventh Edition. Crown 8vo. 6s.

———— The Foundations of Faith, being the Bampton Lectures
for 1879. 8vo. 7s. 6d.

WALES (H.R.H. the Prince of). Speeches and Addresses.
1863-1888. Edited by Dr. J. Macaulay. With Portrait. 8vo. 12s.

WALLER (Rev. Horace). Health Hints for Travellers in Central
Africa. Fcap. 8vo. 1s.

WEIGALL (Lady Rose). [See Burghersh and Princess Charlotte].

WELLINGTON (Duke of). Notes of Conversations with the
late Earl Stanhope. 1831-1851. Crown 8vo. 7s. 6d.

———— Supplementary Despatches, relating to India,
Ireland, Denmark, Spanish America, Spain, Portugal, France, Congress
of Vienna, Waterloo and Paris. 15 Vols. 8vo. 20s. each.

WELLINGTON (DUKE OF). Civil and Political Correspondence. Vols. I. to VIII. 8vo. 20s.

WESTCOTT (CANON B. F.) The Gospel according to St. John, with Notes and Dissertations (Reprinted from the Speaker's Commentary.) 8vo. 10s. 6d.

WHARTON (CAPT. W. J. L.), R.N. Hydrographical Surveying: being a description of the means and methods employed in constructing Marine Charts. With Illustrations. 8vo. 15s.

WHITE (W. H.). Manual of Naval Architecture, for the use of Naval Officers, Shipbuilders, Yachtsmen, &c. Illustrations. 8vo. 24s.

WHYMPER (EDWARD). Travels amongst the Great Andes of the Equator. With 140 Original Illustrations. Engraved by the Author Medium 8vo. 21s. Net.

———— Supplementary Appendix to the above. With 61 Figures of New Genera and Species. Illus. Medium 8vo. 21s. Net.

———— How to Use the Aneroid Barometer. With numerous Tables. 2s. 6d. Net.

———— Scrambles amongst the Alps in the Years 1860—69, including the History of the First Ascent of the Matterhorn. An Edition de Luxe (Fourth Edition). With 5 Maps and 130 Illustrations. £2 12s. 6d. Net.

WILBERFORCE'S (BISHOP) Life of William Wilberforce. Portrait. Crown 8vo. 6s.

———— (SAMUEL, D.D.), Lord Bishop of Oxford and Winchester; his Life. By CANON ASHWELL, and R. G. WILBERFORCE. Portraits. 3 Vols. 8vo. 15s. each.

WILKINSON (SIR J. G.). Manners and Customs of the Ancient Egyptians, their Private Life, Laws, Arts, Religion, &c. A new edition. Edited by SAMUEL BIRCH, LL.D. Illustrations. 3 Vols. 8vo. 84s.

————Popular Account of the Ancient Egyptians. With 500 Woodcuts. 2 Vols. Post 8vo. 12s.

WILLIAMS (SIR MONIER). Brahmanism and Hinduism, Religious Thought and Life in India as based on the Veda. Enlarged Edit. 18s.

———— Buddhism; its connection with Brahmanism and Hinduism, and in its contrast with Christianity. With Illus. 8vo. 21s.

WINTLE (H. G.). Ovid Lessons. 12mo, 2s. 6d. [See ETON.]

WOLFF (RT. HON. SIR H. D.). Some Notes of the Past. Contents:—Three Visits to the War in 1870—Prince Louis Napoleon—Unwritten History—Madame de Feuchères—The Prince Imperial. Crown 8vo. 5s.

WOOD'S (CAPTAIN) Source of the Oxus. With the Geography of the Valley of the Oxus. By COL. YULE. Map. 8vo. 12s.

WOODS (MRS.). Esther Vanhomrigh. A Novel. Crown 8vo. 6s.

WORDSWORTH (BISHOP). Greece; Pictorial, Descriptive, and Historical. With an Introduction on the Characteristics of Greek Art, by GEO. SCHARF. New Edition revised by the Rev. H. F. TOZER, M.A. With 400 Illustrations. Royal 8vo. 31s. 6d.

YORK-GATE LIBRARY (Catalogue of). Formed by Mr. SILVER. An Index to the Literature of Geography, Maritime and Inland Discovery, Commerce and Colonisation. Compiled by E. A. PETHERICK. 2nd Edition. Royal 8vo. 42s.

YOUNGHUSBAND (CAPT. G. J.). The Queen's Commission: How to Prepare for it; how to Obtain it, and how to Use it. With Practical Information on the Cost and Prospects of a Military Career. Intended for Cadets, Subalterns, and Parents. Crown 8vo. 6s.

YULE (COLONEL) and A. C. BURNELL. A Glossary of Anglo-Indian Colloquial Words and Phrases, and of Kindred Terms; Etymological, Historical, Geographical, and Discursive. Medium 8vo. 36s.

BRADBURY, AGNEW, & CO. LD., PRINTERS, WHITEFRIARS.

www.ingramcontent.com/pod-product-compliance
Lightning Source LLC
Chambersburg PA
CBHW031058110726
47900CB00003B/980